HE HELD SE

AND

THE BATRUKH RACED UP ON THEM.

Above the flying beast's hideous, ratlike visage, Evander glimpsed the face of the figure astride its neck. It was not the fell beauty he had thrust his knife into. Instead it was a haggard thing, skull-faced, with huge eyes that glowed with hate.

Then it swept past and for a moment Evander dared to hope, for nothing immediately befell them. But then he saw it: a shining cord descending around them in a single loop like a lasso. It suddenly transformed into a net with a million strands no thicker than a spider's web but far stronger. It wrapped around the flying carpet, Serena, and Evander in a flash. He struggled with every ounce of strength, but the strands were unbreakable. In a matter of moments, they were helplessly bound. Then the rug was pulled up into the air and towed away by the batrukh....

THE WIZARD
AND THE
FLOATING CITY

Christopher Rowley

A ROC BOOK

ROC
Published by the Penguin Group
Penguin Books USA Inc., 375 Hudson Street,
New York, New York 10014, U.S.A.
Penguin Books Ltd, 27 Wrights Lane,
London W8 5TZ, England
Penguin Books Australia Ltd, Ringwood,
Victoria, Australia
Penguin Books Canada Ltd, 10 Alcorn Avenue,
Toronto, Ontario, Canada M4V 3B2
Penguin Books (N.Z.) Ltd, 182–190 Wairau Road,
Auckland 10, New Zealand

Penguin Books Ltd, Registered Offices:
Harmondsworth, Middlesex, England

First published by Roc, an imprint of Dutton Signet,
a division of Penguin Books USA Inc.

First Printing, June, 1996
10 9 8 7 6 5 4 3 2 1

 REGISTERED TRADEMARK—MARCA REGISTRADA

Printed in the United States of America

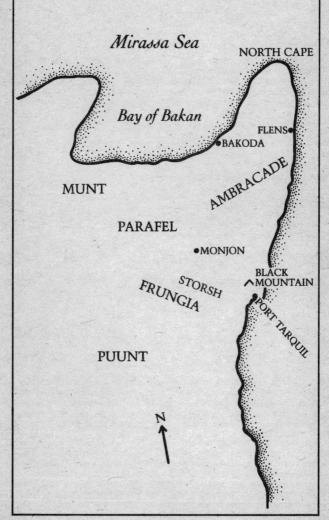

Upper Bakan Coast

Mirassa Sea

Bay of Bakan

NORTH CAPE

FLENS

BAKODA

MUNT

AMBRACADE

PARAFEL

MONJON

STORSH

BLACK
MOUNTAIN

FRUNGIA

PORT TARQUIL

PUUNT

N

The Wizard of the Floating City

The cold dusts swirled and rippled across the hidden contours of the land far below. The ancient Master held the railing for support and blinked in the scattered light of the sun cutting through the hurrying clouds. The white fur on his chest parted in the wind. His long ears grew cold. He had not come to this high pinnacle for many years, though once it had been his favorite place. He did not need to see the ruin that lay below; he knew his world had perished. But now he needed the sky, the widest horizon.

A strange dream had left his spirit trembling. Even now, hours after he had awoken, he felt an extraordinary elevation of consciousness. The mystic center of being still sang a great ode, and his heartbeat raced at the sound.

Had he been visited by the Gods? The question shook him to his core. It was impossible, especially to one grown so old and wise and certain that the Gods no longer existed, if they ever had. But how else to explain the extraordinary dream? If dream at all was what it was.

A golden face atop the form of a giant insect had come to him with soft, sweet singing. The eyes of green glass were imbued with vast intelligence. It terrified him and spoke kind words in no language that he knew, and yet he had understood every word so sweetly sung.

He squinted as the clouds thinned and the harsh light of the sun beat down. The warmth it brought his skin was enough to make other memories erupt.

Once there had been such beauty here. The whirling dusts blew hard across the ruins of far Canax. He imagined the lost grace of that city. Inevitably, his eyes flicked away from the ruins and turned southward.

From the pit of the Dominator rose a pillar of black

smoke, whipped and attenuated by the hurrying winds.
There rested the power, beneath that dark, impenetrable
entity astride the sky. There slaved the millions who
served him, where they burned the very land to drain it
of its riches. There continued the work of the deceiver,
the Dominator of Twelve Worlds.

And now, when all was lost, the Gods had spoken to
him, to ancient Shadreiht, Master of the hidden fortress,
and with their words they had given him the key to the
destruction of the Dominator, the Lord of Twelve
Worlds. A spell to bend the mirror, a spell to trap the
deceiver on the far side of the mirror, and leave him in
limbo forever.

Twelve worlds would rise from the dust. A legion of
lost lives would cry out their thanks for vengeance at last.

Alas.

A tear pressed from his eye and wet his old gray cheek.

Alas, the Gods had waited too long. The power of the
Lords Eleem was gone. The citadel of the enemy was too
strong for what remained of that once proud host. They
had the key, but they lacked all means of using it. Their
enemy was perfectly safe. Their world would remain
ground to dust beneath his heel.

Chapter One

"Evander! Come up and see!" came the shout from the foredeck.

A lithe young man with a tousled shock of sun-bleached hair dropped out of his hammock and ran up the steps to the deck. He wore the simple costume of a common sailor, cotton breeches and a shirt left open to the warm air of the Gulf of Issak.

The sea glistened in the morning light. Ahead was Cape Bakan, with the chalky Tooth of Tormentara looming at its end. The *Wind Trader* was running before an onshore breeze, and Evander could see that they would be in the harbor at Port Tarquil within an hour or so.

"Kospero, you remember your promise?" he cried to the stocky, red-faced man who stood above him on the bowsprit.

"Aye, you young devil, I remember. We'll go to the Wild Parrot just as I promised."

"The Wild Parrot of Port Tarquil!" whooped the young man loudly enough to draw the attention of the ship's mate, who cast a fierce eye over the middeck rail.

"The captain will be giving a short lecture on the evils of Port Tarquil before anyone of you sets foot in the place," he growled.

The youth and the stocky man exchanged warning glances and pretended to busy themselves with the nearest set of rigging. In a moment, however, Kospero signaled that the mate had turned away once more and it was safe to talk.

"My prince, you will find the girls in the Wild Parrot as glamorous and exciting as any in the world."

The youth's face tightened into a glare.

"I'm sorry my ... I mean," Kospero stammered.

"You are forgiven, old friend, but you must try harder.

There is no Prince Danais anymore. He is gone forever, for if he were not, then he might be found, and that would be the end of me."

Kospero shook his head with downcast eyes, "My apologies, Evander, but since I was set to look after you, I cannot forget. I . . ."

They had been on the run for a long time, but the habits of a life at court were hard to drop.

"Enough." The youth brightened. "Tell me again about the girls who come to the Wild Parrot. They wear red sashes, you said, and are confident, outgoing, challenging."

"Indeed, they do, and they are," said Kospero with resumed good cheer. "Of course, they must not be confused with common whores, for they are not that. They are not to be judged by our Kassimi social mores." The lapse was forgotten. Above them the breeze snapped the foresails tight once more, and the *Wind Trader* sailed on smoothly toward the land.

By noon they were docked, and the crew had seen to the unloading of casks of honey from Zeuxas, bales of hides from Issak, and a handful of passengers, five monks destined for the monastery on the high ridge of the Bakan behind the town.

Liberty was but a few minutes away, except that first they had to endure the captain's lecture concerning the evils of the grog shops of Port Tarquil. The captain appeared on the poop deck, where he glared down at his crew, like some ominous cloud of black thunder.

"Ahah, I see that everyone is looking eager and ready for liberty ashore!"

He favored them with a fierce smile before continuing. "While I am not the sort who would wish to curtail your ardor for the pleasures of life, at least not while you are ashore, I feel it is my duty to warn you about certain facts of life here on the Bakanbor coast." The captain studied them for a few seconds before continuing.

"Unfortunately, it has to be admitted, even though I, myself, picked you for my crew, there are fools among you, fools who don't like to pay heed to advice from their dear old captain and let me tell you something . . ." His eyes became even more piercing than before.

"Fools who drink too much in Port Tarquil are likely to wake up in chains in a wagon going over the hill into

Bakan. Yes, chained and gagged and on their way to the auction block!" He thrust out his lower lip and put his hands on his hips.

"So, if any of you fancies the life of an agricultural slave, then please, ignore my advice. Be sure to drink deeply of the Tarquili wines; they are strong, heady, and smooth. When the landlord sees your eyes flushed with wine and offers you the free tankard, take it!"

Captain Inndiby glared out to sea for a moment before returning that fierce gaze to the crew. "And then you can be sure you'll wake up on your way to the auction block in Skola."

The men looked on impassively. Most had heard this lecture, and others like it, before. Port Tarquil was legendary for many things, including the disappearance of drunken shipmates. They would take care of themselves. The captain was not quite finished, however.

"And for those of you foolish enough to go to those hell holes like the Wild Parrot"—here Inndiby scowled furiously at the tall youth with the sun-bleached hair—"I will remind you that Port Tarquil is infamous for corrupting diseases of the flesh. Catch the pox here, and we'll likely be dropping you astern with a stone between your toes and canvas wrapped around before we're halfway home."

Evander blushed. Captain Inndiby's gaze was far too candid, too knowing to be withstood for some reason. Then he laughed at himself for this self-consciousness. After a month at sea up from Zeuxada, he had every right to seek out the company of the opposite sex. To hell with old Inndiby; he was off to the Wild Parrot the moment they touched land.

And at last the speech was over. The gangplank was opened, and they swarmed ashore, glad to set foot on land after the long voyage up the coast.

Port Tarquil was a town of stone houses, huddled below the great chalk ridge that dominated the landscape. The streets were cobbled, or paved in sea stone, as were the plazas and the docks.

But as they tramped up the dock, the men from the *Wind Trader* noticed that something was amiss in Port Tarquil. Gone was the air of festivity that cloaked the place in legend from one end of the coast of Eigo to the other. Gone were the festive flower baskets that hung on every lamp-post. Gone were the bright pennons that announced the world-famous taverns.

Somewhat disconcerted, the crewmen gazed around the deserted grand piazza. Then with shrugs they pressed on, past empty fruit stalls and shuttered shops, up the winding streets into the town.

An old woman watched them go and then spat loudly behind them. A cat wailed. Children scuttled away, and doors slammed up the cobbled alleys.

Finally, Kospero found the right street and led Evander up the cobbles to the famous inn, a three-story structure of white stone beneath a slate roof. The sign outside was emblazoned with a red-and-yellow bird. They pushed open the door and found themselves inside the Wild Parrot. Alas, it appeared that the Wild Parrot was wild no more. In fact, it seemed distinctly tame.

A few old men nursed tankards at tables in a corner. Light streamed in from an upper window, but the atmosphere was one of sour gloom. The fiddlers were absent, and no music thrilled the heart and lightened the feet. Instead of the enticing aromas of a good lunch cooking in the kitchens, there was just a dank mustiness. Worst of all, there wasn't a girl in sight.

"This is the Wild Parrot?" said the youth, gazing around at the empty tables and forlorn barstools.

"We're early. Later in the day the place will be packed," said Kospero quickly. "For now let's take some light wine and go see the rest of the town. The Reburbish Hotel is famous for the grandeur of its lounge. Then there's the walk up the side of the Tooth. We could take a lunch up and enjoy the views of the sea."

"Kospero! I've seen enough views of the sea these last four months to last me a lifetime. I wanted to meet the famous girls of the red sash."

Kospero nodded glumly. Prince Evander, he reflected, was a young man in the full vigor of youth. His impatience was understandable.

A heavyset man with black mustachios pushed into the room from the kitchen and asked them their pleasure in a dour voice.

"Two glasses of the excellent Viognier you make here, if you will, landlord," responded Kospero. "And then tell me, where can we pick up a picnic lunch? We're in from the *Wind Trader*, lying in the harbor, and we think we'll try the walk up to Tormentara today.''

The landlord sucked on his remaining front tooth. "Ah, mmm, well, I'm afraid, gentlemen, that I have no Viognier right now. Truth to tell, I have no good wine at all. The best I can offer you is some Rolaga. It's thin, but not yet soured.''

Kospero blinked, and his fingers ceased to caress his purse.

"What, no Viognier? That's a pity. I was looking forward to your Viognier, so well do I remember it. Ah well, let's have the Rolaga then.''

In a moment two glasses of a pale pinkish wine were before them. "To the Wild Parrot!" exclaimed Kospero.

At the first sip Evander gasped and set his glass down with a crash. "That's horrible," he hissed. Kospero was aware that the prince had had little experience with bad wine. The cellar in the Palace of Sedimo was not only extensive, but was stocked with a fabulous selection of wines from all over Sedimo Kassim and far beyond.

"Certainly it lacks, uh, body.''

" 'Tis thin, and lacks more than body.''

Kospero heaved a sigh and turned to the landlord. "This wine is sour and nigh undrinkable.''

The fellow twiddled the stiffened ends of his mustache. "Nevertheless, it's all I have for sale.''

Kospero blinked once more. "In that case, it would appear that the Wild Parrot has gone down considerably since I was last here.''

The landlord gave them a sad smile, "Indubitably true," he said. This nonchalant acceptance of lowered standards disconcerted Kospero.

"Well, where can we find an excellent picnic lunch then?''

"Not here," said the landlord.

"Aye, but where in the town?''

"Not in Port Tarquil. There's no good lunch here anymore. All our cheese grows mold within an hour of being made. All our wine is soured; the vines will not put forth flowers or grapes. The wheat will not ripen in the fields. We have to bring in oats from over the Bakan. No, you'll not be enjoying your stay in Port Tarquil on this occasion, my friends.''

Evander wore a long face. "Then the girls of the red sash will not be visiting the Wild Parrot tonight either?"

"They most certainly will not. They're all in a savage mood. They'd as soon kill a man as take him to bed."

"Extraordinary," said Kospero, fingering the wineglass with distaste. "What has happened to Port Tarquil?"

The landlord's eyes became furtive as he leaned against the wall and cast an eye out the window to the chalky slope of the Bakan. There was nothing but blue sky and a single white cloud.

"We are under the curse of the new wizard in the Black Mountain."

"What wizard is this?" asked Kospero.

"He has many names; chiefly we call him the Wizard of the Black Mountain."

"Where did he come from?"

"It is said he arrived in Bakanbor one moonlit night, and that he had flown across the ocean from the haunted isles."

"The haunted isles, how ghastly."

"He is most demanding and perverse. From mountains to dales to valleys, he has laid waste to all the lands around. From us in Port Tarquil he demanded a tribute of eight virgins every year. We refused. What kind of fathers does he think there are in Port Tarquil who would give up their beloved children to this monster?"

"What happened when you refused?" asked the lithe youth with the sun-bleached hair.

"He laid upon us a terrible curse. In time we will starve and the town of Port Tarquil will be no more." And with this bleak assessment of the future, the landlord returned to his kitchen.

Thus it was with heavy hearts that Kospero and Evander set off back to the harbor. However, as they passed the empty fish market, they heard the noise of an angry crowd. Shouts, jeers, and outbreaks of clapping resounded up the stone alley walls.

"Let us see what's happening," suggested Evander.

They turned into the empty fish market and passed through it to the broad space of the temple piazza. Here was gathered a throng that seemed to include most of the population of the town.

"What's going on?" Kospero asked a sailor named Herner, who was standing at the back of the crowd.

"The mayor of Port Tarquil is about to read a statement."

A portly fellow in a black velvet jacket, white breeches, and tricorner hat climbed atop the dais near the temple steps. "Citizens," cried the mayor several times, waving his hat to get their attention. Gradually they quietened.

"I, Golpho, your honorable mayor, have to report that our latest bid to open negotiations with the Wizard has not been successful."

Several in the crowd began shouting something at the mayor. He turned upon them with a furious face. "And, yes, I know that some of you think that we should just give up and surrender. But the honor of Port Tarquil is at stake! Never will I, Golpho, surrender to these infamous demands! This evil force from the haunted isles shall never feast upon our daughters."

"Then he'll be feasting on all of our bones!" shouted a man at the front of the crowd.

"Ah, Konoko, a father of two sons, you would have us give in and send our daughters to the monster! What would you say if he were to demand your sons in a tribute instead, eh?"

Many more in the crowd began shouting insults at Konoko, who shouted back with equal fervor. An old hag tried to spit on him, but Konoko's friends shoved her back. The town constables moved in to separate the combatants.

When the noise died down, Mayor Golpho began to read from a parchment scroll he had taken out of his coat pocket. "Hear ye, all citizens of Port Tarquil. Following the breakdown in negotiations, your elected representatives have levied the sum of five hundred ducats from the leading merchants of the town. This sum will be offered to one of the great magicians of Monjon as payment for a cleansing of the Bakanbor Coast and the removal of the evil one from the Black Mountain. Furthermore, we solemnly make public our belief that the Wizard is a bandoor, a slime-hag, an eater of corpse flesh, a creature of the most disgusting sexual habits . . ."

Suddenly, Golpho was seized with a fit of coughing and was forced to stop reading. He coughed for a full minute or more, his face growing redder and redder, until it reached a shade of puce.

The coughs ended at last, but Golpho, straightening up,

let out a great cry of woe. He grimaced and moaned, then took his parchment scroll and began stuffing it into his mouth. In a moment his face had gone black, and he tumbled to his knees on the dais.

With a gasp of fright the crowd gave way and began to stream back up the alleys. Not one went to the aid of the groaning mayor, who was still shoving the parchment scroll into his mouth. Even the constables drew back with looks of uttermost dismay and disgust. This was unclean, a manifestation of the darkness itself. It seemed the mayor was doomed to choke himself on the scroll before anyone would help.

Then Evander pushed forward and knelt down by the mayor. The mayor weakly tried to fend him off. Evander forced the man's hands to his side.

"Come, Kospero, hold his arms for me."

"Are you sure you want to do this, my prince?" Kospero threw a worried glance to the looming mass of the Bakan.

The crowd had scattered.

"Come on, Kospero, hurry it up; the fellow's choking to death!"

Kospero came forward to obey, and Evander pried the mayor's mouth open with considerable effort, and finally jerked the parchment free. He tossed it on the ground and slapped the mayor on the back a few times to help him regain his breath. By the time he had done so, there were tears running down Golpho's face.

Eventually, the mayor was able to speak once more, in a hoarse voice broken with sobs. "I should thank you, young man, I know, but excuse me for saying that I think it would have been better if you'd left me to die. There's nothing to live for now. We will be slaves to the sorcerer forever."

"Surely, it's not that bad," said Evander.

"Oh it is, it is," and the mayor got to his feet and lurched off into the fish market, leaving Evander and Kospero all alone in the piazza. A sudden chill breeze had blown up that swirled twists of insect wool into the air from outside the weavers' shops.

"I don't like this," said Kospero. "Let's get back to the ship."

With a cold wind at their backs they walked quickly down the empty streets to the harbor where the *Wind Trader* idled at the wharf.

Chapter Two

There being little to do in the somber town of Port Tarquil, the *Wind Trader* unshipped at first light and stood
off a few miles to sea to round the shoals beyond Tormentara. Once more the ship made easy progress, rolling
along before a warm wind from the south. The mass of the
Bakan fell behind.

During the day they dropped lines for the silver tonto
fish in migration along the coast, and were rewarded with
the capture of several of these handsome creatures, some
of them more than three feet long.

That night they washed down the grilled tonto with the
last of the dark wine they'd bought in Zeuxada. When the
wine was finished and the songs were done, Evander
headed for his hammock. He was not on duty until the
third watch, at dawn.

As he slept, the full moon rose in the southwest. On this
night the moon possessed a baleful yellow color, as if it
were some old polished bone sent rolling across the sky.
As it crept to its zenith, Evander turned restlessly in his
sleep and began to moan. Soon he started to squirm and
scratch.

He awoke, sweat pouring down his face, dripping from
his body to the floor. Groaning, he stumbled up the steps
to the deck, drawn by a mysterious compulsion to get outside, into the night.

There the moon's rays struck down upon him and com-
pleted the spell. Evander screamed in sudden pain and
writhed as his skin began to lump and thicken. It felt as if
he were on fire.

The rest of the crew, including Kospero, was gathered
around him by now.

"What ails the lad?" asked Borgo, the steersman.

"I know not," cried Kospero, his eyes bulging with concern.

"It be the revenge of that sorcerer," said Herner, who had seen Evander's act of mercy in the piazza at Port Tarquil.

"Wizard's work!" hissed others.

Sailors on the mirassa sea were notoriously superstitious.

"He shouldn't have interfered," growled another.

The skin on Evander's chest and shoulders grew more mottled by the minute. Lumps rose up within it, and gray spots spread and ridges thickened while he writhed helplessly on the deck.

"He's a turning into a thing!" screamed Borgo. "Look at those buboes in his meat."

"He'll be sucking our blood in the night!" said another man in near panic.

"Enough of that talk!" snapped Kospero.

"Call the captain," shouted Borgo. "We have to throw this thing overboard before it destroys us all."

"You shut your mouth!" bellowed Kospero, standing astride the youth on the deck with his fists up.

The captain came. At the sight of the rough, gray skin, lumped and warty, that now covered the youth's chest and shoulders, his face grew grave. He reached down and examined Evander's face, which was red and lathered in sweat, but not marked by the hideous skin.

"What ails ye?" he muttered. "What in the name of the mysteries is this?" He touched the weird, thickened skin on the boy's shoulder. "Fie! It's like a crocodile!"

"Ugh, what a disgusting sight!" exclaimed Borgo.

Kospero flew at the steersman. "You shut your mouth, damn you!"

Borgo snarled and snapped an elbow in Kospero's face. Kospero lashed back with his foot and drove Borgo into the rail. Borgo's knife came out.

"I've had enough of you, Sedimo scum," he growled.

Kospero had no knife handy and backed away.

The captain interposed, swinging his cane down to the deck with a crunch. "There'll be no fighting aboard my ship!"

The youth moaned, rolled over, and sat up.

"My skin burns. Help me, Kospero."

"My prince." Kospero looked wildly around him and ran to get a bucket.

"I say we throw him overboard; that'll quench his fire," growled Borgo.

"You don't give the orders here!" roared the mate.

"Aye, Borgo," growled Inndiby, "remember your place. I'm the captain of this ship."

"Put him out of his misery, and toss the other Sedimese overboard while you're at it. They're nothing but a danger to us. Have been from the first."

"Now, Steersman, they paid good money to be taken aboard, you remember that." Inndiby's voice grew hot.

"Money that's already spent. Over the side with them."

The men surrounding them murmured loudly.

"Hurry, lest we all be taken with the sorcerer's horror," said Borgo.

The captain glared at them. "That's enough of that talk!"

But just then a cold breeze blew over the ship. Equipment rattled, something flapped loudly in the dark, and a hatch slammed shut. Several men screamed in panic.

"The Wizard be coming for us all!" shouted Herner.

Captain Inndiby looked up to the heavens with an uneasy eye. Something blotted out the stars for a moment directly above. Again, the crewmen let out shrieks of fright.

Ignoring them, Kospero returned with a bucket of water, which he poured on Evander's burning skin. The youth groaned his thanks and struggled to sit up.

And then a purple spark flashed brightly above the ship and shook the mainmast. The men were unhinged. Captain Inndiby was swept aside as they reached for Kospero and Evander.

Kospero struck back fiercely and laid the steersman low. But a knife flashed, and the stocky man slumped to his knees.

"Don't let his blood stain our decks," shouted someone, and in a trice he was lifted and tossed over the side. A few moments later, Evander was hurled overboard to join him.

At first the water was a relief to the fire in the skin of his chest and shoulders, but as he bobbed to the surface, he pushed the pain out of his mind and cast about for Kospero, calling his name over and over to no avail.

The *Wind Trader* sailed on, leaving him behind, but Evander paid it no heed. He was a strong swimmer, and he searched for Kospero for a long time, but found no trace of his friend.

At length, his heart grew heavy, and he prepared himself for death. He had half decided to let himself drown right there and then, but the waves lifted him up instead, and he glimpsed a line of phosphorescence in the near distance. The shoreline was relatively close. This discovery gave him new heart, and he began to swim toward the shore with regular strokes.

He felt as if he swam for a very long time, but at last, before his strength gave out entirely, his feet touched bottom, and slowly, he staggered out of the surf onto a moonlit beach, where he sank to his knees and collapsed with a final groan.

Chapter Three

Evander awoke with a start in the middle of the night. A hand was gently shaking him by the shoulder. He sat up, shivering slightly, though the fearful itching and burning in his skin was gone.

A slim figure wearing a dark, hooded robe squatted beside him. Evander could make out only a suggestion of a bony, angular face. Bright eyes reflected the tawny light of the moon.

Then the figure spoke, but in a tongue unknown to Evander, who knew only Kassimi and Furda, the common tongue of the. coast. He tried Kassimi first, but received only a shrug. Then he tried Furda, and after a moment received a response, so heavily accented that he had to concentrate hard to get the meaning.

"Young fellow, how come you here?"

Evander pushed himself to his knees and stared around him at the long, white beach. The combers from the ocean rolled in one after the other and crashed upon the sand. The full moon rode low upon the horizon.

For a few seconds he had no idea how he came to be there, and then he recalled the final frenzies aboard the *Wind Trader* and his inability to locate poor Kospero.

"Kospero must be dead," he began in a broken voice. There was a hard lump in his chest, and he was unable to go on. Tears were starting from the corners of his eyes.

"Young fellow," said the hooded figure once more. "How you get here?"

"I was on a ship," Evander mumbled. "There was a fight, we were thrown into the sea."

"Ah ha! You are salvage then. You must have swum to shore. You are lucky to have survived the sharks; they are terrible on the Bakanbor coast."

At the thought of sharks tearing at poor Kospero's body,

Evander sobbed, but the little man chattered on in a bright voice.

"You lucky, you survive long time, but it is full moon tonight, and the wizard's creatures soon find you if you stay here."

"Creatures?" asked Evander.

Abruptly, a shadow passed across the moon, far out to sea. The hooded figure looked up sharply.

"Terrible creatures, the curse of our time. You better come with me, it not safe here. My name is Yumi, what yours?"

"Evander."

"Good, hurry up now."

Something flapped in the air, and a thin screech cut through the sound of the waves.

"Hurry, we have been seen!" The little man was scrambling up the beach, his cloak flapping in the wind. Evander followed, and they jogged across the dunes and slid beneath the fronds of a grove of palms that grew along the margin of the sand.

"What is it?" said Evander.

"Ssh," hushed the other, gripping his arm tightly and pointing back to the beach.

Abruptly, Evander saw a huge shape swoop down from the sky and pass low over the place where he had lain. For a moment the shape reminded him of a bat, but this was a bat the size of a house. Then it was gone, and only a plaintive screech echoed back to them from the dark sky.

Evander shivered.

The little man, no more than five foot tall, clapped him on the shoulder with surprising vigor.

"You very lucky, Evander! When the moon is full like tonight, Yumi not leave his house. He certainly not come down here to the beach to look upon the ocean. Not in these days with the Wizard on his mountain. But tonight I could not sleep. Something seemed to call to me from the sea, so I came and found you before the batrukh did."

"Believe me when I say I'm very grateful."

"That is good, since you are my salvage, eh? Come, Evander, we have hot soup by the fire. I think you like to get warm. And maybe we find you some dry clothes, too."

They walked on through tattered palms, past small, irregular fields surrounded by stone walls that glowed white in the moonlight. At length they came to a small house, also built of the white stone. There was a round chimney in the center of a thatched roof, from which a thin wisp of smoke trailed into the starry sky.

As they drew closer, Evander saw that this house consisted of several rooms, with a stable to one side. Inside the stable a pair of donkeys solemnly watched their approach.

Amber light flooded out into the yard as a door opened. A slender figure appeared in the doorway, clad in a calf-length skirt and a short, sleeveless jacket. Yumi called out a greeting in liquid-sounding syllables and drew a cheerful response.

"This is Elsu," said Yumi. "Elsu, meet Evander."

Elsu was another slender little person, with brown hair tied back in a bun and large, bright eyes that observed Evander with a distinct air of calculation. After scrutinizing him carefully, she spoke to Yumi once more in the rapid, liquid syllables of their own language. Yumi replied a couple of times and then turned to Evander.

"Elsu says you are a barbarian from the north, maybe a Kassimi, eh?"

"I am not a barbarian, but I am from the north. My homeland is Sedimo, on the borders of Kassim."

More liquid language flew between the pair, followed by laughter from Elsu.

Yumi held the door open for Evander, who had to stoop to enter.

"Elsu says you certainly are barbarian, but a very tall, handsome one."

Evander felt a sudden, odd shyness, then felt a sudden shock of memory and disgust. His torso was covered in strange, lumpy skin. He hesitated to enter the pool of light, but Yumi tugged him forward. The smell of a hot vegetable soup was irresistible.

The interior of the house was cluttered with tables, cupboards, and chairs. A potbellied stove sat in the center with a black chimney rising to the roof. Light struck down from a circular lamp set near the ceiling. In that light Evander saw the skin of his upper arms, now a weird, ridged moonscape in dark gray.

"I cannot come in," he groaned. "I am a monster."

"No," said Yumi. "It is not that bad, you are just a barbarian."

"Look," cried Evander, "see how my skin has grown hard and horrible."

Yumi and Elsu crowded around him with soft coos and cries. Elsu's fingers pried at some of the lumps and ridges on his shoulders.

"Elsu say this must have been powerful magic to cause such a transformation. You lucky to still be alive."

"I am a monster, cursed by the Wizard," groaned the youth. And slowly, with occasional halts, he told the story of what had happened in Port Tarquil and aboard the *Wind Trader*.

Strangely enough, Yumi was not discouraged by this news. He bade the youth seat himself and take a bowl of soup. "You lucky you not dead. We lucky to find you. So much luck! You must be answer to our prayers," he said.

However, this thought merely brought to the surface an image of poor Kospero gnawed by fish in the dark ocean.

Evander slumped upon a stool beside the stove, tears straining to escape from eyes that no longer saw anything clearly.

Somehow he ate the soup they gave him, barely tasting it. Later, wrapped up in his misery, he rolled into a blanket and slept beside the stove.

Chapter Four

The next morning Evander found Yumi and Elsu busily packing several leather pannier bags with clothing and small possessions.

Seeing that he was awake, Elsu went inside and fed him a breakfast of bulgrum cakes and millet, with a cup of hot tea. In the morning light he saw that she was younger than Yumi, but that they were obviously of the same race or tribe. Each had a honey-gold color of skin, with lustrous brown eyes and long, straight brown hair. Yumi's hair, like Elsu's, was tied in a bun on the back of his head.

Elsu's face was an even more delicate caricature of the human norm, with high cheekbones and overlarge, olive eyes. Like her husband, she was less than five feet tall, with the build of a twelve-year-old boy.

Both wore loose-fitting suits of fine cotton cloth in dark earth tones, with silver clasps, buckles, and buttons. Both wore finely-made sandals on their feet. Only Elsu's breasts and hips betrayed the gender difference between them.

Elsu had dried Evander's breeches by the fire, and now she gave him a shirt that she had hurriedly made for him out of a sheet of cotton. Evander was stunned by the delicacy of the work. Then questions came crashing in. How long had he been asleep? Several hours, or days? No tailor in Sedim could have done this in less than a day.

"Good morning, Evander," said Yumi when he came back from loading the donkeys. "We are leaving today, and you are coming with us."

"Leaving? But why?"

"Wizard chase away all our customers. Elsu and I are flower growers. We take our bulbs now and go north. I have an old rug that can be repaired only in the city of Monjon. Have you heard of it?"

"Monjon? Of course. It is the magical city on the Skola."

"Monjon very magical, because of the power of the blessed Thymnal. So we go there and take my old rug. We take you, too; in Monjon you find a cure for your skin."

"But what about your house and your fields?"

"No matter, we will build another house somewhere else. As long as we have our bulbs and our brains, Elsu and I can build our farm again in another place."

This positiveness and casual mobility in the face of adversity impressed Evander. But he was suddenly seized with the hope that Kospero might have survived somehow. Perhaps his friend was on the beach even now, badly wounded, but alive! Starting up with a cry, he ran toward the shore, calling out Kospero's name.

Yumi ran after him and caught up with him by the edge of the dunes.

"Where you going?" cried the little man.

"Kospero! He may be out there somewhere. I told you, he was thrown into the water at the same time as I was."

"If he was on the beach in the night, then he not be there anymore. Wizard's creatures will have had him."

But Evander would not listen and hastened out upon the white sand. He stared up the beach, which seemed harsh and bright under the morning sun. The tide was out. Gentle ripples washed up along the wide, sandy shore. The onshore breeze continued, and masses of white clouds were gathering far out to sea.

And then he noticed a dark shape bobbing at the water's edge two hundred yards away. He ran toward it.

It was a human body, or what was left of one. Gagging in horror, Evander pulled it up the beach. There were no legs and only one arm. Bones showed through where the fish had worried the carcass. When he turned it over onto its back, he was relieved to see that it was not Kospero. Instead, the agony-wracked countenance of Borgo, the steersman of the *Wind Trader,* gazed up with dead eyes and stiffened flesh.

His relief faded and was followed by a sense of desolation such as he had never experienced before, not even when he had been forced to leave his homeland and become a wanderer.

Kospero was gone, probably devoured like this, washed up on some ill-starred strand along the coast. He had lost his friend forever. Helpless tears ran down his cheeks.

Poor, brave Kospero, who had warned him not to interfere in the doings of the Wizard, and had now paid with his life for Evander's good deed. Kospero, who had been his friend and companion ever since the day of banishment, Kospero with the hearty laugh and genial good humor. Kospero was no more.

Now Evander was truly alone, an outcast, doomed to wander the face of the world, loathed by all men for his monstrous appearance, with no place he could call home, and no man who knew his true and rightful identity as Prince Danais, heir to the throne of Sedimo Kassim.

After a while, Yumi approached, carrying a small pick and a tiny shovel. Together, he and Evander buried Borgo's remains in the palm grove. As he dug, Evander wondered at the mysteries of life. Borgo had been their enemy, and now Borgo was dead, while Evander still lived. Afterward, Evander stood for a long while looking out to sea and mourning for Kospero. At last, with a softly spoken oath of vengeance on the sailors of the *Wind Trader,* he turned away.

Back at the house he found everything made ready for their departure. There was a pack for each of them, plus the panniers on the donkeys. Finally, there was the rug, rolled up and stuffed inside a waterproof skin with stout drawstrings to keep it shut tight at either end.

Evander was surprised at how light the rug was. It was at least eight feet long and rolled up to a foot in diameter, but felt as if it weighed only a few ounces. It was strapped onto the panniers of the jack donkey.

The house now seemed empty, although all the chairs and tables were still there. Elsu poured salt on the floor of the doorway and recited a little rhyme while Yumi bobbed his head and hummed along with her. Then she lit a stick of incense and placed it on the ground beside the salt. The door they left open.

"This was good house," Yumi explained. "We built it ten years ago. We leave it now for someone else."

Evander glanced along the trail leading away from the little house. Open fields, with stone walls and clumps of trees, greeted the eye. To their left the land rose up in several humps that he knew would eventually merge to form the great ridge of the Bakan. Straight ahead was a low line of gray hills, while to the right there was flatter ground, with a dark stump some ways off, an isolated mountain that dominated the land around it.

"What is that?" he asked, pointing.

"That is wizard's mountain," said Yumi. "We not go that way, that for sure."

"Which way do we go? And how far is it to Monjon?"

"First we cross over Bakanbor moors to Storsh town. There we sell the donkeys and buy tickets on the stage-coach to Monjon. It take three, maybe four days to get to Monjon."

"What will we eat? Where will we stay? It sounds like it will all cost money, and I'm afraid I have none."

"No worry about that; Yumi and Elsu have enough silver. You are our salvage, so we look after you and see if you can be cured in Monjon. You were sent as answer to our prayers."

"Do you think it's possible?" Evander looked at his thickened, lumpy skin with distaste. How could this be the answer to anybody's prayers? The skin on his shoulders was half an inch thick, like the hide of some monstrous dragon.

"In Monjon anything is possible; it is magical city. It floats. Sick people come from all over the world to be cured by the blessed Thymnal. Surely, Evander can be cured, too."

With this, Yumi urged the donkeys forward, and they began the journey.

Chapter Five

The early afternoon hours passed quickly as the trio moved down the trail past many abandoned farms with overgrown flower fields and decaying, one-story houses.

"Did all the people here grow flowers as you and Elsu did?" asked Evander.

"Oh, yes, soil here very chalky, very good for some kind of flowers. These are houses of Ugoli folk, like Elsu and Yumi. We sold our flowers to all the markets in the Bakanbor coast. Business very good one time."

Evander's eyes lit up.

"Ugoli folk, that's what you are! Of course, I should have known. In my homeland the Ugoli are known only from the storybooks."

Yumi nodded glumly. "There are not so many of us left in this age when big people are so numerous. Once, of course, world was empty except for beasts and Ugoli. But then there came the bigger people, who grew bigger each generation. As they came, so they drove Ugoli folk away and slew the beasts and cut down the trees and changed the world."

"Yes, that is how it was," agreed Evander. "I always did find it rather unfair. There were no Ugoli people in my homeland. They must have all been chased away long ago."

"You come from north, from land of ice and snow."

Evander thought of the burning heat of a Sedimo summer and said quickly, "Well, actually, not really," but Yumi rattled on.

"Ugoli people never like ice and snow, so not many Ugoli ever live there. Then when the barbarians came, they all left. Barbarians not good to Ugoli people."

Evander nodded. "And we've been stricken with guilt by it ever since."

All of the Kassim cradle stories about the Ugoli cast the

smaller people as a good influence. A gentle people who
had offered the tribes of Arna much wisdom and been re-
paid with slaughter and displacement. The most important
of all the stories was that of the "Healer Ugoli," who
stopped to cure King Ginzax of Kassim, who was dying of
his wounds by the side of the road. Five Kassim nobles,
four bishops, three peasants, a dwarf, and a starving child
all walked past the dying king, but the little Ugoli healer
named Muffupu stopped to staunch his wounds and stayed
with the king and nursed him back to health. Later, un-
grateful nobles engineered the trial by torment of the
healer, who was then burned at the stake, becoming a mar-
tyr and a perpetual focus for guilt in all the lands of Arna.

The little Ugoli were creatures of dim myth now in the
kingdoms of Arna, but he, Evander, had found them. Or
they he. Had the Gods sanctioned this? Were the Gods
watching out for him, after all? He needed to talk to
Kospero. Kospero always had an idea about what the Gods
were up to.

And now he was to travel up the valley of the Skola with
these elfin Ugoli folk, like something out of ancient fable.
And their destination was the magical city of Monjon. He
laughed to himself. Who of his friends, still secure in Sedimo Kassim, would believe the adventures that Danais
Evander Sedimo had already experienced? How their jaws
would drop when he told them. If he ever managed to find
his way home someday.

And if he ever managed to shed the horrible skin that
covered his chest and arms, a thought that quickly dispelled
the warm picture of friends and home in his mind.

On they went, climbing now into the central moors. Here
on higher ground the palms and biscuit trees were gone,
replaced in the hollows by giant thistle and scrub oak. Dappled slopes of wildflowers shone beneath the sun. The air
was bright and clear, and the only clouds were far out to
sea behind them.

They crossed several small streams, descending into narrow canyons each time to do so. These canyons were
choked with dense stands of thistle and red furlock.

It was in one of these canyons that Yumi suddenly froze
and held up a hand for silence. Elsu muzzled one of the
donkeys. Yumi signaled for Evander to do the same for
the other.

Cautiously, Yumi stepped forward to the side of the stream and gazed up and down the canyon. The vegetation to one side was much trampled down and broken. He eased his way past this and disappeared around the bend for a moment.

Evander noticed footprints a yard wide in the gravel by the bank of the stream and felt the hairs rise on the nape of his neck. What gargantuan animal made such tracks?

A tense minute ensued as he waited there for Yumi to return. When he did, Evander pointed to the huge prints. "What made these?" he asked in a whisper.

"The Wizard's beast, a thing like a toad the size of a house. It eats anything it comes upon."

Evander examined the surrounding countryside more closely as they climbed out of the canyon and back onto the plateau. The sunny day seemed suddenly all too bright and clear.

"Is this beast active by day?"

Yumi sought to reassure him. "No, it shuns the light of the sun. They say it live in a cave. Since the moon was full last night, it would have hunted on the moors. At other times it is found only in the region surrounding the black mountain."

Evander looked to the north, where the mountain was still dimly visible, a black stump heaved up above the hills. "What does this wizard want?"

"Alas, no one knows. He has a hate for all the world. It is said he very ugly."

"But the world is beautiful; why does he not love it like other beings?"

"Wizard is unknowable. Those who have gone to his castle to plead with him have not come back to tell tales."

On they went, Elsu leading the first donkey, Yumi the second, while Evander walked beside him. They stopped for a quick lunch when the sun was already starting down the sky. Elsu brought out pickleberry preserves and a loaf of bread baked the day before. Yumi produced a bottle of Cantabral wine to wash it down.

"If we keep going like this, we can reach Storsh Town tonight," he said. "We want to be away from moors by dark. Because that when the creatures will awake."

Evander found himself in complete agreement with the idea of being well away from the moors by then.

Later, they climbed a high hill, and on its far side entered a wood of dwarf oak and giant thistle. "This is Severeb woods," announced Yumi. "We halfway now."

These words left Evander uneasy.

Halfway! But the sun was far down the sky now. They had only a few hours left to get well away from this strange region, overgrown with giant thistle and haunted by carnivorous monsters.

To keep his spirits up, Evander asked Yumi questions about this region of the world, of which he knew little on his own account. "Tell me about Monjon," he said finally. "Tell me about the blessed Thymnal. I have heard of its existence, but I know very little more than that. It is only a thing of legend in Sedimo."

"See, you must be barbarian. Everyone in Eigo knows about Thymnal of Monjon."

"My home lies beyond the lands of Eigo, in Arna on the continent of Ianta. My ship came from the great port of Molutna Ganga. Have you heard of that?"

The little Ugoli shook his head. "I know only the cities of Bakan coast, never been across ocean."

"It seems to me that everyone calls any people who live beyond their own experience, barbarians. In Sedimo they say that the people in Molutna are barbarian. But in Molutna, they call the Sedimese 'savages.' Now you tell me that everyone in Kassim is barbarian, even the great king of Kassim himself. I would be interested to know what you would say to the great king if you were brought before him in Gondwal, in the palace of blue marble."

Yumi laughed. "I would say, great 'barbarian' King, I bring you lovely flowers."

Evander chuckled. "The king would accept your flowers, and then he would have your head cut off for impertinence."

Yumi laughed again, amused by the thought of the great king of the savages, who lived in a blue palace.

"Anyway," said Evander, "tell me about the Thymnal. What is it exactly? I had heard that it is made of silver, that it glows too bright for a man to look at without going blind."

"Ah, that wrong. It is one big legend! So many stories they tell. But agree that it come to Monjon in the time of King Donzago. Long ago, when Monjon was young. Since then, it has been kept in a vault beneath the palace. Thymnal give energy, much power. It float the city and make many, many lights shine at night."

"I had heard that there were many lights there; we call Monjon the 'City of Lights' in Sedimo, where we have only candles and lamps. So tell me, what are these lights?"

"Oh, everyone know that! The Thymnal is very hot! And so they put water in tank with him. When water in there for long time, it get hot, too. Then this water is put in glass bowl, and when the sun sets, it glows with bright yellow light. Now every room in the city have a bowl, and there are big ones in the streets. Everything bright as day, all night."

Evander was awed by such a thought.

The forest of oak and thistle gave out and was replaced by birch groves with glades filled with wildflowers.

They climbed another hill and found themselves atop the last bare stretch of the moor. Nothing but heather, grass, and exposed stone lay around them, a dismal stretch.

Far in the distance, however, the greener lowlands of Storsh could be seen, offering an end to the moors altogether.

"Almost there now," said Yumi.

Then Elsu gave a cry of alarm and pointed to the south. Black clouds were massing there and moving swiftly toward them. Lightning flickered around their bases. Distant thunder banged out in ominous rolls.

"We better hurry," said Yumi.

They tried to push the donkeys to increase their pace, but the animals were vexed from their exertions of the day and refused to do more than keep up their steady pace. The clouds gained on them very quickly.

All too soon they were in shadow, and the first rain drops were falling. It grew steadily darker as the sun vanished from view, and a strong wind blew up that sent dead leaves whistling through the woods.

Elsu opened one of the panniers and brought out waxwool cloaks and hoods and a waxwool blanket for Evander, which he wrapped about his shoulders and secured with a strap.

Elsu also produced a hat for him, made of a mysterious material that stretched when pushed hard enough and held its shape otherwise. It was also waterproof according to Yumi, and was called "ugolfelt."

It was just in time, for the rain came down now in sheets, and they could barely see their way through it. Small streams on the moor turned quickly into torrents with foaming brown water kicking over the rocks.

They struggled on, slipping in the mud, with the rain hammering down.

Then Evander saw a large stone ahead, eroded in the shape of a mushroom by the harsh winds of the moors.

He ran toward it for shelter. Underneath the cap it was at least partially dry, and the direct force of the rain was held at bay.

Elsu and Yumi followed, but Yumi urged them not to stay. "This is dangerous place. A beast will come here soon to look for travelers like ourselves, taking refuge under the stone."

"A beast?" asked Evander uneasily.

"Yes, one of the wizard's creatures. They use such stones like men use lobster pots and visit them when storm come."

Evander stared at the sundry stains on the lower parts of the stone, and then noticed with a shudder the skulls and weathered bones that were scattered on the other side of the stone. Once more they went on, pressing forward into the driving rain.

They entered a region of heather thickets, the rain coming now in squalls, driven by fierce, chill winds. They were all soaked to the skin, shivering.

"This storm is from the evil one," said Yumi. "He knows that travelers are out upon the moor. We must get to rope bridge at Taungi Canyon; that's the only safe way out."

The path wound through the waist-high heather, which grew thickly on all sides. Soon Evander began to feel a strange unease, a prickling of some sixth sense. At about the same time the donkeys seemed to sense something, for they kicked and snorted and actually begin to pick up speed voluntarily.

"Something stalks us," said Yumi.

Elsu's eyes were large and bright.

Evander looked back at the next rise and caught a glimpse of something large and reddish brown bustling through the thistle thickets a ways behind. Its movements were oddly mechanical, and the shape was outlandish.

"It's big, has at least four legs, seems to be brown in color," he told Yumi.

"It be wolgonger," said Yumi with grim certainty. "It love to eat Ugoli, big people, too."

Evander searched about for some kind of weapon, but the moor was empty of anything more substantial than a giant thistle bush.

"Come, we run!" Yumi tugged at his sleeve and urged him on down the muddy track.

They ran headlong down into a valley floored with boulders and bare rocks. Here they forded another stream, although this one was in spate, the water above knee level and rising fast.

The donkeys were unwilling at first to enter this stream, but the scent on the wind of the thing that pursued them drove them in. Soaked, shivering, they ran up the far side of the little valley.

Evander looked back, but saw no sign of the wolgonger. Yumi yanked on his hand. "Come Evander, run for your life."

Bewildered, he followed the slender Ugoli who were sprinting across a bare prairie of knee-high grass toward a distant structure, which turned out to be the shelter beside the rope bridge across the next canyon, a much larger, steeper void than any of the others.

The donkeys were running a little ahead of them, the panniers and carpet bouncing on their backs. They all ran though their hearts were hammering and the breath hot and harsh in their throats.

Suddenly, the donkeys accelerated, running as if pursued by lions, and when Evander looked back he saw why. A crablike thing ten feet high was skittering toward them. Arms that ended in heavy pincers waved aloft.

Evander gave a shriek and ran faster than he would have believed possible. He was catching the donkeys, with only Elsu ahead of him. Elsu staggered suddenly, her ankle twisted.

Evander swatted the donkeys on their rumps to encourage them even more and grabbed up little Elsu and ran on with her in his arms.

Ahead loomed a chasm, with walls of white limestone and a brown river roaring far below. Across the empty

space hung a rickety rope ladder, with wood slats and
withes along the sides.

The wolgonger was so close they could feel the ground
tremble under its tread. From its joints came ominous
squeaks and whistles as it stretched its articulated limbs.

The donkeys burst straight onto the bridge without hesitation, and Yumi followed right behind, although the stam-
pede caused the whole thing to gyrate wildly and knock
Yumi off his feet.

Then Evander's foot slipped in loose stones and he fell.
Elsu rolled forward out of his arms with the litheness of a
gymnast and ducked to her right into the heather.

Evander crawled into the heather on his left. It was not
easy to move through, except at ground level, worming forward like a human snake through the twisted stems.

The wolgonger was on top of them. Evander heard it
ripping up the heather with its pincers and stuck his head
up to take a look.

The crablike central body, a disk ten feet across, was
turned to the right, where it probed for little Elsu in the
heather just beyond the path.

Heather was churning up over the thing's back like hay
from a mower. Evander started forward at Elsu's first
scream. Without really thinking about what he was doing,
he leaped back to the path, sprang onto the wolgonger's
hind leg, and heaved himself onward to land in the middle
of its back.

With a tremendous hiss the thing jerked backward and
tried to flip him off. He was flung flat on its upper carapace
and slid to the front. The pincers were swinging down to
snap up this morsel.

Under the carapace was a nightmare visage of gnashing
beaks, feathered horns, and two fist-sized eyeballs on the
end of black stalks, three feet long.

With a shriek of mingled fear and rage, Evander grabbed
the eye stalks and started to knot them around each other.
The wolgonger went into paroxysms, tumbling sideways,
hissing furiously.

Evander clung on desperately and then attacked the eye
stalks once more, tucking one through the other and jerking
them tight. The thing leaped beneath him as if electrocuted,
the beaks gaped wide. Evander was hurled loose and

landed in the heather with a thump that knocked the breath out of him.

When he got back on his feet, he saw Elsu sprinting for the bridge and the wolgonger springing up and down in place as it tried to unknot its eyes with its heavy pincers.

Evander pushed forward through the heather, heading directly for the bridge. It was slow work, and he felt terribly drained. He passed within ten feet of the thrashing thing and kept on, grim-faced, close to total exhaustion. It saw him and attempted to seize him, but its eyes were still crossed over, and its pincers, misdirected, moved the opposite way. An odd wail of frustration escaped it as he slipped past.

At last the heather gave way. At the same time there was a triumphant hiss behind him. Glancing back, he saw that it had untied its eyes. It sprang straight up in the air six feet and landed with snapping pincers.

"Run, Evander!" screamed Elsu and Yumi.

He ran, or stumbled, or staggered, although the bridge seemed miles away all of a sudden. The thing was right behind him, its whistling joints shrieking. Then Elsu and Yumi took his hands and pulled him forward down the swaying bridge to safety.

The monster remained at the brink, its pincers snapping the air in frustration. Tentatively, it put a foot on the bridge, but under the weight the bridge swayed alarmingly, and the wolgonger could not venture farther.

In sick horror Evander watched the mouth parts gnash together in a fray of hooks and beaks. He shuddered at the thought of being consumed in there, as he might so easily have been. Then, wearily, he got to his feet and negotiated the rest of the bridge to join the donkeys, who were unconcernedly cropping the grass on the cliff top at the far side.

Yumi checked the panniers and announced that everything was safe; they hadn't lost a thing.

Elsu suddenly jumped up and threw her arms around Evander's neck and gave him a loud kiss on the cheek. She said something to Yumi and let go. Both Ugoli collapsed together in merriment.

Eventually, Yumi turned to Evander, "Elsu say you definitely answer to our prayers!"

Chapter Six

The nightmarish wolgonger was left behind, stamping on the cliffs. Soaked to the skin, they journeyed on, breathing hard, but glad to be alive. Yumi gestured to the lands ahead, only dimly visible in the rain where the broad Skola River formed a shining snake across the plain.

"We are safe now; this is Frungia. There will be villages soon."

The weather gradually improved, and they spent the last hour of evening light strolling down a well-paved road to the city of Storsh. Farms and houses were numerous, while horse-drawn vehicles passed them on the road.

Storsh was a town of stone buildings five and six stories high with massive roofs of copper and slate. It was the market center for the Duchy of Storsh, on the great bend of the Skola.

As evening fell, warm lights came on in the windows, and streetlamps on each corner lit up as well. Evander remarked to himself the obvious prosperity of the place. There were never so many lights in Sedimo.

They made their way through cobbled streets to a row of stagecoach company offices, each in a separate building of gray stone, with wooden sidewalks built along the front. Here, Evander witnessed the astonishing prejudice against the little Ugoli folk that was prevalent in some parts of Eigo.

One clerk pointedly shut his business window when Yumi appeared, purse in hand, to buy tickets.

Several customers shied away with loud sniffs and angry stares.

"What the hell is a goddamn imp doing in here?" muttered somebody in a loud voice.

Evander was perplexed at first, but soon puzzlement gave way to anger as the Storchese pointedly shunned the Ugoli.

Yumi was a kindly soul and deserved better than this. These rude people were decidedly unpleasant. He suddenly felt ashamed of his own kind.

Evander pushed forward to the next clerk's window. "I want three tickets to Monjon," he said in a voice that would brook no opposition.

The clerk sighed and handed over three rectangles of brown card coded with numbers and the letters MJ stamped in black.

"That'll be six silver ducats, or a monjon crown if you've got it."

Yumi fumbled out six small silver coins, and Evander paid them over. The clerk touched the money gingerly as if it were infected.

"Imp silver," said someone in a knowing tone.

"Well, I'll not ride with an imp!" snapped someone else. "Clerk, my money back, please. I'll take my business to another line."

Evander glared at them and brushed past. He and Yumi moved outside to the loading dock where Elsu and the donkeys waited. Without a word she led them round to the stabling yards, where Yumi haggled briefly with a surly lout and obtained a dozen ducats for the animals.

The lout would have been tempted to cheat the Ugoli and send them away with a thick ear if he complained, but for the tall, fierce-eyed youth who stood behind him. The fellow had the look of a fighter, and the lout wanted none of that.

Elsu and Yumi kept up a constant chatter in their own tongue all the way back to the stagecoach loading dock. Yumi seemed very pleased about something, and so did Elsu, who gave him another bright smile.

When the Monjon stage arrived, they took seats in the cabin. The stages on the Monjon route were large, pulled by five and six pairs of horses. Inside there were four rows of seats. When Yumi and Elsu took their places, the woman sitting next to them gasped and moved hurriedly away.

Evander took her seat, next to the window.

"Since when have imps been given the freedom to ride on Blue & Red lines?" snapped a man in a wide-brimmed leather hat, his face red and his nose overlarge. Like most Storchese, he wore a black cotton suit, white shirt, and ankle-high boots.

Evander looked up, his face flushed with anger. What right had these people to be so rude? He was about to ask them to their faces, when he felt a pressure on his forearm.

"Say nothing, it will pass," whispered the slender Ugoli.

"Why?" questioned Evander.

"It better for us. You see."

Evander contented himself with an angry glare at the man in the wide-brimmed hat, who snorted and looked away. The fellow began reading a small book by the illumination of a glowing glass ball dangling from his lapel.

The light fascinated Evander.

"That is Monjon lamp, small one," whispered Yumi in response to Evander's question.

Evander was deeply impressed by this evidence of real magical power.

The coach started up with a crack of the whip and lurched away down the Monjon highway. The well-maintained road was paved in gray stone slabs; thus they made swift progress.

As they went on, some of the passengers put away their books and dozed. A few stared moodily at the passing countryside. They were in the wine country of the Skola now. On the slopes to their right, they passed wide vineyards ripening toward the harvest. On the lower land to their left were more vineyards, interspersed with fields of wheat and the villages of the vineyard workers.

In the back of Evander's mind certain memories were stirring, of a much drier land that also ran beside a great river. Grapes were grown there, too, but in small plots rather than these enormous tracts.

All that day they traveled on the well-constructed highway, with more than enough room for two coaches to pass one another. Prosperous towns with steep, gray slate roofs and stone walls rose up one after the other along the road and receded behind them.

That night they halted in the wine town of Mainzan, a picturesque place with whitewashed houses around the market place. At the Market Inn, however, they met once more with the Frungian prejudices.

"We have no rooms available for the like of your companions," snarled the concierge. "No imps allowed here."

Evander protested loudly and was seized by the house guards, a pair of burly fellows with overlarge stomachs.

Evander put his elbows into those stomachs and temporarily disabled the guards, who fell back.

"Send for the constables," said one of them.

"This fellow needs to spend some time in the stocks," said the other.

"Keep your hands off me," cried Evander in a fury. "I'm leaving anyway," and he stormed out.

For a while he strode up and down an alley, too angry to think straight. Slowly, he cooled down and got his temper under control. He was a prince of the royal blood, and he had never experienced anything like this. It was hard for him to reconcile himself to it.

Yumi, who had already warned Evander against trying any inn in Mainzan, now led the way down to the stables. And here, although the grooms complained halfheartedly and threatened to throw Yumi into the manure heap, they were allowed to bed down in an empty stall with clean straw on the floor.

They unpacked some of the preserves and waybread they had brought, while Evander bought a flagon of ale and a leek-and-potato pie with Yumi's silver piece.

When he returned, he found the Ugoli man sitting on a bale of hay, examining the unrolled carpet. On a dark red background were diamond-shaped medallions in orange and black, depicting dancing horses.

"That's beautiful," said Evander as he sat down and took a swig of the ale.

"It called Nine Horse Carpet; it very powerful when it repaired."

Evander took another long swig of ale, enjoying the first flush of alcohol. It had been a long day.

Elsu stroked the carpet as if it were a cat. Suddenly, it began to wriggle and twitch.

Evander looked at the ale pot in his hand. The ale here in this strange land was obviously stronger than what he was used to.

Yumi cut the pie in sections and handed one to Evander, who leaned back against the stable wall to eat it. The carpet wriggled again.

"By the gods," he exclaimed, "this ale they make here does strange things to your head."

"It just ordinary ale," said Yumi with a shrug.

"Well, I could swear I saw that carpet of yours moving as if it were alive."

Yumi shot him a look of reproof. "But it *is* alive, silly Evander. It is Ugoli rug from long ago. This is a Xish Wan rug, very, very magical." He stroked it with a slender, boned hand. "You should see this old rug on the night of full moon when the sky is clear! It jumps on the floor. It takes little leaps. It will lift you up an inch or more. It yearns to be free of the pull of the ground."

Abruptly, Yumi's face fell. "But it is an old carpet, Xish Wan was long ago, and it has lost its vitality over the years."

Once more he brightened in his mercurial way. "But in Monjon we will be able to get it repaired. Postrema, the weave witch, has the highest recommendations."

Evander stared at the carpet while Yumi stroked it and murmured sweet nothings to it as if it were an old favored hunting hound lying by the fire.

"Come," said Yumi. "Put your hand on it, feel how soft it is."

Evander was wary, but eventually he reached out and touched the rug. The fibers seemed to quiver, like the fur on a cat's back, then the rug shook slightly. Evander jerked his hand back.

"It *is* alive. I'll be damned."

Yumi laughed happily, and the rug seemed to be laughing with him, its corners flipping up and down.

Later, he rolled it up once more, and they finished the ale and the pie and settled down to sleep. Evander was the last to drop off. His thoughts were still buzzing with magical images, and beyond them his hope for healing from the Wizard's curse.

Chapter Seven

Evander awoke to an odd sound, a scraping, whining, fiddling thing. He sat up and stared about the stall. The odor of horses was strong, and the light was dim, filtering in over the top of the stall from the lamp by the outside door.

The scraping came again. It was a weird thing, quite irregular. Evander rose and went to take a look out the stable door. He lifted the bar that kept the door closed and stuck his head out. Something flashed in the corner of his eye, and he flinched. The blow from the cudgel that should have knocked him senseless fell across his shoulders instead.

It was still a very solid blow, and he went down with a gasp, then rolled quickly to dodge boots that swung at him out of the dark. He kicked out with his own legs and brought one man down with him.

Another stood over him, the cudgel in his hands. Evander dodged and felt it strike the ground beside his head. He kicked upward and caught the cudgel's wielder in the groin.

An explosive gasp came from the fellow, and he crumpled. Then Evander was back on his feet and had the cudgel in his own hand.

Two more grooms, their breath livened by ale, were inside the stall, ransacking the Ugolis' bags. One of them had already grabbed the rolled-up carpet, while the other held a knife to Yumi's throat.

Evander lunged inside and caught the wrist of the fellow with the knife.

"Damn you!" yelled the knave struggling to free himself.

The cudgel felled him. The one with the carpet dashed for the door, and Evander chased after him the length of the stables, past two dozen sleepy horses until Evander's waist-high tackle brought the thief down with a crash on the stone flags. Evander was in a battle rage, eyes wild, the cudgel raised for a lethal stroke.

"No, please, don't," wailed the fellow.

He felt that touch again, on his wrist, a subtle pressure on the muscles of the forearm.

"No, Evander," said Yumi quietly. "Spare this knave. It will be better for us not to spill blood here in Mainzan."

The battle lust faded. Evander lifted the wretch onto his feet by his collar. Yumi took back the carpet and cradled it tenderly. Evander shoved the groom away.

"Go now," said the Ugoli. "Trouble us no more."

The groom slunk away with an evil glance back over his shoulder.

"He does not seem so grateful; perhaps I should go after him," said Evander, but Yumi held him back.

Evander then dragged out the other would-be thieves and sluiced them down with the cold-water bucket to wake them. Then he sent them on their way with a few well-placed kicks.

Once more the travelers settled down behind the securely barred door of the stall. Yumi tried to explain why Ugoli were treated so badly in Frungia.

"The Frungians claim that Ugoli people once cursed their vineyards, and they had years of poor wine as a result. But this is just a story. In fact, they blame us for the coming of the Wizard. They have lost the moorlands and much else to his dominion. They have found that it does not pay to complain to him. So their hatred of him has turned upon the Ugoli."

"Are you sure that Ugoli never cursed their wine?"

"Perhaps in the distant past it may have happened. This was all our forest once, and when the men came and planted their vines, the Ugoli may not have wished them to. I do not know. You would have to ask someone wise in the lore of ancient times, not Yumi."

"But this was long ago, before the Sorcerer came."

"There was no hate like this until then."

"And in Monjon?"

"Ah, Monjon—there things are very different. There are many Ugoli there, and they work in silver and brass and make things that are sold all over the world."

Evander mused on this for a moment. "The Storchese hate the Wizard, but are too afraid of him to hate him out loud, so they hate the Ugoli instead? I'm afraid I don't understand too well."

Yumi gave him a wry smile, "If Storch people dared to hate the Wizard with their voices, then he might hear them and mount upon his batrukh and appear one night at their doors to carry them away to his dungeons. To hate Ugoli instead is safer."

Evander shook his head in perplexity, but Yumi just made himself comfortable once more and was soon fast asleep. Evander lay there in the dimness for an hour or more before, he, too, finally returned to sleep.

Chapter Eight

The next couple of days passed more peacefully. The stage left the wine country behind and entered a landscape of rolling hills, wheatfields, and beech forest.

The river meandered like a great silvery serpent until immense rapids broke as the river descended the Monjonese bench, a shelf of resistant basalt of great antiquity.

Here, the town of Shugalent sat at a crossroads formed by the river road and the first bridge across the Skola. Shugalent was a more tolerant, cosmopolitan place than Mainzen. Accompanied by Evander, the Ugoli obtained rooms in the Hotel Chaume with little difficulty, and while some of the bellboys were disinclined to haul Ugoli luggage, others were eager to earn their coin.

The following day the coach left Storsh altogether and entered Monjon proper. New passengers began to appear in the coach. These were Monjonese, who in contrast to the dour, unsmiling Frungians and Storchese, were happy to see the Ugoli and called out greetings to them as they entered the coach. To the Monjonese, the smaller people were bringers of good luck and were regarded as especially favored by the principal god of the Monjon pantheon, Pernaxo.

A coachful of Monjonese was marked by a roar of chatter, another marked contrast to the sober Frungians and Storchese, who spent their time in the stagecoach reading or glooming out the window. In fact, the Storchese shrank away from the Monjonese with every bit as much distaste as they showed for Yumi and Elsu.

Evander soon found himself in conversation with a couple of herb sellers who were on their way to the market in Monjon. They also spoke Furda, although Monjonese pronunciation of Furda was as strange to Evander's ear as was that of the Ugoli.

"Yes, we have dragon's foot and snerper's tidsel for the apothecaries," said the husband, Donforth, a lean fellow with twinkling eyes and gray hair shorn short around his ears and neck.

His wife, a plump woman with red cheeks with auburn hair, added, "And we have dog's nose and wild iris root as well, for the magicians and wizards."

"There be a big demand for all these in Monjon, especially now," said the husband.

"And why is that?" asked Evander.

"Haven't you heard?"

Evander confessed that he hadn't heard, indeed knew almost nothing about Monjon.

"There be a contest of magicians," said the wife, "to win the hand of the Princess Serena. Very active and wonderful it is now in Monjon."

"Every night they make the skies sparkle with their fabulous displays."

Evander turned to Yumi. "You knew of this?"

"Not at all, but all the better for you, my friend. There bound to be someone in the city who can cure you."

The Monjon herb collectors were brimming over with the news from the city. "Extremely memorable it is, so we've heard. The wizards battle one another on the plains in front of the city, and everyone can watch from the walls."

With this concentration of magical forces in mind, Evander found himself looking forward to his first glimpse of the city with increasing anticipation.

When it came, he was not disappointed. The daylight was waning when the coach came over a rise, and the city became visible ahead, on a hill beside the river. There was something strange about the hill, which appeared to have perpendicular sides, lost in shadow.

Evander gaped at the beauty of the city. A dozen graceful towers rose to catch the golden light of the late afternoon sun, their conical roofs sheathed in glazed tile that glowed in amber glory.

"Monjon," said Yumi beside him, "a magical city, see how it floats!"

And as the coach drew closer, Evander saw that indeed Monjon did float, about ten feet off the ground. The hill was sliced through, as if cut off by some giant's knife, and the top half hung suspended in the air.

Evander pointed to the darkness below the floating hill. Beneath the city was a region lost in perpetual shadow.

"A place of ill omen, but now inhabited by many of the poorest wretches," said a Monjonese in comment. "The crops have been cursed for years by the damned Wizard, and many folk are close to starvation."

Evander saw the heavy ropes that stretched from the walls of the city to a circle of huge pegs driven into the ground. These ropes were the width of a man, and the pegs were in proportion, as he saw when the coach passed several in the approach to the ramp system that led up to the city gate.

"Ropes to hold it in place?" he said to Donforth.

"Exactly, my friend. Otherwise it shifts in strong winds."

Long before they reached the city, buildings had appeared along the road, and closer to the floating city were suburbs of modest two- and three-story buildings in brown brick with thatched roofs.

And now as the light of the sun dwindled, Evander saw hundreds, then thousands of lights twinkle into life in the floating city. The windows in the high towers were red, blue, gold, and green. Lower down, the windows of the city came alive with the softer, amber glows.

Even in the townships surrounding the floating city, there were lights, illuminating the countryside for miles around.

"This is all due to the power of the blessed Thymnal," said Yumi. "Here we will find a cure for you."

The coach rolled on across the plain toward the magical city.

Chapter Nine

"So I have the power of the blessed Thymnal to thank, is that all you can say?" The speaker whirled around to confront her mother, who shrank back into her ermine robe.

"Because Father has made his choice, hasn't he? He has chosen to give *me* up rather than the damned Thymnal!"

"My dear, you must remember that many, many lives are dependent on the blessed Thymnal. We all have to make sacrifices."

"If I hear that rubbish about making sacrifices one more time, I'll scream. You want to sacrifice *me,* that's what you want."

"My dear, after you've been married a while, you'll see; it will get easier. You will cease to share your bed with your husband, you will take your lovers. I promise you this."

"Mother! I sometimes wonder what goes through your head! I don't want to take lovers. I want to choose my own husband. And this isn't a situation in which I'm to be married off to some ugly prince whom I've never met and who may or may not want me, a situation that might make any young lady a little wary. No, you're having a contest between weird old men of the mountains to see who gets to carry me off! I mean, some of them don't even look human."

"Now, dear, they aren't that bad. And besides the royal magician is bound to win. You'll see, old Alberto will win the contest. He has promised me this."

"Mother! Alberto is older than you are. I don't want to marry him!"

"Of course not, dear, and Alberto will gladly stand aside when the time comes."

"But, Mother, if Alberto is powerful enough to win the

contest, why doesn't he take to the field against our enemy?"

The queen had no answer to this. Her daughter bored in mercilessly. "Since the Wizard, Gadjung, cursed the kingdom, Father has been unable to do anything about it. If the royal magician can't defeat Gadjung's magic, what makes you think he can win the contest?"

The Queen wriggled uncomfortably. "My darling, Alberto is a wonderful man; he will find a way, I know it." With that she swept her ermine robe together and left her daughter's chamber.

Her daughter, the Princess Serena, shook her auburn hair in disgust and stared out the window. The situation was simply disastrous, and neither of her parents could be counted on.

Far below in the middle distance, a heavy stagecoach was rumbling up the approach ramp to the city gates. She watched, envying the freedom of the people inside it. They could go where they wanted, could leave the accursed city of Monjon if they liked! Unlike herself.

The bell in Jade Temple began ringing the hour. With a heavy sigh she began to get ready for the evening's round of the contest. She pulled out a new gown of the palest peach silk, and though she was unable to take her usual pleasure in wearing something for the first time, began to dress.

Far from the princess's suite in the high tower, the stage from Frungia rolled in at the south gate. After a cursory inspection of the occupants, the guards let it clatter down the Haymarket to the coach station in the outer ward.

There the passengers debarked, including the wide-eyed Evander and the Ugoli folk. They gathered their luggage from the rear of the coach once more, and stood for a moment staring at the city of lights.

The Monjonese herb sellers had been eager to tell him all about the making of these lights, most of which were circular and brighter than any candle Evander had ever seen.

"The light comes from water that has been energized by the blessed Thymnal. The water is warmed by proximity to the Thymnal, then removed when it is close to boiling point. As it cools, it glows with a yellow light and can be put into sealed bowls, or tubes, or anything made of glass,

and then set into lamps. After many years the water begins
to lose its lustre and will fade, but if it is kept in Monjon,
under the influence of the Thymnal, it merely changes
color, turning red, then green, and finally blue and purple."

Now Evander saw the range of lights around him. Most
were amber and yellow, but on the exterior of buildings
there were many red and green and blue lights. They were
everywhere! There were lights in every window, lights
above every door, and large circular lamps on every street
corner, bathing the streets themselves in an orange glow.
High above on the towers were red lamps on the battlements and purple ones by some windows. Evander gazed
upon it all with awe, until Yumi jerked his elbow.

"Visitors who gawk upward too much in Monjon usually
get their pockets picked clean."

Evander was shocked. "There are thieves in the magic
city?"

Yumi chuckled. "I suspect there are thieves even in the
heavens."

Elsu returned with a luggage barrow, and Yumi and she
loaded their pannier bags. Evander took up the carpet over
his shoulder and followed the Ugoli through the streets to
an inn with a heavy wooden door. Inside was a taproom
filled with men drinking beer and talking in the loud voices
of commerce. Beyond the bar was a small reception area.

Here they were greeted like any other guests. In Monjon
there was none of the prejudice found in Storsh. Monjon
was a positively metropolitan place, open to the world.

Yumi took a small room on the fourth floor, overlooking
the street. There they stowed their possessions, and Yumi
put the rug in the safekeeping of the landlord's vault.

Elsewhere on the fourth floor were bathtub rooms and
even a cold plunge pool. Elsu vanished in the direction of
the tubs.

Evander followed her example with pleasure and soon
felt himself luxuriously clean for the first time in days. The
tubs were closeted privately, although they shared the in-
flow of hot water, pumped out from the Thymnal light
globe factory. Fingering the weird skin on his upper body,
Evander was grateful for the privacy.

When he got back to their room, Elsu had dug out a
clean set of clothes for him, clothes she had modified from

her own while riding in the carriage. Once again he thanked her and received in turn a bright, happy smile.

Eventually, they all strolled out into the illuminated night world of Monjon. First they visited a restaurant, where they dined on baked eels with chard, washed down with an excellent red wine from Mainzan's Purple-Glory slopes.

"For this wine they used the black pearl grape," said Yumi. "The vine gives very small crops, but none can match it for intensity of its flavors. It must be kept in cellar for long time before it ready."

Evander remarked that the wine was excellent and then noted sadly, "The people of Frungia do not measure up to their wines." He rolled the fruity wine around in his mouth. "Perhaps all the sweetness in their land has gone into their wines and thus the people are sour and withered."

Yumi smiled sadly. "Perhaps."

Evander smiled back. "Perhaps that is the curse laid on them."

As they ate, they stared out the window. At one point six burly men in white robes went past, carrying a chair above their shoulders. In the chair slumped a mysterious figure in a black robe and a tall, conical hat. Behind the figure bobbed a series of evanescent dream images, like moving three-dimensional paintings.

In full, bright color the figure of a woman about three feet high, wearing only the briefest of costumes appeared on the side of a precipice. She disappeared and was replaced by a waterfall thundering into a cavern. The woman reappeared and launched herself in a swan dive. She disappeared into the waterfall.

The figure beneath the tall black hat was borne around the bend in the street, and the image spheres vanished with him.

Evander turned astounded eyes to Yumi. "A magician?"

"Of course, and there are more approaching."

Indeed, there were dozens of them, in red and blue and black costumes, usually borne on a gaudy throne above the shoulders of six sweating hulks.

"These are the city's own magicians, members of the high order."

Shimmering wraith dragons in pink and purple floated down the street, ten feet above the head of a witch in white robes and golden casque. Balls of red energy whirled in the

opposite direction, following a tall man with an immense
black beard, who was dressed in scarlet satin from head
to foot.

A little later, they heard bright, sharp trumpets sound.
Six trumpeters clad in silver cloth marched past the restaurant, followed by a town crier, who was calling spectators
to take their places on the walls by the north gate where
the jousting field was sited. A bout featuring the royal magician, Alberto the Excellent, was to begin shortly.

Evander persuaded the Ugoli to hurry their supper and
accompany him through the streets to the north wall.

Once there, they had to squeeze their way in to find a
position from which they could see the smoothly rolled field
below, maintained for sporting events of many kinds.
Evander found himself taller than most Monjonese and had
a good view from a spot beside a tower. The Ugoli scrambled up to a small setback on the tower, about five feet
farther up.

A great crowd was assembled along the top of the wall.
On top of the turrets, which interrupted the wall every fifty
yards, there were tiers of wooden seats and a merry throng
in bright colors. Evander noticed the aristocratic mode of
dress of these people with their frills, ruffles, and long
gowns.

Trumpets blared on the field below. Drums were beating,
and men on horseback were posted in small groups around
a perimeter set with a hundred or more large spheres on
pedestals.

All at the same moment, men removed the cloth covers
from the spheres, revealing Monjon lamps of great intensity
that lit the center of the field as bright as day.

The contesting magicians appeared. One was a tall man
in a gold cloth jacket and conical hat who carried a white
wand tucked under his arm. His introduction brought forth
a great cheer from the crowd and much applause.

"It's the royal magician," whispered Yumi.

The other was a shambling figure wearing a brown
hooded robe and strange, shaggy boots. He leaned heavily
on a carved staff that had a skull set into its top.

"The Wizard with no name!" announced the town crier.

The royal magician of the cloth of gold immediately busied himself. When he snapped his fingers, assistants ran out
with a brazier, and in a flash it was lit and blazing brightly.

The figure in the gold jacket leaped around the brazier most energetically, conjuring with birds and baubles and a long, convoluted spell. Finally, he threw powders and essences into the flame, which erupted in flashes of white light that grew more intense with each application, until at last there was a near explosion, and a giant knight in glistening steel casque and helm was standing there, created out of nothing.

The crowd broke into applause. The knight responded with gracious bows to the audience.

Evander turned stunned eyes up to Yumi. The little Ugoli shrugged, as if to say, "I told you this was a magical city."

Now armorers entered the ring, carrying immense weapons over their shoulders.

The giant knight selected a two-handed sword and swung it back and forth viciously so that it sang savagely in the air.

The crowd applauded again. Shouts of "bravo" came from the higher sections. Favors from the aristocratic ladies floated down to the giant in shining armor. When he stood still to allow the armorers to affix a few of these garlands and kerchiefs to his armor, there was tremendous applause in the seats reserved for the aristocracy.

Now the shambling figure in the hooded robe wandered up to the brazier. The crowd ignored him and continued its huzzahs. The figure looked around in annoyance and then stabbed the skull-stick into the ground. Something not unlike a clap of thunder smote the air.

The crowd was instantly hushed.

The Wizard threw a few fragments into the flames. Thick smoke billowed up immediately, and an evil stench filled the air. With arms raised dramatically, the Wizard made a few simple gestures and called out some words of an unknown tongue in a guttural voice.

The quiet was shattered by deep, terrible groaning. The ground in front of him began to hump and shake, and then to rise up in a mound that became a column that finally stood ten feet high. It shattered and reformed; bits fell to the ground in clouds of dust. Then a monster made of gray stone stood there, towering over the knight.

The crowd gasped in amazement.

"A rock troll," said Yumi in genuine horror.

The contest was begun. The combatants paced around

each other. The eight-foot-tall knight pranced aggressively forward and swung his sword in a cut that would have split a horse in two. Instead, his sword bounced off the troll's rocky hide with an echoing clang.

The rock troll slapped at the knight with a huge hand, but missed its agile opponent, who ducked away to one side and hewed mightily at the troll's arm. Again the sword rang off the stone.

The troll spun, swinging huge fists at the knight, who was forced to dance away in evasion after evasion. His sword just could not cut his monstrous foe.

The knight searched for a weak spot, stabbing at groin, then armpit, and finally the neck, without noticeable success. He grew more desperate, and the troll finally caught him a blow with a huge backhand slap that rang the knight's helmet like a bell and sent him staggering backward.

The crowd gasped in horror. The knight fell and rolled over and away from a huge foot that threatened to stamp him out of existence. He managed to keep rolling until he was clear, then staggered back onto his feet.

He darted away from the onrushing troll, while the crowd cheered in enormous relief.

The knight stared at the blade of the heavy sword. It was notched in five places. He retreated to his armorers and exchanged the sword for a mace with a spiked ball the size of a horse's head upon it. He returned to the fray with the crowd's cheers urging him on.

The troll waited, completely unmoved.

The mace thudded into the troll, and now it seemed to the watching crowd that the troll felt some discomfort, for it backed away and did its best to dodge the wild, swingeing blows of the terrible steel ball. Chips of stone were gouged out of the troll, rock crushed into powder. The troll gave ground, retreating, trying to deflect the blows. In its rage it uttered a weird moan.

The crowd cheered lustily.

The knight sensed victory and pressed his attack with abandon. More rock flew, and more dust rose above the combatants. The crowd was in ecstasy.

Then the troll managed to catch the knight by the arm. The crowd gasped. The troll removed the knight's arm like a man tearing the leg off a chicken.

The great mace fell uselessly to the sand. A vast groan

came up from the crowd as the knight was yanked off his feet into those huge hands.

The troll twisted the knight's head off his body with a quick, convulsive jerk. It tossed the head in the air and punted it over the wall into the city where it disappeared in a trail of sparks as it fell into the streets.

The crowd groaned and hissed. The knight's steel-clad body vanished into thin air with more sparks and flashes.

The troll grew still, a rumbling began in the ground, and the troll deformed back into a rough pillar of stone, which sank into the ground with a steady roar.

In a moment there was nothing left but the two contesting magicians and the brazier with its fluttering flame.

The trumpeters rang for the next bout.

Evander found that his mouth was dry from the excitement.

On a balcony high above the walls, King Agrant of Monjon comforted his queen while she sobbed on his shoulder. The royal magician's magical knight had been defeated with contemptuous ease by the challenger.

"There, there, my dear, Alberto put up a splendid fight; he outdid himself."

But the queen could not be consoled. Alberto, her Alberto, had been defeated in the opening round of the final combats. He could never win the prize now.

Trumpets blew once more as the victor in the struggle was ushered up the steps to the royal balcony to receive a crown of laurel leaves.

The Princess Serena watched the Wizard in the brown hood approach with growing dread. When the victor was standing before the King, he bowed low.

"Wizard of mystery, who goes by no name, we congratulate you upon your impressive victory!" said Agrant in a level voice.

"Thank you, King Agrant," croaked the Wizard, "but it was nothing. That old fool was scarcely fit to be in the ring with me."

Agrant shot him a look of admonishment. But when a page held up the laurel crown upon a scarlet cushion, Agrant took it graciously. "So that we may crown you victor, will you please pull back your hood?"

"If you so order it, King, I will do so. But I should warn you that you may regret it."

"Nonetheless, I do order," said Agrant.

The hood was pulled back, and the Princess emitted a little scream of horror. Others in the gallery gasped and hid their eyes.

A hideous mottled skull was visible. On that bloated head were features that were more those of a toad than a human being, with enormous bloodshot eyes that bulged in the sockets.

Serena wanted to faint, but dared not. She had to confront her father now. This was absolutely impossible! What if this creature won the final round? He couldn't give her over to a thing like this!

Agrant set the laurel crown on the leprous head with hands that scarcely trembled. "And now, may we know the name of today's champion?" he asked.

"Indeed, King, for I am Gadjung of the Black Mountain."

More gasps went up from the assembled court of Monjon.

"Gadjung the Impossible?" the king said in a small voice.

Gadjung's hideous face cracked open, and he gargled, "That is correct."

Agrant swallowed, stared at the amphibious distortion of a human head that wobbled in front of him, and tried his best not to think of his daughter being given to it.

"Welcome to Monjon, mighty Gadjung, champion for the day," he said, fighting for control and succeeding, although with less than his usual royal command.

Gadjung's ugly mouth opened in a toothless laugh. "I expect more substantial challenge in the next round, but all will fall who stand against me. I will place my feet on their necks and break them as easily as twigs."

Gadjung's horrible eyes now fixed themselves on Serena. "And this lovely, is she the one destined to be my bride?" he gloated.

Serena stared at the thing and bit the side of her finger to stifle a scream. Suddenly, she turned away and dove behind the throne, then ran shrieking down the staircase behind the gallery.

Gadjung threw back his head and emitted another hoarse bellow of amusement. He was thousands of years old and had no real interest in the girl, except as a means to take possession of the magic Thymnal.

Chapter Ten

The morning dawned bright and sunny, heralding a perfect day under blue skies with occasional fluffy white clouds floating up the valley from the south.

Evander arose early, his thoughts still buzzing with excitement from the previous night.

Out on the streets he studied the wonders of Monjon in the bright sunlight. The city was built in three concentric layers, which grew progressively taller toward the center. The innermost area, about a mile wide, was dominated by fifteen-story structures, great squares of gray and pink stone. In the center the palace thrust up another fifty feet, so that its gilded onion domes sprouted like enormous flowers in the center of the city. In the palace lay the Thymnal, and from it radiated the power that made Monjon, not only famous, but wealthy.

The streets were soon thronged with Monjonese and a visible minority of traders from other parts of the world. Evander saw some paler Czardhans, quite a few Kassimi, and even some light brown men with the distinctive look of the far distant Argonath, in their twill trousers and short silk jackets.

He strolled up the wide Avenue Fagesta into the center of the city. There the great palace of the kings was set against the squat mass of the Temple of the Thymnal, which bulged out of one wall of the palace beneath an immense roof of green tiles.

Lines were already forming at the entrance to the temple. Hundreds of supplicants—the blind and the lame, men with one limb missing, others carried on litters, too weak to walk—had gathered before dawn to seek the favor of the Thymnal.

With a shock Evander recognized some Kassimi figures, dressed in the characteristic jelab and loose-fitting trousers. A wealthy family from Sedimo Kassim, Evander knew the father slightly; an introduction at a polo match, and then a few dinner parties after the grand fiestas. Evander ducked into the line. The Sedimo family was sitting on chairs at the front of the line. Their family servants were lined up about twenty feet distant from them, ready for the beckoning call, but far enough away not to be too intrusive.

Evander thought of what he must look like. He was lean now, a lot leaner than he had been when he'd left the Sedimo palace. And he was darker of skin, considerably so after all that time aboard ships. He wondered if the man could even recognize him. He was wearing Ugoli clothing after all, most of it a little bit too small for him, despite Elsu's heroic work with needle and thread.

He chuckled to himself, the fear fading away. They would never recognize him. They would never see the brown-skinned, slim youth as the Prince of Sedimo. His secret was safe. The killers would not find him.

Evander studied the crowd. Behind the Kassimi were Bakanors, from all the cities of the fertile plain, and dark-skinned men from central Eigo. A Kraheen noble with scarlet teardrops tattooed on his face stood out by virtue of his height.

A stooped man standing behind him, wearing the fragments of a military uniform, hissed something under his breath about the Kraheen as he caught sight of the tall noble.

Evander half turned. The man was missing a foot, and a rather worn wooden ball was strapped in its place.

The soldier caught his glance. "That be a follower of their prophet. I seen them drinking blood. Cannibal swine." He spat loudly.

Evander had heard of the dreaded "He Who Must" of the Kraheen people, a prophet with a message of pride and bloodshed who had enjoyed enormous popularity in the heartland of the continent. There had been a great war down there; armies from all over the world had united to wage war on the prophet and his suspected allies, the masters of Padmasa. Evander knew of men from Kassim who had gone, volunteers for a crusade called by the ancient Witches of Cunfshon. This wretched figure was probably a bruised veteran of the campaign. His clothes were tattered enough to have been through a thousand miles of campaigning, and his missing foot was mute testimony to a conflict of some sort.

A gong sounded loudly from above. The doors to the temple opened with a groan. Monks clad in saffron robes emerged and began to conduct the visitors within.

Just inside the doors were set great brass collection plates, each monitored by sharp-eyed monks. Visitors could contribute to the upkeep of the Servants of the Thymnal. Those who did so with sufficient prodigality were immediately conducted through velvet drapes at the end of the passage. Those who did not were shunted off into a large, barren room of bare stone.

Monks with square black lacquer boxes on their heads emerged in this room and set up small square tables and chairs. At these tables they interviewed the applicants for the merciful charity of the blessed Thymnal.

Evander waited for an hour before he was summoned to a table. During that time he had seen only one or two of the applicants receive permission to go on, into the inner parts of the temple. The rest had been sent back.

Evander stood quietly by the desk. The inquisitor for the merciful charity of the blessed Thymnal was intent on his files. At length he looked up. "You speak Furda?"

"Yes."

"Your name, and your reason for requesting the rays of the blessed Thymnal." There was very little accent to the man's Furda, as if he had learned it in Molutna Ganga itself.

"Evander, uh, Sedimo, and I have come because of the curse of a wizard."

"Explain the nature of the curse."

Evander did his best to describe the events in Port Tarquil and his subsequent journey to Monjon. The inquisitor wrote notes during his exposition, halting him every so often with a peremptory gesture while the pen scratched away on the clean cream paper.

When Evander finished, the man continued writing for a while before looking up.

"And you have nothing you can contribute to the welfare of the blessed Thymnal?"

"I was thrown overboard. They stole my possessions. I have nothing beyond the clothes I am wearing."

The inquisitor looked at him sharply. "Indeed, it had already been noted that you are wearing the garb of an Ugoli street trader. Yet you are clearly no Ugoli, that folk being of a uniformly high intelligence."

Evander flushed, but held his tongue. He knew now how bureaucracies worked. Kospero had taught him many things since he had left the palace in Sedimo and gone a vagabond. It was best not to respond to such insults. The petty official with a thirst for power, a low-level tyrant, had proved to be common as he and Kospero had sailed around the coasts of Eigo in search of safety. The slightest thing could set such a man against him and doom his effort to see the Thymnal.

"The Ugoli people who found me have treated me with great kindness," he said at last.

"No doubt. They are probably indulgent. What is the nature of your ailment?"

Evander flushed. "Beneath my shirt my skin has been turned to that of some animal, I know not what. I have become a sort of monster. I feel that the rays of the blessed Thymnal might overcome the spell and return me to my previous state."

"Ah, urm, yes, yes." The pen scratched again. Then the beady eyes flicked up.

"Removal of magical taints is not granted very often. In cases of toadskin, or buboes and such afflictions of the skin, the action of the rays of the blessed Thymnal can prove felicitous. However, that said, the Thymnal produces unpredictable effects when conjoined with magics of all kinds. I will apply for you. You will have to wait. Perhaps they will interview you again."

A square piece of pink paper was held up.

"Take this. Bring it when you return. You will be notified within a few days."

The pen tapped. "And it would be much, much easier, if you found some way to provide some silver for the donation. We must all quench the thirst of the blessed Thymnal."

Evander had wondered just how unpredictable things could get. What if the strange skin became covered in fur? Or feathers? The man was looking at him in surprise. He was supposed to have gone away already.

"By the way, how much silver would be regarded as sufficient?"

The face looked up, drawn and accusing. "There can be no upper limit on your generosity to the blessed Thymnal."

"Oh, well, of course, but, er, I must start from nothing, you see."

"It is most improvident of you."

"Well, I did not have much choice in the matter."

"Our lives are filled with choices. Seek guidance from the priests, and bring your silver to the blessed Thymnal."

"I'm afraid I still need to know how much silver to bring."

Annoyance flickered on the man's face. "A minimum of ten crowns can be accepted."

Outside the temple, still cursed with the thick, lumpy skin all over his chest and back, he found it hard to take the same good cheer from the glories of the city as he had before.

The inquisitor had made it perfectly clear, if he wanted to get exposure to the healing rays of the blessed Thymnal, he had to find some silver. Ten crowns, it sounded like a lot, but then perhaps it was not so formidable. Evander had to admit he didn't know how much ten Monjon crowns was worth.

"They turn you down, too, pilgrim?" questioned a voice beside him. It was the soldier with the missing foot.

"Ah, yes, well, they want money. And I don't have any."

"Right, pilgrim, you got it the first try. No silver, no rays from the blessed Thymnal."

"They asked for ten crowns."

"You must have some really terrible disease. I hope it's not easily caught. Please accept my sympathies."

"Is ten crowns a lot?"

"They offered me a chance for a new foot, but they wanted at least five crowns for that. All just to put my foot into the rays of the blessed Thymnal for a few minutes."

"It does seem a bit mercenary of them, does it not?"

"Mercenary? By the breath of ol' Pernaxo, they be avaricious, young friend, they be out and out plain, goddamned greedy, that be what they is."

"Yes, but they control all access to the blessed Thymnal."

"That's the way it is, so things is stacked against you if you've got a real problem, but no silver. I hope to regain my foot. I know it's a lot to ask, but I gave up the foot in the service of the entire Bakanor coast, and I don't think it's too much to ask for a few moments of the rays of the blessed Thymnal."

Evander's interest pricked.

"You were in the war, then?"

"Aye, young sir, I was in the war. All the way down to the lands of the Kraheen. The things we seen. Monsters! Reptiles twenty feet high, I seen them, with heads full of teeth as big as your hand. And then in the lands of the Kraheen, I seen so much cruelty, I almost go insane when I think of it. And that's where I lost my foot. Oh, it was most piteous down there, young sir, piteous and terrible."

Evander nodded sympathetically. The whole business of the crusade against the Prophet of Death had preoccupied the lands on either side of the Mirassa Sea. For a while they'd talked of nothing else in the taverns of Molutna Ganga. Evander's imagination had been fired by countless wild tales of the interior of the dark continent.

"Yes, I was at sea a long time, but in every port they told the tale of the great war in the heart of Eigo and the defeat of the Kraheen."

The heart of Eigo, a place remote beyond mountains and great desert, far to the south and west of Monjon.

The veteran shrugged with a wan smile. "So they say, and there was a great battle. But my memories of the battle were cut short by the thunderbolt that took off my foot. The enemy, you see, projected thunderbolts at us with most grievous effect. They destroyed anything they touched. Even the ground erupted occasionally, right underneath us. Threw men into the air, cut them in half, I seen such things." He paused, stricken. "I don't want to go on no more, young sir."

Evander's eyebrows rose at the thought of this magical style of warfare. It sounded both intriguing and very dangerous. Thunderbolts? After a moment he remembered something else that had always fascinated him. "Excuse me for asking, sir, but I had heard that in this crusade there were men from the far east, and they had their famous battledragons with them. Did you see them?"

"Oh, but of course, young sir, and never have I seen anything like them. Wield a sword as big as a man is tall. Cut down anything with it. But they was dying from the thunderbolts, too, that day. They say we won the victory that day in the popular songs, but old Larzly knows better than that. We retreated for eight days after that battle, and we left a lot of dead men behind. We all thought we was beat, and then the mountain on the Bone blew up. Thought the world was coming to an end, I did. The ground shook. We was down on the coast of some huge lake, and the water came up in a wave fifty feet high. Put boats into the trees. And the whole sky was lit up for hours while this cloud of smoke just welled up and filled the whole sky."

They both paused a moment, rapt at such extraordinary things.

Then old Larzly went on, "It was after that, we won the war, see. We turned around and went back, and the Kraheen wouldn't fight, their prophet was dead, see, and the evil on the Bone was ended. So it turned out well in the end."

They nodded together.

" 'Cept that I didn't have no foot, of course."

They looked at the stump and the wooden ball. Evander surmised that old Larzly could talk for hours about his missing foot.

"I have heard much concerning the battledragons of the eastern realm. They rule the battlefield, 'tis said, and can take the field against the trolls of Padmaz, which hurt us so badly in our wars with the dark force."

"Ah, well"—Larzly cleared his throat—"I wouldn't know about that, young sir. I was just a humble sawyer before I joined up. They took me for carpentry skills, not for fighting, see. But I could imagine them dragons taking the field against anything they wanted to. I saw one chop down one of the monsters in the ancient forest. It was a big, striding one, very dangerous. Dragon took just one blow to finish the beast. Terrible it was. But when the thunderbolts came, they killed dragons just like they killed men and horses and anything else."

Evander shook his head in wonder. The crusade had been every bit as exciting as he'd thought when he had heard the tales being told in the ports around the Mirassa and along the coast of Eigo. Of course, old Kospero had forbidden the very thought of their going on the crusade. As Prince of Sedimo, it was Evander's duty to stay alive, and it had been Kospero's duty to keep him so.

The bells mounted at every large street in Monjon began ringing the hour. Evander made his excuses and set off down the wide Avenue Fagesta. It was time to tell Yumi the bad news.

He found Yumi just returned from a successful reconnoiter of the Weave Witch, Postrema, who was eager to work on this wonderful old carpet. Yumi was very pleased. The witch had been most complimentary about the carpet. He was going to take it to her that same night.

Yumi and Evander went to the taproom, and Yumi ordered two pots of ale, roast eels, and plates of pilaff. They tried to think of a way to obtain ten crowns.

Yumi, alas, could not afford to give Evander the ten crowns himself. He would need every crown to repair the carpet and afford their lodging in the city while they remained. Then he and Elsu would need further silver to buy a little land to restart their flower garden.

Ten Monjon crowns would take Evander years to save up if he took some menial job, a potboy in an inn or hostler in the stables. He wasn't big enough for the relatively well-paid life of a chair carrier for some wealthy person. Six-man chairs, carried at shoulder height, were a common sight in Monjon. And he had no skill, never expecting to be anything other than the king of Sedimo some day.

Then Yumi had an idea. "We go to Ugoli Bank, on the Bund. You take out a loan, pay back later."

"That sounds wonderful, except how will I secure such a loan? I have nothing but the clothes on my back, and those were given me by Elsu."

"True, but we have accounts with the bank; they will listen to Yumi and Elsu."

Yumi promised to talk with Elsu. He wouldn't promise anything, but there were certain things they could use as collateral for a loan of ten crowns so that Evander could be exposed to the rays of the blessed Thymnal.

The first order of business, however, was to take the carpet to the Weave Witch, Postrema, at her shop in the Quack's Quarter. Yumi wanted Evander to accompany him as he carried the valuable carpet through the city streets. Evander's size and agility would be a protection. Like any big city, Monjon boasted its thieves and robbers.

After their eels and pilaff Evander and Yumi collected the carpet from the landlord's safe and set out for the Quack's Quarter, which lay within the intermediary ring of the city. It was dark now, and the fabulous lights of Monjon were coming on. Everywhere was light, from amber in the windows of homes, to great assemblages of colors to form the symbols of the great guilds and societies of Monjon.

On Avenue Fagesta it was almost as bright as daylight.
They strode up the broad thoroughfare unmolested, though
Yumi gave frequent looks behind, still half certain that they
had been followed from the inn.

No such sinister figures appeared, however, although
Yumi's suspicions were scarcely allayed. Then they entered
the second circle of the city with structures of four or more
stories. Almost at once they turned into a narrow street
lined with the shops of medicos, herbalists, dentalists, and
alchemists. Simple remedies for headache and menstrual
cramps were sold from medicine stalls. A poisonous-snake
seller had one stall. Another man sold rats, prepared in
many ways, including sausage.

In this quarter much of the passing throng wore bandages, many around their aching jaws, for it was toothache
that drew the most clients to the quarter. The work went
on around the clock, for the dentalists of Monjon were
famed throughout the Bakan coast. From the brightly lit
windows of the dentalists could be heard the occasional
shriek as one or another tooth was wrenched from its
socket. These cries came from every direction and mingled
with the more normal street barking from the stall holders
and the sidewalk pitchmen, providing an unusual tone to
the sound of this part of the city. Added to this was the
thudding music, beneath the wail of the Ourdhi pipes, that
came from occasional restaurants where the smell of hot
kalut rose irresistibly into the night air. Evander was capti-
vated by the sheer urbanness of it all. Not since he and
Kospero had left mighty Molutna had he seen anything like
this. The cities of Eigo were smaller, far less advanced than
the great conurbations of Arna and Ianta. But here in the
magical city Evander found it again. It made him realize
how long he'd been on the run. It had been a year since
they'd left Molutna Ganga and crossed the Mirassa.

Such memories brought back thought of poor Kospero,
who had helped him so much during his fugitive life—not
to mention before the desperate days began. The young
Prince Danais Evander of Sedimo Kassim had not been
really ready for the life of the streets of such cities as huge
Molutna. Without Kospero he would never have survived.
He sighed inwardly. He missed his friend.

He recalled a distant time when Kospero had rescued
Evander from the terrible disappointment of his first horse

race. It was his first ride on his own horse, and it had been
a disaster. His wonderful Kiprio had run out of control and
lost—lost humiliatingly, going out way too fast and losing
steam in the stretch while all the others thundered past.
Evander had lost control of him and never got it back until
he was run out. Evander had made the mistake of boasting
for weeks that Kiprio was bound to win the race, and now
he was the laughingstock of the palace. He was fourteen
and found this dismal loss quite crushing. But Kospero had
not left him to mope. There was rock climbing to be tackled, and dueling, not to mention archery and weaving. All
the traditional skills of the nobility of Sedimo Kassim, even
down to playing the pipes, had to be learned, and Kospero
was determined that the prince, *his* prince, was going to
succeed in every one. Not just be proficient, but succeed,
which often meant going far, far beyond mere proficiency.
Kospero had been a tower of strength, helping him get
back on his feet after that dreadful humiliation. Eventually,
he had come to learn from it some of the harder lessons
of life without great cost, but at the time it had come close
to destroying him. Alas, poor Kospero had not been so
well served by his pupil.

At length they reached Postrema's shop, indicated by a
wooden sign with a brightly lit patch of cloth attached. Brilliant greens, reds, and browns filled the cloth with color and
pattern that seemed to shift constantly from one pattern to
another, now herringbone, now a paisley, now fleurs-de-lis.

The shop occupied the ground floor of a narrow four-
story house painted a soft yellowish brown. The door and
lintel were freshly painted. All bore the mark of care and
good taste. Yumi thrust open the door, and they entered a
world of weaving. Rugs in fabulous hues hung on the walls.
Pieces of elaborately woven fabric were displayed in
glassed frames. Soft incense hung in the air, and somewhere
above their heads a musician played the Ourdhi pipe.

They were met by a pair of strange-looking men, or not
quite men perhaps, squat in shape with thick lips and bee-
tling brows. Evander thought they might almost be imps,
the foul creatures produced in hordes by the Masters of
Padmasa, but they were more manlike than that.

Postrema appeared suddenly, as if springing out of nothingness. She had a weathered look, as if she had been at

work on weaving for many more decades than she would care to count.

"Ah, my Ugoli friend, you are back." Postrema cast an appraising eye toward Evander, then gave him a brief smile. "And you brought the young afflicted fellow, too."

Yumi nodded slightly, then opened the wraps and unrolled the old carpet. "First we must deal with my rug."

"Of course, of course." Postrema dragged her eyes away from the young man. A very handsome fellow, she thought. Certain wheels already turned in her thoughts.

The rug was the real thing, she knew at once, a Xish Wan weave with powerful magic worked into its very fibers. To steal it would be difficult, and it would be hard to resell without falling foul of Ugoli associations, which were quite powerful in the Bakan. This youth, on the other hand, was more intriguing to her.

Yumi showed her the weakness in the old rug. She noted the lack of tone, the faded colors, and the worn spots. For years the old rug had belonged to a Ugoli woman who knew nothing of its powers and even walked on it! It was laid on the floor and walked on! Yumi's father had rescued it from that indignity, but now it was weak and needed new strength.

Postrema examined the rug with a large magnifying lens and felt the fabric in many places. She even hushed them, closed her eyes, laid her palms flat on the rug, and pretended to be communing with it. All this was largely for show, of course, for she already knew what she would do with the rug and even how much she would charge.

"It will take crowns, many crowns, my Ugoli friend."

"I know that. We are prepared to pay a fair tariff for the repair of our old, faithful rug."

Postrema smiled and gave her price. "Sixteen crowns, and it will be done in three days, perhaps less."

Yumi offered ten crowns. The witch held out for sixteen. Yumi threatened to take the rug elsewhere, to Eiskule the carpet maker, or to Ocanther Mappam.

"They will all charge you more and take longer. Eiskule has little skill with such old styles. He hardly knows a thing about the magic of the old Xish Wan."

Yumi knew this, of course. Postrema had the advantage of him in that she alone in Monjon could boast true expertise with ancient Ugoli magic carpets.

Unwillingly, Yumi raised his offer. Eventually, they agreed on fourteen crowns. Evander pursed his lips. Magic was expensive when you paid for it with silver.

"And now the other work you mentioned." Postrema nodded toward Evander.

Yumi told Evander that Postrema should look at his afflicted skin. She was a witch; perhaps she could come up with a remedy.

There was something slightly sinister about the bony old witch. Her eyes had an odd brightness that made him uncomfortable, but after a moment's hesitation Evander complied. He told himself there was nothing to lose. Perhaps Postrema would charge less for this kind of work.

The Weave Witch's eyes lit up as she gazed at the warty, lumpy toad skin that covered the handsome youth's chest and back. She was a calculating old witch, and she was thinking of retirement soon. A villa on the Zuexatian coast was her dream. She would spend time in her garden, perhaps make wine.

This boy was probably worth a handsome villa. In the Ourdhi market for exotic playthings he would do very well. The outer integument was truly amazing, somewhere between crocodile, snake, and toad. It was hard and glistened, too, like the finest leather.

The tastes of the ruling class in ancient Ourdh had grown quite bizarre over the eons they had sat upon the land. Down in Port Tarquil there was a merchant, name of Negus; he might go half and half on such a prize, and maybe put up half of her half upfront, before he took the youth to Ourdh.

Postrema could almost feel the stones of her Zeuxatian villa beneath her feet. The fresh sea air, the constant sunshine, a life of ease and contemplation; yes, it would suit her perfectly in her remaining years.

Surreptitiously, she took a hair from the youth's head while inspecting him. Then she promised the little Ugoli that she would research the subject of toad skin and other wizardly afflictions and give them a report on the morrow. Thus they parted, and the pair left her shop with hope visibly renewed in their faces.

The Wizard of the Floating City

The call had been heard across the ruined lands of the doomed world of Orthond. The ancient Master called the Order of Seekers to attend him at the hidden fortress above Canax. From hidden hole to isolated peak, from frontier cabin to ruined palace, they emerged and set their gaze toward Canax. No other Lord of the Eleem could summon them thus; they were too proud, too haughty a folk, the horse-faced lords of Orthond. Lack of unity had always been the weakness used by the Great Enemy to bring them down.

Perspax, heir of Sanok, came down from the cold hills of the north. The trip was long and arduous, except for a few stretches where civilization still lingered, kept alive in an isolated county or a string of small hill villages. There one found inns that still kept the welcome lamp lit for the footsore traveler. A mug of ale and a hot meal made the journey easy. But such places were rarer and rarer now. Mostly one slept in the open and made no fire and ate scraps from what might be carried. One moved furtively through the crepuscular gloom of a ruined world, for there were many eyes searching the dead ground, eyes belonging to the servants of the dark spirit of the Dominator, Lord Waakzaam, the enemy of the world.

When they gathered, in what had once been the anteroom to the public baths, hidden below the rubble of fallen cities, Perspax observed with sadness in his heart that there were several newly emptied places in the ranks of his Order. Riok the Mamsetter was gone, taken by micklebear in some northern waste. Spulveen was no more, finally dead from the wasting plague. Rabranka, too, had fallen, hewed down in battle by a foul bewk of the enemy.

Across Perspax's thought trailed a gray parade of lost faces from the past, those who had fallen through the long, bitter years of their wars against the Dominator. Never again would such glory as the ancient hosts of the Lords Eleem be seen. All were now smashed to dust, their bones long interred beneath Orthond's ruined battlefields. At times, Perspax marveled that he lived on, a lonely survivor of those early days. Why had he been chosen to live? Why did the memory of so many repose within him?

At the time appointed, the ancient Master came to them and spoke in prophecy, with words that had come to him from the Gods. In a dream he had seen the Gods and heard them tell him to watch for a sign of deliverance.

He described his dream.

"Was it not said," he asked, "that the works of the Eleem are like ashes, which the wind scatters on a stormy night?

"Was it not said that even as the Eleem had ascended in their glory, so they had laid up in their pride for the disaster that had befallen?

"Was it not said also that to the pure in heart who doth endure, there will come a sign of the end of evil?"

They nodded; all knew these things.

"The sign has come. The gods came into me and pressed down on me with strange, sweet words of terror."

And so he spoke, and they listened. There was coming to them, like a beacon, a sign of the change of times.

Alas, not even the Gods knew exactly what the sign would be, only that it would appear suddenly in Orthond and that it would be the beginning of the last war upon Waakzaam. They must seek the sign! Whatever it was it must not be found by the servants of the Dominator.

Shadreiht was the last of the high masters, and he was mighty in his ways. He had striven for many years against the great enemy, and he knew his thought. He survived, and so did the hidden fortress, which could mean only that the Dominator had not perceived him or discovered his hiding place. All the Seekers recognized him as leader of the Order, and thus they immediately accepted his words.

Was it not said that in the worst of times there would

be a sign, and the sign would lead the folk out of the valley of death and into the uplands of light and air? Was it not said that in the midst of the fire, there could be cool water? That in the blackness of the void, there could come the spark of life?

But in leaving Canax to prowl the wastelands of the world, Perspax could not help but wonder if any power existed that could lift the oppression of Waakzaam the Great, who trod them on his hated winepress till they were but shreds and dregs of the glory of yore.

Chapter Eleven

Evander awoke to the bright moonlight flooding in the window. He had been dreaming of a beautiful young woman who wore nothing but wisps of gauze and a crown of laurel leaves, calling to him from a grove of trees. She had long, honey-colored hair and lips that spoke of sensual pleasures beyond number. Then he was awake, and she was gone, to his intense regret. His eyes fell on the window, and his disappointment began to fade.

The moon was not yet full, but still it bathed the city with its spectral glow. The tall buildings in the center stood as chalky pillars against the night. The onion domes of the palace gleamed. Something about the brightly lit city made him restless. He rose and found Yumi and Elsu fast asleep. Evander took the key and locked the door behind him.

Out in the street his feet seemed to know which way they wanted to go, down the broad Avenue Fagesta, still lit up with hundreds of great, colored displays, and still with sizable numbers of people abroad despite the lateness of the hour. He sped along at a rapid pace, then turned abruptly and plunged into the Quack's Quarter.

It was not much quieter there. The dentalists were still at work, and anemic screams drifted through the night. A quarrel between two rival peddlers of snake oils had drawn a crowd, but Evander did not stop until he reached Postrema's shop.

The door opened, and the squat servants of the Weave Witch ushered him in. He followed them along the hallway past vibrant examples of Postrema's art. He struggled to say something, but could not speak. It was all happening as if in a dream. He hoped he might simply wake up in his bed at the inn with the Ugoli softly snoring nearby. But there was no awakening from this. The servants were pushing him down some stairs and propelling him along a dark, narrow passageway into a small room. He stood there, stupidly staring at the squat men, while one of them pulled open the gate on a large wire cage. Then he was inside the cage and the gate was closed. For the first time the squat servant men became animated. They broke into broad smiles and hearty chuckles. Soon they were laughing uproariously, barely able to stand.

A bell tinkled somewhere above. They fell silent. Their faces lost expression. They left the room, taking the lamp and leaving him in darkness.

Slowly, the spell faded, and he realized what had been done. His concern mounted. Was his disguise penetrated? Did she know who he was? She was a witch, after all, and she was well connected with traders and travelers. Might she have heard of the hue and cry set up for the Prince Danais of Sedimo Kassim?

In which case he was in deep trouble. And he'd allowed himself to be taken with humiliating ease. He'd just walked in here and put himself in the cage!

A feeling of helpless rage filled him until it was hard to breathe. He was doomed. He would be sold back to Sedimo, and his enemies would put him to death. If only Kospero had been with him, he was sure things would have gone better. The thought of his older cousins completing their triumph by murdering him in the dungeon of the palace at Sedimo was truly awful, but it was beginning to seem inevitable.

It was cold in this cellar room, and after a while he was shivering freely. He called out a few times, but received only the echo of his own voice in response. They might at least give him a blanket, he thought.

The time dragged by, hour after hour of miserable reflection. What a stupid fool he'd been. To have shown himself to someone as worldly wise as this witch. Of course she knew who he was. He recalled how her eyes had shone at the sight of him.

It was probably the result of painted likenesses being sent out with news of a reward by his enemies. Kospero had said it was possible, if the new rulers wanted to make absolutely sure of him. Such likenesses would be passed into the regional trade. The likeness would probably have been taken from his official royal portrait, painted the previous year and hung in the room of clocks. And, of course, the little painting of the fugitive prince would be accompanied by the promise of a fat reward.

It was all his own fault. Kospero counseled him not to involve himself in the affairs of wizards. And what did Evander do, but rescue the mayor of Port Tarquil from the wizard's judgment? And now Kospero was gone, and the Prince Danais was taken with the ease of a poacher netting a hare.

His misery was interrupted suddenly by a pale blue radiance that swelled outside the door. A key turned, the door opened, and the blue light came in, too bright to look at. It was difficult to see who stood behind it. Then she moved and he saw that it was Postrema.

He stared at her eyes.

She smiled, but not nicely.

"Gloating is a rather despicable habit, don't you think?" he said bitterly.

"You're going to a very interesting future," she replied in a calm voice. "I'm sending you to old Ourdh. There are wealthy men there who will pay handsomely for such an exotic creature as yourself. I expect you will be exhibited, perhaps taught to perform tricks for the crowd."

He was stunned. She didn't know he was Prince Danais. She was just out to sell him as a thing to be looked at and prodded and laughed at. He'd be kept in a cage in some rich man's house to amuse guests. Evander swallowed heavily. A more dismal fate was hard to imagine.

"Nothing much to say for yourself now, have you?"

"I . . ." It was true; he was too aghast to speak. For a moment he struggled while she giggled. Then he found his voice as anger surged through him.

"The use of magic for abductions is an offense against all civilization. When they catch you, they will hang you, witch!"

Her smile was brief and bloodless. "If I hadn't taken you, someone else would have. You're worth thousands, young man, thousands of crowns. This skin of yours is quite fabulous; such wizardry is rare simply because most victims die in the process, and those that survive rarely live very long, if nothing else because street mobs burn them to death. You are a living testament to the power of great magic. There are those who will pay very well for you. Oh, yes."

"Your honor comes cheaply then, for you do this for
silver alone—selling another human being, someone who
came to you for help. The witches are supposed to aid the
mortal; that's what I always believed. Now I see I was
wrong."

She laughed, but she was offended. She had drifted far
from the moorings of her own order and she knew it.
"Young man, you are going to be taken down a few pegs
in life. Such haughtiness ill behooves a freak!"

The witch turned on her heel and departed, with the blue
glow going on just ahead.

Evander sagged back against the wire. This was the crown-
ing blow, the completion of his disgrace. She didn't know
who he was and thought he was just a freak.

For an hour or more he stared into the darkness, completely deflated, broken in spirit. He could not bear the
thought of the future before him. He would take his own
life, somehow, at the very first opportunity. Better death
than such shame and dishonor.

Slowly, however, his anger relit within the swamp of self-
pity. He recovered himself, resolving not to cooperate any
further in his own destruction. At length he began to take
such action as was available to him. He felt around the
interior of his prison. It was made of wires, woven together,
stout enough to resist any pressure he could exert. There
was just room enough to get one's hand out of the larger
gaps. The cage was taller than it was wide. In fact, it was
too narrow for him to lie down in. He found that he could
span the interior with his legs on one wall and his back on
the other. This encouraged him, and he climbed all over
the cage interior for a while before giving up and settling to
the floor, where he curled up to sleep for a couple of hours.

Chapter Twelve

At first light one of the servant men came stumbling down the stairs, lamp in hand, to check on the prisoner, but the cage was empty, no young man visible. The servant panicked. He scarcely looked around the room, but took the key from the hook and rushed across and opened the cage. Where was the damned youth? How had he escaped? It simply was not possible.

The fool never thought to look up, to the top of the cage where the wire was gathered so thickly that Evander, who was compressed there, was invisible from outside the cage.

When the servant stuck his head inside, Evander dropped straight onto his shoulders and bore him down. The servant struck the floor of the cage heavily. Evander was on his feet in a moment, but the servant remained prone. Evander pulled him inside, took his ring of keys, and locked the cage door.

Teeth clenched to stop them chattering, while a dangerous high emotion pounded in his heart, Evander slipped out of the room and into the lit portions of the house. He had a wild urge to cry out in triumph, but bit his tongue to stifle it. Carefully, he stole up the stairs and reached the ground floor undetected. A long passageway with carpets on the walls stretched to his right. To his left was a junction, a more dimly lit area. His nerves were taut. He was determined not to be recaptured. He moved noiselessly along the corridor of carpets, seeking the door by which he'd entered.

Then he heard movements ahead; someone was coming. He doubled back, passed the stairs again, and went on into the dimly lit section. He turned left and went down a blank passage and then up some stairs that opened suddenly onto a large hall.

This room was strongly lit by Monjon globes hanging

from the mirrored ceiling. Rugs and weaves of many kinds were on display, hung over transoms set across the room. He stole across the parquet floor toward a set of double doors.

He opened the doors and slid into a darkened room, which had a wide window, with a balcony. He determined to climb down the outside of the building if he had to.

He started across the room, but tripped on something that rattled. A hiss came from his left, and a moment later a cover was yanked off a Monjon globe, and light flooded the room. Evander jumped back, startled, and fell over a chair.

The witch was awake and out of her bed, searching for a dagger on the night table. She found it in a moment and whirled around to face him.

"By the Breath, I'll have someone's back bleeding," she snarled. "How the hell did you get loose?" She came closer, holding the knife out in front of her. "Mijjot!" she screamed.

Her hand reached out to a tall, silver handbell on a stand. Evander unfroze and plucked the bell off the stand and flung it over his shoulder out the window.

"You little devil." She lunged at him with the knife.

He darted aside, picked up a heavy cushion, and swatted her across the head and shoulders. It was quite a blow, and it took her right off her feet and dropped her on her rear with a thud. The knife bounced across the floor to his feet. He picked it up and examined it briefly—a handsome weapon with a diskoid pommel and guard and a long, narrow blade. There were runes cut into the pommel.

There came an odd, elongated moment when their eyes locked. It would be the work of a second to step forward and plunge the bade into the witch. Surely, she expected it, but he was not a killer. True, there was a voice in his head urging him to slay her, she deserved it, but something held his hand. It was unjust to kill for a mere night's imprisonment. They'd done him no violence. Still, her eyes were filled with fear, for she read his anger clearly, but yet misjudged him, for he was made of nobler stuff.

Then there came the sounds of feet on the stairs—the servants. He shoved the knife into his belt and darted back to the window and slipped out, Postrema's wails echoing behind him.

He found himself on a slate roof, steeply raked so that he had to lean hard over and make his way with his hands and feet. He progressed perhaps twenty feet before the roof came to an end. Below, perhaps ten feet down, lay another roof, of the adjoining building. There was a commotion behind him. The servants of the witch were in pursuit, driven on by a harsh voice calling to them from the balcony. There was no time to linger.

He jumped, hanging breathless in the night sky for a moment, landed on the next roof, and immediately slid down to the gutter, frantically trying to get a grip on the slates. Only when his body was dangling in empty air did he manage to hang onto the gutter itself. His legs kicked frantically over a three-story drop.

The sun was coming out. He'd be seen in moments, and the hue and cry would be on. He could hear the witch's servants calling out to each other. They were none too eager to climb along the steeply sloping roof. That gave him a little time. He calmed himself and looked around beneath the eaves of the roof. There was a drainpipe about four feet away. He moved hand over hand along the gutter until he reached the pipe. His arms were tiring, but he managed to transfer his grip to the pipe.

There was a window a few feet farther down. He moved down the pipe until he could slip a foot in through the broken shutters and pull them open. In a moment he slid the rest of his body across the sill and stepped onto a dusty wood floor. He breathed a deep sigh of relief. The room was dark, and fumbling around, he knocked over some jars that rolled loudly across the boards. Finally, he found the door and pulled it open with an effort.

Loud voices echoed up from below; he'd been heard. Someone was coming, and he didn't care to confront the owners of the building. At the least there would be questions asked by the authorities. Those wretched likenesses could have reached Monjon by now. Someone might possibly identify him, and then the game would be up. His cousins, the usurpers, had put out a reward for his capture as soon as he'd fled the kingdom with Kospero.

Evander vaulted up a narrow flight of stairs and shortly opened a creaky door that let him out on a flat roof above the sloping one.

As soon as he stepped out onto the roof, he knew he'd

made a mistake. Waiting just above on the witch's upper-most roof were two of her servants. Seeing him, they gave loud cries. One of them climbed over a rail and jumped down to the far end of the flat roof. There were further cries in the street.

Evander fled in the opposite direction, leaping the gap between buildings, scrambling across slanting roofs, trying to find a way down. Unfortunately, what doors were available were locked. He was trapped on the roof of the city, working his way inward to the margin of the Quack's Quarter. He went by leaping the narrow alleys and avoiding the wider streets. This took him to a section dominated by larger buildings, long windowless sheds, blocky warehouses, and the like.

His way took him across the long copper roof of a distillery in the scent trade. The smell of concentrated floral scents rose from the various windows below the roof. Dashing through a steaming cloud of rose-scented vapor, he scampered behind the end wall and found a skylight raised open above a vat of steaming flower juice. He swung himself in and down. He was poised ten feet above the vat. If he fell, he'd be simmered in rosewater. Various pipes crisscrossed the space around him. To his right, some four feet below, ran a metal pipe as thick as his wrist. Some distance farther down the room, this pipe joined a much thicker one, He either got to that small pipe or fell into the vat. There was nothing else to do. With a silent prayer to the old Gods of Sedimo, Evander swung himself again, let go, and reached down for the pipe. By some miracle his hands struck the pipe dead on. He caught it and swung around it up high for a moment like an acrobat, and then lost his grip and sailed onto land astride the side of the vat.

He let out a yelp as hot steam seared the leg inside the vat, and quickly pulled himself up until he managed to stand, balanced precariously on the edge of the vat. The fumes of boiling flowers nearly overcame him, but he managed to stumble a couple of steps forward and grasp the pipe. At last he was stabilized. The worst part was accomplished.

He moved hand over hand along the pipe, which began to grow warm in his hands as the bubbling below increased in volume. His arms were getting very tired, but at last he reached the junction with the second, thicker pipe. This one was warm, too, but he could just haul himself up and over this pipe so that he was lying on top of it. Still, this was no place to rest. He could feel the pipe getting warmer by the second, so he moved to stand on it and began the process of walking along it, arms out for balance. Below was a twenty-foot drop between farther vats, mostly empty. Along the farther wall he saw what appeared to be a ladder. A way out! Now, if he could just keep his balance. He wobbled around a corner in the pipe and struggled, arms flailing to stay upright. For a moment he swung out. He thought he was going to fall, but he corrected himself and then stepped quickly across the last ten feet to the ladder, clutching it like a drowning man grabbing a line.

A large door banged open down below. Several men came in. They had not yet seen him, hidden as he was by the pipes and steam above the central vats. He shimmied down the ladder and reached a gallery space above the main floor at the level of the top of the largest vats. These were twenty feet across and twenty deep, and built of stout timbers. From these the pipes ran to the copper pot stills along the wall.

The men were coming up some stairs to the gallery. They were bound to see him in a few moments. He had to get out of sight. He hauled up a hatch set in the gallery floor and found himself staring down at a huge pile of soggy, spent flowers. There was no time for reflection. He jumped.

The next moment, with a syrupy sound, he sank into the mess up to his neck. It was warm and gave off a vegetal stench. It was hard to move, and when he did, he started to sink deeper. He struggled to make progress to the side of the pile. It was like walking in quicksand, and his head was almost sinking below the surface, when his hand struck something solid and clasped hold. He heaved on it and pulled himself toward salvation. His arm was free, then his head came up out of the soggy mess, and he saw that he'd caught hold of a pitchfork left lying beside the mound of spent flowers. A few kicks later and he broke free in a spurt of muck and was outside, staggering on the gravel, covered from head to toe in boiled flowers.

He could hear the men above him. They would be sure to investigate the open trapdoor. He sprang across the courtyard to the distillery stables and dove into a pile of straw set against one wall.

This proved to be a very wise move, for two of the witch's servants entered the courtyard the next moment, accompanied by the manager of the distillery. They conducted a swift search of the upper decks of the still room, but found no sign of the youth. The workers on the upper gallery had reported nothing. The manager barked something uncomplimentary. The servants turned and left.

Hidden in the straw, Evander waited for an hour or more, praying that they would give up and go back to the witch, before he ventured out of the straw. Scattering scraps of hay and dribbles of muck, he slipped across to the door and peered into the courtyard. No one was around.

He passed through the stables. A dozen sleepy horses dozed in their stalls. Wagons and small carts were pushed up against the walls here and there. Equipment hung left and right.

A long water trough provided an opportunity for a quick dunk to rinse off the worst of the debris. He was still a mess, but not quite so immediately noticeable.

The gateway lay open, except for a small post manned by a sleepy watchman. Evander did his best to assume a front of normalcy and shambled past the watchman with no more than a slight nod. The watchman barely noticed him.

Outside the distillery he ran, fleet of foot, along a straight street that went on past warehouses and a brewery for half a mile. He heard distant shouts at one point and looked back, but saw no sign of the servants of Postrema. Still nervous, he skipped along the side of the street with many a glance over his shoulder.

It was still early in the day and the city was stirring, but the rush of folk to their workplaces had not fully gotten underway, so the streets were virtually empty.

At one point he decided to stop and catch his breath. He turned into an alley and leaned back against the wall. It took a while for his heart to stop racing. He was still thinking of how close he'd come to a sticky end in the flower vats. Sweat dripped down his neck, joining the rest of the mess that covered him.

He was about to move on when he heard a door slam open across the way, in a courtyard that abutted the street. Immediately, there was the sound of men cursing. Then a strangled shriek followed by a wild scream, the sound of a blow, and very voluble cursing.

Evander flattened himself against the wall as questions multiplied in his mind. With a feeling that he was about to jump out of the frying pan into the fire, he peered around the corner.

Chapter Thirteen

A young woman was in the process of being pushed into a waiting carriage by two well-dressed fellows complaining loudly at the kicks the young woman kept getting in as they struggled with her.

All three were screaming at one another in Monjonese. Evander couldn't understand a word. But the young lady was definitely unhappy with what was going on, and the well-dressed fellows were more or less violently abducting her.

Instinct told Evander to lie low, but everything in his training told him to intervene. This was wrong. He had to do something to stop it.

One of the men had the door open to the carriage, and together with his fellow they were shoving the girl inside. Evander stepped forward, crossed the street, and entered the courtyard.

"Why are you doing that?" he said to them in Furda.

The men whirled around, their mouths agape at the sight of Evander, dripping wet, his face covered in slime.

"What is this?" said one in thick Furda.

"My question exactly," said Evander. "Why are you doing this to the young lady?"

The young lady in question chose this moment to lash out with a nicely shaped foot and catch the young man who'd spoken Furda in the crotch. He gave a gasp and sank to his knees.

The other young man swore, grabbed the young lady around the waist, and lifted her bodily into the coach. She struck at him with her feet and drove him back.

Evander was stunned for a moment at this violence.

She looked up at him. "I hope you're not just going to stand there," she snapped. Evander noted that she was rather beautiful, with auburn hair and wide-spaced hazel eyes. Her Furda was good and had very little accent.

Now the heavy young man recovered and slammed the door on her and turned the lock. He turned to face Evander. "Go!" he shouted with a violent wave of his arm. He was red in the face with scratch marks on his forehead.

"Go!" he bellowed again.

The other fellow, still getting off his knees and purple in the face, yelled something harsh in Monjonese.

The scratched one barked an assent, took a truncheon from behind the driver's seat, and advanced on Evander with an ugly smile.

"I tell you go, but you don't go, eh?" he said. His Furda was monosyllabic. He swung the heavy truncheon ominously.

Evander was not one to pick a fight needlessly, but he had been schooled for years in the martial arts. Under Kospero's steady tutelage, he had grown quite useful at the "Three Hands" school of unarmed combat.

This fellow came from the basic stupid bully school of truncheon work. Evander evaded a wild swing of the billy, stepped in, and planted his foot in the other's midriff.

The fellow doubled up with a whoosh of escaping air. Evander had a good right leg; indeed, he'd kicked out of goal for his school team as a boy.

He stood on the truncheon to snap it out of the man's hand and then kicked it away.

The other one had recovered enough in the meantime to stand in front of the carriage door. He was licking thick lips nervously as Evander came close.

"Who are you?" he said nervously. "Whatever they're paying you, I can pay more. I am Bwento Eruxi. My father is the Duke of Eruxi, do you understand?"

"You idiot!" screamed the young woman in the carriage. "I came to you for help, not to elope! Set me free at once! My father will have you flogged and thrown to the lions."

The young man replied with passion in Monjonese.

"I think you better do as the young lady asks," said Evander quietly.

"You dolt! What do you know of this?" snapped the fellow.

His accomplice was getting to his feet. Now he lurched for the truncheon.

Evander grabbed the man in front of the coach by his lapels and hurled him away from the door. He unlocked it and yanked it open.

The young lady thrust her legs out and then slid into his arms. This took him by surprise, and she slid right through them, too, and sat down hard on the ground with a shriek of complaint.

"Sorry," said Evander, picking her up and setting her on her feet. Her dress was of white cotton, and she wore small, delicate sandals. He was holding her hand when he noticed that her wrists were bound with a tough cord. The lovely eyebrows knotted for a moment when she looked up at him, but then relaxed.

"Look, let's just run, shall we?" she said.

The heavyset fellow had the truncheon back and was coming after them. They ran. She was slowed by having her arms bound in front, but not by much, and Evander kept pace behind her. The young men soon fell back and were left, bellowing entreaties in Monjonese.

Evander and the girl cut around a corner, then another, and were in a deserted part of the city, where once a canal had flowed. The canal was now half filled with rubble. The buildings alongside it had been downgraded to subsidiary warehouses. The two ran alongside the canal for a while, passing only a pair of old watchmen. Finally, they slowed.

"I hope you can cut this rope," she said. "We've left them behind. I don't think either of those idiots can run ten yards, let alone a hundred."

Evander found his fingers too clumsy to untie the rope. He pulled out the knife from his belt. The young lady gave a shriek. His hand wrapped around her mouth. She struggled frantically and tried to bite him.

"Stop," he implored. "I'm only trying to cut the cord."

Slowly, unwillingly, she stopped struggling.

"That's a large knife you have there."

"It's all I have with me. It'll have to do."

With a sigh she surrendered to his efforts. The big knife was awkward for such work, and it took time. She eyed him warily while he sawed away at the tough binding. "Who are you anyway? How did you come to be there? Do you work for my father?"

He bridled at her haughty tone. This was a wealthy young lady, used to talking down to others, but he kept his feelings to himself. "My name is Evander," he said in a level voice. "You might say I was a traveler." Suddenly, he fell silent, embarrassed at the thought of explaining why he had come to Monjon. He didn't want this lovely girl to know what horror lay under his shirt.

"A traveler? What is that? You just travel from place to place? That sounds like a drifter. They don't allow drifters in my city."

My city? This haughty lass was getting a little annoying. He stopped sawing away at the cord and looked her in the eye. "I apologize for my lack of skill in describing myself. You could also say that I am a merchant, that I have traveled to Monjon on business. Would you allow me in your city, then?"

Her eyes studied him carefully.

"Yes, I think so, my enigmatic savior. But tell me, why are you covered in muck and old flowers?"

Something sparked in her eyes then, and a smile almost came to her lips.

"A long story, I'm afraid. Perhaps if we have time later, I will try and explain."

He resumed sawing at the tough cord.

"And do you work for my father?" she asked, clearly intrigued.

"No. I have never met him."

"I wonder who you really are," she said. "A traveling merchant? Or a vagabond drifter who should be shown to the gates at once?"

"Is that the thanks I get for intervening?"

"I suppose you did rescue me; you should be rewarded."

The cord finally parted, her hands free. She raised them with a happy cry.

"I guess I did. Who were those fools anyway?"

"Oh, those pathetic idiots are Bwento and Glon. Bwento has been helpful to me once or twice before. He's very well connected at all levels of society, if you follow me."

"A bit of a rakehell."

"Well, perhaps. I wanted Bwento to help me arrange for a carriage and horses should I decide to go, uhm, on a brief tour of the countryside. I might need to get away quickly, you see. But Bwento had convinced himself that what I wanted was to elope with him."

"And you objected?"

"Wouldn't you? Bwento is pimply. Despite appearances, I thought he was intelligent."

"But he is the son of a duke?"

"Oh yes, and Glon is the younger son of the Marquis of Felous. They're wealthy, but impulsive."

"And so they tied your hands together?"

"They wouldn't listen to me. Said I was just protesting as a matter of form."

"And why do you need to get away so suddenly?"

She looked at him sharply. Could he be lying about working for her father? Father was very devious, but he always hired the same types to spy on her, and she always detected them a mile away by their earnestness and general air of stupidity. This youth had been brave and intelligent enough to interfere on her behalf and did not seem at all like the craven types Father always chose.

"Were you not at the walls last night for the magical jousts?"

"Oh, yes! They were amazing!"

She shook her head dismally. "Well, you know the hand of the Princess Serena is the main prize, don't you?"

"Yes, of course."

"Well?" She stared at him, slowly growing annoyed. "That thing, the Wizard Gadjung is going to win, don't you see?"

"Ah, no." Evander was lost. Then a flash of intelligence finally broke through. "My city" after all. "Oh, I see. You are the Princess Serena."

"You mean you didn't know that?"

"I'm sorry, I didn't know what you looked like. I haven't been in Monjon that long. But I agree with you absolutely. You can't be wasted on one of those horrible old wizards."

The eyebrows knotted again, then relaxed. "I thank you, Sir Evander of wherever you come from."

For a moment the urge to tell her his identity almost overcame his caution, but he bit back the words. He could trust no one with that information. Instead, he bowed with a flourish, just as any courtier would back in Sedimo Kassim. This mollified her completely.

They walked inward, along a winding road that fringed a long series of graveyards. The first they passed was that of the nonnobility of old Monjon. The grave markers were simple stone balls, sometimes with flower urns. Few were

even engraved. The second was a place of follies and fantasies in stone. Sprites, faithful hounds, griffins, and elves
danced across plinths and tombs. Spired follies, statues in-
numerable, rose in crowded splendor.

A gate swung open at Serena's touch. Evander was still
in a mental whirl. The events of the night before, followed
by this sudden entrance into the life of a lovely young
woman, who also happened to be a princess of the realm,
now combined to leave him confused. Vaguely, he thought
about getting back to the inn. The Ugoli would be worried
when they woke up and found him absent.

Confusion or not, he was aware that this was a special
sort of day. It was still barely morning, and already he felt
he'd seen enough for a week. Moreover, things had taken
an interesting turn. Despite her haughty manner, Princess
Serena had a liveliness that made her very appealing. Indeed, he could hardly recall a more attractive woman in
his entire experience.

They threaded their way along the paths through the riot
of stonemasonry. The princess chattered brightly, skipping
from place to place, while naming some of the tombs they
passed. She evidently knew the place very well.

"That's my great-aunt Eyura's tomb." She pointed out a
monstrosity in pink marble that involved elephants on the
corners and a statue of the departed great-aunt in her
prime, standing above.

He noticed they'd turned onto a winding path that approached a massive wall. They'd come a long way into the
city. Ahead loomed the outworks of the palace itself, but
on the far side from the main gate and the usual view.

This pathway wound between the tombs of royal bas-
tards, great courtesans, and royal magicians. Near the looming mass of the long-dead bastard Ludiz the Great's tomb,
Serena paused and looked around her carefully, even scanning along the wall above them. There were soldiers on
a tower some ways distant, but trees screened their view.
Signaling to Evander, she ducked to her left down behind
the tomb of an almost forgotten courtesan named the
Goose of Gold. This tomb was modest compared with most
of those surrounding it. There was a column with the woman's likeness carved on it and a small mausoleum of plain
white stone below. On the south wall was a brass plaque,
long since crusted green with corrosion. Serena paused

there and touched the four stars in the corners in a right to left progression. Then she reached up to a second plaque above the first and touched a central feature.

There was a slight groan. To Evander's astonishment, part of the lower wall slid aside, revealing a set of steps leading down into the dark. The princess lifted her skirts and daintily descended the steps.

A few moments later they were plunged into pitch blackness as the stone slid shut above their heads.

"Where are we?" he whispered.

"No need to whisper, silly," she said. "This is a passage that goes to a false chimney in a small room on my floor in the west wing. I think the Goose of Gold used the tomb's construction to cover up her building this passage. She kept the king amused and cuckolded him constantly."

"How did you discover it?"

She took his hand in hers and helped guide him down the stairs. "When I was ten years old, we were playing a game down in the cellars. My cousins Maunce and Plesir and I were hiding from my friend Dosina, who is now the Marquess of Xerx.

"Well, I was determined that she wouldn't find me, so I went all the way down the dark passage and got lost. I had a lantern, so I wasn't scared at all. I just kept walking until I found these steps and came up, and the door opened automatically when I stood on the fourth to the top. Hold on a moment."

She released his hand. There was a scraping sound, and then a soft green glow lit up the place. The princess removed a small Monjon globe encased in a lantern cage, and by its light Evander saw a narrow passage leading to stairs that went down into darkness. The place was dank with mold and was claustrophobic to a fault.

"This way," she said and turned down the passage. With questions forming in his brain, he followed.

Chapter Fourteen

The journey through the labyrinth below the palace walls seemed to take a long time. Slow curving walls, low ceilings, occasional pools of ankle deep water, a cold silence, all began to tell on Evander's nerves. The princess, however, seemed unaffected.

At length they reached a place where they had to duck down and creep through a tight little passage.

"This is where I came all those years ago, when I was a child," she said, knocking off dust from her garments.

Now they entered more familiar parts of the labyrinth. There were many passageways bored through the ground, and now there were sounds. A distant slamming of a huge door echoed past them at one point. At another they heard far-off shrieks, but whether they were human or animal, they could not tell. Later there were bells and drums, which seemed to pass over their heads and then cut off quite abruptly. Serena thought they were a party of priests climbing the stairs to the Temple of the Thymnal after a ceremony at Donzago's Pit.

They were to see the pit for themselves, for not long after she spoke of it, they climbed a short stair and emerged from a low door into a very large space. A vaulted ceiling was lost in the darkness above. In the center stood an old railed gallery built from stone and marble, encircling a large pit perhaps fifty feet across. This hole in the ground sank straight down into darkness. There seemed to be no bottom to the pit.

Evander asked what this place could be, and she replied as if speaking to an ignorant child, "Why 'tis the pit of Donzago the Great, of course. He was the king who brought back the Thymnal to Monjon. The city did not always float, you know."

The pit was accessed by semipublic tunnels, so now they

passed occasional monks, servants of the blessed Thymnal. Clad in dark robes with long hoods, they seemed somewhat sinister figures to Evander in these dark places, but they took no notice of the princess and her young companion. Serena did not seem worried in the slightest about them.

Eventually, they left these passageways and descended several turns on a broad staircase. At the bottom was a circular space from which radiated more tunnels. Without a moment's thought, Serena headed into one of these, and they mounted stairs, climbing for a long time, passing occasional landings with more passageways leading off into gloomy distances. At length she pushed open a door, and they emerged into a room of startling luxury. Lavish rugs covered the floors and walls. Works of art, tapestry and painting, hung on every wall. Rich furniture and elaborate timepieces were grouped in the center beside a large dark wood table. When the door was closed behind them, Evander saw that it was hidden by an ornately bordered silver mirror.

Evander gave a low whistle, but Serena snapped him a warning glance.

"No noise"—she raised a finger to her lips—"until we get to my apartment."

Evander nodded. So she was trying to smuggle him into her apartment without attracting the notice of her parents. He wondered if this wasn't such a good idea. But when she turned back with a wave for him to hurry and follow her, he went without a second thought.

They passed down a hallway floored with malachite and covered in fine mirrors chased with gold. Then they turned into a wooden hall, under the glowering visage of a line of portraits of old men with fierce eyes and narrow lips.

At last they came to a wide door. Serena knocked and was admitted at once by a guardsman in a red-and-white uniform, an unsmiling six-footer who nodded and bowed and stood back to attention until they were past him.

They came to another door, opened by a hidden key. Now they were within Princess Serena's private rooms, situated above the central courtyard, with views of the gardens below. Serena had several lovely Kassimi rugs on the floors and several large, exquisite pieces of Eoran pottery, including a great glowing green vase four feet high. Evander recognized it as Cunfshoni, a fabulous piece from the far east.

In the salon, furnished with heavy Bakanese pieces in dark wood, there was a Kassimi flower rug of great style and antiquity. Evander was impressed. Such rugs were worth a king's ransom.

On the red velvet walls of her intimate little parlor room, there hung paintings from Czardha, the acknowledged world leader in the visual arts. Evander gazed on these jeweled canvases in awe. He recognized one as the work of Giltoft of Leinkessen, perhaps the most famous artist of the previous century. Giltoft's paintings of wild sea scenes, tempests, volcanic eruptions, and warfare in the Czardhan manner were world renowned and fetched astronomical sums at auction. This one was a scene from Czardhan myth, the Dammenor. It was famous, and one of Giltoft's recurring obsessions, depicting the abduction of the fair lady Lamen by the hero Blue Frog. The fair lady Lamen was a voluptuous beauty, trailing silk and glory. Blue Frog was a knight in chain mail and helmet, a great sword, square handled in the barbarous Czardhan manner, belted to his side. Horses danced in fury on one side of the canvas. A battle raged on the other, and over it all writhed the wild orange sky. Evander whistled inwardly at the size of the purse needed to purchase such artistry.

Serena waved him to a seat on a comfortable stuffed divan. She sat in another, opposite him, across a table of exquisite inlay work in different colored dark woods. Evander would have been ashamed to show her his own, former rooms, which were small, a little shabby, and unpainted for years, with scarcely a decent rug in the whole place, except for his Kijans, given him by his grandfather long ago. Who had the Kijans now? he wondered. Which of his cousins had those lovely weaves to treasure?

Serena sat down with a long sigh of relief and sank back into the cushions. "Thank Pernaxo for that being over!"

She took a deep breath and then sat up again. "The first thing I must do is bathe. And then, when I'm feeling like a princess again, I want some breakfast."

She looked at the table. "As for you, my enigma, will you have breakfast with me?"

"Nothing could be more enjoyable."

"Good. You will want to bathe, too. Fortunately, there are two bathing chambers right next door—one of the reasons I took these rooms when Aunt Pulvia passed away."

He found a six-foot tub of steaming water waiting. The water was constantly pumped through the palace after exposure to the blessed Thymnal. Unfortunately, after bathing, he had to put his damp, filthy clothes back on before returning to the parlor. He planned to take breakfast with the princess and then leave before things got perhaps too dangerous. Besides, Yumi and Elsu would be worried. And he had the nagging concern that the Weave Witch might do their rug some harm following her failure to abduct Evander. He felt he had to warn them.

He waited in the parlor and soon found himself toying with a complex, three-dimensional puzzle set up on the table. It was an affair of balls studded with pins, and balls dimpled with sockets that had to be connected in just a certain way. To connect five of them was to solve the puzzle.

Evander lost himself in the puzzle, and so was startled when the door opened and the princess came in, pushing a cart ahead of herself.

She now wore a red velvet robe, buttoned to the neck, with gold slippers on her feet. She had rouged her cheeks and reddened her lips.

On the tray were a set of dishes. "Breakfast!" she announced. "I had the cooks send something up."

Evander was aware that his stomach was growling with anticipation at the smell of toasted graincakes and hot butter. He piled a plate with hot scones, scrambled eggs, sauteed carrots, and took a cup of well-brewed Kalut, the universal hot drink of Ryetelth.

After the first few furious minutes of attacking his food, his hunger ebbed enough for Evander to push the plate back a moment. Serena had reached the same point. They smiled together and fell into a discussion of their escape, laughing over the memory of Bwento Eruxi falling on his ass. Then, after a few minutes, inevitably, the talk returned to Serena and her dreadful fate.

"I won't let them do it. I won't marry some horrid old monster, not even human anymore. So disgusting a thing as you cannot imagine."

Evander, unfortunately, could imagine only too well. Even talking about a wizard made him uneasy. The horrible lumpy skin on his chest and back was still there. He was still a freak.

"Can you not battle the wizard with the power of the blessed Thymnal?"

Serena considered this. "Well, yes, if he was to attack me with magic. But only if it took place in the palace, or the city. The power of the Thymnal operates only within the city walls, that part of it that is risen from the ground. But my father plans to force me to go with the wizard. The blessed Thymnal is famous for defeating all other kinds of magic, but it cannot stop my father's guards from taking me out and giving me to the wizard."

This thought was perfectly hateful for Evander. "There's got to be some way out of this. It's totally unjust for them to force you to do this."

She sighed her absolute agreement. "They say it's my duty, and ordinarily, well, I would have to agree. A princess cannot always suit herself when it comes to marriage. In fact, I had always resigned myself to an arranged marriage. What else could I expect? It was either going to be the Prince of Storch, or the young Duke of Hawban, or some-one of that sort, and if I was very lucky, he'd be somewhat kind and capable of conversation and perhaps, even, family life. As for looks, well, I knew he would not be handsome. But this? This is just madness. None of these creatures is interested in a wife. Most of them would probably put me in a cage like an animal. Those that are still sexually active are prone to repulsive perversions, and the rest are so old their hearts are made of stone. They are incapable of love, or even lust.

"And father is so blind. He can't see that it's the Storch who are behind this. They're so jealous of Monjon. All of them, all the other states of Bakan, they're all in this to one degree or another. They smile in our faces, and then behind our backs they have called in this dreadful wizard to blight our lands."

"What happened?"

"Three years ago the wizard came to Monjon and de-manded that the king, my father, give up the blessed Thym-nal to him."

"And which wizard was this?" In truth, thought Evander, the land of Eigo was haunted by wizards of many sorts. Sedimo Kassim seemed a far less hazardous place to be, unless, of course, you were the true heir to the throne there.

"Oh, he has many names, some call him Gzug, others Gulfcades of the Black Mountain. His real name we now know is Gadjung."

Evander paled. "The Wizard of the Black Mountain, the one who has blighted Port Tarquil?"

"The same. He came to the Bakan at the time of the War of the Kraheen, took the Black Mountain, and made it a foul and evil place. He unleashed his creatures upon the land and drove away the folk."

"I have seen these things," said Evander in a sombre voice. "This wizard is a curse upon the world."

"So are most of them; as a class they are a pest. So are witches and spellsayers of all kinds. But, of course, Monjon floats by the magic of the Thymnal, so it is perhaps hypocritical of us to denounce all magic. There are limits though, and I will not allow them to give me away to that . . . that thing! I will kill myself first."

Evander went cold inside. "Ah, no, that doesn't sound like a good idea. There has to be something better than that."

"My father is deeply afraid of this wizard. At first he refused his impious demands, but the wizard released a storm of silver crickets that devoured the crops."

"Could you not produce counter magic?"

"Everything was tried. The royal magician was worn to a shadow in his efforts. The people prayed to Pernaxo, our old God. They prayed to other Gods, too; many women prayed to the Eastern Goddess, the one they call the Great Mother. Nothing came of any of this. The crickets devoured everything. The next spring a new horde of them arose from the ground, and once again nothing was harvested. The hunger began in the third year. Now Monjon is buying all its food, and the local people are either moving away or else they throng the streets in hungry mobs. There are thousands living in the shadow beneath the city."

"And so your father decided to offer his daughter to the winner of the Jousts Magical?"

"Originally, he thought that whoever became his son-in-law through such a wedding would feel honor bound to go forth and destroy the dark sorcerer."

"I see."

"No, you don't, because now it seems the evil wizard has joined in the contest and is winning every round."

Evander's face creased with shock. "But . . ." he spluttered.

"And if he wins, which seems likely, then I will be given to him. Father thinks that by appeasing the wizard he can find safety. If the wizard is his son-in-law, then he feels he will be able to exercise some authority over him."

"But . . ." Evander groped for words.

"So the contest must go on, and I must be given away."

"I see." Evander did, finally, understand the situation. It was quite horrifying. If Serena escaped, then the king would be forced to break his own promise. He would be utterly shamed. The city would still suffer at the hands of this wizard, and there would be no succor. If Serena didn't escape, then, well . . . Evander refused to pursue that line of thought.

"And so, in a few days' time, when that wizard defeats the rest of them, he'll come and claim me. I'll be given to him, and he'll carry me off to some flea-ridden lair in the hills." Her voice had become brittle. Suddenly, she began to cry.

The next moment he was sitting next to her. He put his arms around her and was trying to comfort her. She looked up at him with blurry eyes.

"Can you save me? Can you be my Blue Frog and I your lady Lamen?"

Madness overtook him. His lips crushed hers. She kissed him back. For a long moment they remained thus before they pulled apart. They looked at each other very closely, eye to eye.

"Who are you, Evander?"

He almost blurted it out, but then as if Kospero's voice had shouted a warning in the back of his mind, he shut his mouth.

"A merchant, my lady, of good family in Molutna."

"Molutna Ganga!" Her eyes widened. "The great city of the world, oh, how I would love to go there." She snuggled closer to him. "You must tell me all about Molutna Ganga."

Experimentally, she ran her hand along his chest. Through the damp shirt she felt a rough, bumpy surface. "But what has happened?" she said. "Were you wounded; are these bandages?" She pulled open the shirt despite his attempt to prevent her. Openmouthed, she stared at the blue-black mottled toad skin that covered him.

Chapter Fifteen

After a few seconds of mortifying embarrassment, he became aware that the noise he was hearing was Serena's screaming.

"No, don't," he began, but she darted away toward the door. He rose in pursuit, but fell over the table. The pain in his shin was truly incredible and brought tears to his eyes. The princess was at the door.

"No," he croaked, struggling to his feet, but it was too late; the princess was out of the door and screaming in the hall.

Evander remembered the guard, a tall, heavyset fellow. He was undoubtedly effective. Evander felt for his knife, but it was gone. He'd put it down when he bathed and forgotten to retrieve it afterward.

Civilized life could do that to you. It made you soft and stupid, albeit nice and clean. Now he was weaponless. He ran down the hall in the opposite direction from the screaming princess.

As he went, he cursed himself for not telling her earlier, when the consequences would not have been quite so life-threatening. The gravity of his situation was now clear. He had to get out of the palace and hide. If only he'd told her before, but somehow it had just seemed impossible. Everything had been going along so well, as if it had been ordained by the Gods.

He ran through a scullery and a small kitchen and then found a back entrance to the apartments, where a spiral staircase descended to what he imagined were the servants' quarters.

Then he became aware of two women looking up at him from the stairwell, their faces filled with apprehension. They, too, emitted piercing screams, disappearing through a doorway at the bottom of the stairs. He heard a lock turn and bolts slam home.

With sinking hopes he tried a stoutly built door to the outside. It, too, was locked and required a key to open. Evander turned back into the scullery and quickly flattened himself to the wall behind the door. Heavy footfalls announced the arrival of the guard, who stomped through the scullery, eyes alight with enthusiasm for the task of running down the rascal who had upset the princess.

In the kitchen he tried the door and then barreled down the stairs to the servants' quarters. Evander fled the other way and reached the front door of the apartment in time to get away down the hall.

The princess's quarters were in an out-of-the-way section of the royal apartments, and the guards had not yet swarmed to the scene. Evander felt a surge of hope. If he could just find a way out of here, he might yet escape.

Then he heard loud voices roaring in outrage. The guards were definitely coming now.

Evander searched for a way out, but the door they had entered through had been conscientiously locked by the first guard. Worse, that guard had now returned to the hallway, fired up with the descriptions fed him by the servants.

Just in time Evander found a door that would open, and he plunged into a long ochre-colored room. Portraits of the old kings of Monjon glowered down. Evander sped by them, feet skipping over ancient carpets.

At the far end was another door, which opened into a dining chamber, lined with shelves bearing fantastic china and the most elaborate porcelain work, further evidence of the wealth of Monjon. This place made the palace in Sedimo seem shabby. He wondered if even the great kings of Kassim could match these Monjonese.

In a further corridor, running on a thick green carpet, past white painted doors, he rounded a corner and came out on a wide landing. Stairs cascaded down a tier past a wall of mirror. On the lower floor were the princess, two guards, and King Agrant, wearing a dressing gown and sandals and looking very put out.

At his sudden appearance on the landing, Serena gasped. The king looked up and roared, and the guards charged up the steps toward him.

"No, it's all a mistake," Evander shouted. The guards

kept coming, urged on by a stream of loud commands in Monjonese. He ran back the way he'd come, but there were more guards. He tried the white painted doors until he found one that opened. Inside, an elderly servant stacking laundry screamed and fell back against the wall with her hands to her mouth. He darted past her to a window whose shutters were open, and thrust out a leg. Peering down, he saw a drop of three stories to a cobbled courtyard.

It was a long way down and a hard surface at the bottom. He would probably break his legs.

But the guards ran into the room, and there was no choice. He started to throw himself out the window when the first guard tackled him around the waist and pulled him back, throwing him to the floor. He scrambled to break free, trading punches with the fellow who had him around the waist. Then he was seized from behind by the second guard. Blows rained on him from two directions. He got an elbow into the face of the second guard, and then a knee into the chest of the other. For a moment he was free and on his feet, and then a third guard whipped his legs out from under him with a sweep of a billy club.

This time they didn't make any mistakes. When he was eventually pulled to his feet, he was sore in a great many places, and there was blood running from his nose. They frog-marched him back to face King Agrant.

The princess wouldn't meet his gaze. She looked away, but then she gave him a sidelong glance, unsure of who or what he really was.

The guards ripped open his shirt and exposed the horrible work of the wizard.

"What is this?" questioned the king in harsh-sounding Furda.

Evander tried to explain, but the king was not listening.

"Some kind of wizard's work then. No doubt of it."

"Yes, sir, it is, but . . ."

Serena was staring at him, appalled.

"There, you've admitted it. Wizard's work! What are you then, a spy? Sent here to harm my daughter?"

"No, Your Majesty, nothing like that. I am a simple merchant from Molutna Ganga."

"Then what are you doing here? Why were you in my daughter's apartment? Since when do simple merchants enter my daughter's apartment without my leave?"

"I, was, uh ... instrumental in saving her from some trouble, earlier this morning. In the process my clothes were ruined. She was kind enough to offer me breakfast and a chance to bathe."

"What? You were bathing with my daughter?"

"No, sir, not at all. I bathed alone. She bathed alone. I assure you that my intentions are honorable toward your daughter."

"Your intentions? What is this nonsense from you? Who do you think you are? You dare to have 'intentions' toward my daughter, without even a by-your-leave. Rampaging around in my palace! Obviously some kind of magical spy. Well, we'll get to the bottom of this, just you wait."

The king turned to the guards. "Take him away, lock him up, and keep an eye on him. We'll investigate this more closely."

"But, sir, I have done nothing. It is all a mistake. Ask the princess."

"Ask the princess Serena? Ask what?" The king glared at his daughter.

Her eyes clouded. "I know nothing," she mumbled.

Desperate, Evander turned to the guard they'd passed at the outer door. "You there, you saw us when we entered. Did I not enter with the princess?"

The guard, stony-faced, denied it. "Never saw you before. Don't know how you got in."

King Agrant had had enough. "Take him away. In three days we'll give him to the lions on the day of all saints."

"To the lions?" said Evander in horror.

"Yes," said the king. "It's been a long time since they were properly exercised. Poor old things, they haven't killed a prisoner in years. Do them good. Crowd will like it, too."

"But, Your Majesty, I have done nothing to deserve this."

King Agrant peered closely at him, then reached out a finger to poke him in the chest where the skin was especially nubby and warty. "Wizard's work! Make a fitting gesture for the last day of the Jousts Magical. Throw you to the lions, and then anoint the winner of my daughter's hand."

This was too much for Serena, who fled up the stairs and around the corner.

"Go with her, make sure she's safe. If she harms herself before week's end, there'll be more than one prisoner for the lions to exercise upon. Am I understood?"

The guard thundered after Serena. The others hustled Evander away.

Chapter Sixteen

Night after night the Jousts Magical continued as wizards battled just outside the city walls. Serena was forced to watch as every wizard with even a pretense to a normal human appearance was eliminated. It soon became clear that the contest was to be settled between the ancient Gadjung of the Black Mountain and the Bluegreen Wizard of Sonkando. Neither was anything less than utterly repellent, both physically and morally. Indeed, Gadjung was the very wizard against whom the king had set up the competition, seeking a champion for the city.

At night Serena wept. All day she prayed, both publicly to Pernaxo and in secret to the Great Mother of the East.

Occasionally, her thoughts turned to the handsome young man who had rescued her from foolish old Bwento. The pleasant memories of their walk back to the palace would then be blotted out by the thought of the horrid skin covering his chest and back. She would shiver with disgust, mixed with remorse. She would recall his tale of woe. He, too, was a victim of the wizard. But she had not spoken up. She had not dared to believe him at that moment. Her father would not have listened anyway, and her spirit had failed her. Now he was doomed, just as she was. The following day would see the last joust. To complete the evening's entertainments, the king had ordered that a wizardous intruder into the Palace of Monjon would be thrown to the royal lions. The climax of the festivities would come the following day when she would be given to the wizard in marriage.

By then Evander would be gnawed down to the bones.

There was so much unrest now in the city that a good piece of barbaric entertainment was absolutely essential. Thousands of poor wretches lived in the shadow under the city, and their hunger had grown sharp. Since the wizard's

curse, they had abandoned their lands and come to Monjon
to live on what they could beg from the wealthy city. There
had been an explosion in thievery and petty crime. The
gates had had to be locked at night and the watch quintu-
pled in size. Still, there were pickpockets in the daytime
crowds and muggers in dark alleyways. Starving wretches
were ready to sell themselves for almost any purpose.
Throwing someone to the lions, which hadn't been done in
ages, would give them all a savage thrill and remind them
that King Agrant was the ruler of the city and possessor of
an army and the Royal Guard. Others might be thrown to
the lions. It would also be a cheap way of feeding the royal
beasts, who ate their weight in meat every few days.

Serena would be forced to watch. The king was insistent
that she attend all public activities and show her resolve to
do her duty for the city.

"Duty"—that was all that she heard from her parents.
She was to do her duty and save the city. Without her, they
could not hope to deal with the Wizard of the Black
Mountain.

In vain had she shouted that the Wizard of the Black
Mountain was openly taking part in the competition and
quite likely to win. Did they really mean to give her away
to their own worst enemy? Her parents were oblivious to
her protests. Serena realized at last that the king intended
to use her to buy off the wizard and that nothing would
stop him.

Indeed, her father had even sent old Caltrabes to give
her a little inspirational chat. He was the High Priest of
Pernaxo, and though not a wizard, he was not overly clean
either. In addition, his teeth were rotting and his breath
stank. He insisted on coming close to her and talking in a
whisper that enveloped her in his fishy stench. "It is that
my words are of an intimate nature, my dear princess. I
must not let the slightest stain fall upon your virginal honor.
I must talk with you concerning the matters sexual. Your
father has insisted upon it."

It was clear from Caltrabes's prune face that he found
this task quite distasteful. Nose wrinkling in more than disgust, she replied quickly. "I know about the matters sexual,
High Priest. I was given instruction by nurse Hanny when
I was thirteen. I know what a man has between his legs,

and I know what my own private parts are, and what they're for."

"Yes, yes, my child, you know about the basic, ahh, quite ordinary practices. However, there are others, those that involve the use of other parts of the body in order to stimulate the partner to orgasm."

"Orgasm?" she had said, shocked.

"Ahh, yes." Old Caltrabes looked so unhappy she would have cooperated if only to ease him through the excruciating embarrassment of it all, but she had already grown too angry. He stumbled on.

"There are various, shall we say, 'arts' of love that the sophisticated wife can employ to satisfy, even enthrall her husband. The king, your father, wishes you to know about these arts and practice them upon your soon-to-be husband. In this way it is hoped that some degree of control might be gained over the behavior of said husband-to-be."

Serena saw red. "They want to wed me to a monster of perversity and then they want me to service this monster with enthusiasm?"

"Ahh, well, I do not, that is, I ..."

"And they have demeaned the very High Priest into coming here and telling me this ... this obscenity."

Caltrabes was retreating into the collar of his robes like a hermit crab into its shell. Serena exploded at him. All the pent-up anguish and fury she had in her heart was vented in a half minute or so of pure rage. Poor old Caltrabes had left in silence, completely extinguished by the blast.

Later, King Agrant had reprimanded her severely and threatened to have her confined to a cell if she did not show the decorum of a proper princess. Her duty to the realm must come first!

Serena knew that she was being monitored. Any signs of attempted flight would be enough to have her locked up.

She had begun to think about suicide. When she took an inventory of knives in the kitchen, she discovered that they'd all been removed. Her medicine cabinet had been rifled and some things taken. Belts and ropes and sashes had disappeared from her wardrobe. If she even tried to throw herself out the window, they'd intervene. Only by carefully toeing the line could she avoid the ultimate humiliation of being locked up.

But could she stand to watch Evander torn asunder by the royal lions? Worse even than thoughts of this horrible event were the gnawing doubts about herself.

First came a nagging call to her duty. For all her kicks against responsibility, deep down Serena knew there were burdens attached to the privileged life she had inherited. Was it possible that her father's crazy scheme was actually the best thing they could do to save the city? In that case, shouldn't she sacrifice herself for the people? Wasn't this the duty of a princess of the realm? Serena had refused to accept this thought before, so much did she loathe that wizard, but now it entered her thought frequently. Did the king know better than she what had to be done? Should she simply obey and go to her fate, trusting in the good God Pernaxo of Monjon?

Something in her screamed defiance.

And then guilt would well up when she thought how she had let Evander down, just freezing there and leaving him to her father's wrath. If she'd spoken up, he wouldn't be facing the lions.

In her heart she knew that Evander was telling the truth. The mad story he'd babbled to the king about Port Tarquil and the Wizard of the Black Mountain was perhaps not so mad after all. Madness had afflicted her world already. That was the same wizard that had lain waste the crops of Monjon. That wizard was capable of the most terrifying magic. His power was clearly of an order of magnitude greater than that of the magicians of the Bakan.

Evander was handsome and brave, and he'd been so charming on their walk back to the palace. She'd been quite ready to melt into his arms. Everything would have been wonderful if it hadn't been for that awful skin, like some monstrous crocodile, thick and lumpy, ridged and bumpy.

She was forced to admit to herself that she had betrayed him quite monstrously. He had begged her to listen to him, and she wouldn't. She'd gone off screaming, and he'd been arrested. And then Daddy had just done the worst thing he could've done. And now Serena would have to watch the most interesting, good-looking boy she'd ever known die in the jaws of the lions.

And she knew he felt something for her. She'd seen that in his eyes. So she would be responsible for killing someone who loved her—someone who had protected her. She remembered how afraid she'd been when he produced that knife. How wrong she'd been about that. He was no ruffian, but a gentleman with the soul of a prince.

And so she prayed to the Mother of the East, the great gray Goddess who knew all and foretold all. Let not the telling of Evander's story end in the lion's pit, she prayed. Let not the telling of Serena's story end with unholy consummation with the dreadful old wizard. Let not this budding love between herself and Evander be destroyed.

At night her dreams were horrible. She would awake, sweating from the imagined embrace of Gadjung, a hairy, ill-smelling thing in the shape of a man, but with monstrous appetites.

By day she saw the few friends allowed to her and wept with them at the approaching end of her life. When she was taken away by the wizard, it would all come to an end.

She was not completely alone, however. The princess had many friends in the city who were deeply distressed by the king's actions. Shock had given way to other, more dangerous emotions. Some of the hotheads were plotting. Day and night they moved around the city, holding meetings, rousing others to act to save the princess. Among those who came to the meetings was Bwento Eruxi, who had already forgiven the princess for spurning him. Like the others, he was determined to save her.

Messages came to her, but trapped now within the palace, under constant scrutiny, Serena felt little hope. Sometimes she even wished that she'd let Bwento carry her off; at least she might have gotten out of Monjon.

On the other hand, those fools would have simply been caught at the gate. They'd taken precious little precaution against discovery.

How could such incompetent fellows help her? The one who had really tried to help her was locked up and waiting for the lions because of her silliness and lack of courage.

Her sobs racked her chest as she closed herself off in her room and knelt down by her bed to pray to the great Goddess, the fount of all life, the principle of existence. She prayed fervently, unschooled in the correct rituals of the east where the great Goddess was widely worshipped. Nonetheless, her prayers were heartfelt. Whether they would be heard was, of course, unknowable.

*Was it not said, that at the beginning and at the end there
shall be nought but the humblest of creatures? That the
finest and the mightiest shall be pulled down, and all shall
be equal in low estate?*

*Was it not said, further, that they who had been raised
up from animals should go henceforth and climb to the
stars?*

*Was it not said, by all the mages, that it was best to live
as do the meek in spirit, for they are the pillars upon
which the world is built?*

*Was it not also said, that it was wise to fear the doings
of the lowliest, for where there are pillars, they can be cut
down, and where there are jeweled vaults, they can be
leveled unto the dust?*

In the darkness they dared him. They crawled in cold
slime to reach his throat, unseen. Had he detected them,
he would have made them pay most horribly. But they
were the meek, the humble, with no panoply of war or
bright armor to wear. To him who bestrode their world on
iron-shod feet, they were of little account, save as slaves.

In this, perhaps, he was in error.

Like ants they burrowed beneath the roots of his stone
walls. With wondrous stealth they dug their way toward
him, for kenspeckle activity would be detected. Annihilation, they bore in their hearts, death, they carried to him,
unseen, untasted death.

In dank tunnels they slaved. The lantern caught myriad
cabochon eyes agleam in turtleheads. Small, lumpish bodies struggled in the freezing mire.

Where they cut the rock, they used acid and felted pry
bars. Bare hands, a multitude, carried away the lofted
blocks. On they groped, feeling their way through the
stone, living on mud and paste, existing in utter darkness,
withstanding the cold and damp, with determination to go
on until they reached him and brought the fear of death
to him, the soul killer, the ruler of Twelve Worlds, Waakzaam the Great.

Chapter Seventeen

The day was winding down in the market square. Most of the market stalls had been dismantled and wheeled over to their storage places, under the lee of the gate tower. The last few vendors were closing up shop, and the Wheatsack tavern was full of thirsty market folk having a wet before trudging home. Times were hard, but the traders and stall holders clung to their comfortable tradition.

Outside the tavern's warm glow, however, the market-place was the scene of a shift in population. The regular customers were gone, and now the horde of the starving were picking over the rubbish heaps.

Here someone found half a bun, a little muddy, but still a bun! There a woman found a cabbage, a bit rotten and wormy, but there were a few good bits. Over there a group of frantic people were picking through the debris around the peanut seller. Every so often they would press something to their mouths, and their jaws would work frantically.

This ragged horde was let in at the end of the day to find what they might. The guards were supposed to keep an eye on them, but, of course, there were too many hungry folk and too few guards. King Agrant should have come down to see the consequences of his charitable order, but he did not. In these troubled times the king stayed in the palace.

Indeed, the king was a worried man. He did not care for either of the remaining wizards in the competition, but there was nothing to be done about that. The prime question remained—would the winner accept that he must defend the city now that he had won its princess? Once he wed into the royal family, the victorious wizard would be required to uphold the system, and that meant keeping the Thymnal safe inside its vault in the Palace of Monjon. Both the finalists were creatures of unguessable habits of mind. They gave him, the king, little respect. They leered openly at poor Serena. The king felt for his daughter. He was not a man with a heart of stone, but he was determined that she do her duty. Duty was essential. They would survive only if they all did their duty.

While the king occupied himself with endless calculations of the nature of wizards, the ragged folk driven away from their farms picked through the leavings in the market. Had Agrant known how many of them there were, he would perhaps have rescinded his order allowing them in. They were hungry and they were angry. They had been farmers and townsfolk, people who had worked all their lives, and then seen the ruination of their hopes in three years with no crops at all. Now they lived on scraps and dirty vegetables, and rage boiled in their hearts.

There came a sudden stir at the high end of the marketplace. A group of well-dressed young men stepped down the cobbles with a determined stride, ignoring the looks of frank dislike they received from the hungry.

While a few men pulled a stall out of storage and pushed it into the middle of the place, others grouped themselves around it with folded arms. Several called out for the attention of the people.

Onto the stall bounded a young nobleman with overlong hair of a pale, tawny yellow. He pulled at the sleeves of his goldcloth jacket and began to harangue the crowd in angry Monjonese, denouncing the Jousts Magical and the plan to force the princess to wed an ugly, unknown wizard.

The yellow-haired youth, Impitan, son of the Duke of Baroche, was, he informed them, a natural leader, so regarded by all his friends. Thus, the people could trust to his abilities. He and his fellows, the cream of the young aristocrats, would lead them on a march to the palace, where they would demand freedom for the princess.

This speech was met with relative silence. The crowd eyed one another. Who were these young madmen, wearing puffed jackets and gemstones for buttons? Why should the starving care about the Princess Serena, who could loll on her comfortable bed with a full belly?

Impitan of Baroche sensed the crowd's reluctance. He took another tack, more certain to win approval. "It is all the fault of the Storchese!" There were always folk who hated the Storchese. "They're the ones who put this wizard up to it. We demand war on the Storchese. Bring an end to the depredations of the wizard by going to his paymasters. War to the Storchese!"

This produced an ugly murmur and some scattered shouts of support. People were pouring out of the taverns, the Wheatsack, the Blue Boar, the Grapes. The crowd was swelling rapidly. The guard at the gate sent an anxious message to the palace.

Sensing the possibilities, other elements were already moving to join the crowd. Among these elements were some frankly criminal ones, the thugs who controlled the protection racket in the outer ward.

The mob was getting roused by now. Between Monjon and Storch existed perennial rivalry and dislike. Monjon had outshone Storch ever since the Thymnal first floated the city of lights. The Storchese had never accepted their secondary status. The wizard's campaign to wrest away the Thymnal? Of course, they were behind it. War to the Storchese!

A lot of others, particularly at the front, were enraged by the mere sight of these well-fed young men, glittering with jewels, dressed in a year's pay, standing there and demanding loyalty of them, the starving of the land. The first rotten vegetable flew out shortly and splattered off the stall. A mutter went up. Someone made a crude joke, producing a guttural growl of laughter.

The young aristocrats looked to each other with dismay. They sensed the coming storm. They understood that they had aroused a tiger, and that it was focusing on them. Impitan of Baroche raised his voice and begged them to listen. "Hear me, good people, please listen to my message!"

Another rotten vegetable whizzed by. The front of the crowd started hissing and groaning. Things were disintegrating.

Then another figure bounded up onto the stall, assisted by a knot of heavyset fellows who had suddenly muscled the circle of aristocrats aside. He wore the plain garb of the market people, dark blue coat and round porter's hat, and when he was up on the stall, he turned a well-known face to the crowd, causing both shouts and boos. He was the Nob Hat of the Outer Ward, an up-and-coming thug in the criminal underworld.

"It's Glukus!" someone shouted.

Another crude joke was called out, and everyone laughed. Glukus responded with a similar joke, casting doubt in the first jokester's parentage, wits, and sexual ability. More laughter followed.

Glukus, the Nob Hat, raised his hands.

"Truth of the matter, friends, is that what we really need now is food. You're starving to death here, and up in the palace they're eating pheasant and drinking Skola wine, just as they always do. They don't care a whit for your suffering."

This brought an immediate roar of approval. Shouts of "Glukus!" filled the air. "Hark to the words of the Nob Hat!" bellowed one of the biggest thugs.

"The king is wealthy! We all know that. Why doesn't he give up some of his great wealth to feed his starving people?"

Another roar went up. By now the crowd was extended back through the main gates, which had been left open by mistake and kept that way by Glukus's boys. Now it was too late. The word had gone back into the nether regions below the city, where thousands upon thousands of starving wretches were camped. A stream of people was pouring up the ramp and into the city.

Impitan and the other young aristocrats realized that things had slipped out of their hands completely. Moreover, they knew they'd get the blame for whatever might happen. Impitan tried to retake the initiative from Glukus. He started shouting about the princess over Glukus's voice, calling on the crowd to march to demand Serena's release. A heavyset man stepped up to his back, and the prick of a knife against his kidney cut off his pleas. The thugs quickly shoved the aristocrats back to the margins. There they grouped in a gloom-struck line while some looked for a way out.

Glukus continued his harangue. "Now, folks, don't get me wrong. The king is a good king, and I am his loyal subject. That I know he is good makes me think he just does not understand the problem of the poor people in these lean times. I think that if we could just make him aware of the problem, he would distribute food from the city granaries right away."

"Right away!" came the shouts.

"Good ol' Nob Hat."

Glukus now raised the issue of the dungeons. In the palace dungeons there were dozens of unfortunate farmers who'd been imprisoned for debts, or for stealing some bread in the city. It was time they freed those farmers. It was time the king fed his people. They just had to tell the king how they felt.

"Food and freedom!" shouted Glukus. "Food and Freedom!" The crowd took up the chant.

"Free our brothers who demanded food and were jailed."

"Food, food, food," roared the crowd.

Glukus and his followers jumped down and started up the avenue toward the palace. Ahead of them were the young aristocrats, retreating at a trot, appalled at what they had stirred into life. The sight of the young, well-feds did something to those in the crowd who saw them retreating. An angry roar broke out, and the mob began to surge down the avenue in pursuit.

A line of Royal Guards appeared across the way. They drew batons and ordered the crowd to halt and disperse. Glukus gave a shout, and his boys charged the guards and wielded clubs of their own. The crowd was encouraged by the sight and came on, quickly overwhelming the guards who were beaten senseless and disarmed.

The roars of the hungry echoed through the city. A restaurant was rushed, the customers robbed, and their meals taken and devoured as if by locusts.

A carriage was overturned, the horses driven off in panic and the coachman beaten. Then the aristocratic ladies inside the coach were pulled forth and assaulted by having their fine clothes ripped off their backs and their fanciful hairpieces torn to shreds. They were pushed to the front and driven on, screaming with horror and rage, while the braver of the aristocratic boys returned to close around them and lend them jackets and hurry them away.

The mob went on, out of control now, venting the pent-up rage of a once prosperous people reduced to rags and empty bellies.

Outside the palace stood a rapidly deployed platoon of the Royal Guards, armed with spears and shields. More guards were running up to join them. The sharp calls of command rang off the walls. Horns were blowing inside the palace, and drums began to beat.

Running up, the young aristocrats called to the guards to let them through. The guards ignored them. Indeed most of the guardsmen were quietly looking forward to the opportunity to hand out a few whacks to the arrogant drunken fops who so often caused trouble in the streets of the inner ward. The aristocrats were about to be sandwiched between the guards and the mob.

What nobody counted on was Glukus and his boys. The guardsmen didn't realize that this was Glukus's only chance to get into the royal dungeons and slit a certain prisoner's throat. Alive, that prisoner was sure to identify Glukus in an upcoming trial. Dead, he was no threat at all.

Glukus and his boys pressed up hard behind the aristocratic youths, forcing them against the guards who beat them with their spear butts. Some of the youths fought back as best they could while others cringed beneath the blows. Thus things might have stabilized if Glukus himself had not reached past the bent form of Bwento Eruxi and struck home with his club and knocked down a guardsman. A gap appeared in the line. Glukus's biggest thug surged into the space and exchanged blows with the next guardsman over on the right while Glukus kept the fellow on the left busy. The rest of the boys came piling in the next moment, trampling the prone form of Bwento Eruxi. The guards' line buckled and broke and the guards withdrew, slowly at first, and than at a gallop, when they heard the main gates of the palace start to winch shut behind them.

The mob roared forward until it lapped up around the main gates, catching them still partly open. Once again Glukus was there first. The gates remained open. The palace was breached.

A few guardsmen appeared on the battlements above. The king had been informed of the looming disaster. He was debating whether to appear to the crowd to try and calm them. Of course, his appearance might merely enrage them further. Nobody could be certain. There had been some excellent circus entertainment lately, but there had been very little bread for a long time.

While King Agrant dithered, the mob took things into its own hands. The palace food stores were broken into—then the wine cellars. In no time there was a sizable part of the mob clutching bottles of wine. Rampaging bands went off in all directions in search of loot, but parties of guards were holding the main staircase in the center of the palace, plus the balcony of the outdoor staircase on the second floor, thus preserving most of the palace from the mob.

The starving mob was interested in filling its belly before anything, and this altered the pattern of the riot. As the mob cleaned out the kitchens, the guards began to take the initiative. Reserve guards were coming up from the middle ward, but slowly enough that chaos still reigned.

Someone set fire to the kitchens, and a blaze erupted in the small servant's wing. Some of the guards were diverted to fighting this blaze. Some of the rioters actually rushed to help the guards put out the fire, their sense of Monjon pride overcoming their hunger and their rage. The great palace could not be allowed to burn. It contained such a treasure trove that even the dispossessed would not let it burn. The guards did not question this sudden shift in alliances. Water tanks reserved solely for firefighting were kept in the high attics of all the central buildings. Hoses were seized and hauled into position, and water streamed from them when the stopcocks were turned. Choking clouds of smoke arose mixed with steam. The guards were thus able to suppress the fire quite quickly, before it caused any major damage.

While this effort was in progress, grimmer work went on in the dungeons below. There, Glukus and his thugs had broken in, beaten the jailers unconscious, and gone down the rows of cells, breaking out everybody. Glukus made sure the criminals he'd released remembered to whom they owed the favor. Then his men seized the poor fellow they'd been hunting, and in a moment his head was leaving his shoulders under repeated chops with a blunt sword. His wails rang out for a dreadful length of time as the thugs hewed at him.

Evander, released along with the rest, witnessed this murder and backed away quickly.

"Remember what'll happen to you if you sneak on the Nob Hat," said Glukus to the newly freed prisoners.

Evander ran through the palace, noting a strong smell of smoke and a distant din. Parties of ragged men were moving through the rooms, smashing fragile objects, stuffing other things into their pockets and packs. A howling roar came from the main hall.

Evander looked out. A party of guards were beating a mass of rioters with their spear butts. The guards were trained in this kind of work, and now there were enough of them to do the job. The rioters were on the run.

Evander found himself well placed, however, since the guards had left an exit unguarded. He was through it in a moment and sprinting across the piazza outside the palace in the next.

Chapter Eighteen

Evander ran all the way to the inn through streets alive with excitement and fear. A great cloud of steam was still rising from the palace, and the stench of smoke was thick in the streets. Still, the riot seemed to be winding down. The guards were regaining control.

A sullen mass of rioters hurried down the avenue, many staggering under their loot, which included everything from sacks of grain to incongruous pieces of royal furniture.

Inside the inn he found Elsu. She jumped up with a peal of joy, hugged him, and gave thanks to Pernaxo, the Monjon god.

This almost brought tears to Evander's eyes. Elsu's genuine feeling melted his heart. She was completely oblivious to the wizard skin under his shirt. For a few moments he was barely able to speak, then he noticed Yumi's absence.

"But where is Yumi?"

"There is much trouble with our carpet. He will return very soon. Tell Elsu what happened. Where have you been?"

Evander explained. Elsu's face hardened when he described Postrema's plot to kidnap him. She uttered little gasps of horror as she heard of the prison, the injustice to Evander, and then the riot.

While Evander tore off his filthy clothes and bathed, Elsu brought him food and hot Kalut. He was starving after the days in the dungeon. King Agrant was not generous to prisoners, and the jailers had stolen most of what was allotted for Evander, declaring that there was no point in letting it all go to the lions. The smell of a piece of vagabond pie had him salivating. He sat and ate everything with leonine speed and concentration.

He had barely finished, when Yumi returned, greeting him with a fervent embrace. Yumi then fell on his knees to thank the Gods for their favor. He sat beside Evander and listened intently to his tale. Occasionally, Elsu would add a stream of rapid fire Ugoli, and the two of them would speak back and forth in that ancient, liquid-sounding tongue. Then they would turn back to Evander with those big eyes. Yumi nodded sadly, as if he were hearing confirmation of his worst suspicions.

"Terrible injustice," he said when it was done. "I did not understand before. We did not know where you had disappeared to. I even began to think that you had abandoned us. I asked after you all over, but there was no report of you. I am sorry now to ever have doubted you, Evander."

Evander clasped the little Ugoli man's hand.

"We will have to hide you from the king."

Evander had been thinking about this same point. He could hardly hide in the inn. The guards would soon be checking all such obvious places, and then the king would surely put out a reward. No, there was no possibility of staying at the inn.

"But what about the rug?" Evander asked. Yumi's face darkened.

"The witch has refused to return the carpet of my ancestors. I have been to see the Ugoli council. There will be action taken."

Elsu's eyes went wide, but she said nothing more than a muttered prayer.

"She tried to take me captive by witchcraft," growled Evander. "Isn't that illegal?"

"When this trouble with the king is cleared up, we shall have grounds for calling for her arrest. But first we must take the carpet. She has even threatened to damage it."

Elsu gasped.

Evander looked grim. "I want to help you get back the carpet."

"Good, we will need you, Evander. But first we must go to the house of Ornizolest. He is leader of the Ugoli Council in Monjon and a good man. You will stay there until we can work out a way of smuggling you out of the city. The gates will be watched now."

"What about the Princess Serena?"

The Ugoli gave a helpless shrug.

"She will go to the wizard, whichever one wins tonight."

"You think the contest will still be held? After the riot?"

Yumi nodded somberly. "It is the only way to bring an end to the depredations of the Wizard of Black Mountain."

Evander shook his head, depressed terribly by this thought. Poor Serena, he felt certain that she hadn't really wanted him thrown to the lions. She'd been frightened. She was already in a state of acute anxiety, and she'd been through a lot that day. In her panic she'd lied to her father.

His feelings for her hadn't altered a bit. To have to sit still while she was given to the wizard, was too awful to contemplate. Evander chewed his lip. What could they possibly do to save her?

"We take Evander to Ornizolest's house," said Yumi. "He will be safe there for now. Better there than here anyway."

Outside, they moved quickly, boldly, through the streets. There were still crowds outside, and order was far from completely restored. Most of the rioters had slipped away down the avenue, and parties of guards were jogging up and down, searching for stragglers. From the palace came a somewhat reduced din as the guards mopped up the drunken residue of the riot that had been trapped in the palace. The Ugoli had not been involved in the riot, so the guards paid them no attention. They ignored Evander as well in his clean clothes and freshly scrubbed face.

They crossed into the middle ward and turned onto a broad street lined with large four-story houses. One of these belonged to a wealthy Ugoli merchant, Ornizolest. When Yumi pulled on a heavy chain, a bell clanged inside. Following a long silence, the door swung smoothly open. Several beaming Ugoli welcomed them into a warm interior of wood and white walls.

They passed through low-ceilinged rooms spanned by dark wood beams before coming to Ornizolest's parlor. Here they were met by their host, an unusually plump Ugoli wearing a suit of dark blue velvet with a golden chain hanging around his neck.

Yumi and Elsu spoke with Ornizolest in Ugoli for a few moments. Then Ornizolest stepped up to Evander and embraced him with a shout of welcome. He switched to Furda after that.

"A good friend of the Ugoli people is always welcome in the house of Ornizolest," he said warmly. "Particularly welcome are friends of my friends Yumi and Elsu, the greatest flower growers of our time. Who will ever forget the purple orchids they grew for the millennium ceremony? Or the tangled vestia they gave to the Ugoli Queen in the Decadion? More beautiful than roses they were, such vestia has never been equaled!"

The small crowd of Ugoli in the room, composed of other merchants and their servants, broke into polite applause.

"You will stay in this house until we can find a way to get you out of the city. I do not think it will be difficult, nor will it take long."

Then the talk shifted to the purloined carpet of Yumi's ancestors. Evander sat by a window, where he was served a goblet of chilled wine and a bowl of nuts. He looked out on the garden courtyard of the house. It was typically Ugoli with a virtual riot of blooms, many of them set against each other in dramatic clashes of color—orange against dark green with pink highlights, blue against yellow, with red salvia and white tendernots everywhere as borders.

The Ugoli became quite excited during the talk of the witch and the carpet. Then Ornizolest spoke in a loud voice, and they fell silent, listening for several minutes. Then they began to plan in earnest.

Evander watched, Elsu translating occasionally for him as they hatched their plot to break into Postrema's house. It was simple enough. They intended to move at once, charging her front door and breaking it down. By the speed of their attack they might be able to prevent Postrema from destroying the carpet. Once inside, they would fight their way to the rug, and seize it, and fetch it back.

To Evander this began to sound rather improbable. He ventured to say so after a while.

Ornizolest looked up. "Why so?"

"Because the witch has many servants, and they will put up a fight. It may take longer than you think to overcome them. And during this period the guards will be sent for."

The Ugoli stared at him silently. There was wisdom in his words. Even though they wished to go at once and grapple with the witch, it might be better to try another plan.

After a few moment's of internal struggle, Ornizolest realized the truth of this. "Evander is right. Our plan would not work. We are only Ugoli folk; we cannot fight so well.

We might not even overcome the servants of the witch. We must think again."

And so for hours they mulled the problem. In the end Evander came up with the only likely ploy. It made him uneasy, but it seemed the only way.

He would be the bait. Postrema would be eager to recapture him. They would inform Postrema that they would exchange Evander for the rug.

When Postrema came to inspect the captive, they would spring their trap and take her prisoner. Then she would have to give up the rug to obtain her freedom.

"She will use magic," warned Evander. "And she will have some of her men with her."

"Any magic will be weak. This is Postrema, the Weave Witch, not the Queen of Mice," said Ornizolest.

"May the saints preserve us from that!" said someone else.

"She has power, too," said Evander. "Believe me, I know."

"We have power, too," said Ornizolest. The others fell silent.

Ornizolest nodded slowly to himself.

"Evander has good idea, certainly better than ours. We can trap the witch, but we must beware her magic."

They were soon decided.

Chapter Nineteen

After the food riots King Agrant became more determined than ever to push through his plan. Serena would wed whichever wizard won, and that was that. Only by forging an alliance with some powerful wizard could the city be saved and the Thymnal preserved.

Serena was moved to a small room, a "cell" as she declared it, and a guard was set outside. She had but a single window, on the sixth floor of the tower. From it she could see the roof of the lion's den, a green cupola thrusting up among the trees.

Her only visitors were her cousins Amili and Luipa, loyal friends, and fortunately great favorites of the queen. So she was not utterly alone.

"It does not occur to my father the king that his grain policy might have something to do with the riot," Serena fumed. "I wonder if it would have ever happened at all if he had disbursed some of the grain in the palace stores. We should have done more to alleviate the hunger of the truly wretched."

Amili and Luipa were more concerned with the state of the royal decor. "But Serena, the entire ground floor has been destroyed. Be thankful you can't see it, my dear, it'd break your heart. Vandals, that's what they were. Tore the Vespalline tapestries down and ripped them to shreds."

"I know it's awful, Amili, but think how angry those men must have been. And they are poor folk. What do they know of the art of Vespal?"

"They smashed the stained glass of the convent. All that beauty gone in a few moments of brutish rage," said Luipa.

"Well, they have been starving down there in the dark."

"Serena, you are the soul of social generosity. I grant the starving the right to protest, but not to destroy priceless works of art!"

"They can't eat art! Why does the king not send out grain to the starving?"

Her cousins nodded in agreement. "Indeed, why can he not do that? That would have prevented all of this," wondered Amili.

Luipa countered at once. "Well, he'd run out of grain and then we'd all starve."

They fell silent for a moment while Serena sighed wearily and glanced out the window across the courtyard. White doves were hooting softly on the farther roof.

"I still can't believe my father is sending me to be wife to one or another ancient, bad-smelling wizard, all whiskers and foul breath."

Their lips compressed. Their eyes glistened. "Poor Serena," they sobbed together.

Serena was dry-eyed though. Her predicament was far too serious for tears. There had to be some way out. But what? Escape seemed out of the question.

In all their news from the outside world, Amili and Luipa said nothing about the fight inside the prison or the mass escape of the prisoners. Nor did Serena dare to raise the subject of Evander. She could not afford to set her cousins, sweet as they were, to gossiping about herself and Evander.

Later, when they were gone, she did weep when her guilt and remorse over her treatment of Evander overcame her once more. He'd been so sweet to her. She'd felt a kindness in him that was coupled with a ferocious demeanor when he was aroused to protect someone. Like herself.

Cry folly! She wept. Poor, handsome Evander, who had rescued her once and then been betrayed by her and condemned to the lions.

It was just that she had this horror of deformity. There was a little, retarded cousin, who could barely talk, and being with her was profoundly uncomfortable for Serena. Often she had prayed to the God Pernaxo for help with this fear of the deformed. It seemed so mean and uncharitable of her, she felt soiled by it sometimes. Alas, Pernaxo had not heard her prayers, and no relief from this meanness of spirit had come. And now, through this weakness, she'd lost the man she knew she loved, and her heart would be broken forever.

The lions were roaring loudly over in their dome. They'd been tormented briefly by a few rioters who'd thrown rocks through the bars of their cages, and now they were in a mood to do violence themselves.

Serena contemplated the window. She could always throw herself out of it and end it all—except that she was afraid to die. She was young and beautiful and had a wonderful life ahead of her, or at least she ought to.

And with that came thoughts of what awaited her—the filthy clutches of one of those disgusting old wizards. She sank to the floor in utter misery.

The lions were loud that night and could be heard clearly across the city.

Evander was sitting out on the highest balcony of Ornizolest's house. He gave thanks to the Gods; but for their grace he might be listening to those huge, hungry cats from his cell. There had to be something divine in the sudden stroke that had spared him.

It was a lovely night, the stars were bright, yet the air was not chill. Evander looked over the strange city and wondered at all the things that had happened to him since he had fled his native land. He wondered, for a moment, how he would someday tell his relatives at home about his adventures.

Just thinking of home brought up too many thoughts for him, and he pushed them away with an effort. Yet, he prayed that his cousins had been merciful. They had no reason not to be. His father and mother were both dead, his sister married and safe far beyond Sedimo. Any killings in the family would simply be gratuitous. Cousin Madees, now the king, was a cautious man, Evander knew this very well, so the chances were good that young Florio would have been spared, as well as Kamia and the other younger cousins. Perhaps, if the Gods were willing, he would someday sit out on the battlements at Sedimo and tell Kamia and Ri and even Florio about his sojourn in Monjon, the magical floating city of the Bakan. It didn't seem too likely, but it was a strange world he had discovered, and the strangest things could happen.

Such was made obvious by his rescue of a beautiful princess with whom he'd shared a kiss and fallen in love. Unfortunately, the curse of the great wizard had turned him into a half-monster, and thus he had lost her love, most sweet and precious substance in the whole world. Or, perhaps

not; he was still confused about her. She had failed to come
to his aid, but that had happened when she was in a most
flustered state, and under the awe-inspiring gaze of her
regal father. He could understand her reluctance, her hesitation in his cause. So, did she love him? For there had
been that spark, unmistakable, between them on the couch
in her apartment.

He would soon leave this city, so magical and yet so
cruel, but escape would not help him with this sense of
enormous loss. While he might save his skin, horrible as it
was, poor Serena would be married off to one of those
ghastly old men. Poor girl, she would die a thousand deaths
and he, her prince, would be completely unable to save
her. It was such a wrong that he wanted to cry out and go
at once to the king and demand freedom for the princess,
even if it meant his own return to the dungeons.

The lions grew loud again suddenly. Their trainers had
come to throw meat to them. Since the prisoner selected
for their dinner had escaped, that part of the evening's
entertainment had been reluctantly canceled, although the
king had considered feeding them with some of the rioters.
His advisors had counseled caution. The mob might easily
be stirred once more, and hunger was still widespread. The
lion's roaring chilled Evander, and he turned his head away
and stepped back into the room, closing the door to the
balcony. It muted the sound of hungry cats.

King Agrant had decreed that the Joust Magical should
be held on time, as if nothing had happened. The needs of
the city of Monjon came first. The rioters would be dealt
with later. For now, the gates were shut and the guard
quadrupled on the walls.

Evander looked at himself glumly in the mirror on the
wall. There was nothing he could do about any of this. He
just had to get out of Monjon as best he might. And that
meant they had to get back Yumi's precious "Nine
Horse" carpet.

The plan was proceeding. A message had been sent to
the witch, and her reply was expected at any moment.

While the Ugoli prepared, Evander was to rest in this
room. He dozed for a while on the settee and soon fell into
a striking dream. The walls of old Sedimo appeared to him,
crystal clear in late afternoon light. He was but a boy of
eight, and usually he yearned to be free of all authority,

but now he was going to his mother, his beautiful mother, who would die the following year in childbirth. Her round chin, merry brown eyes, and long dark hair were framed against the warm walls of old Sedimo, bathed in golden light. He was going to her with the news of some inexplicable small victory of childhood, his heart alight, words bursting from his lips. He saw her teeth flash as she laughed in joy at his words. His father was there, too, his normally stern face broken into a rare smile while his eyes were squinting against the flat rays of the late afternoon sun. They were all three together in that wonderful moment, a shining time in childhood—in that time when all their dreams still lived and Evander Danais was destined to be king in his father's footsteps.

He woke up when the dream ended, which it did abruptly, turning to darkness in a moment. He awoke, but the images remained with him, especially the haunting sight of his mother's face. It had been a long time since she had crossed his mind. Would she still be proud of him? he wondered. After all that had happened?

Yes, he was sure, she would have accepted what he'd done. She would know that he was not a coward. He had done the best thing possible, he was sure she would know that. Would his father have agreed? To let the throne go without a fight? Evander knew his father's pride was immense. He would not have gone easily. But Evander also knew that his father had been in a much stronger position and was never outmatched so badly as Evander had been. In those circumstances, when civil war would have ravaged the land, Evander thought the old king would have done his utmost to prevent war, even if it meant accepting exile.

He moved restlessly around the room, disturbed by the dream. At least the lions had ceased making so much noise. He could open the door to the balcony again and let in the sounds of the city.

The Monjon lamps were on outside, and their warm light illuminated thousands of windows right across the city, making a uniquely bright cityscape on the world of Ryetelth.

After a while, moved by curiosity, he pulled away the cover of the Monjon lamp in the room, and immediately, it was filled with a warm amber light.

He caught sight of himself, bare-chested, in the wall mirror again. He examined the strange skin on his torso. It was now a solid, lumpy crust, part callus, part translucent and flat. Sometimes the dark, hard ridges itched, and he would scratch futilely at them. Under his fingers it felt like the skin of a crocodile, not that of a man. In the light it was possible to see into some sections, where a creamy translucence had replaced the initial black and brown. Inside the creamy areas were visible the dark threads of veins. He picked at the stuff, at times seized it and tried to pull a piece of it off. If he pulled hard enough, there was serious pain. There was no doubt of it, the horrid stuff was connected to him.

When he turned back to the pallet, he could feel the hard excrescences chafe against the inside of his arms where his skin was still normal, a horrible feeling. Would he ever be free of it? Would he ever be anything other than a sort of monster, that would fetch a good price on the curiosities market in Ourdh? No wonder the princess had run away, screaming.

He stirred, put on his shirt, and went back out to the balcony where he did his best not to think too much.

Chapter Twenty

Evander was to be exchanged for Yumi's magic carpet in Izzum's ostler yard, in the outer ward near the main gate.

As her sedan chair was borne through the city toward Izzum's, Postrema, the Weave Witch, pondered the situation.

She knew the Ugoli would try to trick her. They were famous for trickery in business dealings. Nasty, treacherous little things, more like elves than people. She swore to herself that she would out-trick them. She had decided that she had to have both the young man and the magic carpet. The Ugoli would get nothing.

She needed to move quickly. Her friend who traded with Ourdh was making up his cargo for his next voyage. If she could get the boy to him, she could realize a small fortune.

She was well aware that the rug was worth far more, but only if it could be made to obey her and to carry her. As it was, it would not fly. In fact, it behaved with hostile intent each time she trod upon it, wriggling unpleasantly.

She sniffed to herself. After all she had done! She had repaired it, reviving it visibly. Its colors had brightened, and its very fibers had gained in strength. She had seen it rippling on the floor in the moonlight, as if eager to be up and away.

However, when she came to it, it refused her feet.

Of course, the rug was very old, the Xish Wan was one of the schools of the Old Red Aeon, and the spellsay involved was enormously complex and powerful. She was sure she could learn much by eventually deciphering it.

That was enough on its own to ensure that she must keep it. Such artifacts were very rare. So she would keep the rug and work upon it, and in the fullness of time she would unlock the puzzle and bring it under her control. That would turn the old rug from a curio to a working flying carpet, capable of flying tens of miles in a day. Such things were fabulously rare, outside of the network of Ugoli merchants and traders.

Postrema had another thought, and a cruel smile flickered over her thin lips. Perhaps the little devils were actually thinking they might just overpower her at the appointed meeting spot.

Just let them try it! Her men, Griffin and Luksli and the rest, would be with her. If the Ugoli tried anything, they'd wind up with a good thrashing.

Beside her Postrema carried a rolled-up rug placed within a fine silk carrying case. The rug was the same size as the Ugoli one, with the same pattern of nine diamond-shaped medallions in soft orange with black horses rearing upon them. Even the borders had the same yellow and black scallop work.

It was, however, nothing but a modern carpet, mass-produced with slave labor in Ourdh, an inexpensive copy of a famous and ancient pattern.

Postrema had slicked the cheap rug with a spell, making it seem much more like the Ugoli's rug. She was sure it would fool the Ugoli for long enough for her to make her getaway. She was very confident in her spell up to the point when someone tried to make that cheap Ourdhi carpet fly.

She would not want to be there then. She would be well on her way home with the whole deal, the rug and the boy. She would sell the boy to Negus the trader, and then she would retire. It was time to leave Monjon, which for all its excitement was becoming crowded and somewhat dangerous these days. Once, wizardry had seemed quite wonderful and unusual. Now, with this terrible old man on the Black Mountain, there was a definite surfeit. Postrema thought it was high time she retired and took that villa on the coast. There she would live quietly in the sea air while she worked on the carpet and brought it under her control. Just think of it, an ancient elf rug all her own. Such a thing was worth more than its weight in gold, worth more than *her* weight in gold!

And who knew, the rug might even be one of those rare ones that could fly in daylight. Things from the Old Red Aeon had a way of surprising one.

She giggled to herself, an unpleasant sound, sharp and

hard that made the men carrying her shiver slightly. No man enjoyed working for Postrema, the Weave Witch, but she paid well, and that was what counted.

She arrived at the ostler's yard to find it empty. There were a few horses in stables on the far side and mounds of straw in several places. On the far side of the square space stretched storerooms and a blacksmith. Haylofts were arranged above.

As she got down, she chuckled to herself. She had already pierced their designs. The foolish little Ugoli were hiding in the straw, thinking to jump her at the right moment.

"Griffin," she snapped. "There are wicked little Ugoli hiding in the straw here. Take your men and beat them soundly. Don't kill them, however; I don't want any lives on my hands. These are troubled times, and the guards are liable to be difficult about killings."

Once she had captured a few Ugoli, she would soon force them into giving up the youth. Then she would have it all.

Griffin and the others took stout staves down from the rack on the sedan chair and advanced upon the straw.

Evander was concealed on the upper floor. He had been against the Ugoli plan, but their pride would not allow them to accept his counsel in every detail. Now he saw that things were taking a disastrous course.

Postrema stalked back and forth while her men charged into the hay piles with their boots flying and their staves thumping. With cries of pain the Ugoli who'd been hiding there were roused and beaten. They were simply too small and weak to put up a fight with these large men and their heavy staves.

Postrema strode up and down, encouraging her men with harsh cries, giving no thought of the hayloft behind her.

Evander judged the distance carefully, then retreated as far as he could to the wall of the loft. He pushed off and ran to the edge and leaped out into space. For a moment he was suspended above the struggle, and then he landed in the hay pile he'd aimed for. It was hard getting out of the pile of hay, and for a moment he almost panicked. Then he got his legs going and kicked his way free. He was out of the hay and running for the witch, who had failed to notice any of this, so engrossed was she in the beatings being handed out to the hapless Ugoli. A moment later he

cannoned into the witch and bore her down to the ground
with a last shrill squawk.

Before Postrema could utter another sound, he had
pressed his knife to her throat. The irony escaped them
both.

"Tell them to stop, Witch."

Her eyes went so wide when she saw who it was that he
thought they might explode from rage.

"You . . ." she hissed. He pressed harder with the knife,
and a drop of blood ran down her neck. "Stop them or
die. I swear it."

Her eyes flashed murder at him, but she was helpless.
The knifepoint dug a little further. "All right," she croaked,
"enough." She raised her voice and called to Griffin and
Luksli and the others and bade them desist.

Their eyes tightened when they saw Evander and the
knife held to Postrema's throat. The witch was difficult to
work for, but she paid well. If he killed her, they'd be losing
a good wage. They stood back and put their staves up.

At Evander's order she made the men leave the yard
and stand in the street.

The Ugoli rose, unsteadily, groaning with pain.

After a few moments to recover, they fell upon the silk
case and unrolled the rug. Even Yumi was fooled at first.
The design was the same, the same medallions, the deep
red borders, the skillful dark lines. But then he smoothed
the rug with his hand and called to it softly and bade it
rise and show its strength, and in that moment he knew it
was not the rug.

The spell broke then, and Yumi saw that the rug was
but a crude substitution and not possessed of any magical
power whatsoever—no more capable of flight than an
Ugoli.

The other Ugoli were confused by the spell still, but
Yumi spoke up and the spell collapsed. In rage they turned
on the witch, still held tight by Evander, with that knife
pressed to her throat.

"Put her into her chair, bind her, and gag her mouth.
We'll take her to her house and retrieve the carpet."

And thus the sedan chair returned. It went less swiftly
than before as the Ugoli were not as good at carrying its
weight. Evander brought up the rear, the knife in his belt,
staring down the hard-eyed men who came after them.

Ornizolest sent messages to his house, and within a few minutes they were joined by his footmen, Pilsuren, Dulk, and Chamweed, who took over the task of fronting off Postrema's servants.

They reached her house without incident. The city was still alive with the sounds of emergency. The stench of the fire lay thick and heavy, but crowds were out and moving in the direction of the main gates, heading for the Joust Magical that would determine the Wizard of Monjon.

At knifepoint Postrema led them to the rug, bound up and stuffed into a corner. In a few moments Yumi had freed it and unrolled it. It was unharmed. Indeed, it had been repaired. Postrema had done the work they'd agreed on.

Yumi announced that he would pay the witch, and he called on witnesses to observe him place the pieces of silver on the table for her—exactly the sum they agreed on. Yumi wanted them all to see that the Ugoli always kept to their side of a bargain.

Taking the carpet, the Ugoli left Postrema's house.

Outside, their men continued to face off with Luksli and the rest of Postrema's servants.

The witch shrilled curses after them, and Ornizolest replied with traditional Ugoli gestures, holding up a palm as if to cup some flour or salt, then taking an imaginary pinch with the other hand and tossing it over the shoulder. All the Ugoli laughed heartily at his performance, and they hurried on their way to Ornizolest's house.

There they began an immediate celebration in the carefree and lavish manner of the Ugoli. A huge dinner was ordered. Wine was brought up from the cellar. Fiddlers began to play, and the Ugoli set to dancing, and everyone came to toast Evander, who had saved the day and made sure they rescued Yumi's ancient magic carpet.

The merriment was in full swing, but Evander was troubled. Yumi could see it on his face and came to sit beside him and ask him what was the matter.

Evander explained that the final Joust Magical was being held at that very moment, and that Serena would then be given away to the wizard in wedlock. There was very little time left.

Yumi agreed that this was very sad. But what could they do about it?

Evander thought for a moment and then pointed to the rug, which was now unrolled and hanging on the wall above the happy throng of Ugoli. "Can your rug fly now? Could it help me rescue her? I think I know where she is."

Yumi swallowed heavily, his eyes popped. "Of course you can. The rug itself owes you this much. I know it will fly for you, and it will take the princess as well; neither of you are that much heavier then Ugoli folk."

"Thank you."

"Of course, the king will be marvelously angry if you abscond with his daughter."

"We will be in great danger, but I cannot leave her to be given to the wizard either."

Yumi sighed heavily. "I agree. It would be an abomination."

Chapter Twenty-One

Postrema had done a good job of repairing the ancient rug, for it flew strongly now, even at a height of one hundred feet, which was most unusual for a flying carpet. Its preferred pace was that of a brisk walk, though it was capable of matching a runner when it was flying just a few feet off the ground. Yumi thought that it would show great endurance, which meant that it could travel as much as fifty miles before it became exhausted.

Now the rug flew smoothly along the side of the top floor of the palace at a steady walking pace. To guide it, Evander stroked its sides with his hands. Rubbing the pile forward sent it on. Backward rubbing produced a reversal of direction. Rubbing more one side than the other produced turns, and the intensity of rubbing controlled the tightness of such turns. At the same time the rug seemed to sense its surroundings, for it refused to fly into walls or other obstacles.

Evander had willed himself not to look down. He was sitting on nothing but a tautly stretched carpet, suspended over one hundred feet of thin air. This knowledge would not go away. His mouth was dry, his heart hammering no matter what he did to control it. But his mind was made up. He would do whatever it took to save Serena from the wizard. The Prince Danais of Sedimo Kassim was not about to lose the princess to one of those horrid old creatures.

Outside each balcony he slowed to a halt by pressing down on the rug on each side. To descend one pressed on the front part, and to ascend, on the rear. Again, braking speed was determined by how hard one pressed on the rug, which always maintained a perfectly flat plane with no dent to mark the weight it bore.

After a moment of careful listening, Evander would climb off the rug, always a heart-stopping thing at this height, and go over the balcony and explore the apartments beyond. Almost all were empty. He did see one woman dozing on a divan, and a pair of elderly servants preparing dinner for someone in a well-lit kitchen, but only their pet cat saw him and it merely stared.

Of the Princess Serena he found no trace.

He had identified her rooms, after a search, for the Giltoft painting was unmistakable, the knightly Blue Frog and the lady Laman. He strode through her lovely little apartment, but found it completely empty. Something about the still air in these rooms told him that she had not been there for some time.

With a sigh he'd returned to the search. It would all have been much easier if she'd been in her rooms. Now he had to hope he could find where they'd moved her.

As he went on, he wondered if he was too late, and she was already being hustled off to be handed over to the champion wizard. Was all his effort futile? He gritted his teeth and refused to countenance the thought. He would not give up.

Back upon the rug, he sped along the palace walls, searching window by window. Time was getting short. The Jousts Magical were begun, and how long the final combat might take was unknowable. One of the remaining wizards might get an advantage in the first clash of magical horns and quickly finish off the other. Or perhaps two equal opponents would battle for hours. He could not afford the risk of an early victory, but this process of searching the whole palace from the outside took time.

He rode the rug up to the roof level and passed into an interior courtyard. There were a few windows lit up here, mostly on the lower floors. Only one window on a high floor showed a light. Evander pushed the rug closer.

As he approached the window, he heard someone sobbing. When he paused outside, hovering beneath the moon, he heard the cries distinctly.

He disembarked and entered. He found a young woman dressed in rich garments of red-and-gold cloth, who turned a tearstained face toward him in shock when he strode into her room.

"Who are you?" she asked in Monjonese. "What are you doing in my room?"

He replied in Furda. "I am a friend of Serena's. I'm going to take her away from all this."

The young woman's eyes went round. Her tears dried up. Her Furda was accented and clumsy, but intelligible.

"You're the one who was going to be thrown to the lions."

He nodded to convey that this was true, but now irrelevant.

She compressed her lips. "Oh, friend, you are too late. She was taken away an hour ago. Soon they will give her to the wizard."

"It cannot be." He refused to believe that he'd failed.

"Oh, friend, it can be. And do you know the worst of it?"

"No." His heart felt poised over an abyss.

"One of the wizards came on a batrukh. It flew here on one of the fell things that fly from the Black Mountain."

"What can it mean?"

"Why, it means that the wizard is the very wizard who has brought lamentation to Monjon. And he will win. He has practically destroyed us with his plagues and pests, and for that he has been given the royal princess in marriage."

The worst imaginings had come true. "Where will they hold their . . . uh, ceremony?"

"It will be atop the High tower."

"You say a batrukh?"

"A foul man-eating batrukh."

He rubbed his jaw and concentrated on the problem.

"Poor friend, I am sorry that you are too late. I am her friend also; Amili is my name. Now I think my heart is quite broken."

The woman sank back on a divan and fanned herself desolately.

Evander suddenly turned and took himself back to the rug still hovering patiently beyond the balcony.

Behind him he heard her exclaim, "Wait, friend! Where are you going? And where did you come from, anyway?" But by then he was on the carpet and heading up and over the high roofs toward the central tower of the palace.

Atop the tower he could see pennons fluttering. Musicians had been gathered. A red carpet unrolled beneath a dozen powerful Monjon globe lamps.

It was obscene, he thought. They would give away Serena to their own worst enemy and serenade him at the same time with triumphal music! Perhaps the wizard had already unhinged the king. Perhaps this was all some elaborate play of humiliation, unleashed by the wizard on his doomed victims. Perhaps the king was under some sort of spell.

Except that there was the power of the blessed Thymnal. The Thymnal, strange, unpredictable beast that it was, lurked below. The wizard would not dare do magic in its proximity.

And yet there were many subtle schools of wizardry. Who could be certain that some such school could not have learned a way to work around the prohibitions of the blessed Thymnal?

Perhaps the king was caught up in some bizarre shadow play invented and choreographed by this noxious sorcerer. What else could explain so cold a father's heart as that of Agrant?

Evander rose smoothly up beside the wall of the great tower until he could peer just above the battlements. The communication with the carpet had improved steadily. It seemed to understand his brushing movements better every time.

A squad of guards was drawn up along the far side. To their right were the musicians—drummers and sundry horn-players—and to their left were the Princess Serena and a burly-looking pair of women guards who were posted there to keep her from jumping. Serena's face was drawn and tight, but she had her shoulders squared back and not a trace of a tear. Something about the set of her jaw made Evander enormously proud of her.

King Agrant emerged from the stairwell, surrounded by guards and close advisers. Serena stared fixedly at him, but he refused to meet her eyes. He would not look at his own daughter while he gave her away.

A signal was given. The musicians crashed out a roll of drums and a fanfare of horns. They played for thirty seconds and fell silent.

All eyes scanned the heavens.

Evander slipped across the tower, keeping to the darkest shadows. He crouched behind a catapult not twenty feet from where Serena stood. No one had noticed him.

And then out of the dark sky came a shrieking cry, and on massive wing beats the batrukh came. With a vast fishy exhalation it landed on the battlement and dug great claws into the very bricks and mortar. It gave a short, chilling shriek as it folded its vast wings.

From its shoulders emerged a tall figure wrapped in a black cloak. This figure slid toward the king with a slow, elegant stride. When it drew close, it let the cloak drop away to reveal the beauty of bone, with cold, white skin, dark, hooded eyes, and bloodred lips. This tall, well-proportioned man was clad in a perfectly-cut suit, all fine wool and silk, but the face was so perfect and so cold that it sent a thrill of horror through Evander.

King Agrant appeared greatly relieved. He had been dreadfully nervous since the conclusion of the final bout between wizards. Once again the stone giant had triumphed, crushing the black octopoid of the Bluegreen Wizard Hejeemis under its massive feet. How would the victor choose to show himself? He had already appeared in two guises, as a foul old man covered in an eldritch filth, and as a "thing" with pustules and a drooling tongue. Both times the king had to struggle to hold in check his disgust and anger. Agrant had been forced to swallow much of his pride during this troubled time. To be compelled to grant an audience to this sorcerer, this shape-shifting monstrosity, and then to have him appear in such disrespectful and disgusting manner was almost more of an insult than Agrant could stand.

Thus the king was grateful that on this occasion, at least, the wizard's appearance was virtually normal.

Though it must be said that a side of the king was appalled on behalf of his daughter. He was a loving father, in a remote sort of way. He cared for her and felt the vulnerability of all fathers of beautiful daughters, and still she was going to a loathsome fate as a plaything for this monster. Unfortunately, it was an essential piece of diplomacy. This wizard had to be bought off and made an ally, nothing else would save the realm. Serena's charms were the only thing left to bargain with, except the throne and the Thymnal itself. Never would Agrant give those up.

Evander forced himself to calmly study the sorcerer, who appeared no more than thirty years old, perhaps less. His black hair was grown long and tied back behind the ears. His dandyish way of moving and the long, slender scabbard for a swordfighter's foil indicated a rakishness that was belied by the coldness in the face.

Evander calculated how far he might get if he tried to rush the wizard. A distance of fifty feet lay between them.

It did not look good. Anyway he visualized it, he could not imagine reaching the target before being noticed and blasted with some wizardly magic and destroyed. There was nothing to do, but to wait and watch events and seethe inwardly.

"My king," said the wizard with an elaborate bow and a slightly mocking smile.

Agrant nodded and raised a hand in benediction. He calmed his raging heart and spoke in a gentle voice. "You have won the contest. How shall we name you now?"

"Call me son, Father!" said the wizard with a laugh.

Agrant forced a smile to his own lips. "That I shall do, and gladly. You shall wed my only daughter as I promised."

The sorcerer preened. "So, dear Father, you have brought me my prize?"

In his heart, Agrant was encouraged. Serena was a beautiful girl; surely this monster's heart would be melted. Even a wizard must be inclined to satisfy the joys of the flesh once in a while. If Serena played the coquette correctly, she might win over this strange, terrifying man. And thus safety for Monjon could be bought, for a while. Agrant did not consider his daughter's feelings, for the throne itself was at stake.

"Yes, my son. I have brought the Princess Serena. Here she is."

Both of them turned to Serena, standing but fifteen feet away in front of the burly women who guarded her. Agrant smiled fondly in her direction, but did not actually meet her eyes.

The wizard, however, licked his lips suggestively and blew her a wet-sounding kiss.

Serena looked back at him stonily and then turned away with a sniff of disgust.

The wizard threw back his head and laughed happily. "Such spirit! Does it not raise a man's blood?"

Agrant tried to smile, but it was getting rather difficult.

"Oh, the poor little thing," said the wizard, "she has mistaken me for some of my more uncouth shapes. They are upsetting, aren't they? You must understand, dear Father, that sometimes I have to take other forms. A shapeshifter must shift his shape, you see."

Agrant nodded, smothering any further response. For a

long moment they stood there silently, and then the wizard nodded faintly back.

"She will recover. I fancy that we shall become a famously well-regarded couple." The wizard strolled across to where Serena was now held firmly by the matrons. They were taking no chances with her now. He smiled roguishly at her. "I fancy they will write poems about our great love. We will be held up as an emblem of the erotic power of our age."

The sorcerer came close. Evander could see his face quite clearly and hear him perfectly. He watched as the wizard took Serena's jaw in his hand.

"My dear," he said in a fell voice. "I am so glad that you are to be my bride. It is only for the thought of you that I endured this dreadful tournament. Can you imagine the kind of spell-mumbling old fools I've had to deal with? And yet, throughout my ordeals, I fortified myself with the thought of you. With your spirit, you shall excite my existence. With your beauty, you shall slake my passions."

Serena barely suppressed a scream. He put a hand on her arm and tenderly stroked her skin while the matrons held her in place. He laughed lightly at her shudder.

"We shall have such pleasures together, my love," he whispered.

Serena wanted to spit at him, but he held her jaw tight in his hands and prevented her by main force.

Evander crouched barely twelve feet away. No one saw him in the shadows. His brain was boiling. He felt the knife in his hand. Did he dare it? If discovered too soon, it would be his death warrant. But then, he had come this far. He was risking his life already, and what else could he possibly do? Serena had to be saved from this.

And still, young Prince Evander Danais of Sedimo Kassim did not want to die. He loved life, even accursed as he was with the skin of a monstrous toad. While he had life, he had the hope of somehow being freed of the sorcery. Sweat started from his forehead as his hand tightened on the dagger.

There was no conscious decision, but a few moments later, he was in motion, stepping out of the shadows and sliding quietly toward the wizard's back.

Time suddenly slowed, and there was an unreality about the scene, as if someone else entirely were stepping along here as quietly as he could, while his heart hammered in his throat.

He was halfway there, the knife in his hand, when Serena noticed him coming and gaped in astonishment.

Fortunately, the wizard was enjoying himself too much to notice her. He was looking over the city spread out before him with an acquisitive eye. This would all be his soon. And it would come to him quite legally and in proper course. He would inherit the throne of Monjon. Indeed, he had made plans already to do that very soon. Agrant was immune to magical power because of the Thymnal. He was not immune to poison, however. The cooks in the palace would soon be approached by his agents. A way to the king's stomach would be worked out. Thus engaged in gloating, he missed the first warning in Serena's eyes.

Evander gained another two yards.

Then one of the matrons let out a scream and struggled to free her baton. A shout went up behind, a sort of angry bellow from twenty throats.

The wizard whirled around. He was very light on the balls of his feet, the sign of a good fencer. His hand flew to the hilt of his sword, but in all he was a fraction of a second too late, and Evander was a second too early, and the knife drove home, sinking into the wizard's chest.

The sorcerer staggered. The beautiful face crumpled, and with a look of appalled horror, the wizard collapsed. On the ground he gave out a long, peculiarly soft-sounding cry and writhed slowly like a worm.

Evander stood there, shocked by the act. He had killed a man. And yet the thing was so strange, the moment so perverse. It had been like cutting into a pumpkin, not a man.

Evander looked at his knife blade for a moment. Scarcely any blood showed, just a pale slime. What was this thing? For it was certainly not a man. Then a stinking cloud of brown smoke arose from the figure on the floor.

On the battlement the batrukh let out a terrible scream and then another. It opened its vast wings as its cries echoed from the walls.

Evander came out of his state of shock. The thing on the stone flags was not dead. Strange, choking sounds, a gobbling of mud and stones, came from its throat. There was not a moment to lose.

Evander turned around, saw Serena's eyes widen in fright, and jerked his head sideways just in time to dodge a vicious blow from the baton wielded by one of the matron guards. It still struck him on the shoulder and sent him reeling.

He recovered, spun about, and kicked the woman in the belly. She collided with the other guard and then sat down with a gasp of lost breath while he pulled Serena into his arms.

The princess took all this in with near disbelief right up to the moment when he picked her up and ran for the side of the tower.

She realized he had no intention of stopping and assumed that he intended to jump to his and her deaths. So this was how she was going to die. Still, it was preferable to being the plaything of that monster. Behind them she clearly heard her father shriek commands at his archers not to fire.

Evander sprang up onto the battlement without a backward glance. Then he took the fateful step into the nothingness beyond, and Serena closed her eyes.

A moment later, she bounced in his arms as he landed on a surface that gave ever so slightly. He set her on her feet on a carpet suspended in thin air. Her mind whirled as he pulled her down to a sitting position.

"Hold on to me," he said and dug his hands into the pile of the carpet as it moved abruptly forward and downward.

Serena started to slide forward down the rug and flung her hands out and caught him around the neck. She could feel the bizarre, lumpy skin beneath his shirt, but mastered her revulsion.

Looking back over Evander's shoulder, she saw her father staring after them amidst a crowd of guards. For the briefest of moments their eyes locked. Then they were gone, dropping down into the street of the inner ward, hopping over a wall and into an alley.

Back on the tower King Agrant spun around, his face taut with inexpressible emotion. He stared with bulging eyes at the shape-shifting thing on the tower floor. Terrible sucking sounds came from it, a wet staccato.

It had been a large ornate knife, and the king had seen it driven into this thing, and yet it lived and writhed on the stones. How had it survived? Was it simply unkillable?

When it sat up again, his blood suddenly cooled. For a second the king teetered on the brink of fainting as the hideous visage of a thousand-year-old man stirred, flesh like stale dough, and began to pull itself to its feet. King Agrant wondered if he was going insane, but realized sadly that it was the world, not himself, that had gone mad.

Chapter Twenty-two

Through the alleys and small streets of the middle ward, they flew at shoulder height with the speed of a fast runner. An occasional startled observer would let out a cry as they went by, but for the most part they went unseen. The crowds were still out on the avenues, following the finale of the Joust Magical. The alleys were silent, the houses dark.

Evander steered for the city wall, using the palace behind him as a landmark. There were lights all across its top now, and he had no doubt that pursuit was being organized. Yumi had warned him that fast horses might overtake the carpet on level ground, but if he could evade horsemen, then the carpet would be able to carry them fifty miles in a night, before resting for an hour or two in the sun. It was a strong carpet, imbued with great magic.

Evander would go south. It was a clear night, and he remembered what Kospero had told him. Razulgab and Zebulpator, the red dragon stars, would point the way south.

Once past Frungia they would meet Yumi in the Bakan town of Caddik. From there they would go into hiding on the Ugoli network. Ornizolest had made arrangements that would get them secret berths upon a ship heading east. Evander already had plans to go to the fabled city of Kadein, the leading city of the Argonath. It was under the protection of the witches of Cunfshon, and thus might offer safety from the wizard.

They would make a new life for themselves in that distant city ruled by law and constitution. Evander planned to work for an Ugoli merchant until he had enough of a stake to be able to strike out on his own. Of course, it wouldn't be the same as being the next king of Sedimo Kassim, but at least he would be alive, and perhaps he could win Serena's love.

He pressed the rug across the meridian street and into the outermost ward of the city. Here the houses were small, for this was a district of workshops and artisans' dwellings. The streets were relatively dark for Monjon. There were only a handful of the Monjon globes aglow on any street.

They cut down a long alleyway, dank and narrow, startling a motley group of dogs before turning into the tinker's lane that edged up against the city wall. Now they floated silently past a stable occupied by sleepy donkeys, while a cat looked on in wide-eyed amazement from its perch on a post.

At the wall Evander stroked the carpet to make it climb, which it did, but more slowly than before. Evander knew that it was not quite so fresh as it had been. It was dark, so no one noticed them as they rose beside a buttress, partly shadowed by it.

Then they were over the wall and descending in a long, smooth downward glide, building up speed and then flattening out at the preferred height of five feet from the ground, which was covered in squatters' shacks and mounds of debris shoveled over from the city above. Monjon loomed behind and above them, the lights glittering from a thousand lamps floating in the darkness, an unreachable fairyland to the wretches below.

Now they were on the open ground, and Evander steered for the nearest cover, a grove of trees lying some distance ahead across flat, open space. Speed was everything now. They had to trust to the cover of darkness that they would not be discovered.

As they moved out across this vulnerable terrain, Serena suddenly murmured in his ear. "You're making quite a habit of rescuing me. I want you to know that I appreciate it."

He turned his head, and she kissed him lightly on the lips. In her eyes were reflections of the distant lamps. "I think I'm falling in love with you, Evander."

He felt his heart soaring on high. "Even with the monster's skin?"

"Even, but we will go to a witch somewhere and have it removed. I just know you can be cured of that."

He turned back and kissed her. "I wish I could have come earlier, spared you that horror back there."

Serena shivered at the memory of the cold, beautiful face of the great wizard and almost broke into sobs.

"We'll be safe now," he said.

Serena wasn't so sure about that, but she refrained from any comment.

Then Evander had to turn back to navigate as they moved down a ridge of debris and on toward the trees. He pushed the rug through a passage between two heaps of ill-smelling rubbish, but his heart was still singing within.

She did feel for him, much as he felt for her! Evander was certain that he had never experienced anything so joyful in his entire life. Life could be simply amazing with the tricks it threw one's way. Here they were, in love, it had to be, and both of them born to royalty and both forced to flee, penniless, from terrible fates. But if they could stay together, no matter how they lived, Evander would be content.

They were getting close to the trees now, and once hidden by their sheltering shadow, he thought the pursuit would be unlikely to detect them. Once the rug had taken them a few more miles, they would be safer still, and then it would be a matter of staying out of range of those horsemen.

Evander looked back. The city was now far enough behind them to be made out clearly as a single great entity, a glowing cloud of lights. Evander recalled when he had first set eyes on the fabulous, floating city, and how high his hopes of it had been. And here he was, escaping with the beautiful princess of the city, who said she loved him.

Then a shadow fell across them, and he looked up. The batrukh's scream rang across the land.

Serena stared upward with appalled eyes and gave a sad groan. "Undone, alas, my love." She kissed Evander again.

The batrukh swung down toward them in a broad arc, and as it came, he saw a figure riding astride its neck. Undoubtedly, the wizard had survived.

Evander was stunned. He remembered the pumpkin flesh of the thing—how the knife had gone home to the hilt. No man could have lived through that, but clearly this wizard could.

Evander pressed the rug to move at its quickest pace. It

responded, but only to the speed of a good distance runner. It was covering ground, but the batrukh was capable of far greater speeds. It would come up behind them in just a moment, and there was nothing they could do about it.

He held Serena in his arms and watched as the batrukh raced up on them. Above the flying beast's hideous, ratlike visage, Evander glimpsed the face of the figure astride its neck. It was not the fell beauty he had thrust his knife into. Instead, it was a haggard thing, skull-faced, with huge eyes that glowed with hate.

Then it swept past, and for a moment Evander dared hope, for nothing immediately befell them. But then he saw it, a shining cord descending around them in a single loop like a lasso. Spinning about them in a shining ring, it suddenly was transformed into a net with a million strands no thicker than those of a spiderweb, but far stronger, that wrapped around the rug, Serena, and himself in a flash. Evander struggled with every ounce of strength, but the strands were unbreakable. In a matter of moments they were helplessly bound. The rug jerked to a halt. For a moment there was a tremendous contest of strengths between the rug and the flying monster, and then the rug was pulled up into the air and towed away by the batrukh.

The rug was strong, for a rug, thought Evander, but it just couldn't match up to a wizard's batrukh. Anymore than he himself had measured up to the wizard with his desperate knife blow. He tried not to think what the wizard might do to him. Impalements, carnivorous slugs, acid baths all passed through his thoughts briefly. He refused to dwell on it. There was no point in adding to the misery. Perhaps there would come one more chance, a stray unguarded moment. Evander swore he'd try to kill the thing again if an opportunity presented itself.

The batrukh beat steadily on, however, and soon they were back at the high tower of the palace, where the king and his court were still gathered. The batrukh landed on the battlement again, and the wizard slid down from its neck. The rug had come to a sudden halt as it bounced against the wall and hung suspended in midair. The wizard took up the magic cord and pulled the flying carpet in like a fish on a line and grounded it on the tower.

Evander and Serena stared up into the thing's face. The eyes blazed, and sounds quite unlike speech came from the mouth. Neither of them could move a muscle. The wizard leaned down to look them over and gave a ghastly little chuckle before resuming human speech.

"I recognize you now," it rasped. "You were the impertinent youth that prevented my justice being carried out in Port Tarquil. As I recall it, I punished you with a particularly revolting spell. But you should not have a manlike appearance. You should be a toad of some kind. Your impertinence knows no bounds, it seems."

"I never meant—"

"Silence! And then you came back to plunge a knife into my vitals. Such violence in a young man. Oh no, no, no, I shall have to make an example of you. Of course, I do commend your courage. No one has tried to stab great Gadjung Batooj in eons.

"But there are further reasons for extreme penalties. You have sullied my bride. With my own eyes I have seen your kissing. For that I shall blast you into nothingness in front of these witnesses. Console yourself with knowing that it is a far quicker death than anything else I had planned for you. But it will be good for all assembled here to witness what I, their Lord Gadjung, will mete out to any that does violence to my person or to that of my beloved bride."

The thing turned its baleful eyes on Serena. "And because my bride-to-be was so eager to embrace you, I shall let her remain entwined with you when I vaporize you, so that she shall feel your agony and remember it well. Indeed, her very spirit will be burned."

The wizard raised his hands above his head and lifted his voice. "Ohgg nok rigujj, pladst un virkul . . ." His voice had become huge, like that of a brazen bull bellowing at the sun.

With a shriek the king jumped forward with his arms up. "No! My son, no, do not use great magic here. This is the place of the Thymnal!"

But the warning went unheard. Ancient Gadjung, gzug of the Old Red Aeon was too caught up with the tremendous spellsay and the conjurement of power. He ran off the lines in the ancient tongue, and the spell was cast. Then, he raised his hands, while the king screamed for him to stop, and hurled down a bolt of pure fire at the couple on the rug.

In an instantaneous reaction, the entire world flashed red in their eyes for a second. When it was done, the very stones in the tower were glowing red, but not from heat. Evander and Serena were still together, unharmed.

The great taboo of Monjon had been broken. For a long moment everyone trembled. The wizard's magic had failed. Gadjung could scarcely believe it. Then they felt the Thymnal's wrath as a second volcanic flare of red light flashed from the very stones of the tower itself. Mismagic ground in the matter of the world for several seconds with a sound like huge teeth splintering.

Evander felt himself lifted, the rug was moving, and he raised an arm and knew that the magical cord was gone from around them, yet he could see nothing except turbulent clouds, patterns of darkness.

This lasted for perhaps a second, and then he felt a sudden sensation of plunging into much colder air. There was a stink of burning, and something worse.

He landed heavily, falling a foot perhaps, and tumbling on hard, gritty ground. Everything was lost in white and gray fog. The carpet was gone. Then Serena appeared next to him out of the fog.

He caught her in his arms. Together they stared out into a limbo of gray mist and shivered in the cold.

"Where the hell are we?" muttered Serena.

Hell? It might very well be, thought Evander.

A sudden breeze cut the fog into tatters, and the stench grew stronger. Now a dim, diffused light was visible through the gray clouds above. And through the wind-driven dust they saw ruins towering up here and there, vast structures broken into shards and spines.

Nearer they saw a pile of shattered statuary at least fifty feet across, set by some twisted structural members that rose up in knotted ribbons. Dozens of stone horse heads stared, blank eyes gazing with mute dismay.

"What is this? What has happened here?" questioned Serena in a voice dulled with shock.

"All I know is that this isn't Monjon."

Then, suddenly, Serena gave a cry of fright and pulled back her foot.

Out of a deep gulley cut in the gray ground popped a small gleaming figure perhaps a foot tall. It was manlike, a tiny man, dipped in blue silver, with eyes like emeralds glowing in a featureless face.

Chapter Twenty-three

Evander pinched himself. The stinking wind continued to rip through the gray mists.

"I don't believe I'm seeing this," Serena said as the small metallic figure stopped in front of them, put its hands on its hips, and leaned back with its head up, looking at them with that pair of gemlike eyes on the otherwise blank face.

"Believe," said Evander. "I'm seeing it, too."

"I don't suppose either of you know how we're going to get out of here, do you?" said the little man in a sharp voice and good, accentless Furda.

"It speaks," she said in awe.

Evander swallowed heavily, unwilling to admit that he'd been just as surprised, even as frightened as Serena.

"Of course I speak," said the tiny metallic figure. "I spoke before, but you could not hear me because I was just a rug."

"What? You are the rug? Yumi's magical carpet?"

"Of course, I am, as I was conjured by great Zambalestes in the long ago. My name is Konithomimo, which might translate to Little Prince of the Air in this barbarian tongue, Furda, which is all you seem to speak."

"Well, I'm sorry we're so linguistically uncouth," said Evander, feeling stung, "but Furda is the language most people know in this part of the world."

"Furda!" snorted the little man with considerable contempt. "Whatever happened to Senshwy and Ood? Those were far superior languages."

"I don't know," said Evander. "I've never heard of them. But tell me this, what has happened to you? If you were Yumi's rug, why aren't you a rug now?"

"I don't know. I rather hoped you might enlighten me about that, seeing as how you managed to get us transported here."

Evander felt his jaw drop. "Pardon me, but we are here because of the foolishness of an evil wizard."

"Of course," snapped the testy little metal man. "But if you hadn't been risking the anger of that wizard, then we'd still be in our own proper world."

"Since when do rugs talk back to their owners?" muttered Serena in disbelief.

"You don't own me! I am my own person. Though I am a rug, I operate for the Ugoli family Yumitura, of which Yumi is the current leader. Indeed, he is the last of the family, and if he and Elsu do not have young, there will be no more of the Yumitura, and I will be free at last of the ancient spell of Zambalestes of the Xish Wan."

Evander was stunned even further. "Free?" he mumbled.

"A free carpet, if I want. Or something else. I haven't decided yet."

"Haven't decided . . ."

Serena finally put all the pieces together. "The wizard used great magic directly above the chamber of the Thymnal. I saw the red flash. The Thymnal was angered."

"What might that mean?"

"Almost anything. At a minimum, I'd suggest that we are no longer on the world we call Ryetelth."

"And rugs turn into small metal men that talk."

"I am not a metal man," the rug said querulously.

"I'm amazed that we're still alive," said Evander.

"I am afraid, Evander."

Their eyes met for a moment.

"We'll find our way back somehow," he murmured.

"Of course," she said, equally unsure. "But where are we?"

He tried to smile, wishing he felt more reassured himself. "Well, that's the first thing we have to find out."

Serena hugged herself. "I'm so cold."

"I'll give you my shirt."

"Oh, no, then you won't have anything at all."

And the hideous wizard skin would be visible, too. Evander understood. It was better for both of them if he kept his shirt on. It really was cold, too. He was shivering constantly. He looked over toward the nearest ruins, dimly visible piles and spires about a quarter mile away.

The sound of the wind playing over the twisted ruins was overridden by a long, wailing cry of peculiar malevolence.

It was repeated twice more, and then an ominous silence fell across the dismal scene.

One question was settled for Evander. This place was inhabited.

"Perhaps we should seek concealment," said the tiny metal figure.

"Perhaps we should hurry," said Serena, and with no more ado they ran away from the shrieking cries.

The bare, open expanse turned slowly into tumbled rubble and broken walls after half a mile.

Evander saw two humanlike figures in the near distance vanish into a dark doorway as he watched. He decided not to mention them to Serena. He was having a hard time accepting all this, and it had to be even worse for her.

They pressed on, dogged by the little rug man, Konithomimo, who bounded along with immense leaps, easily longer than their own. Konithomimo was clearly capable of much greater speed, but hung back to accompany them. Evander was still trying to comprehend what had happened to the rug. The magical forces involved in all this were too much for him to comprehend. He pushed it to the back of his mind and concentrated on getting to some sort of safety. He really didn't like being out here on the gray flats.

They passed the first building, a ruin, and then more, many with the look of jury-rigged shelters built from the rubble. Here and there a structure had fallen in ruin and lay in a heap. Eventually, they found themselves in a street with broken-up tenement buildings on either side. Windows gaped like eyes above a series of dark mouths where doorways opened wide.

"Do you think anybody lives here?" Serena said in a whisper.

"I don't know," said Evander.

"Should we hide?"

"I think so. Until we know more about this place, it might be a good idea."

Evander jumped at the touch on his leg and then looked down to see the rug man.

"Better get inside, something's coming."

Evander looked up, and in the next moment he shoved Serena into a doorway and slid in after her with his hand on her mouth. "Not a sound," he whispered in her ear. Her muscles were taut with tension, her eyes wide.

A deep, muddy grunt sounded outside. A heavy tread went by. He peered around the edge of the doorway as something passed, and glimpsed a thing the size of a bear, with huge arms and legs, but no head, just a glistening socket from which stubby pink tentacles stirred.

Evander felt the blood drain from his face. The thing was both sinister and filled with tremendous power. He slid his head back into concealment and listened, his heart beating.

The heavy footsteps slowed for a moment, and his heart leaped in his chest, but then they resumed their former definite tread. For a long second he scarcely dared to breathe.

The thing had gone on. Evander was just about to breathe a sigh of relief when a loud shriek of rage came from somewhere above and nearby. It was followed by more cries filled with obvious anger. Another, deeper voice began to reply. The two voices, one deep, one higher pitched, both very loud, continued to shriek and bellow.

A loud bang echoed, as if a door had been slammed.

Outside in the ruined lane Evander heard the tentacle-headed thing returning. It trod back the way it had come, and now it was virtually trotting.

It had not gone very far when there broke out a dreadful snarling interposed with a bizarre whooping sound and then a long, loud crackle, as if an enormous moth had burnt to a cinder in a fire. Finally, a thud shook the ground slightly.

Tension-filled silence enveloped them. Evander wondered what the hell had happened. Then his ears cringed as a triumphant bellowing broke out. This continued, but moved away from them, into the warren of ruins. They heard something or someone climb above in the ruined tenements, and it seemed to be the source of the bellowing, which now sounded like a triumphant monologue. Eventually, there was another bout of screaming between the bellower and the higher-pitched voice and another slamming of a huge door.

Silence returned to the ruins. Evander and Serena looked at each other.

"This place is pretty terrifying," said Serena.

"I agree."

Evander waited a full minute before he dared peek

around the corner. In the ruined street lay the massive thing, the tentacles burnt to a crisp.

Serena was shaking a little. "I don't like this place, Evander. I'd like to go home."

"I second that proposal," said the little rug man, who was hiding behind Serena.

"Ssh." Evander held up a finger to his lips.

Fresh noises erupted outside—scurrying feet, the sound of a file rasping on metal; a sharpening?

"What the hell is happening now?" she whispered.

"I'm not sure."

Carefully, Evander took another peek into the ruined street. A group of man-sized things, with large beaks and enormous black eyes were butchering the carcass of the dead monstrosity. They wielded long knives and silvery hatchets—a disturbing intensity about their work.

There were no good answers to any of the questions pounding in his brain. He pulled back inside. "Let's go farther inside and try to hide. I need to rest a little, I think."

Serena nodded, and together they inched into the gloom of the interior of the ruined building.

Most of the walls were still standing, and so were most of the ceilings, but the doors were broken open throughout. In some places the ceilings were down, and they could see through into the upper parts of the structure. It had all the appearance of a ruined apartment building—narrow corridors, lined with doors, all broken away long ago.

They found a dark nook hidden within a room with intact walls and ceiling. In the nook they could not be seen from the door. It wasn't safety by any means, but at the least there was a feeling of some protection.

Evander was exhausted. He let his back rest against the wall behind him and then slumped down until he was sitting on the hard, gritty floor. He was cold and very tired.

A loud screech came from outside, followed by similar screeches, until it sounded as if a flock of gigantic crows were at work.

"What is going on out there?"

"First there was a large creature, big as a bear, looked ugly. Then something came down from up above us and killed it. Now there's a bunch of smaller things attacking its body, which is lying out there in the street."

Serena sat beside him, and they put their arms around one another and huddled for warmth. The small metal rug man stared at them for a moment.

"Is this the best you can do?" he snapped.

Evander stared at the little gleaming figure, his eyes dull. "Hey, let me get my breath back, will you?"

"Bah, I will be better off on my own. You are too weak and watery for this world, I think."

Before either of them could say a word, the little metallic figure left the room and ran down the steps.

"Konithomimo," Serena called vainly.

Evander suddenly felt completely exhausted. "I never thought a rug could be so hard to get along with," he said.

Serena gave a single laugh. "What did he expect of us?"

"I don't know. I don't understand how a rug has transformed itself. I've had enough wizardry for the rest of my life."

Serena buried her face against him, against the leathery, knobby skin under his shirt. They were both cold, getting hungry, and very, very tired.

Evander didn't want to sleep, but at a certain point it became inevitable. Serena was already snoring softly in his arms.

Chapter Twenty-four

Through the gray mists came the seeker, by name Perspax, heir of Sanok, child of the Miggenmorch, and once the bearer of high rank in lovely Orthond.

He had sensed them far away. Their thoughts radiated widely in the thin ether of Orthond. From the type and temper of their thought, it was clear that they were unlike anything that he had ever encountered before. This whetted his curiosity.

He knew that if he could sense them, so could other, more predatory seekers. Thus he made haste bringing sword and dagger, with poison for micklebear and good steel for multipedes.

His fur spread back by the cruel winds, Perspax covered the ground quickly on his long, gray legs. Everywhere he went he passed the desolation of Orthond. In Canax he jogged beneath the ruined towers of Gebizon, the shattered roof of the chapel of the Green Saint still standing above the remaining walls like a fragile cry of complaint at the damage done to such beauty. Perspax would have wept if he had but tears with which to do so. Alas, all tears had long since been shed. The world of Orthond now groaned beneath the heel of a mightier lord than any king in Orthontower. Hope and beauty had long since been ground to dust.

He came up on the locale after a long run at full power to cross the flats. The ground had been tortured here by the dark lord's full power. Much was absolutely bare, but there was a fringe of wretched habitations. The ones he sought were hidden in a cranny within.

Perspax found a group of Jooks butchering a fallen Glosh in the street. He sensed a pair of his own kind lying up nearby. They ruled this wretched ville. One of them, the male, had slain that Glosh very recently with a fully charged "musket." Both of them were oblivious to his presence, lost in the power of the rut. They were crude, unlettered, hardly sensitive at all on the higher planes. They were not folk of rank and quality. Ignoble and often cruel, they were of the type that managed to survive in the new era. He who had slain the Glosh was still exulting over the killing even as he mounted his lovemate. Such brute insensitivity sickened Perspax.

The Jooks in the street never saw him as he slipped past beneath an invisibility spell and entered the tenements. The minds upstairs were absorbed in the rut and remained unaware of him. Perspax was thankful. It would be better to extract the newcomers from this zone without the possessors ever knowing about it.

He eased himself carefully into the room and surveyed the sleeping humans. They were small things, weak in appearance. It was incredible to him that they could be here. What possible power could they have that enabled them to survive on ruined Orthond? He knew they were not of Orthond itself, and he recalled no intermediate steps in the development of such creatures. So where had they come from? And why?

This brought the unwelcome thought that they were creatures of the Dominator, brought into existence for his evil purposes. And yet they didn't look like the creatures that normally served the Dominator. They possessed no armor, no spines, no long, raking claws. They looked virtually helpless.

Perspax felt something twitch the ether. Something else had arrived on the scene and was already climbing the stairs. He left the small sleepers and withdrew into a hiding place on the landing one floor down. He waited but a moment before the patter of the twenty-four feet of a multipede came up the stair. The little ones were very fortunate, indeed, that he had come in time. When the multipede drew close, he stepped quickly out of concealment and drew sword.

The spade-shaped cephalon froze. Its stupid, carnivorous gaze lingered on him for a moment. It would like very much to eat him, but it was afraid of the steel that glittered in his hands.

It backed away, huge round eyes looking for any opportunity to get past him and go on up the stairs to where the food things lay. Alas, the biped standing in the way was an Eleem, and it had long steel in hand. Steel in the hands of Eleem was deadly. The big cephalon swayed slowly from side to side.

The multipede backed away farther, considering its position. Perspax waited. Driven by raging hunger, it and its fellows had scoured lovely Orthond since the fall and devoured everything they could catch. Nonetheless, their intelligence was limited, and he had little fear.

Suddenly, it leaped at him, moving from decision to execution with the usual instantaneous quality. Mouth parts whirred as it reached for his flesh.

Perspax had anticipated the attack, and his sword removed a limb and cut back across the thing's jaws on the return stroke with such speed that the blows were almost instantaneous.

Jerking back, it rose up, hissing, dark blood pouring from the severed limb, legs waving. Perspax cut at its belly, and with a shriek it rolled down the steps, hitting the lower floor with a thud and curling up in a ball.

Perspax felt the Eleem upstairs awakening to the situation. Nobody wanted a multipede around. They would be bound to take action, especially with all those Jooks to feed.

The next moment he landed beside the multipede and thrust home his blade, skewering the thing through its small, miserable brain. It made no further sound, and its thoughts were cut off as if they had never existed.

The Eleem above were concentrating on the Multipede now, he could tell, but they could not feel its stupid thought anymore. For a moment it had been there on the mental horizon, and then it was gone. He sensed that they had relaxed. It had been just a wanderer out there in the flats. If they felt it again, they'd go on the offensive, but for now it could be ignored in favor of the rut.

Perspax kept his thoughts on very low power and drifted up the steps. It was fortunate that they had been so concerned with picking up the multipede. It had kept them from noticing the thought of the little strangers, who were now wide awake.

Indeed, they were watching from the top of the steps. The male pushed to the front, a knife of an unusual shape in one hand. His thought radiated anger and fear in equal proportion, and yet there was a determination to die if need be in defense of the female.

Perspax laughed inwardly. The small one had courage, being a third shorter and half the weight of a male Eleem. But his fierce display made Perspax think that perhaps the little creatures were not quite so unconditioned for life on fallen Orthond as he'd thought.

He stepped back to the landing and sheathed his own sword. Then he looked up at them very carefully and bowed.

They were astonished. They had been prepared for the worst, prepared to die fighting. Perspax was surprised at the stubborn determination he sensed in their minds.

Then he spoke to them in their language, in words that he filched from their minds. They knew nothing of the process, and he quickly realized they were transparent to the mind of an Eleem trained in the ancient arts. As he learned their tongue, he glimpsed something of the beauty of their world and sensed the tragedy of their young lives. And such tragedy as only grew worse, for now they were marooned on poor, broken Orthond, beneath the Dominator's heel.

"Greetings, travelers from Ryetelth. Greetings, Evander and Serena," he said. The alien tongue tripped lightly from his own. Indeed, it was fair to speak and to listen to, not as fair as the tongues of the Eleem, perhaps, but still very fair indeed.

He noticed that they had instinctively clutched hold of each other in sheer fright.

"How do you know our names?" squeaked the female.

"The same way I know how to speak to you. I read it in your mind."

"You read our minds?"

"Life is very different on your world."

They nodded.

"I would welcome you to my world, but as you can see, very little is left. It has been destroyed by the evil one."

This answered several questions for both of them. Perspax watched the emotions course through their faces. They were such intelligent creatures, beyond anything he knew, except the Eleem.

"What do you call yourself?" the female asked.

"I am called Perspax . . . "

"What do you call your world?" the male said a little unsteadily. Perspax could feel him fighting for self-control.

"This was Orthond."

"Orthond," they said together, each trying the word, and in truth Perspax did not find their saying of it ill-formed at all. He found these little ones both comely and well spoken.

"But hark, my friends, you must come with me, and swiftly. Those whom I would call the owners of this place have not yet detected your presence. It would be better if we left before they did."

"Who are they?" said the male, the one called Evander.

"They are like me, but they are considerably less, ah, sophisticated, shall we say. I wish to rescue you and convey you to a safe place. They will probably think of cooking you over hot coals for lunch."

They exchanged a look of bafflement. What was this creature, this nightmarish thing like an eight-foot-tall, two-legged horse, except that the head sprouted feelers and things that might have been stubby little horns?

Strangest of all were the big eyes, manlike eyes, but the size of a man's fist, and filled with keen intelligence. They seemed kindly eyes, however, and this thought left Evander baffled. More questions mounted with every second. And how did it manage to pluck words out of their minds?

"You speak excellent Furda," Evander said as politely as possible.

"Thank you; let us hurry." He motioned them down the stairs.

Perspax moved ahead of them, swift and lithe, with the deadly grace of a great cat.

Evander had already taken note that Perspax wore armor and bore a long sword at his waist. Evander was aware that that sword was longer by far than even the great two-handed sword of the sultans in Sedimo Kassim. The creature was not only enormous, but armed with a skill weapon, for that sword was no brutal tool of butchery. Not even the terrible trolls of the Doom Masters of Padmasa could match this creature for deadliness.

What kind of world was this Orthond?

"Be as quiet as possible," said their bizarre guide. "There were Jooks outside earlier. You needn't fear them, not with myself at your side, but it would be best if they didn't see you. That way the owners I mentioned will never know you were here."

Holding back the tide of questions bubbling in their minds, they followed him back down the ruined stairs and out through the rubble-strewn hall to the street. On the first landing they passed the curled-up carcass of the multipede. Evander saw the sword cut through the crocodilian skull and shuddered at the bristling teeth in that carnivorous mouth. He looked up quickly to the retreating back of Perspax. He had saved them from this.

In the street the Jooks were still busy carving the Glosh. Perspax put forth the invisibility spell and did his best to cover the little ones with it.

The Jooks never noticed a thing and continued with their butchering while the unlikely trio stole to the end of the ruined street and slipped away.

Beyond the drift of broken tenements they worked their way through heaps of rubble toward the open flats.

Serena suddenly squeezed Evander's arm. "What about the rug, Konithomimo? Are we going to leave him behind?"

Evander looked back in confusion.

"He left us. I don't know if he would come even if we could find him. What I will tell my friends Yumi and Elsu, I don't know."

Serena looked back helplessly. There was nothing they could do. They couldn't stay. This world was too inimical. They needed the protection of their strange savior.

"I feel terrible leaving him behind."

Evander shrugged. "I don't know. Maybe he'll find his way back to Ryetelth. He didn't seem to like us much."

Perspax strode warily ahead of them, his eyes scanning the flats ahead. Normally, there'd be no danger. He could outdistance any multipede or micklebear, but he was not alone. Could these little people run fast enough for long enough, if they were pursued?

They crossed the floor of a long since ruined building. The marble was cracked and pitted, but still mostly intact. The walls were gone, and there was hardly even any rubble remaining.

The long shrieking cry they had heard earlier echoed out of the ruins. Perspax looked around carefully for the micklebear. Seeing nothing, he felt for it with his mind and detected it at last deep within a nearby pocket of ruined buildings. Micklebear were tricky like that; their thought was not loud. It had not seen them, did not even suspect them. It was intent on digging out a feral family of Neild. The Neild were digging deeper in a desperate attempt to escape the monster's jaws.

Perspax would have liked to try to save them, but he could not risk the strangers, so the Neild would have to fend for themselves. They seemed to be good at digging, at least.

"What is it that makes that cry?" asked Evander as the sobbing malevolence died away in the distance.

Perspax turned those huge eyes on him. "Micklebear." To be stared at full-face by the Eleem was frankly intimidating.

"What is that?"

"Micklebear is death. It kills and eats everything it catches. No one, not even the Eleem can fight such a monster. We use poison, but even that is risky since it takes time to kill the micklebear. They are very tough, incredibly difficult to kill. We best avoid them."

Evander had no trouble in agreeing to this concept.

They had just renewed the march when a sharp cry behind them turned their heads. Evander saw a tiny figure bounding toward them, gleaming faintly as it came. There was no doubt who, or what, it was.

"Konithomimo!" Serena exclaimed.

Konithomimo caught up in a few more bounds. Evander was impressed by his energy and pleased to see the strange rugman or whatever he was. Evander was still hazy about the little man's origins and nature. Konithomimo, however, was bubbling with complaint.

Hands on hips, he scolded them. "No thanks is what I get. I go out scouting and what happens?"

"The small creature is one of your party?" asked Perspax in considerable surprise. The small one gave off no mental emanations that he could detect at all.

"Yes, I suppose so."

Perspax stared in wonder at the little creature. It gleamed like polished metal and was no higher than his ankles, but it could jump eight feet into the air while running and exuded tremendous energy. Most astounding of all was that it was invisible on the mental plane. In Perspax's experience, only a great wizard could do that.

The small blue metal being failed to take notice of Perspax, too intent on its complaint. "It's just another example of the way humans always treat me. I always give thanks that I belong to the Ugoli. They at least know how to treat a treasured possession. They don't go running off, leaving one behind."

"I'm sorry," muttered Evander, not quite understanding why he was bothering to talk with the personification of a rug, if that was truly what it was.

"You walk out and leave me all alone back there and don't even have the decency to warn me. There are things eating each other in the street back there!"

Evander finally lost his temper. "Well I'm so sorry. After you left us, damning us for being useless, we fell asleep. Unlike yourself, we are not magical, nor do we have inhuman strength. We are people, and we get tired and need to sleep for a few moments every so often."

"You could have called for me! I was not far away. It was fortunate I saw you leaving the end of the street, or I'd have missed you completely."

"Perspax warned us to be silent. We couldn't call you."

"Who is Perspax?"

Evander nodded toward the giant Eleem. "He is."

At last the small, perfectly sculpted metal head craned backward to take in the looming figure of Perspax.

"Perspax was there when we woke up. He was killing a multipede. If he hadn't reached us first, it would have killed and eaten us."

The little head turned to focus the green gem-like eyes on Evander. "Everything on this terrible world is either killing or eating. Why did you bring us here?"

They felt a slightly amused presence looking down at them from above.

"I didn't, that's preposterous."

"And what is this thing that you follow?" asked Konithomimo.

"I don't know really. He calls himself an Eleem."

At this point Perspax had had enough. "My name is Perspax of Xerranon, a knight of Orthond," said the Eleem. "Although I suppose I am a knight no more, simply a fugitive."

Konithomimo gazed up at the Eleem. "I am Konithomimo. I am thousands of years old."

"Welcome to Orthond, Sir Konithomimo. I wish my world were in better condition to welcome you properly. But as you can see, fair Orthond has been devastated."

"Why do you allow this to happen to your world?"

"We tried to prevent it, but we were not strong enough. We were overwhelmed by a power from beyond our world, a power we could not match."

"I am Konithomimo, and I am free in this world."

Perspax frowned. "None of us are free in Orthond, my little friend. Orthond lies beneath the heel of the Dominator of Twelve Worlds, Waakzaam the Great."

Chapter Twenty-five

They went at a fast walk, a pace that seemed most natural for the long-legged Perspax. It was faster than comfortable for Serena, but she made no complaint. For hours they went on across the cold, featureless landscape of the flats. Evander soon lost any idea of how far they had come. He tried to help Serena along with encouraging words, but this seemed only to annoy her, and they both fell silent, withdrawing into themselves. She kept up the pace, putting one foot in front of the other. Evander decided that for a slightly spoiled princess of the realm she was tough and dogged enough. His own feet hurt, his legs ached, and from his lips to his lungs he was dry and caked with dust. He would gladly have lain down and slept for a week. She gave no sign of discomfort, despite the cold and their lack of warm clothing. Evander was impressed.

Konithomimo, of course, was not content to hang back with them. He spent his time quartering the landscape ahead, zigzagging back and forth with boundless energy.

Evander had many, many questions that he wanted to ask Perspax, but his mouth and throat were too dry for talk. And after a while he was too tired, anyway.

The sun was still invisible behind a thick haze of gray clouds. The cold wind came from behind, stirring the bare, brown dust beneath their feet into little rills and wave fronts from which it streamed away into the air.

Thirst was their greatest problem. Perspax was suffering badly. He, more than his two charges, needed water desperately. He had gambled, perhaps with his own life, wanting to avoid the micklebears on the margins of the flats. He had decided to make a direct crossing through the center of the flats to the ruins of old Putchad. This meant he must find water in the middle of the emptiness. Perspax was convinced he could. Straight ahead he had sensed

Neild, just faintly, but enough to convince him that he was
right. And wherever there were Neild, there would be
water.

Visibility in any direction was very limited. Gray clouds,
mist, and smoke closed in all around the horizon. Evander
wondered how Perspax was able to navigate. There were
no landmarks; in fact, there was nothing to be seen but the
clouds and the dust. And still Perspax strode along, with
no hesitation concerning his direction or destination.

Occasionally, they would halt. Perspax calling for it with
a raised hand. Then he would stand still for a moment
while the short antennae on his head moved, shifting in
one direction and then another.

It was a strange, uncanny thing to observe. The first time
Serena, seeking warmth and shelter, moved close to
Evander. She was oblivious now to the wizardly skin on his
chest and back. Evander wrapped his arms around her. It
was a great comfort to touch another person, especially one
as dear to him as Serena. Thus they gained a little comfort
in a world gone mad, a world they could barely
comprehend.

Perspax had said there would be water, but it would be
a long trek to reach it.

Every so often the diminutive figure of Konithomimo
would bound in from the shadows to tell them there was
nothing to report on the surrounding flats.

Another hour went by. The glow in the sky grew dim.
The cold wind slowly ceased to blow from behind them.
Instead, a wind was beginning from the opposite direction.
They paused for a rest.

Serena dropped to her knees in the dust. "I need water,"
she said flatly.

The Eleem nodded, gasping. "I, too. It has been too long
since I drank, but there are few springs in this barren district. However, I suspect that there is one not too far ahead
of us now. I can sense that there are Neild there."

The horse-headed Eleem had mentioned these Neild before. Evander had gained the impression that Neild were
farming folk, people that improved the land.

"Way out here in this emptiness?" Serena said, feeling
her doubts resurface about the strange-looking monster
called Perspax. Yes, he had saved them, but what might his
real motives be? He might easily be planning to do them

in himself. Serena commanded herself to stop. She was frightened enough by this terrible place not to be scaring herself further with conjectures.

"Yes," Perspax said in that uncannily perfect Furda. "I suspect they have hit on a very good way of surviving. Micklebear must stay near water; they are thirsty brutes. So the Neild are safe from their great enemy."

Micklebear again. Evander did not like the sound of the micklebear. On the other hand, the Neild sounded like a good idea.

They went on, trudging forward across the cold wastes.

"How can you sense these, uh, Neild," said Evander.

"In the same way I can sense you," said Perspax. "Their minds give off a signal that the trained and educated Eleem can detect easily. The Neild have always fed the Eleem, who have protected them in turn. Some would say the Neild are slaves for the Eleem. Others would call them pets. The truth is that Neild were raised up by the Eleem and bred for their skills. After many generations the breed was improved to the point where the Neild began to speak. This might have lead to complications, for those who can speak can also complain."

Evander smiled here, thinking of Konithomimo, who complained about everything.

"But always the Neild were content to serve the Eleem. And the Eleem have always doted on their Neild."

Evander turned these things over in his mind, wondering if he'd heard it all correctly. He questioned Perspax a bit more and then fell silent. Orthond was a very different world from that which he knew.

He and Serena tried to make sense of all that had happened to them since Evander had appeared on the tower top to try and rescue her.

"You came to me just as the hero Blue Frog came to the lady Lamen."

"Blue Frog?" He chuckled for a moment remembering Serena's lovely painting. "I'm afraid I didn't rescue you so much as just get you in worse trouble."

She put a hand to his cheek. "You rescued me all right. Nothing could have been worse than that monster, not even this."

They exchanged wan smiles.

They walked on toward an infinitely distant gray haze.

And then quite suddenly they came on a change in the landscape. First came Konithomimo's excited report. There was something ahead, like an island with vegetation all over it.

Perspax came erect with an audible snap. He fairly leapt in the air with a grunt of triumph. "They are there. Come on."

Soon the dust beneath their feet thickened and, incredibly, grew tough-looking clumps of a stringy yellow grass. Even the smell of sulfurous burning faded and was replaced with one of mud and rotting vegetation. As they went on, the clumps became more numerous. Eventually, it became difficult to walk since the clumps were treacherous to tread on, and it was hard to find footing between them. Then the clump grass gave way to a forest of trees scarcely taller than Perspax. Their progress slowed even more as they forced their way through a tangle of thickets overgrown with thorned vines that Perspax had to take a sword to.

They struggled thus for perhaps an hour before the tangled forest finally came to an end. The ground was now hard-packed soil, with larger trees shading out the smaller ones. And then there was the first pond—a circle of water perhaps thirty feet across, fringed with reeds. From the reeds came the sounds of vigorous life, a croaking, batrachian cacophany. Insects buzzed through the air above.

They knelt by the side of the pond and drank from cupped hands and slaked their thirst.

"Neild are watching us," said Perspax, "you can be sure of that. If they thought we meant them harm, they would have discharged a musket by now. They are not defenseless."

Evander chewed his lip. Everything on this world that he had met or seen had appeared dangerous. Surely, Neild would be no different.

Now they passed more ponds, and these grew larger and were surrounded by boggy places. And from the bogs arose biting insects that flocked to them with eager whines. Their efforts to push on were intensified, and they stumbled along at the best possible speed through thickening marsh. Just when the insects seemed overwhelming, with millions arising around them, the tall Eleem bounded up a bank to drier ground, and they left the marsh behind.

Another hundred paces and they were in what was unmistakably an orchard, with rows of identical trees bearing thick, round leaves, and standing perhaps ten feet high. Along their branches were little brown pods, some of which had fallen to litter the ground below.

Past the pod bean orchards were small green fields filled with white pod and other grains. Dark green peg moss and tawny nutbush grew in others. All the fields were immaculate.

The scenery spoke of intense husbandry. It seemed as if every leaf here had been individually inspected.

And then they saw the first buildings, one-story houses built low to the ground, with round windows and rectangular doors. Closer yet, Evander could see their mud walls and woven withe roofs. Around them were gardens of small plants with many flowers.

It was in such a garden that they spotted their first Neild. A small, round-shouldered figure, wearing a head scarf, was working on a bed of tiny blue flowers with a spade. Evander, at first, thought it was a rather diminutive woman. Then it turned its head and he gasped. Enormous round eyes dominated a face like that of a tortoise.

It saw Perspax and let out a low, moaning cry, but the moan was a happy one. The little creature danced toward them with flapping arms, making a series of moaning barks. Perspax responded with similar barks and started slapping his big hands together. The Neild wriggled like a puppy.

Evander, Serena, and Konithomimo stared at each other.

More Neild were appearing in doorways and garden arches. More happy-sounding whines and barks went up.

As they came closer, Evander was reminded of beavers, or especially fat dogs, with the faces of turtles. Turtle-beavers, with hands of skill, each with four black fingers and a startlingly white thumb.

The eyes were the most astonishing thing. They were enormous, with pupils the size of a man's entire eye. They bulged from the wrinkled turtle-heads in a quite alarming way. Yet in those eyes was a warm, happy intelligence. The little creatures seemed clumsy, but, in fact, their movements were consistent and deft. Their eyes sparkled with love of Perspax. They flocked around the tall figure with its wolfish body and horselike head and danced, wriggling and slowly shuffling their feet while they sang in a strange voice, almost a howling, almost a song.

They wore brown tunics and leggings, small round hats and scarves, and none came up to Evander's chest. Some would barely have cleared his navel.

"These are good Neild," said Perspax, patting them, hugging them close to his legs and knees for a moment, scratching them under the chin.

Evander noticed the fine beadwork and embroidery that covered the clothing of the Neild. Their garments were impeccably tailored, if simple. Some of the round hats bore elaborate designs in pearly sequins.

"These are a folk with great skills," he said.

"Good Neild are never still. Their fingers are constantly at work."

Chapter Twenty-six

The Neild made a good caper for the coming of the Lord Eleem. Before him they bowed, and then danced to welcome him to the well-watered manor on the land.

Alas, they had to confess, they knew not whose the land was. No lord had visited them before. They were alone. They had been left to defend themselves from the foul enemies of the world. They begged the lord's pardon if it was his land, but when they had come there, the spring had been plugged and the land was desolate. No lord was making use of it, and everything they had done had been to improve it and make it bountiful.

They were unsure of their position and begged him for the mercy of the Eleem. All they were sure of was that it was safer than their old gardens in the ruins on the margins of the flats.

And when they thought of the gardens in the ruins, they let out a wail of lamentation for the memories that such thoughts brought back. Ravening micklebears turning over the rubble for young, tasty Neild. Multipedes swarming after the old ones.

And so they capered in hope and submission and welcomed the lord to his home, if he would but take it. For they were Neild without a lord to worship. And if he wished, he would be their lord, and they would serve him gladly. Above all, they were most concerned to impress upon him that they were good Neild, extremely good Neild.

"Let us serve you, Oh, Lord," they cried out again and again as they fell upon their knees and bowed down.

When they finally quieted enough to let him get in a word, Perspax sang to them in their own tongue, the sonorous language of Nessor, and he thanked them for their service. He blessed them as being good Neild, worthy to serve himself and his guests, whereupon he pointed to

Evander and Serena and the little metallic figure of Konithomimo.

The enormous eyes examined the guests as if for the very first time, as if they had never seen them before, as if all this time they had been so intent on the figure of the Lord Eleem that they had never noticed the bizarre, small, pink creatures, and the even stranger little blue one.

A long solemn moment passed as the enormous, chelonoid eyes regarded Evander and Serena. Perspax sang to them and told them of the people of Ryetelth and how Evander and Serena came to be amongst them. Konithomimo he did not explain, nor did they ask him to, for all could see plainly that the small figure was a representative of some great magic. It was enough that the great Lord Eleem, their Lord Perspax, child of the Miggenmorch, had brought these creatures to them. They would care for them and worship them as lords, too.

Then they turned back en masse to regard the lord. "Long have we dwelt here alone, Oh, Lord," cried the Neild. "For we came here to escape the micklebear and the multipede that devoured all of our people."

Perspax blessed the good Neild who had suffered much.

"We have worked on this land, Oh, Lord, and now it is a well-watered land, where once there was only dust."

Perspax blessed them again.

"And we have made from the spring twelve good catch ponds, and each we have dug out with our hands. And around the twelve good catch ponds we have planted the holy plants and sowed the fields with white pod."

Perspax blessed them. And they went on to sing of how they had brought up good gardens with withe and water. And how they had built homes for themselves, and how with more withe and water they had raised up a habitation for their lord, if he would but let them lead him to it.

And Perspax blessed them once more.

The Neild begged the lord to take up residence in the house they had built for him, and Perspax accepted. And so they were led through a narrow street between the low thatched roofs of the little houses of the Neild until they came to a low wall of whitewashed plaster, round windows, and a low set door of polished wood. Neild prostrated themselves around the door, which swung open to reveal more Neild, also prostrate, lining the rooms within.

"We are your servants, Oh, Lord!" sang the Neild.

Evander and Serena found themselves in comfortable rooms lit with small lanterns set in the corners. The cream-colored walls were decorated with framed weavings, tapestries of exquisite skill. Brilliant green and white rugs covered the floors. All wood surfaces gleamed with polished podwax. Neild surged around them, wriggling in joy at the opportunity to serve the lords.

The doors opened, and they were struck by the pleasant aromas of freshly baked bread, roasted meats, and pies in the oven. Food was ready for them, a table laid.

Perspax sang his thanks to the Neild and requested baths and hot water. At once they were ushered to bathing rooms where they were able to soak in hot tubs and remove the dust and dried sweat of their long, terrible journey. While they bathed, their clothes were taken apart, examined, and remade. Several new items were run up, including warm outer shirts for Evander and Serena, who were obviously underdressed for the rigors of doomed Orthond. Evander found these new clothes a perfect fit. The materials were similar to the finest linen and wool cloth.

Serena now wore thick trousers of a woollike material and a long tunic of darker wool, lined with linen. She felt warm for the first time on Orthond. Her worn-out palace shoes had been replaced with stout new boots of soft gray leather.

Evander, too, had received new boots, and just in time, for his old ones were worn to holes. Clean and with fresh clothing, Evander felt something of his normal confidence return. Their situation was desperate, but at least they would be comfortable while they visited with the good Neild. Outside this oasis there stretched only the nightmarish desolation of ravaged Orthond, but here they were enveloped in a warm glow of hospitality.

Evander and Serena had rooms side by side. Perspax had a larger space on the other side of the hall. They met outside the doors and were ushered down the hall to a room dominated by a long table of dark wood, gleaming with polish. Upon the table were placed platters and plates of dark red porcelain. Clear crystal goblets were filled with fresh water. They took their seats and were immediately surrounded by ecstatic Neild.

Of Konithomimo there was no sign. They were informed

that the little blue man had gone out into the fields to explore. They were asked whether the little figure took nourishment. Evander explained that as far as he knew, Konithomimo did not. In his own world he was a carpet. His transformation had been most perplexing.

Perspax understood. This was clearly the product of great magic, and such things could be most unpredictable.

For the Neild, the meal was an epiphany. They reveled in this chance to serve the lord and his guests. Throughout their service they sang the sweet hymns to the Lords Eleem that they sang at all their religious festivities. They sang as they poured the berry wine and the water. They sang as they brought dumplings and tiny pancakes rolled around stuffings of nutty flavors. They sang as they brought the first pots of stew, and they continued to sing as the feast went on, for eight courses at least, Evander decided.

It was good food, surprisingly tasty considering that the ingredients were not familiar to his taste buds. Only the rather burnt shreds of an animal with goat-like flesh had been unpalatable. These shreds, however, were of great importance to Perspax, who took several and ate them with much show. This seemed to raise the spirit of the Neild even further than before.

They were all very hungry, and thus they fell silent for a while as forks scraped on plates. Evander had a second goblet of the wine, which was excellent, reminding him faintly of some fruity Eorha wines that were popular in Kassim when drunk very young.

After they had eaten their fill, they pushed their chairs back and relaxed. Perspax quizzed Serena and Evander politely about their world.

Serena described the floating city of Monjon, and Perspax was struck with awe. He declared that the power of the blessed Thymnal was clearly very great indeed.

At the conclusion of the meal, they were shown to the verandah at the rear of the house of the lord. From the low-slung verandah they stepped down onto a long, neatly clipped lawn. To either side were flower beds, largely invisible in the murk of early night. And yet the scent of flowers was strong here, and no longer did Evander smell the burned stone of Orthond, that reek which had grown so familiar in the desperate hours they had strode this tragic world.

Beyond the inner gardens they saw pools of lantern light, dotted across the scene. Each pool of light revealed work parties of Neild. They seemed to be everywhere. There they rebuilt a bridge across a water channel. Here they dug a ditch to better drain the bean field. Over there they pulled weeds from a patch of white pod. Everywhere one looked the land seemed to boil with working Neild. The soft sound of their hymns came floating across the air.

They came to a small pond, where groups of tiny Neild children waded, wielding little nets to catch the larvae of annoying insects. The larvae were retained in shoulder satchels for later consumption by pond fish.

The presence of the lord was soon noted by the baby Neild, and an excited muttering and whistling went up among them. An adult called them to move away, lest they annoy the Lord Eleem, and with many worshipful, backward looks the young Neild moved away across the pond.

Perspax paused and gazed back through the gardens. Patches of lantern light glimmered here and there where the good Neild worked with their cunning hands. The wind soughed through the trees in the orchards.

Behind them came the sound of Neild rapping the nut trees to bring down more ripe pods. The sticks beat out a steady rhythm to which the Neild voices sang their hymns of joy.

Evander thought the scene had a peculiar, moving beauty.

Perspax sensed his thought. "This is how our world used to be."

Evander heard the note of sorrow in Perspax's voice. "You said you would tell me what happened to your world."

"I will try, but only one knows the truth of all this, and he is the cause of our destruction."

"You mentioned him before."

"His is a name we do not use in Orthond, for we know that it is a name of treachery and infamy only."

"You said earlier that we would go to Canax. Is that still your plan?"

"It is. We will rest here first. These are good Neild."

"Amazingly so, such gentle servants can scarcely be imagined."

"The Neild exist to serve."

For a moment Evander tried to imagine what the faintly shabby palace of Sedimo Kassim might look like if there were Neild to take care of it. "I would like to know how such a world could be ruined so."

"Ah." Perspax looked away and his words were bitter. "Only the wise ones really know the answer to your question," he said. "I remember only that there suddenly came a time when there was dissension across the lands. The issues of the day produced great controversy, and the contention grew to hatred and finally to conflict. We had been spared the evil of war for an eon. And yet once again we fell into the ancient barbarism, and we slew one another and formed cliques and armies to do so. The fighting went on and on, until we were decimated. Great heaps of dead and dying warriors decorated every battlefield.

"Some say the evil one was already among us at that time. And that he had been the secret mover of the political struggle that had consumed us. They say that secretly, with great magic, he drove us to ecstasies of extremism and sowed the seeds of the hate that later brought the wars."

"The wars went on?"

"The wars gradually consolidated into a single war. It went on without cease, rotting our nations from within, destroying our traditions, killing our best and brightest. At last it ended when we were completely exhausted. Everything was broken down; the dead were no longer buried."

"And then?"

"Then came the dark one in power, and he wielded a magic mirror, the same that sits in Orthontower. And with it he brought to life a fell army of evil beasts, and with them he began his reign of terror.

"He claimed to have come to save us from ourselves, and for a while there were those among us who were fooled. We consented to allow his arbitration in our disputes. Then we learned that he had betrayed us and that his fell army was already at work, destroying the Neild. Then we understood our enemy at last.

"At first we sought to join together and form a great host to go up against him. And, indeed, the hosts came from east and west and joined together. But, alas, our wars had devoured our strength. At Cruach Calladan we fought the enemy, and for two days the host of the Knights of the Miggenmorch held the field, surrounded by a sea of bewks and micklebear. But in the end the knights fell, and the dark hordes swept over us.

"Since then, the bewks and multipedes have gone across the world, systematically destroying everything. Micklebear have eaten the Neild. Everything they worked so hard to create has been destroyed. The remaining knights of Orthond grew hungry. In time we starved. Our numbers dwindled, our power fell away. One by one, the kings of the Eleem were seized and brought to kneel at the enemy's steel-clad feet and there beheaded with the axe."

"And now?"

"Now we are but remnants, hiding in the ruins. Many have lost the great arts and become savages like those I took you from."

"And your enemy?"

"He sits in dreadful majesty in Orthontower. His creatures devour our world for minerals. Great mines have been bored to extract our wealth in gold and iron. There is very little we can do."

A sense of intense desolation came over Evander, and he fell silent. Instinctively, he and Serena held each other for comfort in the most primal of human responses.

"I am terrified, Evander. How can we ever escape this world?"

"There must be a way."

The Eleem turned his tragic eyes upon them. "We will go to Canax. There we will consult with the venerable one. To Shadreiht we shall go."

Chapter Twenty-seven

Their room was snug and their bed uncannily comfortable. The exhausted pair slept deeply for a dozen hours and awoke greatly refreshed.

Only then did they realize what had happened. Before they had been too tired, and too used to a desperate intimacy since they had arrived on Orthond to even take note of what they were doing. They had huddled together for warmth and psychological comfort, instinctively, naturally, and without a second thought.

Now they had slept together, naked, albeit without ever making love. Still it brought a blush to Serena's cheeks. She had never slept with a man before.

Then she giggled at a sudden thought. "By common law in the old days we would now be man and wife."

He grinned. "Then I wish common law still prevailed." They laughed together, and he leaned over and kissed her, and for a precious moment their predicament, even the hideous skin covering his chest and shoulders, was forgotten.

"Wait a moment," she said suddenly, pushing him back. "I still don't know who you really are, Evander the Enigma. I surely don't believe that you are a trader from Molutna Ganga."

"You don't?"

"No, not in the slightest."

"Oh." He'd been quite sure she'd accepted his hurriedly patched-together tale. It was curiously discomforting to learn that he'd been completely wrong about this. Now he confronted the need to actually confess the truth.

"I am not sleeping with a man who won't even tell me his real name," she said, scrambling back a little.

"Yes, of course, I can understand that. Look, I know it

must seem strange, that I should hide my origins, even my true name."

He paused, not to be dramatic, but to try to marshal his words carefully. "I can only say that I have reason to hide. There are those who would like to kill me if they could find me."

"Kill you? Other than the wizard and my father, of course."

"Of course. These are powerful men who usurped the throne in my homeland. If they ever find me, they will kill me."

"But why do they want to kill you?" she asked, half-believing him, but clutching the blanket to her chin.

"My real name is Danais Evander of Sedimo Kassim." This did not have quite the effect he had expected.

She smiled. "That is a nice name, I like it. Where is Sedimo Kassim?"

"On the northeastern edge of the empire of Kassim. Almost as far as Czardha."

"That is very far, indeed. But I still don't see why they want to kill you."

"My father was King Danais the Sixth. I would have been Danais the Seventh."

Her face had grown pale. "I knew it had to be something like this. I knew you were not a trader. But what happened? Why were you in Monjon?"

"My father died too soon. I was too young to win support in the outer fiefs of the kingdom. My powerful cousins combined to usurp the throne. Madees sits on it, but is childless, Domijia's son will inherit. They had the support of the east, the west and the north, I had only the southland behind me.

"I knew that if there was war then my side would lose, and the subsequent slaughter would be widespread and vengeful. I also knew that Madees would make a good king, he is stern, but he is just. The nobles will fear him and obey him."

"What did you do?"

"I left. Took along my old friend and tutor, good Kospero, and rode south to great Molutna. I planned to make a new life for myself. I had some gold, enough to last us for a long time, if we lived sensibly."

"You abandoned your Kingdom?"

"I would have lost it. And then I would have lost my

life under the headman's axe. I couldn't see the point in sparking a civil war when I had no chance of surviving. The southland would have been devastated for decades."

"Oh, Evander, I'm so sorry."

"Don't be. If I hadn't fled Sedimo, I never would have met you, and I never would have been truly happy."

Her eyes widened at his words.

"Neither would I."

He smiled at the utter seriousness in her voice.

There came an interruption in the form of a gong ringing loudly not too far away. Tentatively they rose from the bed.

Almost as soon as they were on their feet, the doors opened and bustling Neild brought them breakfasts on trays. They both received plates of hot grain cakes dipped in something that tasted very much like butter. Then came slices of salted fish, finely sauteed in a nutty tasting oil and pieces of fruit, some of which were much like apples, served in small, exquisitely made baskets of withe. All was washed down with crystal clear water.

When they had breakfasted they went out on the patio. There was no sign of the Eleem. Evander tried to question some of the Neild, but none of them could understand him. Only the Lord Eleem could speak Furda.

Serena was still troubled, although a sound night's sleep had put a little of the customary bloom back into her cheeks. Her eyes betrayed her state of mind. She was clearly haunted by something. She took his hand in both of hers.

"Evander, I've been thinking. We must make a plan."

"A plan?"

"To get home. We can't stay here. I'd go mad if I thought I would never get home."

"Of course we'll get home, Princess, of course we will." Exactly how they would do this, he could not imagine. Furthermore, he forebore to mention the fact that home, by which he assumed she meant the city of Monjon, was decidedly dangerous for them both. If home was meant to mean his home, then it was even more dangerous. On the streets of Sedimo Kassim he would be taken and slain in no time.

"Of course we'll get home." He slid an arm around her to try and reassure her. She wriggled closer. If she even thought of his hideous skin she showed no sign of it.

"But how, Evander? I keep trying to think of a way, but I can't."

"Well, we will have to put our trust in our strange new friend, the Eleem Lord. We know hardly anything about this place yet. We have to know where we are before we can begin to chart a course for Monjon."

"We don't know anything, and everything we do know terrifies me. I want to go home, Evander."

She was shivering, and not from cold.

"Well, we shan't stay here." He sounded brave. "Perspax said we would have to go to a place called Canax. He has a friend there, a sage of some sort who can advise us."

"Look." She nodded toward the nearest bushes where a dozen pairs of bulging eyes were fixed on them. "They're everywhere."

"They are, and they are such wonderfully hospitable creatures. We have been treated very well since we arrived here."

"I think they're fattening us like prize pigs. When we least expect it, they'll come after us with axes and we'll be in the ovens in no time."

Evander squeezed her gently and did his best to project a confidence he barely felt. "Don't worry, Princess. We'll find a way to get home. We can't stay here."

Serena straightened her shoulders and squared her chin. She took a deep breath to help master the fear. It was a general, all-encompassing fear, not the old fear of the wizard that she had struggled with for weeks. This was an all-encompassing whirl of terror. At the thought of being trapped here on this desolate world, utterly removed from home, friends, and family, her heart quailed. Even the "noble" horse-headed thing was an absolute monster. Listening to it speak Furda was the weirdest sound she had ever heard. It looked as if it ate babies, raw, and yet wore the garments befitting a knight of chivalry.

"You're right, dear Evander, and now we must be brave. I must remember that I am the Princess Serena of Monjon." Her eyes were bright. "And for the Princess of Monjon, the city of Monjon is not exactly the safest place in the world."

He put on an encouraging smile. "You have a point. We want to return to Ryetelth, but we don't want to return to Monjon. If we just got back to Monjon, we'd be in worse trouble than we're in here. In Kassim we call that jumping out of the cauldron into the firecoals."

For a moment they forgot the Neild peering at them and the desolation of Orthond and clung to each other for warmth and security.

They were interrupted by a small, high-pitched voice calling loudly as it approached. They pulled apart as a small blue-metal figure came bouncing across the lawn toward them. It came like some hurtling ball, bouncing along at fifty-foot intervals.

"Welcome," said Evander as the miniature figure jumped smoothly up to the top of the polished wooden balustrade that edged the patio. He spun there like a beautiful ornament for a moment with his arms extended above his head like a dancer.

"Hello, inactive ones," said Konithomimo. "I have been out since before dawn, and I can say that I have now thoroughly explored this place."

"Congratulations. And what have you found?" asked Evander.

"It is not very large. In area it is less then twenty square miles. Much of that is covered by useless thorn forest. The arable heartland is perhaps only a third of the total. The arable land swarms with these servile creatures. There are thousands of them. They infest it like roaches in a greasy kitchen."

Evander felt this to be an inappropriate description of the world of the Neild. It was fantastically neat and tidy and comfortable. What did it matter if it swarmed with Neild? They were the ones who had created it and constantly improved it.

"They have made it a beautiful place," he said.

"Surely, that is a matter of opinion," snapped the little blue man, who was now doing stretching exercises and hopping from one leg to the other. "Their design is strictly utilitarian, flat, boring, a scheme with little to recommend it to the decorative eye."

Evander took a moment to digest this.

"I did not know you were such a judge of agrarian systems."

"All activities of intelligent purpose fall within the purview of the artistic mind. I was made of the greatest art of all, and thus I can view things only from the artistic lens."

Evander looked helplessly to Serena. She rolled her eyes.

"Have you seen our horse-headed friend?" asked Serena.

Konithomimo spun to face her. " 'Horse-headed' did you say? You are very impolite to the noble Perspax. I shall inform him of what you said."

"Please don't," Serena said in distress, regretting her slip. Konithomimo spun away for another turn before deigning to answer.

"The noble Lord Perspax has been called to adjudicate certain disputes among the Neild. He will join us for the midday meal. I, of course, do not require the ingestion of gross foodstuffs, so I will not join you during the digestion ritual."

"Ah, yes," said Evander, "I had been wondering about your needs regarding food."

"You do not need to concern yourselves with my welfare," the little man said sulkily. "I am perfectly equipped to survive here. I do not need to return to Ryetelth at all."

Evander recalled Konithomimo's distress at an earlier juncture. "You have changed your views then on that question?"

"I have?" said the little figure in an ominously querulous tone.

"When we were forced to leave you at the ruined village, you seemed quite worried about your ability to survive here on your own."

Konithomimo was unabashed. "It is most inconsiderate of you to speak of such matters. Common standards of politeness would expect that you would not raise them." The little blue man sniffed disdainfully and hopped away along the top of the balustrade and did a pirouette.

"Come now, be reasonable," Evander called after him.

"You are quite hateful; I will not speak with you." He hopped down and disappeared into a network of shrubbery.

"Well, I never," said Serena. "Who would've imagined such impudence from a rug?"

"Not I," said Evander. "A lot of things have changed in my views of the world. I find that things are vastly more complicated than I had ever imagined."

They strolled through the gardens. Neild were everywhere. Those huge liquid eyes were turned on them from behind every bush, from holes excavated in the ground, from below bridges, and from above them in the trees. The

Neild swarmed in their well-watered land. Evander began to feel the pressure of constant observation oppressive.

Serena had noticed. "You see how it gets?"

"I agree. One could soon yearn for privacy here."

"Can we go back to the house? At least there are fewer of them back there."

They turned back through the bonsai park, with miniaturized trees, pools, and structures, so that walking through it made them seem like giants. Young Neild were at work on the tiny trees, watering, clipping, removing dead twigs. Others were digging a new pond farther on.

They reached the far side of the miniature park. A neatly clipped hedge enclosed it, and when they passed through the entrance, they found themselves back in the world of normal-sized things. The effect was startling.

"The Neild are very ingenious, are they not?"

"The Neild are almost too ingenious. I don't know why, but they frighten me."

Ahead was a low-slung bridge across a wide channel. Below them a party of young Neild were playing, jumping from rocks into the pool.

This was such different behavior from the usual industriousness that Evander paused to watch for a moment. The young Neild were even more like turtles than their elders. They leaped with happy noises into the pool and emerged again a few moments later, tossing the water off their backs and wriggling out onto dry ground again.

Something had changed. Evander looked again. One of the young Neild did not resurface. The others kept on diving, not seeming to notice. Evander continued to watch.

"What is it?" asked Serena.

"There were more of these youngsters down there a moment ago. One of them didn't come up."

Serena looked at the water with a worried eye. Did it conceal some fresh menace?

"Is there something down there in the water?"

Evander leaned over and called to the young Neild. They stared up at him with astonished eyes. He pointed to the water and called again. They simply stared back, completely overawed. They appeared unaware that one of their companions was missing.

Time was passing. The little Neild might be drowning. Evander pulled off his warm outer shirt, kicked off his boots, and then dived over the side of the bridge the next moment.

The water was colder than he had anticipated; he half expected his heart to stop from the shock. But it was also reasonably clear, and he could see right across the pool. The bottom was flat and unmarked except with patches of weed. At the edges were forests of roots from the trees that lined the pond. Where was that missing child?

He turned about, seeing nothing, and was about to head back to the surface when he caught a flicker of something moving. Tiny legs kicked desperately among the roots.

He turned at once and in two long strokes was on the scene. The baby Neild was caught up in the roots of a tree that was virtually overhanging the pool. In its blind struggles it had wrapped a root as thick as a finger around its middle.

Evander reached in and hauled on the little Neild. It kicked at him in its panic and broke his grip and spun him around. He felt himself running short of air. There wasn't time to waste. He pulled his knife free and slashed at the roots. They were tough and had to be sawn through with a back-and-forth stroke. He had to release the little Neild to get enough purchase on the roots with his free hand while he sawed away. The damned roots would not give up! He was on the verge of blacking out when the roots gave way and the little Neild dropped free and kicked itself into the mud on the bottom, disappearing under a cloud of disturbed sediment.

Evander felt a pounding in his ears. His chest was horribly tight, but he dove into the cloud with his arms outstretched and ran headon into the little Neild, which had rebounded and was heading for the surface. The concussion knocked his head sideways and added stars to the bad music pounding in his brain. He had to breathe. He kicked with almost his last strength. The surface seemed to float dreadfully slowly toward him. There was water in his mouth, and then air, and then he was coughing and gasping and floundering in the water beside the narrow bridge.

Serena gave him a hand. He caught it and almost pulled her in. Then the baby Neild floated by, and he grabbed it and hugged it to his chest with his free arm. It clung to him with hard little fingers, and he felt the desperate energy of the small animal. When he let go, it gripped him around the neck.

He caught hold of the bridge, still sputtering and spitting out water, and slowly hauled himself out onto the decking. The baby Neild remained attached. Serena knelt beside him. He shivered from the cold, and she wrapped his Neild shirt around him. The other Neild children were standing on the bank, staring at them.

They examined the little Neild. Its fur was wet and slicked down like that of a seal. The body was tubby, but graceful, the eyes enormous, but hidden now behind expansive lids.

"Will it live?" she asked.

The Neild suddenly began to cough, and he set it down as it vomited up water and sucked in air with high-pitched little whoops.

"I think it's going to make it," he said.

"Don't look now, but we're not alone."

Indeed other Neild had appeared out of the landscape and were gathering around. Quite a crowd had arrived already, and more were on the way. Some of them began to sing one of the long, slow-tempo songs they were so fond of. Evander found himself walled in by the eyes of Neild.

"Why do you think they sing all the time?" she asked.

"I don't know, but they seem to like doing it. By the Gods there's a lot of them though."

And more were coming all the time.

Serena grew apprehensive. It was uncomfortable being surrounded by hundreds of Neild. They seemed to be closing in. "Let's go back to the house."

Still carrying the little one, Evander walked toward the wall of Neild adults. It parted before him, and he walked on, through the gardens toward the house. A path opened up in front of them through an almost solid mob of Neild. The singing was getting very loud. They were throwing fronds onto the path before their feet.

"What is all this? Do you think they're worshipping us?" asked Evander, finding the thought incredible.

"Whatever they're doing, I wish they wouldn't."

As they passed some groups of Neild, there were outbreaks of mass pant hooting and body wriggling that up till then Evander had only seen them do around the Lord Eleem.

They were soon back on the main lawn approaching the low-slung house, which was so deeply bermed into the ground under gray thatched roofs that it seemed to grow organically out of the land.

At the steps to the patio they were met by Perspax, who towered above the Neild that surrounded him. Evander came to a halt. A pair of old, wrinkled Neild came forward and took the young wet one away.

"Well done, my friends," said Perspax. "You have convinced the Neild that you are protectors. That is the most sacred attribute to the Neild; therefore they now worship you, even as they worship the Eleem."

"All I did was fish a youngster out of a pond. He was caught up in the roots of a tree."

"I have heard every detail of the story already, three times over, with different emphasis each time. The entire village is awake with it and already singing the hymns of praise to the new Gods."

"Well, I accept their thanks, but I am no God."

"To the Neild you are. The Neild were bred to worship." Evander realized how strange this world was and how different his thinking must be from that of a creature like Perspax. He tried to shield his thoughts and hoped that the Eleem would not be insulted if he happened to be reading his mind. Perspax seemed unaffected, however, and continued to wave a languid hand to acknowledge the adulation of the Neild.

They were ushered inside and greeted with hot drinks and fresh, dry clothing for Evander. Perspax had news for them.

"If you are rested sufficiently by tomorrow, I think we should push on for Canax. The sooner I can deliver you to the wise one, the better. He will know what to do. Do not despair, Princess Serena, the great Shadreiht is very wise and learned in the ways of our enemy. He will know a way."

Chapter Twenty-eight

The flats stretched ahead of them, drear and desolate. Evander had difficulty understanding how the landscape could have been made so barren. It was a manifestation of the Dominator's great power, Perspax explained. The world had burst into flame here. The very land had burned.

On this day the mists had faded, and the sun had come out. But it was harsh, white and small, not the comforting sun Evander was familiar with. The flat emptiness was gray and stretched off in all directions to a bleak horizon.

They had already walked for hours. Perspax assured him they would walk for many more. At least they wore comfortable clothing and carried food and water, courtesy of the Neild.

Perspax had confessed to some nervousness about the next leg of the journey. They would soon leave the flats and enter a wide section of ruins. Among the ruins were still a few traveling vagrant Neild, settling briefly in one place, growing a patch of bean pod and then moving on. Hunting for these Neild, and anything else that still survived, would be micklebear, the ravening beasts unleashed by the evil one.

Micklebear were especially dangerous because they were hard to detect on the subtle plane when they were hunting. Even the most sensitive Eleem could be tricked by an old, wily, micklebear hunting upwind, thoughts shielded. In the beginning micklebear had fed well on Orthond. Those easy days were long gone, however, and micklebear now were generally starving and would therefore keep up pursuit until the bitter end. Since those early days of catastrophe, the surviving Neild had become much more sensitive on the higher planes of perception. Feral Neild had also become far less tractable; they were no longer really "good" Neild.

The mention of the Neild was enough to drive Konithomimo away, leaping across the flats ahead of them.

Evander was still interested in the origins of the Neild. To have actually bred intelligence into a lower animal was an astonishing feat, or so it seemed to him. "So, if Neild are left to themselves, they turn feral, in your terms. Do they then cease to serve the Eleem?"

"Alas, these are Neild that have never known protection."

"Ah, yes, that is the Eleem side of the social bargain. You protect them, and they serve you in everything else," Evander said. "Tell me, what were the Neild originally? What was their role in life as animals?"

"They were small delvers in the streamlands. They built dams of sticks and logs and created lakes in which they built their lodges."

Evander fell silent for a while, rubbing his chin thoughtfully. "I'm sorry, Perspax, but I'm troubled by the thought that the Eleem literally bred the Neild up from pure animal life to that of servants."

"The Neild had to be bred for a long time, to bring out intelligence and skill with hand and eye. There is a legend that claims it took one hundred generations. Actually, I think it took far longer. There were many breeders among the Eleem, and they competed with each other to produce the best, newest strains of Neild."

"And over time the Neild changed from their wild state and became more tame. You bred them until they could understand you."

"In time they became good Neild."

"Still, you took from them what had been theirs."

"I suppose that is true. Perhaps the Neild were forced to sacrifice. Yet it served a greater purpose. It saved the Eleem. It saved our civilization. Having the Neild proved more satisfactory than other systems that had been previously pursued."

"Such as?"

"Such as the employment of Eleem as servants for other Eleem. The Eleem are a proud race, incapable of servility. Service was never very good or prompt. Systems to enforce service inevitably became harsh. Rebellion flared. Bloodshed followed. There was even war. Then the wise ones saw the answer and began to breed the Neild.

"We protected them from the loping alu and the other predators of the old forests of Orthond. Those were their natural enemies. Alas, they are no more."

"And what has happened to them?"

"All killed and eaten long ago by micklebear and multipede."

Serena spoke up. She had been quiet for some time, just concentrating on putting one foot in front of the other. She was hot and dusty and wanted some water, but refused to allow herself to be thought weak. So she waited for Evander or the Eleem to broach the subject. "Every tale you tell us of this world ends like that. Isn't there anything joyful left here?"

The Eleem found this an odd question. "I do not think so, Princess. Orthond belongs to the great enemy now. Perhaps there is joy in his heart, but that must be the only place left for it."

Serena found this thought profoundly disturbing. "What if he comes to our world?" she asked, voicing her deeper fear.

"Then your world will be devastated and your peoples will be scattered and hunted down."

Evander nodded, but was not entirely convinced. There were great wars already on Ryetelth, and terrible wizards with awesome power. Certainly, this Dominator of worlds that had brought down the Lords Eleem would have a lot of enemies if he came to Ryetelth. Could he overcome all the wild wizards and dreadful sorcerers that already abounded there? Could he defeat the kings of Czardha, or the wise Emperor of the Rose in the uttermost east? And yet the destruction of Orthond was so complete that fear did grow in his heart. The peoples of Ryetelth were already warlike. They might easily be manipulated into endless wars that would weaken them. Perhaps the same thing that had been done to the mighty Eleem Lords could be done to the nations of Ryetelth.

"We must go home so we can warn our people about this enemy."

Perspax thought about this for a moment and then nodded approvingly. "Very good idea. We will ask the wise one, old Shadreiht. He will know how it is to be done."

Serena shaded her eyes with her hand for a moment staring out to their front. "How far is it to Canax?"

"Still a ways. We have yet to reach the ruins. When we do, we will have to move more carefully."

Both Evander and Serena took deep breaths. Their strides became firmer.

Evander wondered what it was that drove Perspax to risk death for them. There was something dreadfully sad about the Eleem people. Endlessly noble, but quarrelsome and proud and completely dependent on the Neild. They followed a knightly code, which Evander could see had many similarities to the code of chivalry that ruled the lands of Kassim, but despite the value of this code, it had helped to destroy them because it had encouraged intolerance in disputes.

Evander had managed to learn the value of tolerance during the vicissitudes of his recent life. Becoming a fugitive from the usurpers who sought his life to cement their hold upon the throne of Sedimo Kassim had put an edge on things for him, sharpening his appreciation of the hazards and pleasures of existence. He had lost the sense of superiority that he'd grown up with as a young prince and grown to accept that he was really just another person, like any other. In his travels he had seen so many different peoples, all with different customs, that he had given up the notion that any one people had a monopoly on truth or wisdom.

He admired the Eleem for their beauty and heroic defiance of their monstrous foe, but wondered at the impiety of their role in creating the good Neild. Had the Eleem perhaps tempted the Gods to intervene? Had their arrogance brought on their demise? Evander had no idea if the Gods of Kassim and the Bakan, or any of the Gods and Goddesses of Ryetelth exercised authority here on Orthond. He had only the haziest idea of where Orthond might be, and all he could be certain of was that it was not Ryetelth. Were the Gods universal? Or were they restricted and therefore incapable of affecting such widely separated locations as different worlds?

Another hour went past, with the travelers all quietly lost in their own thoughts. Perspax could sense other minds now as they approached the horizon of the ruins of old Putchad. The sun was lowering. A dense fog arose, and the temperature dropped quickly.

They were soon walking forward into dense mist, through

which they could barely see ten yards ahead. Perspax walked forward with his thought straining ahead of them. The ruins were close now, probably well within view. He sensed Jooks squabbling in a tower way off to the left. He also sensed several multipedes off to the right. They had nested after feeding on the carcass of a dead micklebear. Beyond them were other minds, including Neild, hidden feral Neild, living hand-to-mouth in the ruins. He did not sense micklebear. This made him uneasy. They were sure to be there. What had the multipedes eaten after all? Perhaps that had been the only one? Then why were those Jooks way up in the tower? There was still light for micklebear to hunt by, so it was a dangerous time.

They went on this way for another hour, and then abruptly Konithomimo appeared, leaping out of the wall of mist ahead of them. He bounced across to them, huge leaps of twenty feet at a time.

"I bring you warning and alarm. Two large, ill-smelling beasts approach you from that direction." He pointed off to their left. "They are ponderous creatures, quite enormous. I think they intend you harm; their purpose is most direct."

Perspax looked off to the left and strained to find them. It was not easy. They were almost completely shielded from him, but at the last he had them, both strong and very hungry.

"Micklebear all right, and they are charging. We must hurry. We will angle to the right, and we must run for as long as we can, at least to the ruins. I can outrun micklebear. The question is whether you two will be able to. I had hoped to spare you this. Come."

The Eleem turned and began to jog. Evander and Serena followed him, with many a look backward into the gray mists for a glimpse of that which pursued them. Nothing betrayed itself. The mists remained unbroken. They ran for their lives.

Chapter Twenty-nine

The menacing thud of huge feet behind them was getting louder by the minute. No matter how hard they pushed themselves, the damned things were gaining. The problem now was they had covered a mile, and both Serena and Evander were getting winded. Neither was really in good enough condition for running any distance, not at least at these speeds. Energy depleted, they were running on fear.

The micklebears, on the other hand, were quite capable of a speedy trot for miles. For the Eleem this was not a problem; Eleem were built to run and could easily outdistance any predator. For the Neild, however, it had meant disaster, just as it seemed to for Evander and Serena.

On they sped across the flat land through thinning fog. The ruins were visible ahead, perhaps another half-mile to go.

The thud of predatory feet was so loud that Evander jerked his head back to see. What were they, these creatures that Perspax feared so? The things had to be close enough now so that he could see them. Then he did see and immediately wished he hadn't.

Like enormous swine with huge bloodshot eyes the micklebears loped forward on long-striding hind legs, front legs tucked up below their chins. As he glanced back, one opened its mouth to taste the air, revealing rows of daggerlike teeth. Their skins were a pinkish white, lined with cracks and crevices . . .

He heard gravel crunch and skitter behind him. Huge feet dug talons into the cold ground and pressed their owners forward. There was no time for anything but a frantic race for survival.

A feeling made him look over to Serena. He saw at once that something was wrong. She was fading. Her heart might be willing, but she did not look capable of staying ahead of the monsters for half a mile farther. The micklebears were only thirty yards behind now, and clearly visible.

Something had to be done—she was slowing down, stride by stride. "Serena," he shouted in her ear. "Look behind you!"

She looked back and froze for a moment, then with a yip of fright she jumped a foot in the air. She almost lost her footing then and stumbled along, staggering for several strides before regaining her balance. By then her face was set in a rigid mask. She had now confronted the unimaginable. She'd seen those champing jaws. She found a new source of strength, somehow.

One of the micklebears emitted that awful, chilling cry of theirs, loaded with hunger and malevolence. Perspax turned around and drew his sword.

"Run for the ruins," he called. "Hide there. Now run!"

The sword swung easily in his hand. Evander noted the Eleem's easy familiarity with the weapon. Add to his knightly attributes that of a swordsman. Evander saw the weight of that blade and was glad not to be facing the Eleem in combat.

The ruins were barely a quarter mile away now, a lacework of broken shapes of stone, piles of rubble, and some possible shelter from the monsters that pursued them.

An extraordinarily loud series of grunts and roaring broke out from the monsters and was echoed and repeated. Evander looked back and saw Perspax actually engaging one of the great brutes. The other had halted, too, and was swiping at the air around its head with its foreclaws.

Perspax's sword flashed in an arc of silver, and the beast was blooded in the next moment. It gave a roar of pain and rage and stepped backward.

Serena had stopped to look back, chest heaving as she sucked down lungfuls of air.

"Come on, Serena," he said, pulling on her arm. "The ruins, we've got to hide."

The micklebear swung its tail like a club and almost caught the Eleem, but he had read the move and was already out of range.

His sword glittered as it swung again, and the micklebear shifted its bulk back another step. Its head swayed in a most calculating way for a moment, and then it danced ponderously sideways and around the Eleem. Perspax stepped back. It lunged quickly with great jaws snapping. Perspax lurched back off balance and swung and missed. The beasts had great speed in their snapping attacks. It darted at Perspax, and he was forced back again, his riposte missing the huge head, which snapped back as if on a spring. This process continued, and Perspax was driven back and back, and then finally forced to run when the other micklebear came at him from the other side. The chase was resumed, but in those precious few moments Evander and Serena had gained thirty yards or more.

Evander concentrated on running; Serena was already five yards ahead of him with her arms coming back from her shoulders while her legs were driving at full extension.

The next few minutes were a daze of running, way past exhaustion, in a hazy world filled with weird, terrifying sounds, as the micklebears drew very close. Evander and Serena ran with the air burning in and out of their tortured lungs and the sound of those huge feet thudding closer and closer, for though they flagged, the micklebear did not. The predators could keep up this pace for another mile or so.

They ran across an ancient piazza, its flagstones cracked and heaved up. A row of columns, snapped off above their bases, fringed one side. The other was buried under rubble. Ruined tenements of more recent times arose just beyond the piazza's edge.

They heard Perspax shout something, but they didn't look back, just sprinted for the shadows of the ruins.

At last they were out of the open space, where there were walls, structures that could hide them all around.

"Quickly, up there," Evander said, pointing to a stair ascending into a tenement building that still retained most of its stories and walls.

They darted through the entrance into a dimly lit interior smelling strongly of mold. They could hear Perspax call their names, but from a distance. Evander was glad to know that Perspax still lived, but he dared not reply.

The stairs were worn and irregular and wound around the inside of the shaft with a central empty gap. They struggled up them, slowly at first, but then more quickly, impelled by the sudden thunder behind them as one of the monsters arrived at the entrance of the building.

The whole structure shook, and dust rained down upon them. Evander heard terrible sounds of devastation as the micklebear dug its way into the building, ripping wood and bricks alike out of its way as it widened the passage.

They climbed, forcing exhausted bodies far beyond their limits. The sounds of pursuit had reached the bottom of the steps.

Evander dared to peek over the edge of the steps. The bloated thing was pushing itself into the stairwell, and sliding upward like some enormous white snake. Its huge reddened eyes fixed on his with an implacable stare. A stench came from the thing, like the smell from a slaughterhouse on a hot day.

Serena gave a shocked cry when she peeked over, too. "How?"

"Must have cartilage instead of bone," muttered Evander. "Come on. Have to get higher."

As they climbed, the floors were more devastated. Gaps above let in more light. The floors were broken out in many rooms. The stairwell remained firm, however.

The micklebear followed, slowly but steadily squeezing its enormous bulk into the stairwell and ascending in pursuit. It virtually filled the space and was climbing with all four limbs.

If they went too high, they'd be trapped.

Evander called to Serena and pointed down a ruined corridor. It ran directly to a distant wall, and there was a black space there. The floor was filled with small gaps, and the stones were loose.

She looked up and realized that the stairwell would remain strong enough to support the monster, and they would have nowhere to go to get away from it at the top, where the building frayed away.

They ran, eyes searching for breaks in the floor, once or twice driving a foot through a rotten place and having to be helped out by the other. At the end was a dark hole in the wall. A space beyond it was filled with the unknown.

A roar from behind announced the arrival of their nemesis. The building shuddered again, and for a moment Evander thought it might collapse as the micklebear tried to squeeze itself into the passage. Then the floor gave way, and it was forced to cling to the stairwell entrance, snarling in frustration.

Evander ducked through the hole into the darkness. The

smell inside was vaguely familiar, but he could not pin it down. "Come on," he whispered.

The micklebear was trying to force itself backward out of the stairwell—a task more difficult than the ascent. It roared in frustration and shook the building.

Serena joined him in the dark. "That smell," she said. "It's familiar, but I can't place it."

"Me, neither."

"What are we going to do?"

"I don't really know. Try to find Perspax. We've got to get away from this place."

They went on down a long passage. At some point Evander got the notion that they were being watched. He felt the hairs stand on the back of his neck. Something was out there.

"There's a little light up ahead," said Serena.

He noticed it, too, a paleness in the dark ahead.

They hurried toward it. Evander had the knife out, ready to engage whatever it was that followed them. They came upon a broken doorway leading to a balcony. Below the balcony was a large courtyard, surrounded by the walls of an old, but well-built tenement. The courtyard had filled up with debris, now covered in the omnipresent dust of Orthond. In one corner was a pond of dank water.

Evander estimated that the drop from the balcony down to the ground was only seven or eight feet.

He swung a leg over the ruined rail. Serena was not so sure.

"It's a long way down."

"Not that far." He dropped down and felt his boots impact the semihard surface and absorb the shock. It was easy.

"Jump," he hissed.

Serena looked down and closed her eyes for a moment. When she opened them, she didn't hesitate. He tried to catch her, but although he broke her fall, he was knocked off his feet. They both landed on their backsides with a thud.

He pulled her to her feet.

"My hero," she said sarcastically, and they both found the energy to laugh.

There were no micklebears in the courtyard. But the one

they'd left in the other building was having more suecess
extricating itself.

"We mustn't give up, right?"

"Give up? Never, Princess."

They crossed the courtyard. On the far side the buildings
had fallen, and there were just remnants of the lower walls
and piles of rubble. Here and there were harsh clumps of
thorn bushes. The rest was lost in the mists, which were
thickening again, carrying the stench of burned stone. Perspax had said the stench came from the gigantic mines of
the Dominator.

Ahead was a low ridgeline built of rubbled brick. A ruined tower was briefly visible beyond it. Evander and Serena set out for the tower.

Skulking through the tumbled tenements they kept a
keen eye out for some sign of Perspax. They didn't dare
call out in case it brought one of the monsters down on
them. Evander had to fight off a sense of panic when he
thought of losing contact with the Eleem. Everything he
had seen of this world had been horrendously dangerous.
They knew virtually nothing about the place. Without the
Eleem, their chances would diminish sharply.

The rubble ridge was cut by an alleyway. It seemed the
quickest way through the mounds. The buildings along the
alley had survived in part, their lower floors at least. This
had kept the alley open. They went past gaping doorways
all jammed with broken brick. Knee-deep pools of water
filled the alley in places and had to be waded through. They
were going to have to sit down and rest soon, preferably
somewhere warm, or they were just going to collapse.

Evander wondered dully why they had ever left the Neild
settlement. They had been wonderfully comfortable there.

The alleyway seemed to be sinking deeper into the
ground. It was dark farther ahead. Mushrooms grew between the cracks, everywhere.

"I don't like this, Evander," Serena whispered.

"But it's the quickest way through. We'll have to climb
otherwise."

"Let's climb." She was adamant, and rather than argue
about it, he allowed himself to be swayed. They turned
about and made their way cautiously back to the point
where the alley petered out. They started to make their way
up the rubble hill. Thorn bushes grew out of a depression in

the side of the hill. Thick mists whipped across the scene, and visibility was down to a few yards.

They had climbed some fifty feet when Evander slipped on a damp brick and started a small landslide. The rubble downslope added itself to the moving mass and soon a medium-sized slide crashed down into the lower areas with a roaring sound. A pall of dust went up in the aftermath, and silence gripped the scene.

Then, straight out of the cloud of dust, poked the head of a micklebear. With a scream of triumph, it started up the slope in pursuit.

With sinking hearts they tried to stay ahead of it, but they were so weak now, and it was much better at climbing than they. Evander realized it would have them in no time if they climbed. He pulled Serena off along the side of the slope, aiming for a place thick with thorn bushes. Narrow gaps between the bushes allowed just enough room for him and Serena to crawl through on hands and knees. They scooted along and emerged on the far side of the thorn bushes.

The micklebear was working up the slope to get around the barrier presented by the stout thorn bushes. They kept on along the slope, leaning into it to keep their balance. Quite abruptly, it was cut through by another alleyway—a near vertical drop of thirty feet into a pool of dark water that had filled up the alley here.

"How deep do you think it is?" asked Serena.

"I don't think it matters." He grabbed her and kissed her, hard.

The micklebear was on top of them.

"I love you, Serena of Monjon."

It was reaching for them with those long arms when he jumped, carrying her with him, dropping free. Her scream rent the air until it was cut off by the water. They went down, and he felt the bottom strike his feet, hard, but not hard enough to break bones.

They rebounded and found themselves on the surface, gasping for air. The water was very cold, not far from freezing.

Thwarted, the micklebear filled the alley with its screams of rage.

"Are you all right?" he gasped.

She nodded. "I think so."

They hauled out onto a slime-covered ledge of dressed stone that ran ten feet below the ruined top of a massively built wall.

"Where to now?" she asked.

He glanced upward. The micklebear had gone, retracing its steps with anxious speed back to the bottom of the mound. If it could trap them in this alley, they'd be easily taken.

"We go on; it's not giving up."

They shuffled along the ledge, which had once supported a course of much larger stones. After fifty yards they reached a place where rubble had spilled from above to block the alley and allow the water to build up into the deep pool. They had to scramble over this and slide down the other side where the alley had been obliterated for a space, and there was a deep pit. Their ledge continued, with the pit falling away on their right. Beyond the farther edge of the pit a section of the old alley was still intact.

A few strides farther on, Evander slipped on moss and would have gone over the side if Serena hadn't managed to grab him when his fingers were scrabbling for purchase on the slick stone. She held on as he got a handhold.

Behind them they heard the sounds of their pursuer. It was coming down the alley, hidden from them by the mound of debris. The pit would hold it up, but not for long. Evander had a grim feeling that this time they were really trapped. It might have been better if the water had been only a few inches deep and they'd not survived the drop.

He called out for Perspax in desperation, but his cry merely echoed mockingly off the ruined walls and was instantly overwhelmed by a gleeful roar from the micklebear.

They came to a place where the great wall had recessed once, probably into a large entranceway. Corner stones rose up above them for twenty feet before being cut off like the rest of the outer wall. The entranceway was filled with tightly packed brick and rubbish—no way through there. They would have to go on.

The micklebear came into view, already climbing out of the pit. It had seen them.

They ducked into the recessed place. It was dark. The micklebear would be on them in a few moments. Serena leaned back against the wall, her eyes empty.

"I can't think of anything else we can do. We don't have any weapons. There's nowhere to go to get away from it."

Evander gripped the knife tightly, but he knew how futile it would be against a brute like a micklebear.

"You could kill me; that would be a mercy," she said quietly.

The monster was out of the pit.

Evander stared at the knife, then at Serena. It was the only thing to do. Kill her and then kill himself. Could he bring himself to do it?

Serena had shut her eyes and put her hands over her ears.

The heavy tread was close. He drew back his arm, preparing to thrust home the blade, tears filling his eyes.

There was a sudden touch on his arm. He almost jumped out of his boots.

A small figure stood forth from the recessed shadow. A door had opened silently behind them. It was a Neild wearing a flat metal helmet and carrying a sword. The shock of its appearance had left him dumb.

It made a motion with one hand. A universal movement that said "come with me."

The monster was on them.

There was no time to dally. Evander pulled Serena along and stepped into pitch darkness. Behind them he glimpsed the huge head of the predator swing down into the recessed space.

Then the door swung shut, leaving them in cool darkness. Outside, the micklebear screamed in rage and attacked the stones of the ancient wall.

"What happened?" Serena asked, taking a breath.

Evander hugged her tightly. "Someone saved us. Neild; I saw one."

A pale light shone into the space suddenly as a door opened. They saw a figure silhouetted in the doorway, the Neild in martial costume. Then it beckoned to them and vanished.

"Different kind of Neild, I think."

Serena had found a final reserve of energy. "Come on," she said.

They slipped through the second door. It swung shut behind them.

Chapter Thirty

A dark cloth was removed from a lantern, and yellow light spilled over them. Around them stood a dozen Neild, all wearing chain mail and blackened steel helmets, a few with spikes projecting from the top. Some held spears, others just their swords. Their resemblance to turtles and beavers was much reduced. They seemed more like short, plump men of war, except for their gargoyle faces.

"Thank you," said Evander in Furda, his voice shaking a little. "You saved our lives. We are indebted to you."

Evander's words brought hissing from the Neild, who shook their turtlelike heads vigorously and put fingers to their mouths to command silence.

Evander swallowed. The monster outside was still venting its rage against the wall. It was not to be encouraged by any sound from within. He nodded to show he understood. Serena did, too; they exchanged a long look.

The silence continued. The Neild studied them for a long minute or so. The micklebear continued to roar and scream and pound on the stones, but they were too strong and well cemented for even one of that brutish kind.

Then one of the spiked helmets moved over to a screen and pulled it aside to reveal a narrow entrance. Through this they exited, with the spiked-helmet Neild in front, carrying the lantern, and the other Neild behind, carrying their spears.

In silence they wound their way along a narrow, curving passage that had been bored through the tightly packed brick rubble. There was a rank smell, like that of many animals packed together tightly.

Eventually, the passage opened up into a room that had small wheelbarrows stacked along the wall. It was hard to see much in the darkness, but the walls seemed covered in equipment, rakes, shovels, and the like. An earthy smell invaded their nostrils. They went on into larger rooms in which tier upon tier of flats rose up around them, each filled with beds of mushrooms. Neild, dimly visible, with panniers over their shoulders, worked in the mushroom gardens. The earthy odor was strong.

More rooms followed in this underground warren, like a village carved into the depths of the rubble pile. There were numerous Neild, but not so many as there had been at the oasis on the flats. Nor were these Neild as plump. Clearly, survival here was a struggle.

At length they entered some very well-appointed rooms that boasted lanterns in the corners, textured wall hangings, fine Neild furniture, and giant pots. In one of these rooms they were introduced to several ancient Neild wearing blue satin coats and red slippers. Their faces were lined, and their eyes seemed to droop in their huge sockets. For a few moments the Neild and the prince and princess stared at each other. Evander wondered if he and Serena were supposed to bow and scrape. A polite murmur came from the Neild. One ancient, wearing a golden plate hung from his neck, stepped toward them and held out what was clearly a large skull. Evander noted, the hair rising on his neck, that the skull was that of an Eleem—furthermore, that it was glowing slightly.

The ancient continued to push the skull at them. As if to ward it off, Evander instinctively raised a hand, and it accidentally brushed against the skull.

"Welcome" said a voice in his head. He heard it as clearly as if someone had spoken aloud. There was a mental contact, and then it was broken as his hand moved away. Evander once more felt the hair on his neck stand up.

Again the glowing Eleem skull was pushed toward them. Feeling somewhat apprehensive, he touched it lightly with his fingers. It glowed more brightly, and he felt the thought of the other at once. "Welcome, strangers-to-our-world. We regret the condition in which you find it."

Evander composed a thought, a conscious reply. "We thank you. We have been transported to your world by a strange accident occasioned by a clash of powerful magics. We are seeking a way to return to our home."

"And where is your home?"

"I do not know how to tell you that. All I can say is that it is not in this world."

"Yes, we can tell that you are not of Orthond. Nor do you appear to be creatures of our great enemy."

"Indeed, we are not."

"So why were you searching for your home in the ruins here of old Putchad?"

"We weren't, really. We were following an Eleem."

Evander felt a sudden chill in the other's thought.

"What do you mean, 'following'?"

"He saved our lives when we had first arrived here; he killed a thing with many legs that would have attacked us. Then we went with him out onto the flats."

"A Seeker?"

"A high one of the Miggenmorch?" Evander caught this thought from one of the others, who reached out and touched the skull.

The glow intensified.

They wanted an answer.

"I do not know. He was from Canax, he said."

"Canax?"

The Neild hand was pulled back, and the other thought fell away. The glow subsided.

"What's going on?" Serena nudged him in the ribs.

"When you touch that skull, you can hear them. And they can hear your thoughts somehow, maybe in the same way the Eleem do. It's uncanny."

"These aren't like the other Neild at all."

The long horselike skull was held out again. Evander touched it and heard their thought once more.

"You crossed the flats?"

"Yes. We went to a place where Neild, like yourselves, had made a fertile land. They were very generous to us."

The Neild spoke among themselves in feverish voices. The overtones grew strange. Two more blue-coated Neild touched the skull.

"You saw servile Neild? You saw them welcome the Eleem Lord?"

"Yes."

The thought grew chill, then sardonic. "You will not see such a welcome here."

"Yes, I understand."

"We are free Neild."

Another touched the skull; he wore the blue coat, with small decorations of gold and silver worked on the breast.

"We watched you for a long time as you tried to escape the micklebear."

Evander remembered that feeling of being watched in the dark places, and the smell that at the time he could not place, but now knew had been that of Neild.

"We were not sure whether we could trust you with the knowledge of our existence."

Evander wondered why it had to be secret.

Other Neild hands reached out to the skull. "We are still not sure we can trust you."

Taken aback, Evander murmured, "We can be trusted. We will keep your secret."

"You were found by a Seeker. He will read of our existence in your thought. You do not shield your thought."

"Perspax would not harm you," protested Evander. "I know him. I have never felt evil in him."

The thoughts did not warm.

"He is a Breeder Lord. We are free Neild. He will not welcome our existence."

"Well, you can be assured I don't know how to find this place, so reading my thought won't help him locate you."

He sensed confusion.

"My point exactly," said the thought of the first voice, the Neild with the gold plate. "Where was the Eleem taking you? Did he tell you your destination?"

"Canax."

"Then he was taking you to the wise one there, to Shadreiht."

"That name is familiar."

"The Eleem was a Seeker," said the thought of another voice.

"But he is also a Breeder Lord. Do you want them back?"

"The Seekers will not harm us. They know the world has changed. We must ally with them if we are ever to defeat the great enemy."

"A Breeder Lord. They will be here to demand our love."

"We will not give love in the old way. We will give alliance only, as equals."

The arguers withdrew and muttered among themselves. At this point three elderly female Neild, wearing pale blue satin coats and black lacquered shoes, moved to the front.

One of them held the Eleem skull. The others joined their hands to hers as she extended it to the couple.

Evander touched the other end.

"You are exhausted," said a new voice, more friendly than the old males.

"You're right, we're close to collapse."

"We will shelter you. Take food, then sleep. Later we will discuss what to do."

"Thank you."

Evander and Serena were shown to a bustling kitchen area and seated at a small table. Neild carrying baskets of fungus over their shoulders trod past into the storehouses. Neild of both sexes bustled about the kitchen in leather aprons and white leggings.

A young female brought jugs of water and a strongly flavored bread tasting of fried mushrooms. Evander and Serena ate and drank in silence while Neild constantly came and went, their clogs clattering on the floors.

When they had taken off the raw edge of hunger, they talked, secure in the knowledge that no one could understand them in this place. Serena had overcome her worst fears. These Neild, although so different from the "good Neild" they had known earlier, did not seem to wish them any harm. They realized that they could only trust the Neild and see what developed. Soon their exhaustion had their heads down on the table, and they fell asleep where they sat.

Neild came and took them away on stretchers. They were undressed and placed on pallets in a small room, behind a thick wooden door. A pair of guards took up positions outside the door.

When they awoke, there were basins of hot water and another meal of the mushroom bread, washed down with a pleasantly bitter drink, not unlike bitterleaf tea. Their clothes had been laundered and ironed while they slept.

Later, clean and refreshed by several hours of sleep, plus two meals, they were escorted back to the ceremonial rooms. The group of blue-coated Neild had been joined by another group wearing coats of other colors, some light blue, some pink, some yellow.

The aged one with the gold plate on its chest held out the Eleem skull. "Welcome, Evander, stranger-to-our-world."

"Thank you, aged master."

They both bowed.

"You came here with an Eleem Lord. Where is he?"

"We were running from the micklebears. We were separated before we reached the ruins."

"So you do not know where he is?"

"Correct."

"We do not serve the Breeder Lords anymore. We are free Neild."

"Yes, I can see that."

"We do not wish to meet with the Eleem. Their power over us is still very great."

"They could protect you. Isn't that their job?"

Again there was that chill in the other's thought. "No. That is the old way they enslaved us. We served them for a thousand generations, but they failed us. With their quarrels and their treachery they let the great enemy in. Once it had established itself, it destroyed us. And remember that it was Neild that built the beauty of the world, not Eleem. Their skill was always in the breeding of animals, especially of Neild. They couldn't even design these buildings that we built for them. When we were first bred to the consciousness of speech, the Eleem still lived in caves. No, we will not go back to them. We are free Neild now, and there are many of us, spread throughout the ruins. We wait for the day to rise and destroy the great enemy."

"What do you intend to do?"

"We have found a way to enter his domain in secret."

"By telling me this, you have made me dangerous to you, if I understand you correctly. Do you intend to kill us?"

"No. You will go back to your Eleem Lord. We want the Seekers to know that we have a way to reach the enemy. We need the help of the Seekers, but we fear the power over us that any Eleem has."

Genuine fear pervaded the other's thought. Evander began to understand. He had seen the utterly slavish Neild of the oasis. They had wriggled like puppies for the Eleem. Perhaps, even now, these Neild feared that in the presence of an Eleem Lord, they would become cringing slaves once again, "good Neild" as Perspax would have it.

"I understand, I have seen that power."

For a long moment the Neild and he gazed at each other. Then it sighed. "You will be taken to a place near where the Eleem Lord is lying up."

Evander gasped; so they did know where Perspax was. They had been testing him for truthfulness.

"He is accompanied by a tiny blue white demon, which flits around him at a tremendous pace. Do you have any idea as to what this demon is? Is it harmful? It appears peaceful, at least so far. We are much puzzled by it."

Evander swallowed. How to explain the bizarre appearance of Konithomimo? "It is a magic spirit being, at least that is the best description I think I can come up with. It is the spirit of a great piece of magic. On my world that spirit inhabited a carpet that could fly through the air. When we were transported to your world, we were actually flying on that carpet, and it came with us. However, on your world, the magic was altered for some reason, and the spirit was no longer a carpet, but appeared as a miniature person in the form you have seen."

He sensed astonishment. More conversation in Neild, and the entire room grew excited.

"This spirit, is it controllable? Will it help you if you ask it to do something?"

Evander shrugged. "It might, though it has a mind of its own. It does seem to have formed an attachment with the Eleem. Perhaps it would do as he asked."

Another long moment of silence followed. Then a whispered conversation in Neild.

"We have decided that you must go to Shadreiht. Tell him what you have witnessed here. Tell him that we, the free Neild of Putchad, have found a way to reach the lair of the Dominator, Waakzaam. Tell him that we need the aid of the small blue creature. Tell Shadreiht that we wish to meet with him, only with him. We will not meet with any other Eleem."

"How will he give you a reply?"

"He will send us his answer in writing. He will use the old master's language. An Eleem can bring it to Putchad and place it on the grand piazza in a bottle. We will fetch it in at night and replace it with our answer."

Evander felt the Neild's fear of the Eleem. "I will tell them."

Chapter Thirty-one

Following directions from the free Neild, they came upon Perspax, curled up in a piece of broken statue of heroic proportions like a nut inside a shell. So fully asleep was he that he did not sense them until they shook him awake.

He came then alive like a steel spring. An enormous knife, grooved for poison, appeared in his hand like magic. The big slate-colored eyes were fixed on them, wide and sharp. For a moment enormous danger hung in the air. Then recognition bloomed, and the oddly horselike face broke into an Eleem smile.

"Ah, hah! You came back! I knew you were alive. I could sense you were still here, but I could not locate you precisely."

"We were underground."

"That explains it then; it is very hard to trace thoughts through the ground."

Clearly very curious, Perspax looked them over, but did not pry into their thoughts, as that would have been discourteous now that he knew them so well.

"I am glad to see you looking well rested and recently fed. How is this possible?"

"We were sheltered by some Neild. They have excavated a village down there; it's quite amazing. They say they are free Neild."

"Free Neild?" Evander heard sharp disapproval in the voice of the Eleem.

"Yes, they live beneath this very ground, tunneled throughout these ruins. They carry weapons and wear armor."

Perspax stared around him uneasily. He had known the so-called free Neild were growing in number, but he had not expected them here in old Putchad. Micklebear and multipede had ruled the place for a long time. This was a surprise.

"They treated you well?" he asked. His control of Furda had grown with use.

"Very well; they gave us food and water and a safe place to sleep. In that, they were much like the other Neild. There was a very different tone, however. They really are free Neild."

Perspax's face stretched in an expression of discontent. "I am relieved to hear that they knew their duty and performed it by serving you well. That they refused to acknowledge myself or to pay their respects, I find harder to bear. They are not good Neild."

"They admit that; in fact they insisted it was true. They serve only themselves now, they say."

"They are not good Neild!" said the Eleem with increasing vehemence. He raved for a moment in another tongue, high words of great emotion.

Serena squeezed Evander's hand. Her eyes were filled with concern. Was the Eleem all right? Evander tried to indicate his unconcern. The Eleem would recover his stability any moment.

After a few wild-eyed seconds Perspax brought himself under control.

"They want us to go to Shadreiht," continued Evander. "They also say they want to meet with him, and him alone."

"They wish to meet with the wise one? They ask much for Neild, especially wild Neild, beyond the hand of the benevolent trainer." Passion rose in his voice.

"They will not meet with any other Eleem."

Perspax ranted again in his own tongue, then broke back into accentless Furda. "Deep down I am sure it is different. Deep down I must believe that these Neild still love the Eleem. They are rebellious children, that is all. Some day, when the enemy has been defeated and Orthond restored, we shall reconcile with the poor, battered Neild. Terrible has been their suffering, hideous the death toll. Nine out of ten have gone to the bellies of the creatures of the enemy. Those that survive are troubled.

"They feel that we, their protectors, the Lords Eleem, did fail them. And in truth, they are right. However, that cannot change the order of things. Long ago the Eleem made the Neild to serve them and beautify the world. In time they will see the inevitability of their position. They will return to their calling. We shall overlook their insolence."

Evander met the Eleem's fierce gaze. "I think they will not serve the Eleem ever again."

Perspax swelled a moment. "They will not serve the Eleem? Then they are not good Neild!"

"Well, that may be true. But they also claim to have discovered a way to get to your enemy. They want to discuss this with Shadreiht. They also want Konithomimo to help them. They think he could be very important."

Perspax straightened up at this news and stared at them for a long moment. He took a deep breath. "What?"

"That is what they said. They wish to talk with Shadreiht, alone. And this is what they plan to tell him."

For a long moment Perspax struggled with this information, then he surrendered to it. "Great news!" He shrugged his huge Eleem shoulders. "Except for the last part. Konithomimo has no love for the Neild." He shrugged again. "Konithomimo dislikes many things, especially Orthond."

"We'll put it to him that this is the best way for him to get back to our own world."

"Ah, yes, to return to your own world, Ryetelth. He has expressed himself to me many times upon that subject. He admitted to some confusion. He dislikes Orthond intensely, yet is not sure that he wants to go back to being a rug, having to carry you and others like you around until he's exhausted."

Evander and Serena exchanged glances. It sounded like the little rug man all right.

"I wondered how long he might take to begin to think like that," murmured Serena.

"Oh, he has thought about it a great deal," said Perspax. "However, I think that his dislike of Orthond is even greater than his dislike of life as a rug, and so he might be persuaded to help. Against this course, in his eyes, will be his unfortunate feelings toward the Neild. It is quite irrational, and I told him so, but he appears to harbor a tremendous loathing of the little handy folk."

"Oh, no!" cried Serena. "And I suppose the little monster ran away again. Which is why he isn't here to criticize us."

Perspax nodded slowly. He knew as well as they that if Konithomimo were present, he would be complaining about something.

"Yes."

"He usually comes back," said Serena. "We'll just wait for him, I suppose."

Perspax raised a problem with that at once. "We cannot wait here for very long. You are too easily traced by micklebear. In fact, it would be best if we were to leave the vicinity immediately."

"Micklebear can find us here?" asked Serena.

"Yes."

She and Evander exchanged a look.

"Let's go then. Konithomimo will find us if he wants to. He always has before." Neither Evander nor Serena was prepared to risk micklebear again if they could avoid it.

For himself, Perspax was sure that Konithomimo was immune to the perils of fallen Orthond, except, of course, for the great enemy himself, who was unlikely to be seen outside Orthontower. Konithomimo was much too fast for either micklebear or multipede. Perspax could leave the little monstrosity here and not be concerned for him. His first priority was to remove the prince and the princess to safety.

Accordingly, he led them out of the ruins into the gulleyed lands that head up quickly to the hills around Canax. In the gulleys and canyons there was less danger of micklebear, but there were numerous multipedes, orthoraphs, and small blegs and biters.

The ruins of Putchad fell behind them, and as they were in gulleys most of the time, they lost sight of them completely. Quite quickly, they found themselves in the foothills and passed many ruined monuments of the old culture of Orthond.

They saw multipedes, again and again, and were harassed by a pack of small biters, ratlike things that could kill and eat children, especially if they found them asleep. Evander threw stones at them, and after scoring a few hits, drove them away. The multipedes left them alone, not wishing to encounter an armed Eleem. Eventually, they left the evil creatures behind as they climbed onto the plateau. Here the creatures were much less numerous, and for good reason. They were hunted and destroyed by the Eleem, who were hidden here in the ruins.

At Gebizon they passed below the broken spires. At Palemorx they walked along the remains of the once mighty walls. They climbed the stairs of the ancient hill lords to the vaults of Canax. All were long since smashed and looted by the minions of the Dominator, but hidden amidst them was the fortress of Sklees, and this the enemy had never found.

Amidst a jumble of broken stones, some the size of boulders, they slipped into a hidden space. The Eleem led them into a long dark passageway that bent again and again, first left and then right. The passage narrowed. Suddenly, lantern light fell on them. A pair of Eleem wearing armor plate, swords in hand, appeared before them.

Perspax had been anticipated, the guards merely following the routine precautions, in case they had been trailed by a stray multipede.

A third Eleem appeared out of the dark. He wore little armor and carried no sword. "Perspax of Xerranon, greetings!" he said.

Perspax bent the knee and bowed low to this unarmed Eleem. He spoke in the formal tongue of Orthond.

"My lord, I have brought back the visitors that I spoke to you about."

"I see. We have been eagerly awaiting their arrival. There is much we can learn from them, I am sure."

"I found them on the far side of the flats. We came back by the direct path across the center."

"Remarkable! How did you carry enough water?"

"We did not. We had little to carry in the first place. But there are Neild in the very center of the wastes. Good Neild, and they are begging for lordship."

"Good Neild! That is wonderful to hear. We will make contact at once. Good Neild are to be treasured."

Their thoughts touched. Perspax passed on some aspects of the language Furda to his commander. Switching to Furda, he introduced Evander and Serena. They bowed. The Eleem bowed back.

"This is Kobbox of Pelgil, the greatest Seeker of all Canax, a lord of the Miggenmorch."

Taking the Furda words from Perspax's thought, Kobbox addressed them in similar, accentless Furda. "Welcome to Orthond, Princess Serena and Evander. I regret the inconveniences you have had to endure on your journey to our fortress. But, as you are aware, we are engaged in a long struggle with our most dreadful enemy. He has devastated our world, and we operate now in much reduced circumstances."

"Are you reading our thoughts now?" asked Serena.

"Not in the least, Princess. I am taking the words of your mellifluous language from the Seeker Perspax."

"I am unaccustomed to such invasions of the mind. On our world it is unknown, except to wizards, perhaps."

"Ah, yes, your world; we are eager to learn all we can of your world."

Evander felt a twinge of unease at the eagerness he detected in the other's words.

Kobbox drew them down the passageway. "Come, it is time to enter the fortress of Sklees. You are tired and worn. When you are clean and refreshed, we will take you to see the ancient one. He has expressed a desire to meet with you as soon as possible."

Chapter Thirty-two

Within thirty minutes they were ready, fresh from a plunge pool of cold water and a quick meal of wafers smeared with a salty paste.

They followed Kobbox through the adits that led to Shadreiht's shadowy lair, deep within the hidden fortress. Perspax brought up the rear.

The place was huge and cold. Evander wondered how it could have remained a secret so long. At one point, when they crossed a wider space, a central node of some kind, and were walking in line abreast, Evander turned to Perspax and asked this question.

The Eleem turned briefly to him. There was something slightly baleful in his look. "That is a secret that I am not at liberty to divulge."

Evander understood that he would learn no more from Perspax, and he fell silent.

They passed other Eleem during this journey, and at one point they saw their first female Eleem. A group of five females wearing long, loose gowns of brown and gray were sorting through a cart of cloths of brighter hue. Evander noted that the horselike heads were narrower than the male pattern. The bones were less robust, and the graceful qualities of all Eleem were even more pronounced.

Other females were later glimpsed, but they were few and far between. Indeed, there were not that many Eleem to be seen at all. The hidden fortress was surprisingly empty, at least when compared to the bustling hidden village of the free Neild.

At length they came to a suite of rooms, clearly the apartment of an important person. The furnishings were sparse, but built on a heroic scale. On the walls were Neild tapestries of great artistry depicting scenes from the agricultural round of old Orthond. Under the watchful eyes of

Eleem Lords, good Neild worked the land. Other scenes showed Neild netting wild creatures by the banks of a brook.

Within the largest room stood a single dais, on which sat an elderly Eleem wrapped in a white sheet. His face was illuminated by a single lamp that glowed at the base of the dais. The eyes of the Eleem met their gaze, and in their depths Evander felt a gentle soul, a mind brimming with the accumulated wisdom of a very long life. Evander wondered briefly what this ancient saw in the pair of scruffy princelings from Ryetelth who had been brought before him.

A bench was brought out for them to sit on. Perspax and Kobbox sat on another bench. They waited expectantly. A long moment passed in complete silence.

Suddenly, in a soft, husky voice, the sage spoke, and he spoke in Furda, as had the other Eleem, who plucked the words from their minds.

"Welcome, strangers-to-Orthond. You have come a long way, much farther than any have ever come before in order to see Shadreiht of Sklees. I am honored by your presence. I have many questions to ask of you, just as I expect you have many questions to ask of me."

Evander and Serena exchanged a brief glance.

"We thank you for your welcome," said Serena, who then lost her head and rattled on. "In fact, we desperately need your help. We're trapped here in this awful place and we want to go home." She put a hand to her mouth. "I'm sorry, you must think I'm horribly rude."

Evander sensed only a gentle amusement in the ancient Eleem.

"Not at all child; I know that you need help. You want to return to your own world. Rest assured that I will do my utmost to assist you. And perhaps you will be able to help my world, which as you know is in great need of help."

"We would be glad to."

"Good. But first, perhaps you might relate the events that led up to your first appearance on Orthond. There is much I need to know."

Serena explained all that had happened and what she understood of the magical cataclysm that had hurled herself and Evander to this other world.

"You see, it's well known in Monjon that great magic

performed close to where the blessed Thymnal lies is fraught with peril. The wizard ignored this, and instead of slaying Evander, his energies drove both of us from our world to yours in the wink of an eye."

Shadreiht was silent for a long minute after she finished. When he spoke it was with a great weariness. "You are also afflicted with evil wizards then, on your world?"

"Oh yes, Master Shadreiht, I'm afraid we are."

"But the wizard that has destroyed our world is the most terrible that has ever existed, at least to my knowledge."

The cold winds scoured dead Orthond outside the hidden fortress. In their high wail was the cry of lost multitudes. Shadreiht paused again, the withered horse face stilling abruptly, losing all animation for a moment and then reviving.

"Your story, child, sounds like something fit for the books of fables that so vivify the minds of our young. I salute your courage in refusing to accept your fate.

"And I must praise your companion, the gallant Evander of Sedimo Kassim. There is much courage in that young heart. Princess Serena, you are fortunate in having such a companion. Evander, you are young, but already you have learned much of the treachery of the world. I sense that you are no friend of wizards."

"None, sir, though, well . . ." Evander fell silent. He forbore to mention that for all he knew, Shadreiht was a wizard himself. In fact, the distinction between Shadreiht and other sorcerers was less than obvious.

Shadreiht understood the youth's confusion and was not angered. "Fear not, my friend; I am no great conjurer of the dark arts. What powers I have are weak and depend on subtlety for their consummation. You are safe here. Certainly old Shadreiht shall not harm you."

Ashamed, Evander spoke quickly. "I apologize, sir, for my unworthy suspicion. I put myself at your service and only hope that I can help you in some way in your struggle."

"We will see about that. The situation grows complex. I have detected strange swirls of fate in the patterns of the great sphereboard. But now, Princess Serena, please tell me more of this fascinating object you described that catapulted you from your own world to mine."

"The blessed Thymnal?"

"The same."

Taking a deep breath, Serena gave a brief description of the popular conception of the blessed Thymnal, ending with a warm, familiar thought. "The Thymnal has blessed the city of Monjon for many years, and the city has prospered greatly in that time."

Once more Shadreiht pondered a while. "The magical object is kept hidden?"

"Oh yes, Master Shadreiht, it is never seen except by the priests. Its radiance is used for many things, from curing the sick and the lame to illuminating the famous lamps of Monjon."

"Lamps?"

"Yes, the rays of the Thymnal invigorate water which is then poured into glass globes of various sizes. After being exposed to the Thymnal, this water glows, for many, many years. These lamps, in many sizes, have been spread all over our part of the world."

"Ah, I see. This manifestation is a leak from some higher plane of being, the energies involved strong. Tell me, now, I think you said that it also causes the city itself to float in the air."

"Oh, indeed, it does. Monjon is the only floating city in the world."

"Most mysterious; such power is inexplicable."

"No one truly understands the Thymnal, not even the priests. The speculations concerning its nature fill whole libraries in the temple. It will never be understood."

"Do you think it is a manifestation of your Gods?"

Serena shrugged. "I do not know such things. The priests claim that it is holy, but I'm not sure. Our Gods are very old, older by far than the Thymnal. Perhaps they made it, but they never explained why. The priests of the Thymnal's cult are greedy and well fed; there seems little that is holy about them. It is all very confusing."

Shadreiht sympathized. "Indeed, the world is a tissue of confusions. Why, I ask myself, was poor Orthond chosen for destruction? Our world was a model for others. We had abandoned warfare. Our culture was high and graceful, the arts of our Neild wondrous to behold. Of all the many worlds that dwell in the universe, why was ours taken? Why did the enemy manage to find us? Why were our lives destroyed and our lovely Neild devoured?"

Shadreiht paused a moment, as if overcome by sadness. Evander imagined the big horse eyes moistening.

Shadreiht continued, but his voice was unmistakably husked by strong emotions. "Perhaps it was a punishment from our own Gods, who we abandoned long ago. Some say it was the mere caprice of chance, and that it had nothing to do with us or our behavior. A smaller group say it was a curse laid on us by the dying Gods of Orthond, whom we had long since usurped and forgotten. We grew complacent in a lovely land and were laid low in the end because we had forgotten the need for humility."

The old Eleem turned its equine head aside, the eyes seeming to stare off into a dead infinity.

Now Evander spoke. "From the Seeker, Perspax, who saved our lives many times over, we have learned a little concerning the Dominator, this wizard Waakzaam. I am curious about him."

Shadreiht seemed to shrink at the mention of the enemy's name, and he closed his eyes. When he opened them again, he spoke in a voice of ashes. "Many are the worlds that tremble beneath his heel. Twelve worlds in all, he boasts. Imagine that, child, a creature that bestrides a dozen worlds, peopled with his slaves and nothing else."

Serena shivered inwardly while striving to keep an outward calm. The wizard in Monjon was bad enough, but even his power was limited to a single world. The monster that held Orthond in its claws was clearly of a greater order of existence. The universe of worlds was a more perilous place than the princess of Monjon had ever imagined when she was younger, and safer, and thought only of which fair prince might be her husband and which fine castle she might dwell in.

Shadreiht continued in a low voice. "We call him the Deceiver, for in the beginning he came to us with smiling face and pretty words. Alas, we were divided then and failed to understand our peril. He set us against one another, and we destroyed ourselves. That is the terrible irony of his success. He spoke to us with honeyed words, and we believed his fantasies of power and wealth and dominion over all other Eleem. 'Restore the power of the Orthontower!' he said, and we thought him wise. We even allowed him to arbitrate our disputes, so weak-witted were we. He spun pretty tales and we fought on, killing each other while he secretly built up his strength. Through great magic he brought creatures of his own to Orthond. In hidden pens they bred, and he begat an army of them. When we woke up at last to the danger, we were no longer strong enough to overthrow him. Our last great army was defeated, and we have not raised another. We have been hunted down like vermin and reduced to a bare handful. We scratch for existence beneath the stones."

Evander nodded for a moment. "And yet I think I feel a power here in your hidden fortress. I have become sensitive to wizardry, having suffered somewhat from it."

"Ah." Shadreiht's long equine head swung slowly. He had been informed of Evander's unhappy experiences and the bizarre skin that covered his torso. "You are keen in perception, Evander. Though you are insensitive to the thoughts of others on the nonverbal plane, you are bright enough in all other ways. Not to be underestimated, eh?"

"Still," said Evander, indicating his surroundings, "all this is hidden from your foe. It seems hard to understand, considering his powers."

"Well, you are correct. I expect you understand our secret. I, Shadreiht, keep this place hidden from him. Ever does his thought reach out to find me, and ever do I hide from him. I have that much strength. But compared to the Deceiver, I have no power. Ask yourself this, who rules Orthond? Is it Master Shadreiht sitting hidden in the dark of Canax? Or is it the Dominator wrapped in golden majesty within the Orthontower?"

Shadreiht closed his eyes for a moment.

"No, the world has passed on, child. The Eleem and their civilization is gone and will never return. Just another victim of the iron-shod will of the great enemy, who will go on to other worlds. He must constantly seek fresh worlds to conquer, for he is driven by the urge to expand his genocidal empire. Billions of lives has he taken, this affliction on the universe, this sore upon the very fabric of being, and billions more will he take if he can."

"Who is he? Where does he come from?"

"From the void, child. From some hell of deep and most horrid corruption. In truth, no one knows the answer to those questions, not at least on doomed Orthond. To us, he is named Waakzaam the Great, a disease to all hope, a curse to the worlds."

"Why does he do such wickedness? What urges him on?"

Shadreiht raised a hand eloquently. "We have pondered this question again and again. I believe he is driven by the knowledge of the implacable laws of his kind. If he stops expanding, then he will inevitably begin to contract and to lose power to others. So he must expand forever, extending his rule until either he be overborne by a yet greater power, or surprised by sudden death."

This thought spurred Evander's memory. He remembered the message he bore. "Well, to that end, perhaps I can bring you some good news. We were rescued from a micklebear in the ruins of Putchad by free Neild. They have a whole village buried there. They claimed to have found a way of reaching your enemy. They wish to meet with you, in private, with no other Eleem present, to discuss this information."

"Free Neild?" Shadreiht seemed displeased.

There was a short exchange between Shadreiht and Perspax in their native tongue. Their minds touched thereafter, and Shadreiht read all he needed to know.

Evander and Serena noted the universal distaste among Eleem for "free" Neild.

"These were not good Neild, you understand." Shadreiht grew very solemn. "We cannot give them countenance."

"Not even when they might have a way to assail the Dominator that has destroyed your world?"

Shadreiht hesitated, struggling within himself. "Not even then. It would set a bad precedent. We must have dealings with the Neild even after the Overlord has gone."

"Gone?" questioned Serena.

"He prepares to leave us. There is nothing left here for him except minerals, and his servants are busy extracting those. There are few Eleem or Neild left to slaughter and nothing left of our civilization to destroy. So he will leave us. He will exit the Orthontower for the last time through the black mirror that he keeps in a high chamber. For quite a while now, his eye has been directed elsewhere. Because of this, we have been able to probe his defenses, very discreetly, and discover much of his thought. He has discovered a skein of new worlds previously unknown to him. He wishes to explore and conquer them."

Serena shivered at this thought. Was Ryetelth among these "new worlds"?

"But if he was slain, then you might regain control of your world. You could end his depredations with a stroke." Evander was astonished that the Eleem had refused to meet the free Neild.

"You could negotiate later with the Neild. You could begin a new life," implored Serena.

Shadreiht closed his eyes, then he spoke as if reciting holy writ. "We made the Neild to serve us. You cannot ask us to set them free. They are animals, no more. We are the Eleem."

And, suddenly, Evander could see the fatal weakness that had been exploited by the enemy to bring down the Eleem. They were too rigid, too hidebound by their traditions and their ancient ways. Their world had been too perfect, too unchanging, and too dependent on the Neild.

He squeezed Serena's hand when he thought she would say something unconsidered. They exchanged a glance. Now was the time to be guarded, except that neither could be sure that Shadreiht was not reading their minds.

"Do you know where your great enemy intends to go next?"

"I do not. Such things are beyond the powers of old Shadreiht."

For a moment they stood in silence. Shadreiht gave a long, sorrowful sigh. Then he roused himself and moved, slowly, painfully off the stone plinth.

"In truth, I am getting too old for this stone I sit on. Your friend here, Perspax, is older than your own fathers, and yet to me he is a child. My heart grows heavy with the approach of death. I who was born amidst unsurpassable beauty will die beneath the ugliness of hell, like a rodent driven beneath the ground."

Again there was a silence. Shadreiht beckoned them to follow him. "Come, our talk has grown far too gloomy. All is not completely lost, I assure you. Let us take a small meal together. You must speak to me of your world. Tell me of its wide lands and wider oceans."

Chapter Thirty-three

In a narrow, darkened chamber, while Shadreiht ate a bowl of warm mush and half a small fruit, Evander and Serena told him stories about Ryetelth. It was cold, and they shivered despite the warm Neild-made clothing they wore. As they spoke, he divined their feelings of fear, loss, and homesickness. He sympathized. Like his own people, they had been violently dispossessed. Worse, they had been sent to Orthond.

Evander spoke first, and he told of the world as he had discovered it in his wanderings. He had covered a lot of ground since he had fled his homeland, accompanied by poor Kospero. The world, he had found, was much more than the gentle place described by his teachers in the palace school. Its beauty was tinged with tragedy and terror.

Alas, poor Kospero!

Still, as he went on, he painted a pretty enough picture of the oceans he had crossed. The Merassa sea, the Great Western Ocean, and the Indramatic, he had sailed on all of them. As he warmed to his subject, he recalled classroom learning and described the lands of the higher cultures, beginning with Kassim and the Bakan city states, for those he knew best. Then he proceeded to tell of the northern lands of Czardha, where dwelled a golden-haired folk who were perpetually at war with each other and the outside world. The saga of the Czardhan wars between the states of Lankessen and Hentilden was the longest poem ever created, and the fighting still continued, with occasional outbreaks of peace. Every year the poets and the singers gathered to add new verses to this extended list of woe.

Shadreiht nodded as he listened. The Czardhans had more than a little resemblance to the Eleem states in the good old days. Such quarrelsome states would be easily victimized by such as the Great Deceiver.

Later, while they sipped warm tea together, Serena described the tropical lands of Eigo where dark-skinned peoples had raised empires. She also told of the legendary lands of terror in the heart of the great continent where dwelled huge beasts from the primordial world. Shadreiht assembled a mental picture of the lands of Eigo, which sounded warmer and lusher than Orthond. He saw vast mountains, hot seething jungles, great savannahs and plains, a world of great beauty.

He marveled at their descriptions. The more he learned of the universe, the more Shadreiht learned humility.

Serena went on to speak of the distant Empire of the Rose in the far east, a society famous for its equal treatment of the sexes and its uncorrupt government. The emperor of that bizarre land actually served his people and ruled with absolute benevolence. Serena was at pains to point out that though everyone mocked the Cunfshoni people for allowing their women to share power in their society, it was the white ships of Cunfshon that effectively girdled the world.

Not to be outdone, Evander described his first sighting of some of those great ships. It had come during the voyage out of Molutna Ganga, fleeing the mercenary bounty hunters who were on his and Kospero's trail. To cross the Merassa, they'd taken passage on a three-masted bark, *Salut*.

The bark was a stoutly built vessel of two hundred tons, but when they passed through the fleet of white ships, it had simply been dwarfed. Vast pyramids of white canvas flew above gleaming white-painted walls higher than the cross trees on the bark's masts. These great ships, ten or twenty times the size of *Salut*, surged by under great press of sail, heading south and east for the Indramatic Ocean and their distant island home.

From the nearest of them had sounded a long, mournful foghorn, followed by a sharp high note. Along the rail stood a few sailors looking down at them as *Salut* passed behind. A last wave and they were gone, and *Salut* was left rocking as she rode through the greater vessel's bow waves.

Shadreiht had finished his tea. Their own was long gone, though Evander still felt a pleasing warmth in his body from it. He mentioned the sensation to Shadreiht.

"The tea is an invigorative," Shadreiht replied. "Like so many things, it was something that the Neild developed."

"Ah, yes, the Neild." Evander had been waiting for the chance to bring up the Neild again.

Shadreiht would not be drawn in, however; he shifted tack at once. "The world you described rings with beauty; I can hear it in your voices. Verily, believe me, it was once like that here in Orthond."

Serena broke down. "Oh, great Shadreiht, do you know of any way that we can return to our home?"

To Evander's great surprise, Shadreiht responded in the affirmative. "Yes," said Shadreiht. "The Deceiver wafts himself through the wild ether between the worlds. He performs this great magic with the aid of a black mirror that he keeps in the Orthontower. I have read his thought concerning this magic. He thinks himself immune to mind reading, but of late he has grown careless. He believes that all the sages of Orthond have perished. Lowly Shadreiht, dwelling like some rodent beneath the ground, has escaped his notice. He knows nothing of me or of my thought. But at times his thought has been clear to me, and I have heard his incantations to the mirror."

Evander and Serena were stunned, and yet hope quickened in their hearts.

"It is by this method of travel that he rules his empire of twelve worlds. It is also how he finds new worlds. If, somehow, we could enter the chamber in which the mirror is kept, we could send you back to your world."

Evander felt a chill run down his spine. "Then that means the enemy may already know of the existence of our world."

"Oh, yes, he does, and he intends to visit it himself."

Evander and Serena stared at each other aghast.

"We must warn our world!"

"Perhaps we could send you back through the black mirror."

"Then we can go!" exulted Evander.

"Alas, there is no way to arrive at the chamber alive. No force on Orthond could break into the Orthontower as it is now held."

"What do you mean?"

"It is guarded by a great army of his fell creatures. There are not enough Eleem in the world to make a single regiment, let alone the divisions that would be required to take the tower."

Evander's heart sank. "Then we are doomed," he said wearily, feeling all hope evaporate.

Serena was yet undaunted. "Tell me, dear Master Shadreiht, where lies the Orthontower?"

"Not that far from here; in fact, on the other side of the mountains, perhaps a month's journey on foot."

"Then we must go there and spy upon the enemy. We will discover some weakness."

Shadreiht seemed to consider this for a moment. "While you were in the mountains, it would be safe for you, but on the lower lands surrounding the tower, it would be impossible. The land swarms with micklebear and multipede—not to mention his other monsters."

"But wait," said Evander, desperate to make his point. "It is not just our lives that lie in the balance, but that of another world, many other worlds. Surely, it is your duty to help us in destroying the enemy. If the Neild have found a way to reach him, how can you refuse to meet with them and learn what it is?"

Shadreiht's face closed down, his eyes growing cold in the long horselike face.

"Evander is right," said Serena, determined that somehow, someway, she was going to escape from this hellish place.

Shadreiht blinked, then shook his head slowly from side to side. Suddenly, he raised a hand and dismissed them. "Shadreiht goes to meditate upon this. Leave me. The Seeker will guide you to a room where you can rest."

They left the Eleem Magus, who went up to a high place, where he could look out across the sere plains of old Orthond.

Chapter Thirty-four

For two whole days, and days were long on Orthond, they heard nothing. They were closed up in the same small room, and after a while the tension grew unbearable. Without words, they came together after a while, seeking comfort. Evander took Serena in his arms. After a brief, initial reluctance, which melted away, it was as if a dam had burst. There was no stopping. Throughout, of course, he kept his shirt on.

Afterward they lay entwined, laughing softly together.

"We are married now, in common law at least."

"I am so glad to hear that."

"Normally, we would go by your name alone, of course," she said with a mischievous smile.

"We don't want to do that, or I won't live long."

"Then we'll have to invent a new name for ourselves, because we can't use my family's name and we can't use yours."

"Our marriage will start out with a completely clean slate. We'll be new people."

Then she grew quiet, withdrawing into herself.

"Come, Serena, what is it?"

"We've got to get home before we can be any of that. We've got to get home."

Evander tried not to think how hopeless their situation really was. It wasn't easy.

Eventually, they slept, awoke, and were given the same warm mush as the previous day. All day they sat together, talking quietly about their past lives.

"Tell me more about Sedimo."

"Well, as I said, it is not a wealthy country. Certainly not like your fabulous city. At night the city has only oil lamps to light the way, and it's not as large as Monjon, not by half. But there are other things in Sedimo that are

wonderful. The countryside is beautiful. It's a land of small
hills, dappled farmland, and forest preserves. Up in the high
hills the views are magnificent. I would take you riding up
there; I think you would enjoy it."

"Oh, I would. I pray that someday we will be there
together."

Evander nodded sadly. "I fear it's unlikely we shall ever
see old Sedimo."

They sighed together.

"I wish I were out riding my old mare, Tilda. We go out
in the king's park, and it's always so lovely out there. Tilda
loves it, too."

"And how old is she?"

"Seventeen now. She still likes a gallop though, and she's
the easiest ride. We always got along very well."

"Well, I wish I had old Kiprio. He never won any races,
but he was still very fast."

"Why didn't he win then?"

"He could never hold himself back at all. He would just
gallop at full speed until his strength ran out, and it always
ran out before the race ended. We always led for the first
half of any race."

"The rider is supposed to hold back his horse."

"Old Kiprio would not be held back; he was amazing
that way. As soon as the race began, he refused all control
until he was blown and slowing down."

"What did you do with him?"

"I had to sell him in Molutna Ganga. We were going to
sail away, and I had no friends there I could stable him
with."

"That must have been hard."

"It was. I hope he is well treated by whomever has
him now."

"Well, he sounds very spirited. I like a horse with spirit.
Even old Tilda has spirit, but at her age she doesn't care
to gallop for that long. Oh, how I miss my old horse."

"Perhaps we'll find a way to get her back for you. The
Ugoli could buy her, if the royal stables would sell."

"Do you think so?"

"If they'd sell, I can't see why not. The Ugoli are an
amazing folk."

"Well," she said bravely, "if we ever get home, then

, we'll see the Ugoli and ask. Maybe I will see my old Tilda again someday."

They made their happiness despite everything, but desperation lurked behind their eyes, within their lips, present all the time. In their sleep they had terrible dreams in which micklebear pursued them through endless ruins.

Then, late on the second day, after an evening meal of the usual warmed gruel, with disks of a powdery bread, they were visited by Perspax. Accompanying Perspax was the unlikely figure of Konithomimo. Both Evander and Serena cried out at the sight of the little blue man.

"No thanks to you that I am here," he said with his customary truculence. "Only the fact that the good Perspax has begged me to come brought me here at all."

"Well, we're glad to see you anyway. Someday, I hope, you will become more accepting of human frailty."

"Perhaps," said Konithomimo with a near audible sniff. "In the meantime, you should know that I don't intend to return to the other world. Perspax informed me that you were hoping to make use of some magical device to travel there. I wish to remain here, where I am free."

Evander had been expecting this. "What will I tell the Ugoli?" Evander said.

"That I have served them long and well and that I am free now and will no longer be their flying carpet."

"They will be saddened by this news."

"That can't be helped. Konithomimo will remain on Orthond."

Evander turned to Perspax. "Where did you find him?"

"He found us. Apparently, he has crisscrossed all the county between here and Orthontower in his search for the fortress. Our pickets spotted him and brought him in."

"He seems as cranky as ever."

At this, Konithomimo gave a little snort, while Perspax emitted a hearty-sounding chuckling noise. "Indeed, you are correct."

"What did you see on your travels, Konithomimo?" asked Serena.

"Ruins, in every direction there are ruins."

"Of course, what else?" Serena turned away in dismay.

Perspax had news and an invitation. The news was greatly encouraging. After lengthy meditation and consultation among the High Eleem of the fortress, Shadreiht had gone to meet with the Neild of Putchad.

Evander could not repress a whoop of joy and enfolded Serena in a bear hug.

Soon Shadreiht would return. In the meantime they were invited to attend a reception, where they would be formally welcomed to Orthond and given status as ambassadors from their world. Lord Kobbox would be their sponsor. Discussions would ensue on some way of making contact possible between Orthond and Ryetelth.

Perspax and Konithomimo left them, and they spent the night in fitful sleep, poised between hope and despair.

The following day they attended the ceremony, which was held in a large hall filled with perhaps two hundred Eleem of both sexes. The couple were given ancient, Neild-woven robes to wear and made to stand on a stage beside Kobbox and Perspax while Kobbox made a long speech to the assembly. Perspax translated the speech, in which Kobbox described their arrival on Orthond and their subsequent journey with Perspax. The reception was warm, or as warm as Eleem were capable of.

Afterward, they were introduced to most of the Eleem present and then given warm tea and small cakes, sweetened and spiced in a way they found too strong for human taste. The introductions eventually came to an end, and the reception was over almost immediately thereafter. Throughout, Evander thought, it was somewhat graceless and limited. The Eleem had no music, no arts of their own. He realized once more that their culture had depended entirely on the Neild for all the finer things.

Much later, they returned to their lonely room and fell asleep once again. That night Serena had the usual bad dreams, and Evander awoke and took her in his arms and comforted her until she fell back to sleep. After that he lay awake for hours in the darkness, trying to imagine what lay ahead. There had to be a way to escape this hellish world, there just had to be. They couldn't be trapped here for the rest of their lives.

The next day, around noon, Perspax escorted them to a meeting with Shadreiht. This time they climbed a series of spiral stairs cut into solid rock that took them high above the hidden fortress, to a pinnacle that offered views far across the damaged land below, whenever the fogs and mists cleared sufficiently.

They found Shadreiht waiting for them in a gallery room cut around the top of the pinnacle. Evander assumed that the work had been done by Neild.

"Welcome," said Shadreiht. "I have met with the so-called free Neild. It was an experience that I could not have imagined in the old times, to be spoken to by Neild as if by an equal!"

Shadreiht fell silent for a moment. "But such things must be endured in these times of torment. Furthermore, in my meditations I have discerned a great swirling in the patterns of destiny. It is vital that the pair of you are somehow returned to your home world so that you may deliver a warning to your people. The Deceiver must be stopped, destroyed if possible."

Evander's joy must have showed itself on his face. Shadreiht fixed him with that wall-eyed stare. "You are happy, Prince Evander?"

"Well, happy in a relative sense, great Shadreiht. I am naturally pleased to hear that there is a chance that we will be able to return to our own world. I don't doubt that it will be difficult to achieve this."

"You are correct."

Shadreiht pointed out of the gallery in what Evander assumed to be a southerly direction, since the glow of the sun was visible there, behind the ever-present gray clouds. Mountains rose up like the backbone of some enormous creature that had collapsed and deposited its bones in a heap.

"Over those mountains lies one of the enemy's mines, a pit that he digs deep into our world in pursuit of minerals. Beyond the pit, perhaps two days' march, lies the Orthontower. The Neild have infiltrated the mine. They have discovered that there exists a tunnel, driven by the Deceiver's slaves between the mine and the deep levels of the Orthontower. The tunnel is large enough to allow wagons drawn by fell beasts to move minerals to the tower. It is always busy and therefore unsuitable for our purposes."

Evander was concentrating hard. If the tunnel was useless, then how were they to reach the tower?

"The surface is haunted by micklebear, and we cannot use the tunnel. I am at a loss," said Serena.

"There is a smaller adit, a drainage conduit, that runs directly below the main tunnel. Water seeps constantly into the main tunnel and has to be drained away to keep it open. The drainage tunnel is large enough that Neild have used it to crawl all the way to the Orthontower and back. We, too, will have to crawl, or at least be towed along by the Neild."

"We?" Evander wondered what this might mean.

"Towed by the Neild?" questioned Serena.

"Yes, for this is the only possible way of reaching the Orthontower alive. And I have been informed that it is very important that you escape back to your own world."

Serena nodded vigorously; she couldn't have agreed more. Evander wondered who had informed Shadreiht on the matter.

Shadreiht had paused again, as he so often did. Then he said, "If, and when, you do return to your home world, you must go at once to visit some creatures called witches who dwell on some islands in the east. You will tell them all that has happened to you. You will warn them that Waakzaam the Great has targeted their world for destruction."

Serena and Evander exchanged a long look. Evander returned to his questioning thought. "Did I hear correctly? You said 'we' are going. Are you coming, too?"

"Shadreiht is the only one who can operate the black mirror. I have read the mind of the Deceiver and heard his incantations. I know where his Concordance of Worlds is kept, and we shall need that to locate your world precisely. Furthermore, I will be needed to cloak our presence from the mind of the great enemy, for he is extremely sensitive to such things."

"So we're going to travel together," said Serena.

"Yes. We will also need the odd little creature that accompanied you to our world. The Neild believe he will be essential to the success of the mission."

"That may not be possible; he isn't exactly very friendly right now."

"We will try and persuade him. In the meantime, the Neild have readied everything. I was surprised by how much they had already achieved."

"The Neild are very capable. When you bred them, you bred them well."

"These are not good Neild!" Shadreiht sounded very upset by the thought.

"Whatever they are, they are our only hope."

"Indeed. We must prepare for a great ordeal. Go and take food and water, then rest. On the morrow we begin to march to the Orthontower."

Evander made the return trip down the long staircase, still wondering how they would persuade Konithomimo to come with them.

Chapter Thirty-five

The trek across the mountains was arduous. The easy routes were all subject to raids by the enemy's troops and could not be risked. Thus they scaled cliff faces, wandered through biting winds in snow-covered passes where the thin air seared their lungs, and stepped across high ridges of windswept rock that seemed to form the roof of the world.

At night Evander and Serena slept wrapped around each other inside a crude tent fashioned from hides. The Eleem slept in the snow, carving holes that they crawled into headfirst.

Their food was the ash-flavored bread of the Eleem, and for drink there was snow melt. The bread was frozen and required long and vigorous mastication for each mouthful.

Evander thought he was going to die during the first week. He was so cold and tired he felt he might expire at any moment, but he made it over the hump, rebounded, and even gained strength in the second week. As long as there was sufficient food, his body merely hardened and grew stronger. As did Serena's. The princess was already a far stronger individual than she had been on that day, so far behind them now, when she had been hurled into Orthond. By the second week of the march she was in near perfect health, but heartily tired of eating nothing but bread and bitter herbs. She longed to sleep on something other than rocks, and to drink something other than freezing cold snow melt.

Konithomimo, who had consented to accompany them after a meeting with Shadreiht, complained about everything, of course. He'd ignored them at first and traveled at the front of the march, alongside Perspax and Tekax, who led the way. Evander had decided to be outwardly calm and polite with Konithomimo. They needed him, and he was very volatile. Serena, too, did her best not to annoy him, but it was difficult because almost everything annoyed Konithomimo.

In addition to his other skills, it now became clear that Perspax was a great rock climber, as was Tekax. The enormously long Eleem bodies were naturally good at climbing. Old Shadreiht was not so adept, but even the ancient mage was capable of climbing rock faces fifty feet high, given enough time. To begin with, neither Evander nor Serena knew how to climb. Evander had tried a little rock climbing back home in Sedimo Kassim, but that had been many years before, when he was but a boy.

Now Evander and Serena learned how to climb by simply climbing. During the first week there were many frightening moments. Then they grew more skillful, and the climbing became almost routine. Their Neild-made boots proved good for the task, being both tough and flexible.

In the second week of the trek, Konithomimo got into an argument with the Eleem. He forsook their company and inflicted himself first on Shadreiht and then on Evander and Serena when Shadreiht was too incommunicative.

Konithomimo found the going easy enough, but he was sensitive to the cold and now requested that the humans take him in with them at night and warm him between their bodies.

Volatility be damned, Evander was inclined to refuse, but Serena accepted at once for both of them. Whatever Konithomimo needed, Konithomimo was going to get as long as it helped them find their way home.

Thereafter, they slept with the hard, cold little body of the rug man stuck between them, curled up like a kitten. He was always very cold when they first lay down and seemed to suck the heat right out of their own bodies until they were shivering together. At length, he warmed up and then, so did they. He was a restless sleeper, however, and moved around a lot, causing Evander and Serena considerable loss of sleep.

There was nothing to be done except to endure it. The days of walking across the top of the world continued, from one high, windswept ridgeline to another, until late in the third week when at last they began to descend. First they left behind the snowfields and the bare rock. Then they

were among high meadows, dotted with flowers and a pale
flush of grass.

Shadreiht explained that these highlands had never been
sullied by Waakzaam. They offered little apart from beauty,
and thus the Dominator had never felt the need to rav-
age them.

The next night a wave of warm air came up from the
south and brought with it the stench of burning stone. The
next day they could see smoke rising on the far horizon in
an enormous cloud. As they proceeded down through a
steep-sided, rock-strewn valley, the cloud of smoke seemed
to grow larger, as if they were approaching a volcano. The
smoke, Shadreiht explained, arose from the mines of the
Dominator, which lay just over the next ridgeline.

That night they continued marching to make use of the
cover of darkness. The territory here was patrolled by the
enemy and prowled by micklebear.

As they marched, the air grew cold, and a dirty gray
snow fell from the clouds. The stench of molten rock grew
very strong. The morning light found them downslope right
above the edge of the mine with views out across it and
then the plain beyond.

Evander was stunned at the size of the pit. At least two
or three miles across, it descended into the ground in a
series of concentric levels until it vanished into the dark,
still a mile wide. From that darkness arose clouds of smoke
and steam.

Now they could see swarms of slaves streaming antlike
up and down the sides of the pit. They bent under heavy
loads of debris over their shoulders. Huge creatures, manlike, but bigger than bears, stood over the slaves, cracking
whips with brutal force.

Evander wondered if the slaves were Neild. Sadly, Shadreiht confirmed that they were. The Neild that had survived the micklebear had been rounded up and put to work
in these vast mines, covering Orthond like gaping sores.

At the base of a crag that overhung the pit, they found
two of the free Neild waiting for them. The Neild gestured
for maximum caution. Micklebear fed well here on slaves
attempting to escape, or perhaps seeking the release of sudden death,

Doing their utmost to be silent, the group followed the
Neild into an opening that lead to a hidden, vertical cave

formed by a fault line in the crag. Using a series of holds carved by the Neild, they climbed down the near vertical face.

At the bottom of the cave they came upon a much wider space hollowed out by the industrious Neild. Here quite a crowd of Neild were waiting. Evander marveled at how many had risked coming here.

These Neild were a sober, silent group. Their huge goggle eyes fixed upon them, their turtlelike faces unreadable.

The Eleem had also fallen into a deep silence. The Neild did not caper for the lords. The Neild did not give worship. They were not "good" Neild. The long, pale Eleem faces tightened, their eyes slitted up.

The Neild hardly took any notice, but busily produced the glowing skull to communicate with Evander and Serena. Shadreiht and the other Eleem refused to touch the thing. This was Neild magic and none of their own, and they feared it like a deadly pestilence. As they explained their plan, Evander sucked in a deep breath. Bit by bit, he began to realize just how much they had yet to endure.

In the plan ten Neild, harnessed like dogs to a sled, would pull a narrow, wheeled wagon in which Shadreiht would ride, lying prone. The others would crawl, like the Neild, using pads of fibrous material to shield their hands and knees from the rough rock of the tunnel. The Eleem would have the most difficulty because of their greater size.

There would be several sleep periods, for it was impossible to crawl more than a few miles a day. The tunnel was wide enough for Neild children to run down, and they would fetch supplies of food and water. Adult Neild would also be in attendance at every point of the journey. The Neild had no illusions. Even with all the help they could muster, the journey would be very difficult.

They ate and slept for several hours before the signal came down the tunnel. All was ready.

And thus they came to the worst part of their journey, an experience none would ever forget. In close to utter dark, they began to crawl through freezing sludge and water that varied from an inch to a foot in depth. The cold was bitter. After a few hours Serena collapsed, shivering uncontrollably in hypothermic reaction.

An alarm was given, whispered back into the dark. Evander was pushed aside as Neild rushed past him. They lifted Serena out of the sludge. Fortunately, the water here was not deep. Then they surrounded her body like bees surrounding a queen, and their body heat overcame the deadly chill. After a while she came out of near unconsciousness and was made to eat bread and bitter herbs at once. There was a rest period to recuperate before the crawl continued. Serena expressed her uttermost determination to continue the journey. She would endure whatever she had to for the sake of Ryetelth.

When they stopped to sleep, Neild brought forward small pallets, dry clothing, and ointment to treat the blisters on their hands and knees. Still, Evander and Serena would have perished in the cold, dank tunnel if Neild had not warmed them with their body heat to stave off hypothermia.

The second day was worse, because their shoulders and thighs ached intolerably from the previous day. Both Serena and Evander collapsed from exhaustion and the cold. Even the Eleem were suffering by that time, except the old one. Shadreiht had put himself into a meditative state that was beyond mere discomfort, but Perspax and Tekax were weakening. In the next sleep period they, too, had to be swarmed by warm Neild to fight off incipient hypothermia. How they adjusted to being aided in this extremely personal way by freed Neild was unknown, for neither of the Seekers spoke of the experience.

The third day was the worst. They were weakened, and their bodies ached so that every movement forward was torment. Their knees were agonizingly tender, a mass of bruises and blisters. They had to pause every couple of hours to take food and regain strength. Unfortunately, this was the deepest part of the tunnel system. There were long stretches where mud had coated the bottom of the tunnel and others where the water was almost head high. All of these had to be pushed through, despite the chill. At the other end, often, they would be revived by a huddle of Neild. Dry clothes were constantly brought up for them by swarms of Neild children.

During this part of the trek Evander began to realize the scale of the undertaking by the free Neild. A huge effort was underway, and hundreds of Neild were risking their lives. He also understood that the Eleem and he and Serena could not have made it even to this point on their own.

The fourth day, thankfully, was a little easier. Their bodies were still racked by blisters and bruises, but some of the soreness was actually fading as the muscles got used to the strain. Best of all, they were tending upward, and there was much less mud or water. They were dry almost the entire day and avoided any further collapse from the effects of the cold and damp. They were also bouyed by the knowledge that this was the last leg. The next day they reached the hidden base of the Neild, burrowed into the very basements of the Orthontower.

Shadreiht could sense the awesome mind of the Dominator, high above them somewhere, on a distant floor of the tower. The mind was preoccupied with calculations and visits to other worlds—its terrible attention turned to faraway horizons. Thus Shadreiht was able to build his cloaking spell with little fear of discovery. When complete, it hid them to everything except intense scrutiny.

Now they crawled out into a warmly lit, wider space. A lantern was hanging above them, and a dozen Neild were there with blankets and dry clothing. Food came, the delicious feel of a partial thawing, more blankets, and somewhere dry to lie down. There they fell instantly into deep sleep.

Chapter Thirty-six

When Evander awoke, he found Serena shaking him by the shoulder. He was shocked for a moment at how thin and pale she'd become. But there was a fire burning in those green eyes, and his heart went out to her. If there was a way to rescue her from this hell, he would dare it, whatever it was.

All around them were the soft movements of Neild.

"Lady Lamen," he whispered.

She smiled. "Evander Blue Frog." He started to sit up and groaned as stiff muscles complained. Crowds of Neild were in motion nearby. Crudely worked stone blocks stood close at hand. The rough-hewn floor was bare rock.

All at once he remembered where they were. For a moment he felt a tremor in his heart. A chill feeling swept through him as he realized they were in a catacomb beneath the very center of the enemy's power. If they were detected here, they'd be captured in no time. There was no likelihood of escape back down that awful tunnel. Indeed, there was no going back; they either succeeded in this venture or they perished.

"Evander, we've got to get ready. There's some food coming. Then we're going on."

He shook the sleep away and struggled up, pulling the blanket around his shoulders.

"It's always so cold," he whispered.

"It'll be warm where we're going."

"Home."

Her eyes met his for a long moment, then slipped away. The shadow's power was broken once more, and his heart lifted. His eyes took in more of his surroundings.

Shadreiht was nearby, slowly chewing some of the hard, brown bread that was all they had to eat. Neild were at work behind him, and more Neild were coming and going through the tunnel entrance. The shelter was a crowded thoroughfare for Neild, but it was a strangely silent one. The usual hubbub of Neild conversation was absent.

Perspax made his way through the Neild until he loomed over them. Evander noticed that Perspax wore clean, dry clothing, and then realized that so did he. The Neild had clothed him during his sleep, and he had never noticed. He imagined the small hands, so soft and deft, stripping him and then fitting him with fresh clothing. It was faintly unnerving, and yet in some bizarre way it also helped dispell the chill of fear that lay over this place. The Neild were amazing, the hardest workers Evander had ever seen. It was plain to him that one Eleem saying about the Neild applied whether the Neild were "good" or "bad"—Neild were never still.

Evander had been dreading what was coming with a slowly mounting sense of desperation. His previous clashes with powerful wizardry had gone badly. He still sported the skin of a monster on his chest and shoulders. He had been blasted right out of his own world and condemned to ruined Orthond. Worse might lie in store.

Perspax nodded to Shadreiht, who made a gesture of blessing with one hand. The Seeker looked to Evander. "We have just had the word. The enemy has left the tower through his black mirror. Now is the time for us to strike."

"Where has he gone?"

"Who can know that, but Waakzaam? He travels constantly, attending to the affairs of twelve whole worlds. His concerns span areas that I cannot imagine."

Evander didn't want to imagine either, but it was easy to visualize mass slaughters, devastations, and eruptions of the ground.

Serena was holding his hand and arm very tightly. She, too, was fighting the fear. She had not been born to battle mighty wizards like this.

"It'll be all right," he said in a firm voice.

She steadied and relaxed her grip. "We have to do it, Evander. We have no choice." Her eyes were fierce once more.

"We can do it," he said. "We learned to climb on harder walls than this. There'll be handholds, for the Neild have prepared the way."

"That is true," said Perspax. "The Neild have worked very hard here, and they are quieter than mice."

Evander nodded. He knew why. "They have learned that art living in the ruins of Putchad," he said.

Perspax looked up, the horse face knotted in suppressed anger.

"They need never have hidden there. They should have come to us. We would have protected them."

"The Neild are not children anymore, Perspax. They have served their time."

"It was a good life for all when Neild served and Eleem ruled. Neild were safe. Eleem were content. Orthond was beautiful."

The tension was broken by the sudden appearance of a small blue steel streak that bounced out of the crowd of Neild and stood on a stone slab beside them. "Well, as you can see, I'm back," he said in that sharp, unmistakable metallic voice, always tinged with a whine.

They looked at him questioningly.

"I went up to see where the Neild have broken the wall to get into the gallery. It's quite a spectacular climb. We'll be going up between the two walls of the tower, climbing on the outside of the inside wall, if you see what I mean. This tower is absolutely enormous, far larger than any building I have ever been in before. I really don't think you two are going to make it."

"Oh, thank you, Konithomimo," said Serena. "But we will have to try."

Konithomimo's mood had clearly not improved. "No, I don't think you should. I think we should give up on this madness and go back to the fortress where we were safe at least. I am a Xish Wan weave spirit; I must have tranquility. I must have peace for my inner soul. All this has become very tiresome."

Now Serena's voice filled with iron. Evander had to smile.

"We have to go up there so we can get back to our home."

Konithomimo gave a mincing step and then a pirouette. "I don't want to go back and be a rug."

"Then you can stay here."

"I don't want to stay here."

A moment's shocked silence followed.

"You don't? I thought you said you did."

"I am cold. I am always cold now. My energy is running down. I cannot stay here."

"Then come back to Ryetelth with us. You'll always have a job there."

"It is not nice being trapped in a piece of fabric. Once a Ugoli woman laid me on the floor and walked on me! I was kept in one place on the floor for a year, and walked on! Can you imagine such a horror? To be unable to move except upon an owner's command? Any beast of burden has more freedom than I do as a rug."

"Then you must choose. Stay here and grow cold, or return and resume existence as a rug. I will tell the Ugoli about your transformation here. Perhaps they will try and liberate you from your service."

"They will not. They will say that I am too valuable. There are not many rugs left in the world with the sort of power that I display."

"True, but at the least you will be warm, eh? Tranquil, too."

Konithomimo fell silent, brooding. Evander took some bread and began chewing. He was ravenous. The dried, ashy bread actually tasted good to him.

Konithomimo spun on the ball of one foot. "Oh, well, there's nothing to be done. Now that you've woken out of your stupor, I suppose we'll have to go on with this farcical attempt to escape. We'll go on until you are captured or slain by the Dominator's creatures."

"What creatures?" asked Serena, alarm tingling.

"You didn't think that Waakzaam the Great would leave his chamber unguarded, did you?"

"No, of course not," Serena said in a small voice. "Why would anything be simple on this terrible world?"

"A demon was left to guard the room. You will have to overcome it before you can use the mirror."

"What sort of demon?"

"I do not know much about the different kinds of demons. This one is purple, about the size of an Eleem, perhaps larger. Certainly it is more massive. It has a small pack of things with many teeth to help it. It has not yet detected the Neild hole, however, so it is not omniscient."

Perspax nodded. He had been briefed by the free Neild. It'd been a disturbing thing, to be spoken to as an equal by the little Neild warrior in his leather armor and pot helmet. The Neild had bored an eyehole right into the uppermost part of the chamber wall. They had actually witnessed Waakzaam in his chamber and watched him disappear through the black mirror.

Perspax leaned down for a moment. "We shall deal with the demon, Tekax and myself."

"Well, I certainly hope so, because if you don't, then I'll really be in trouble. I mean, I'll be dancing around in there trying to stay out of harm's way while it chases me."

"Chases you?" Evander was taken aback.

"I am to be the decoy. While the thing pursues me about the chamber and anywhere else I can escape to, the rest of you will break in. I just hope you can do it quickly."

"Once we break in, then what?" asked Serena.

"Then we will slay the demon," said Perspax.

"What about the other things that help this demon?"

"Neild and yourselves will deal with them if you have to. You will be given swords, I understand."

Evander nodded to himself; it sounded plausible. Two Eleem Lords, armed with great blades of steel, should be able to kill just about anything, but while they were busy, the others would have to subdue any smaller creatures that might be on hand.

"What else did you see, Konithomimo?" asked Serena quietly.

"Oh, he has the most awful taste in furniture. Huge chairs carved with fierce faces. Cages filled with abominations he has created. Tall glass jars, all with his horrible experiments inside them. These things cover the tables, everywhere, all these experiments."

"What horrible experiments?" asked Evander slowly.

"The Dominator appears to be researching diseases. He seems to prefer baby Neild for his research animals."

"Diseases?"

"I was told that the Neild have seen baby Neild inoculated by the Dominator himself. This kind of work is his passion, it seems. It is a personal quest for knowledge. The babies are then confined in glass tanks. The baby Neild subsequently sicken and die, in various intriguing ways."

Serena had grown even paler, if that was possible.

Konithomimo continued, unfazed. "Apparently, he spends much of his time dissecting baby Neild."

"Enough details. We will see it all for ourselves very soon."

"If you can manage the climb, that is. It is long, and as you know, it is vertical. This is an amazing structure. Far more impressive than anything I ever saw on Ryetelth—"

"What?" said Serena. "More than the palace in Monjon?"

"The grand palace would fit inside this tower with room to spare."

Serena fell silent, oppressed by this thought.

Shadreiht had finished his bread, and he suggested that they eat everything they could. They would need every scrap of strength for the ordeal ahead.

Perspax hesitated for a moment before speaking. "The time has come. My friends, I don't know if we will survive the coming struggle, but I do know that if we succeed, you will be gone and will never be seen again on Orthond. I want you to know that you will always be remembered among the Eleem for your courage. Arriving suddenly on our ruined world, you bore yourselves magnificently, despite everything. On behalf of all the Seekers of Orthond, of the Miggenmorch and the ancient lords, I bid you fond farewell."

Evander and Serena instinctively took each other's hand and squeezed it tight. After a moment Evander replied for both of them. "Noble Perspax, please accept our thanks for all you have done for us. We shall never forget you or your struggle against the great enemy."

The Neild were signaling. There was no more time.

Chapter Thirty-seven

Up a rough stone wall they climbed, using handholds marked in phosphorescence, into a great vault of gloom. They went slowly, with frequent halts to rest tortured fingers. Bodies ached, muscles screamed from days of abuse, and fingers cramped easily and had to be exercised patiently for minutes before they could be used again. Although there were constant handholds, they were made for Neild and thus were too small for comfort for Evander and Serena, not to mention the Eleem. Of especial concern was the ancient Shadreiht, but he continued to climb with a methodical persistence that amazed them all.

The Orthontower was vast, with two massive concentric walls built to withstand any attack. The wall had been doubled so that if the outermost was breached, there would still be the innermost to defend. They were climbing up the outer face of the inner wall, hidden from view, toward a niche that would be their point of entry to the inner fortress.

From the beginning they had seen a faint purple radiance high above in the deep gloom. Now, almost halfway up the wall, the purple glow had intensified. A beam was shooting out of the inner wall and forming a bright violet circle on the outer wall, illuminating the upper part of the vast, gloomy vault between the walls. Occasionally the circle was cut by shadows, and the flickering light flashed ominously.

They were not the only climbers. Several parties of the free Neild crawled past, going up or down, using different sets of handholds to either side of the main trail.

Using an acid gel that ate stone and mortar alike, Neild had created a few niches where climbers could rest with both feet secure.

As they drew closer to the source of the violet light, they rested more and more frequently. They were all tiring, even the mighty Eleem Lords. These rests, though necessary, were resisted by the Neild. The great enemy was gone, but there was no way of telling when he might be back. They had much to do before then.

Now the purple light was getting bright enough to make them squint away from it. The way grew easier for a while, with several good holds. Then they pulled themselves up a rope and were squinting against the light as they climbed into a room dug out of the inner wall. This space narrowed dramatically as it drove farther into the wall. The wild violet light emerged as a beam from a fist-sized hole at the end of the passage. This was the peephole of the Neild. The Neild had gnawed all this out of the Dominator's wall without his sensing them.

If he had known that he was being spied on in this way, his fury would have leveled whole continents, but so subtle were the Neild and so disciplined that he had never detected a thing.

The glowing purple space was quickly crowded when three great Eleem stood up in it. Neild were at work all around them, attaching ropes and arranging gear. All moved with a near manic speed, as if their lives depended on it, which they did.

In the wider part of the room Neild began mixing substances from small barrels. A sweetish, sour odor filled the air and grew strong. The tips of their tongues prickled, and their eyes smarted briefly.

The plan had been explained to them in detail. They would have to climb a little farther above the hollowed-out space and wait while a specially trained team of Neild would then work to remove stones that had already been partly freed in the room. Quickly, the peephole would be enlarged, and Konithomimo would be sent through.

Once he had aroused pursuit by the demon, they would begin the larger work. Special teams of Neild were already in position below them, waiting to carry down the stones removed from the wall.

When the gap was large enough, the Eleem would go through and Evander and Serena would follow them. They had been given Neild swords, short but serviceable blades, in case the small guard beasts got past the Eleem.

Before they started, Shadreiht came up and put out his long, Eleem hands to touch each of them on one shoulder.

They felt his mind reach out to them.

"Have courage, my young friends. Stout hearts will win the day and see you safely back on your own world in a matter of hours. And if we should not meet again for any reason, allow me to wish you well and to commend you for your courage."

"Farewell, Master Shadreiht."

They swung out onto a set of ropes and pulled themselves up a few feet above the opening. There they waited, while from below came a swarm of Neild.

The chemical smell grew strong again and stayed that way. The Neild began to work fast and hard. Inevitably, there were sounds. Stones scraped, metal struck and rang, feet slapped. Neild exhaled with the effort.

A signal, a short whistle, went down in the dark. Konithomimo had gone through.

The work resumed with even greater speed and intensity. More Neild emerged from the dark into the pool of violet light. Ropes were attached, gears ratcheted.

Suddenly, there came a bone-shivering roar from within the tower. It was followed by sustained shrieking that rang through the very stones. Konithomimo had been discovered.

The Neild worked on in a frenzy. Stones were going out over the edge on the backs of Neild and carried slowly down into the dark. Other stones, the great ones, were lowered on ropes. Neild seemed to swarm in the darkness.

The screaming went on and on. Evander felt sweat starting from his forehead. He looked over to where Serena was waiting. Her face was stark in the flashing violet light.

She saw his look and flashed him a nervous smile. He wondered how familiar she was with swordplay. In her pampered life in Monjon, the need had surely never come up.

They said these guard beasts were true horrors, ratlike but the size of small dogs, and very fast. Tekax had warned them not to underestimate them.

By the Gods, Evander thought, the screaming noise was close to unbearable.

The uproar continued, now punctuated with occasional loud crashes as heavy things fell to the floor and shattered. With each one the roaring redoubled in fury, but the high shrieking went on and on with never diminished intensity.

The Neild worked harder, if that was possible.

Still, the work took time, and the noise grew louder. The crashing resumed, and with it the bellowing. The purple light was getting much brighter now as the stones came out of the innermost wall. Then the noise grew impossibly loud for a few seconds before dying down somewhat. The purple light flickered around Neild in motion.

Then, at last, came the signal. Down! The moment Evander had been dreading had come.

They went down toward the screaming, which grew louder with every step and became a gale as they swung down into the little room.

The breach was now much larger, the size of a door, and the violet light blazed through it. Perspax moved forward at once, sword in hand, hunched over into the gap. Tekax rushed behind him.

Two free Neild soldiers carrying stabbing spears went next, and then it was their turn. They were ushered forward into the domain of the Great Deceiver and Lord of Twelve Worlds.

Chapter Thirty-eight

They emerged into blinding purple glare. They were high above the floor, on a gallery overlooking a huge room, with a wall of glass cabinets on the far side. The wall behind them was filled with bookshelves, miles of them it seemed.

Everything was on a grand scale. The floor below was filled with enormous tables on which stood rows of tall glass jars. Tubes, bottles, and cabinets of all sizes made a forest of fantastic shapes. The ferocious purple light sparkled on every shard of crystal and threw utter black shadows across floor and table alike.

The roaring noise of the chase came from somewhere to their right, beyond a series of kilns that bulked up from the floor like huge onions built of brick.

Suddenly, the noise increased in volume. Evander looked up just in time to see a silver streak bound across a table-top, ducking through a set of retorts, before it disappeared past a row of tall cabinets.

Behind it came a huge shadowy shape, massive, predatory, fluid in movement, darting between the tables, leaping on and over them when necessary. Evander glimpsed it for a moment against the mirrorlike background of a cabinet. The demon had a tail and a head that were pantherlike, long apelike forearms, and massive hind legs, heavily muscled. Then it, too, was gone, lost from view behind an immense fireplace in which still smoldered the remains of a large fire.

The source of the screaming came into view a moment later as a dozen or more ratlike beasts the size of dogs scurried by. Evander shivered at the sight of them. They, too, vanished behind the big fireplace. At the same time, Evander noted the many carcasses hanging on butcher's hooks above the fireplace. Many were Neild; some were Eleem.

Perspax was signaling furiously. Tekax was waiting for them just a bit farther down the gallery. A rope was already over the side, and two Neild had descended to the floor. They seemed dwarfed by the furniture and equipment all around them.

Perspax went down next. The rope tightened under his weight, but did not give, and then he was down beside the two armored Neild. The uproar of the pursuit sounded as if it was coming back in their direction. It was time to hurry.

Another Neild went down, and then Tekax. Now it was Evander and Serena's turn. Evander went first, rappeling down the rope, bouncing against a pillar to the floor. They had learned to rappel on fifty-foot drops in the mountains, and now it came to him quite easily.

On the floor he found the tables stood as tall as his head, and the jars set on them were filled with baby Neild in various stages of disease and death.

The Eleem motioned him to move into the shadows behind a cabinet. The noise was getting louder all the time. He looked up. Serena had started down the rope.

The noise was deafening now. Then for the briefest of moments he saw Konithomimo, leaping at full speed, rising onto a table, and then bouncing off it into black shadow. Right behind him came the demon, red eyes glowing, tail straight out behind. It had the mass of a bear in a body almost nine feet tall.

On the tabletop it skidded and knocked over a retort stand. Glass shattered, and a pungent acid struck the tabletop. Eye-watering vapor rose at once in a dense cloud.

Oblivious to this havoc, the demon sprang along the table, then leaped down right behind Konithomimo like a huge cat behind a tiny silver mouse. A swipe with a huge hand missed the little man. A slap almost pinned him, but he squirted free, bounced up onto the next table, and saw Evander waiting in the shadows.

Konithomimo changed direction the next moment and bounded toward Evander, waving his arms and shouting. "Well at last! At last! I thought you'd never come."

The pantheroid demon rose onto the tabletop in pursuit and then skidded to a halt as it caught sight of Serena, who was still halfway down the rope. It flashed its fangs and let its booming roar of rage echo throughout the vast chamber.

Huge muscles bunched, and it threw itself toward the gallery, intending to pluck Serena from the rope.

Several things happened at once. Evander charged from his hiding place, Serena let go of the rope and fell the last ten feet, and Perspax and Tekax rose up with long steel gleaming in their hands.

The demon shuddered to a halt. The swords flashed, and its body shivered away from the steel as if it were made of elastic. With a weird wail it flung itself backward, crashed into a table, and skittered away out of range in the wink of an eye.

Evander dove full length to try and catch Serena. Her body struck his on the way down, enough to break her fall a little, but not enough to break his back. As it was, he landed so hard it drove the breath from his body.

Serena was slow getting up, but still faster than he, and it took several seconds before he could gather a breath again. In the meantime, she had drawn her sword as they faced off with the ratlike things. The demon had disappeared into the acid fog with a vengeful shriek, leaving its beasts to hold them at bay. The creatures formed a ring around them.

Serena insisted that she was perfectly all right, although Evander could see she was shaking a little and her sword point wavered around in the air.

Those seconds were among the longest he had ever known, as he struggled to get a breath back and draw his own sword. The fat beady eyes of the things were the size of grapes and filled with awful hunger.

He had successfully drawn his first breath when four beasts tried to get at them by slithering along under the tables. They emerged with joyful shrieks and plunged toward them.

Then the swords of the Eleem flashed brightly through the purple air, and the first two creatures fairly exploded in blood and viscera as they were cut in two. With wild shrieks of fear the others scrambled back. Tekax caught the hindmost a blow, however, and it rolled with its death shriek under the table.

Perspax charged toward the rest, and they scattered and ran with further shrieks of alarm and rage.

After the noise there was now a weird quiet, and through it they heard little gasps and sobs coming from the jars all around them. Little Neild were dying all through this terrible room. Evander shivered to his marrow as he contemplated the evil of the place.

Perspax and Tekax undertook reconnaisance of the surrounding area. The Neild soldiery took up defensive positions while Shadreiht descended to the floor.

Once the sage was on his feet again, he began to cast a cloaking spell, mumbling the words of power while he concentrated all into a great gesture. He drew the power down from the very air itself and then cast it forth in a net that would hide them, at least partially, from the demon.

Konithomimo had decided to stay for the time being in the company of Evander and Serena. He was agonizing over his decision to go back to Ryetelth. He knew it would mean resuming his existence as an heirloom flying carpet. Until the very material he was made of disintegrated, he would fly on command for whomever sat on him. He disliked this idea very much. Yet if he stayed on Orthond, he would burn up his life force in less than a year. The struggle to decide had reduced him to mumbling to himself, for which both the prince and princess were grateful.

Meanwhile, the pack of ratlike things had largely disappeared from view out beyond the far tables. The acid vapor was still thickening, and the air was becoming horrible to breathe.

Shadreiht's cloaking spell fell over them all as if someone had drawn a shade across the fierce purple light. Its intensity was reduced by half, and a gray veil seemed to filter down around them.

Perspax and Tekax had returned from the fog. It was time for them to move away from the acid that was eating up the table. Tekax would lead and Perspax would bring up the rear. They would head across the room to a massive dais that bulked up beyond a row of forges. The dais was the place of the black mirror.

They had moved perhaps a hundred feet, and the air was improving fast, when the demon suddenly returned. The cloaking spell had not produced any effect on its ability to detect them. Shadreiht groaned in dismay.

Worse, the thing now had weapons of its own, sword and dagger of immense proportions. With a roar of pleasure it gave its challenge and then dropped down to engage Tekax.

Perspax moved up the line in a hurry. The Neild had

gone into a defensive crouch, aiming their spear points outward.

The demon concentrated on Tekax. Their blades clashed, and Tekax was forced back. He ducked a swipe from the dagger and parried the next overhand blow of the main sword, but when the demon closed, he was forced to turn away and evade.

Evander and Serena stepped back, and the demon's sword scythed the air where they'd stood a second before. When they scattered, Evander collided with Perspax and was sent flying. Perspax was left wrong-footed. He barely parried the demon's wild slice at his head and then had to scramble back before the next.

Tekax drove in to divert the demon which engaged him with its dagger. The blades rang off each other, and with the click of a spring the demon activated sword-breaking teeth that opened in the side of the blade. Tekax whipped his sword back quickly enough to free it, but now the demon swung hard at him with its main sword. Though he parried it with a grunt of effort, he was driven back several steps by its force.

The demon met Perspax's next blow with its sword, but perhaps overconfident, it misjudged the speed of the Seeker of the Miggenmorch. Perspax's backhand return was too fast for the demon's parry, and he struck home, slicing into the demon's shoulder.

Black blood spurted in the violet light. The demon uttered a howl and struck furiously at Perspax, ignoring its wound. He defended, but was crowded in with Serena on one side and Evander on the other.

Tekax struck in again, and once more the demon took his blade on its big knife and tried to trap it with the spring hooks. Again it failed, and now Tekax came on with a will, and the demon gave ground as it parried his blows. It moved back with a springy stride, and Tekax pressed it. Perspax followed up, looking to get past and finish the demon.

With a crash the demon pulled down a tall jar filled with baby Neild in various stages of slimy decomposition. A hideous stench arose. Another jar came down, its contents nothing but foul sludge that slopped across the floor. Tekax lunged forward.

And then one of the ratlike things leapt in from its hiding

place under a nearby table and sprang up on Tekax's chest, its teeth aimed at his throat.

Tekax brought a hand up in time, but the thing was anchored to his wrist the next moment, and it pulled him off balance. At that moment the demon turned, sprang back, and struck down with every ounce of strength. Tekax's sword shattered with a flash of sparks and left him helpless. The dagger swung, and Tekax gave a great cry as it sank home.

Too late, Perspax was there, and his blow went wide. Once more the demon flesh shimmied away from steel with an uncanny elasticity.

Tekax sank to his knees, barely able to keep the beast from rending his throat. Evander leaped forward and stabbed down, and the ratlike thing screamed and squirmed around and almost got its fangs into his leg. He danced wildly with it for a moment before he was able to get his sword into it. His blade struck ribs twice before going home and cutting to the heart. At last it died in a gush of stinking blood.

Evander broke free of it and looked to help Tekax, but the Eleem had fallen facedown and would move no more. The demon had only Perspax to face. If he were to fall, then they would surely all die here, or worse, be captured and kept alive for the amusement of the dark master of this palace of horrors. They had to help Perspax. Evander stepped forward to try and come at the demon from the flank. It towered above him, its body with the strength of some great cat. It eyed him with those peculiar glowing orbs and then gave a great laugh. The dark blood had dried and crusted already on its wound. It was still invincible.

It feinted at Perspax, who ducked back, then it came sharply at Evander, huge sword whirling over its head. Evander hurled himself forward, getting inside the blow and trying to strike home with his own small blade. Somehow the demon's leg quivered out of the way. Evander's backhand cut was met by the knife. The trapping spring snapped shut, and Evander's sword was torn from his hand. He stumbled back, with nothing but a knife to defend himself with. The demon's eyes glowed brightly as the sword came up.

Then a Neild soldier ran in from the far side and jammed its spear into the demon's leg. It gave a sudden shriek and jumped as if it had springs in its legs rather than muscles. The Neild, alas, was too slow to escape and was cut down in the next instant.

Evander was back on his feet again and stumbling away. One of the dog-sized ratlike things sprang up at him, but Serena was there, and she stabbed it through the chest with her blade.

He spun around as ancient Shadreiht stepped forward, gripping Tekax's fallen sword.

The demon roared with laughter at the sight of the ancient, withered and wrinkled, daring to challenge.

Then Perspax cut in with every ounce of strength in his great frame. The demon was forced to defend. Steel blades rang together beneath the wild purple light. The demon fled backward again. Evander took up the sword of the fallen Neild soldier and moved beside Shadreiht. Serena came right behind them with the other Neild. The ratlike things followed closely.

The demon leaped onto a cabinet of drawers and skipped down the other side. Perspax started to follow when the demon turned the cabinet over on him. Drawers fell open to disgorge the results of hundreds of dissections. Perspax was knocked to his knees. Shadreiht moved to cover him.

The vast demon stood over the ancient Eleem, but he never wavered. The demon swung, and Shadreiht ducked with remarkable rapidity.

Perspax was having difficulty getting back on his feet. The cabinet had stunned him.

The demon swung again, and the clash of blades almost drove Shadreiht to his knees. The demon gave a grunt of triumph even as it was pulled slightly off balance by the pull of its own blow.

Evander struck in, and his sword went home in the demon's other leg. It screamed. Evander stabbed it again, but a huge hand grabbed him and thrust him down. A foot was going to grind him to pulp.

And then Shadreiht brought the long sword down and sank it into the demon's neck. The blade bit deep, black blood spurted widely, and the demon's great glowing eyes dimmed. It flailed up with a hoarse cry and staggered back, before falling with a crash into another cabinet and spilling a wealth of saws and scalpels across the floor. It rolled over, struggled back onto its knees, and then with a final croak expired.

The chamber of the black mirror was in their possession.

Chapter Thirty-nine

He had seen it all foretold in the dream—a thing of dreadful luminosity in his memory, never to be forgotten. Shadreiht had experienced much in his long life, but nothing would ever match that particular dream.

First there had been the strange singing, high voices, incredibly sweet and beautiful. The sky above was pink. A golden insect appeared, taller than a man, with green eyes that glistened like wet glass. It spoke to him with gentle words like the music of a flute in a quiet garden. Without any effort he had understood the words. Shdareiht knew he'd been touched by the Gods, he knew it, and yet it had not left him happy.

Now the Neild spoke to him in their harsh, overly familiar tone, just as had been foretold in the dream.

"It will not be the way it was, Master Shadreiht. We have made good use of what we were able to save from the old library of Putchad. We are not ignorant Neild anymore. We are not animals."

The purple light caused the round steel helmets to coruscate in blue fire. Shadreiht shuddered within himself. Once more the Neild had demonstrated their frighteningly swift intelligence. Their huge eyes glared up at him across the divide between Neild and Eleem.

He nodded to the Neild leader. The Eleem understood.

The Concordance of Worlds had been easy to locate. It was a book, five feet by four, resting on a giant's lectern beside the dais of the black mirror.

Unfortunately, the Concordance was written in a tongue unknown to Shadreiht. Shadreiht was a master of written symbols. He knew dozens of languages and had expected to be able to decipher the Concordance after a little study. Alas, he had found that the Concordance was recorded in an alphabet completely unknown to him, although it had a passing resemblance to the vertical rune-script of Astansha. For a horrible moment he thought he had failed, and the entire mission would have to be aborted.

Then had come the shocking surprise. The solemn Neild faces ringing him, the eyes boring into him.

"We have decrypted it already, Master Shadreiht. There is one among us who can read the signs now."

And yet the golden insect hadn't given him the coordinates. It meant for him to endure this humiliation in front of the Neild.

Neild standing on the shoulders of other Neild were already turning the big pages, looking up the entry for Rye-telth. Shadreiht again felt the strange distaste, almost fear, these Neild aroused in him. They were so competent, so capable, and so brave. As brave as Eleem. Selfless soldiers ready to give their lives for their cause. The Dominator might return at any moment. If he caught them, they would all pay with their lives. Their deaths would be slow and agonizing. Yet the Neild worked on methodically, quite calmly in the face of great danger.

After a few minutes' searching in the enormous book, they brought him the coordinates for Ryetelth. He prepared himself, sinking into a comfortable position on a high bench.

For a moment Shadreiht marveled at the freak chance that had sent the two young humans to him. Then he recalled the golden insect, and he wondered if it was a freak of chance after all. Their arrival had acted like the first stones of an avalanche. Now he was actually in possession of the chamber of the black mirror in the very heart of Waakzaam's domain.

And Shadreiht knew exactly what he had to do, for out of the dream had come the other message concerning the black mirror. A way to turn it into a lethal trap for the Dominator when he tried to return.

It was hard to accept that the Gods would take on the appearance of insects. Secretly, Shadreiht had long doubted even the existence of the Gods. Then to discover that the Gods existed, but did not resemble Eleem! It was a shattering blow to some deeply buried structure of his own self-confidence. The stable nature of the universe itself had been overturned in his mind.

He comforted himself with the thought that at the least

the Gods were trying to help them save Orthond. The destruction of Waakzaam the Great would be an enormous blessing for the worlds he ruled. And they had chosen him, old Shadreiht, to forge the weapon that would undo the Dominator.

He composed his thoughts, settling into the calm that was so vital to spellsay. The mission was simple. First they would send the young humans back to their own world. Then he would use the spell to distort the mirror ever so slightly. Waakzaam would never notice it. The mirror would beckon to him, but it would not open to him either. He would be trapped in the swirling ether of the chaotic realm. There he would be torn to pieces by the savage creatures that ruled that awful zone.

The golden insect had foretold it all.

With an inward sigh he began. First it was vital to achieve complete inner peace. He closed his eyes and adjusted his breathing until it was long, slow, and deep. In a few moments his thought grew limpid and smooth like the surface of a pond on a calm summer's day.

The spell was not enormous, but it involved arts of which Shadreiht had little knowledge. The casting of volumes and the other megapunctuations of this kind of spellsay were relatively new to him. He had practiced, however, and had learned something of these higher arts.

Again had come the chastening realization of his people's limitations. They had mastered the reading of minds and the breeding of Neild, but these higher sorceries were almost unknown to them.

Still, with his far "sight" into the minds of others he had listened to the Dominator's casting this spell on many occasions, and had memorized it after a while. The technique was complex. He still marveled over the things he had learned since first mastering the use of "volumes" of sound. There was, for instance, a sound so low it was beyond the hearing of all living things, and it caused solid objects to vibrate and even shatter.

Now he began the work. Eerie sounds echoed in the huge room. Bands of pressure expanded outward, making everyone's skin itch momentarily. The fabric of the world was tensing suddenly in this grim chamber of horrors.

Perspax, on guard, watched Shadreiht prepare himself, and a mixture of emotions washed through him. He was triumphant. They had done what he had privately thought would be impossible. But he was still recovering from the blows he'd taken—blows both physical and mental. His friend Tekax had fallen. And fighting alongside Neild had shaken him. The sight of Neild wielding weapons in battle brought home to him more than anything the knowledge that the Neild would never be "good" Neild again.

Not only was the old world of lovely Orthond smashed forever, but now in its place would rise a new world, the world of the Neild. How long could the Eleem survive in a world run by free Neild?

Shadreiht began to murmur the slow syllables of power. Perspax shifted into motion. He was stiffening, sore in many places. He glanced about the room. The demon sprawled full-length amidst a sparkling scattering of surgical tools. Eye-watering vapor was still rising in the near distance. The place stank of chemical reactions. The purple light blazed down, throwing angular black shadows across the gleaming surfaces. Shadreiht sat on a high stool in what seemed a state of trance.

It was time. Evander and Serena waited anxiously near the dais as Perspax approached them. "The Master prepares the way for you, Prince Danais Evander." Evander looked into the eyes of the Seeker.

"I have not heard that name for a long time, Perspax of Orthond."

Serena gave them both a sharp look.

"I bid thee farewell from old Orthond. Remember us in your world of light and freedom."

"Orthond will be free again. The tyrant will fall."

"Our world cannot come again, but we are resigned to our fate. The Eleem can only dwindle. Now comes the time of the Neild. Farewell, Evander. Farewell, Princess Serena, your courage was a sign to us that hope can always exist."

"We will not forget you, Perspax."

"And we will never forget the beautiful Princess Serena. Good-bye."

Shadreiht had begun to intone words that stretched and wobbled and seemed to be torn away by nonexistent winds. As the words rolled on, there came strange implosive bursts that caused hair to stand on end and mouths to go dry. The power in the room was building rapidly.

"The time has come," said Perspax. "You must go up

onto the dais. Be calm. The Master said there will be a short dislocation as you cross the ether, but that it will be brief, and then you will be back on your own world."

"We are ready. Thank you for all you did for us, Perspax, most noble knight of the Miggenmorch."

"I wish you well on your own world, Princess, though I know that great troubles await you there."

Serena had tears running down her cheeks as she ascended the dais.

The little blue man bounced up to join them. The cold was really bothering him. He had burned up a lot of energy staying out of the demon's reach for those long few minutes. The demon had moved unpleasantly fast.

"You will plead my case with the Ugoli folk, will you not? I do not want to exist forever as a rug."

Evander nodded. "I will tell them how things stand. They may decide to release you. The Ugoli are good-hearted folk."

For once Konithomimo did not snarl some mean-spirited reply. In a strange way Evander actually felt sorry for the small blue-white demon. Evander promised himself he would do his utmost to free this creation of great magic from long ago.

They stood there on the dais, invisible waves of power pressing against them as if from winds that did not disturb the air. Then Shadreiht's spellsay culminated in a rippling crack like a lightning bolt in the air above the dais. A long dark line stretched from the floor to a point above their heads. The line widened, spreading out to form a circular mirror surface. But the reflection was hidden in random motions within the mirror, for it was truly a window into the chaotic ether of the subworld. Chaotic patterns pinwheeled before their eyes.

Serena and Evander stepped forward toward the mirror. As they drew close, their hair stood on end. Heavy static charges were building up.

A voice in their heads said, "Step through the mirror, now." They did so, and it was like stepping into icy water. One moment they were in the purple light, and the next they were through the mirror, and for a terrifying moment they whirled, upside down, spinning through the madness of the chaotic ether. Then they shot away through it as if they were arrows released from the bow of the hunter's god.

A tiny beacon glowed in the dark far ahead, but they could not breathe; the chaotic ether was so cold it felt as if their skin would crack and fall away. Could they last long enough to reach that far-off glimmer?

Chapter Forty

With an ear-splitting crack, they emerged into warm air once more and promptly fell six feet into a muddy alleyway. They hit hard, unprepared, and there wasn't nearly enough muck on the cobbles to absorb the blow. Evander's lungs were still seared from the freezing ether of chaos, but before he blacked out, he caught a noseful of stinking garbage and mud. That gave him a moment of triumph. He knew they were back in their own world. Somehow that garbage smelled different from anything on Orthond.

Shadreiht had pulled it off, an amazing feat.

Then came the darkness.

He awoke after a little while, aching in every part of his body. He got to his feet, unsteadily, and found his nose was bleeding.

Serena lay curled up on her side, unconscious, but breathing steadily. The rug was nowhere to be seen, unless that was a corner of it sticking out of a pool of muddy water a few feet farther on.

High brick walls rose on either side of the alley. Rubbish was piled along one wall. A doorway led into a big courtyard, a four-story building beyond it. From the lights and sound Evander was certain it was a tavern.

He noticed more lights, up above the windows of other buildings. No doubt about it they were definitely back in Monjon. Which meant they had a serious problem.

A scraping noise came from above, and someone looked down from an opened shutter and called something to him in Monjonese. He replied in Furda, "Just travelers." He saw some other people looking down from another window, but they made no comment. Then the shutters scraped shut once more.

He had tried to think this through, to prepare himself,

back during the long, arduous days in the mountains of Orthond. For some reason it didn't seem to make things any easier. For a start it was hard to think at all; his thoughts seem to congeal like cold porridge. Secondly his whole body hurt, another effect of the strange and terrifying journey through the nothingness of chaos. The slightest movement brought on spasms of pain from a variety of muscles all over his body.

The first thing was to get somewhere quiet and safe. The nearest place he could think of that would fit the bill was the house of Ornizolest. The difficulty was that he was close to blacking out, and he seriously doubted he could walk as far as that. He knew he couldn't carry Serena that far either.

Standing up was hard enough. He wobbled, alternately sweating, then shivering, and weak as if he had a high fever. He had to lean against the wall for support.

A few moments later he heard a small sound and opened his eyes and saw that a narrow door had cracked open in the wall opposite where he stood. An elderly couple, faces round and rimmed with white hair, were staring at him intently.

The man lifted a hand and spoke in Monjonese.

"Travelers," blurted Evander. "We're travelers."

The old woman came close and stared up into his face. Then she spoke in very crude Furda.

"You get beat up?" was the gist of what he understood.

He tried to frame some simple but eloquent explanation and failed. What was he to do in this situation? It was beyond anyone's experience. Worse, he couldn't think properly. He was just so utterly weary.

The two old folk were now examining Serena, who under the old woman's ministrations slowly came back to consciousness. She groaned loudly—her body also ached in every limb—and heaved herself up into a sitting position.

She saw Evander leaning there, and her eyes went wide at the sight of the blood that had stained the lower half of his face and all down his front. "Where are we?" she asked.

"Monjon."

Visible relief washed through her face.

"Thanks be to Pernaxo and all the Gods."

"Actually, thanks to old Shadreiht."

"Yes, you're right; many, many thanks to the old Master."

The old couple were gazing at them.

Serena turned to them and speaking in Monjonese discovered that they were in the back alley behind the Wheatsheaf Inn. The old couple were named Feerd and Unta, who were retired from active life and lived in a small house behind that door. They had heard a sudden loud noise and had looked out after a while and found Evander and Serena, dressed in foreign style and seemingly the victims of a robbery, beaten and bloody.

Now Feerd stepped up to help Serena to her feet. He called out something to Evander and led Serena through the door into their garden.

Unta was looking at Evander expectantly.

Serena called over her shoulder.

"Come on, Evander. They'll make some kalut; I could die for a cup of kalut right now."

It was a good idea. Get off the streets, recover their strength a little, learn what had been happening since their abrupt departure. Evander made a big effort and staggered across the alley and into the garden. Unta steadied him as he went.

Feerd and Unta's place was a tiny two-story dwelling squeezed in between larger buildings that took all the street front, leaving them access only through the back alley.

Inside was a small, warm kitchen area, the floor tiled in red brick, the walls whitewashed, the ceiling sooty from the cook fire.

Feerd set Serena down in the comfortable chair. Evander sat on a small bench against the wall. Unta busied herself at a stove and soon had water boiling for kalut. She brought Evander a basin and a scrap of rag with which to wash the blood off his face. Feerd pulled out another chair and a stool from the other ground-floor room. He said something to Evander, who shrugged his incomprehension.

Serena spoke up, first in Monjonese to Feerd, and then to Evander. "He's asking if you'd like a shot of brandy with the kalut."

Now there was a good idea. Evander nodded and smiled at the old man, who produced a bottle and some battered tin cups, then poured a splash for each of them.

"To our safe return!" said Serena in Furda, holding up

the cup. The old man was puzzled, but held up his cup anyway. They toasted their survival.

The fiery brandy brought a flush to their cheeks and instant giddiness. Serena laughed, for the first time in days, perhaps weeks. Evander laughed with her. Old Feerd grinned and nodded and said something to Unta who chuckled as well.

Then came the hot kalut and some wheat porridge mixed with butter and salt from little Unta.

"What shall we do, Evander?" asked Serena.

"Rest up a little while here, then go to Ornizolest's house."

"We better find Konithomimo first."

"I think he fell into a big puddle in the alley."

"Oh, dear, he'll be furious."

Evander smiled, not unkindly, at the thought. "He will be, but they'll clean him up once I return him to Yumi and Elsu. I will put his case to the Ugoli. They are a good-hearted folk and will release him someday."

"Oh, Evander, we made it. We survived Orthond. We're back."

He pursed his lips and nodded. After a moment her face fell.

"Right," she said, stricken-faced. "Which means we are in deep trouble. We have to get out of the city somehow. I can never go home."

The brief euphoria from the brandy had vanished.

"The Ugoli will help. We'll find a way."

She nodded after a moment. "I'm sure you're right. If we could escape from Orthond, then we can surely get out of Monjon."

"The first thing we need is some information," he said. "I wonder what old Feerd and Unta know about the current situation."

She turned to Feerd and Unta and asked them what had been happening in Monjon in recent weeks. Unta laughed and asked her where she was from that she didn't know that! Serena explained that they were traders down from the north. They'd heard there was a riot and a long series of Jousts Magical in Monjon, but no more than that.

Feerd chuckled to himself on hearing this, a trifle bitterly. Unta quickly filled in. Since then so much had happened it was hard to keep it all straight.

The king had issued a death warrant for the wizard Gadjung following the mysterious death of his daughter. The funeral for the Princess Serena had been held only a few days before. The occasion had been rendered even grimmer than might have been because there had been no body to bury. Princess Serena had completely disappeared in some kind of magical explosion. It had woken the entire city; indeed, it was heard for fifty miles around. Some said there'd been a red flash and a vision of angels, others just a red flash, and others saw flashes of other colors. The king had blamed the wizard for angering the blessed Thymnal.

The terrible wizard had responded by laying a new curse on Monjon, dooming the city to die of starvation. He had also offered a huge reward to anyone who brought him the Princess Serena, alive or dead. An equal reward was offered for the young man who had tried to abduct the princess from the rooftop of the palace. He, too, had disappeared in the same explosion.

Serena shot Evander a frightened glance. They had disappeared, presumed dead, but the damned wizard had still put a heavy price on their heads.

Unta rattled on though. Now there was war brewing with the Storchese. Agrant had accused the Storchese of being allied to the wizard. Trade disputes had turned ugly. A Monjon fiddle maker had been hanged in the marketplace of Mainzen. Agrant had ordered his ambassador home. Guard posts on the border were set to turning back any Storchese who tried to cross.

It went on, of course. New pests were appearing in the crops. The famine in the countryside was becoming general. Unta's voice took on a singsong quality as she recited the litany of discontent.

Evander nodded off somewhere along the line, too exhausted for even kalut's restorative powers.

He awoke briefly, sometime later, and found himself lying on a pallet in the smoke-smelling darkness of Feerd and Unta's kitchen. Serena was beside him, snoring softly. He reflected that just possibly the tide had turned. The wizard had withdrawn to his lair on the Black Mountain. The king thought Serena was dead; indeed, they'd had her funeral. Perhaps, with the aid of the Ugoli, they could slip away and start new lives in the far east. That was where they had to go anyway, to carry the warning to the great witches of Cunfshon. If they went that far away, surely no one would ever come after them. Perhaps the witches would hide them. He lay back, and sleep reclaimed him.

When he next awoke, he was being shaken roughly. A small Monjon lamp was shining on him, and a circle of faces peered down.

"There's one of 'em awake," said a voice in thick Furda.

"The Nob Hat's coming," said another voice in Furda.

Evander struggled to sit up. "Serena?" he called.

"Evander?" She was being held in the corner of the room. He tried to stand, but found his legs too wobbly to support him. A couple of the men grabbed his arms and held him up.

"Here, young fellow, you look pretty well worn out."

"Who are you?" he asked.

"Who are we?" said a fellow with a big red nose and cruel little blue eyes standing behind them. "We're the committee of local investigations. We were appointed just a few minutes ago in the snug over at the tavern when we heard that a handsome young couple had mysteriously turned up in the outer ward. We also heard that this couple had been taken in by old Feerd. So, we sort of appointed ourselves to the committee and came over to look into it."

"He called out Serena, I do believe," said another fellow who wore a tight leather cap.

There were some chuckles.

"Had a skinful, has he?"

A thick-necked, burly fellow in a fine leather coat pressed close. His nose had been broken many times, and he had the look of a fighter. "What Serena is this?" he asked.

"No Serena," he mumbled. "I said Belina."

"He lies," said the thick Furda accent.

"Interesting," said the leather-coated thug.

A moment later he was joined by a face Evander did remember, the Nob Hat, who had broken into the jail and freed Evander.

Glukus, the protection boss of the outer ward, stared down at him. Glukus had a hard face, all flat planes and sharp angles with piggy, close-set eyes.

"So, what have we here?" he said in Monjonese.

"Almighty great bang, a flash that could be seen in Storch, and these two were found lying out there in the alley. Old couple took them in, gave them a place to sleep. Neighbors told us, and we thought we'd better investigate."

"What have they got to say for themselves?"

"Not much yet, except this one called the girl Serena."

The Nob Hat's eyebrows leaped, and he pushed his face down close to Evander's. "Serena is it? That's very interesting. Very interesting, indeed."

"What should we do?"

"Right now? Bag them, put them in Sid's warehouse. We'll take a look at 'em and see what they're about."

Evander cleared his throat, still seared by the brief exposure to the bitter cold of chaos. He glimpsed old Feerd, blood running down the side of his head, sitting tight in a chair in the corner.

"Kind sirs, we're in need of rest and shelter."

"Speaks Furda all right. That's what the reward paper says."

Evander felt his heart grow cold.

"Bag 'em."

Men were thrusting the princess into a large brown sack. Other men were doing the same to him. Evander struggled weakly, but he was spent. The experience of the black mirror had taken his last reserves. They were burly men, porters and part-time enforcers for Glukus's gang. The bag soon closed over his head, and he was lifted and carried away.

After a short journey, perhaps two hundred feet, he was dropped unceremoniously on a hard surface. As the bag was opened, he glimpsed a stack of bales of straw.

Glukus and the others stood around them. Serena was pulled to her feet and tied to a post. Evander was pulled up and held by a pair of heavyset men. The place had once been used to stable horses. There were haylofts above and a faint, residual odor of horse. Chests and bales were stacked high around them. Monjon lamps glowed above.

"Where did you go?" asked Glukus in thickly accented Furda.

They looked blankly back at him.

"You can't fool me; I know who you are. You're the Princess Serena, and you're the idiot who tried to steal her from the wizard."

"I don't know what you're talking about," said Evander. "We're travelers."

The thug in the leather coat hit him in the mouth, not hard enough to break anything, but painful nonetheless. He sagged for a moment in the grip of those who held him. Then, spitting blood, he straightened up.

"You consider your words, my fine young gentleman. Now, before you start telling lies again, you think about what my friend Stuggles will do if you do."

Stuggles had a nasty smile.

"Look," said Evander, determined not to give in.

"It's no good, Evander," said the princess. "They have likenesses."

It was true; Glukus had a small drawing done of the princess, taken from a court painting, held loosely in his hand. "And it's a very good likeness, too," he said. "The royal artist is to be commended for his work."

Glukus held up the picture.

"So, don't deny that it's you. It won't do you any good, and you'll be wasting my time. Before I ship you off to your, uh, final destination, I want to know where you disappeared to. Were you really hiding in the city? Or did you sneak out somewhere?"

Evander closed his eyes for a moment. How to explain? "Look, you wouldn't believe us if we told you where we went."

"Why don't we let me be the judge of that?"

Evander stared around helplessly. "The magical blast threw us completely out of this world and into another, a world called Orthond."

Glukus's eyebrows rose for a moment. His eyes narrowed. "Go on."

Evander tried to describe Orthond and its inhabitants.

After a while Glukus hushed him with a curse and gesture. "Enough of your damned nonsense. Now, one more chance. Where have you been hiding all these weeks? Tell me with who or Stuggles is going to hurt you."

"But it's true," wept Serena. "He's telling the truth; that's exactly what did happen to us."

Glukus squinted at her. "What is this?"

"We really did leave this world. Look at these clothes; have you ever seen any like them? No one in Monjon would make clothes like these, and no one could sew them so finely. These were made by Neild."

Glukus stared at her for a long moment. He turned

around and raised a hand to send Stuggles in, but then
thought better of it. The wizard didn't want them bruised.
And while it would be nice to know who'd hidden them,
it wasn't worth having to damage them to find out. He'd
been prepared a few moments ago to have Stuggles work
on the idiot, but if they were both suffering from the same
hallucinations, then it might simply not be worth the risk
of incurring the wizard's wrath. The reward was a fabulous
amount of gold. No point in risking all that.

He spat and muttered something in Monjonese and then
turned on his heel and left. The men bound and gagged
them, then rolled them up inside bolts of cloth. A tube was
thrust down inside the roll to ensure that at least some air
reached them, and then they were heaved up onto a cart
along with other bales and left to stew in the dark.

Evander lay there long enough to become profoundly
uncomfortable, in part from the claustrophobia of being so
completely enclosed. He had to fight hard to keep from an
insane panic.

At last they heard horse hooves clattering on cobble-
stones. The wagon moved as the horses were coupled to it,
and then it dipped with a driver's weight. A few moments
later a whip cracked and the wagon rolled forward.

Evander felt utterly lost. This was not the way he had
imagined his return to Ryetelth. If they were going straight
back to King Agrant, Evander would soon have a date with
the royal lions, and Serena's wedding to the Wizard of the
Black Mountain would be hastily rescheduled. However, as
the journey lengthened and grew bumpier with jolts coming
almost continuously, other possibilities grew stronger. Perhaps they were being spirited away to be held for ransom.
The king would pay handsomely to get the princess back.
Evander he would probably leave to the thugs to dispose
of in their own way. After Evander's experiences at the
hands of the weave witch, he did not care to imagine what
horrors might be arranged. The curiosities market in Ourdh
beckoned once more.

The journey lengthened, then finally halted. The cloth
was unrolled, and Evander and Serena were propped up
on some hay. The gags were removed. They sucked in air
and gave prayers of thanks for their deliverance from the
dark confines of the bales of cloth. It was night, and they
were in a stable. A pair of huge, unsmiling men gave them

a few bites of bread and a little water. Evander tried to question them. They said not a word, nor did they trifle with Serena. They might as well have been handling statues.

Serena suggested that he save his breath. "We have to come up with a plan, Evander. We can't fail now, not after we've come through so much."

"Well, we've traveled a long way in this wagon, so I don't think they're taking us to your father."

Serena sobbed. "Then they are taking us directly to Gadjung."

Now that Serena had put it in words, Evander realized that was exactly what was happening. He simply hadn't wanted to accept the inevitable.

He spent some time examining his bonds, but they were expertly done with waxed cord that could not be stretched or loosened. Neither of them was going to get free without help.

Later, the gags were reinserted. Fresh horses had been purchased, and the journey continued. Fortunately, they were not rolled up in the cloth anymore, but were just left to lie on top of the bales as the wagon jolted along. They were joined by a pair of horsemen who rode on either side of the cart.

The wagon jolted across increasingly rough terrain, and hours stretched on into a future filled with dread.

Chapter Forty-one

The sacks were opened, and Serena and Evander were dumped out on a smooth stone floor. Evander looked up straight into the ghastly face of the wizard, a mottled horror of wrinkled doughy flesh hanging from his bones.

The wizard smiled at Serena. "My bride," he gloated. "You have returned to me." He threw back his head and roared with laughter. "Against your will, perhaps, but you have returned to me, your loving husband-to-be."

Serena was ashen-faced, unable to speak for once.

"Oh, my beloved," rasped the ancient creature, "how I long to take you to bed. To ravish you thoroughly as you deserve."

Evander finally found his voice. "Leave her alone."

The wizard's eyes flicked across to him. "You! I shall deal with you, too. But first I will have the answers to some questions. And in the meantime, If I wish to take my lovely bride to her nuptial couch, who are you to deny me?"

"I love her. You do not."

"Love, is it?" Again, the ancient threw back its head and roared with laughter. He glared at Evander, who felt his head gripped by some monstrous force.

"I'll show you love, you piece of verminous filth. You dared to defile my lovely bride with your advances, did you?"

Evander choked, unable to speak.

The eyes glared madly at him and blinked. He could speak again. "I'll not play your game."

"It's no game, child. I will lift your skin from your flesh inch by inch and scour underneath with acid. No fragment of you will die without your wailing for it a thousand times over."

He stroked his doughy chin. "But first some questions must be answered."

Evander felt like a rabbit, run to ground by the hunter's dogs. Since that fateful day when he'd stepped ashore at Port Tarquil, he had been marked for destruction by this sorcerer.

"Bring them!" snapped the wizard, turning away and shuffling slowly across the room, a large echoing hall. Men naked but for leather aprons came forward to seize them and carry them, unprotesting, in the wizard's wake.

Evander turned his head and felt a shiver run through his marrow. One of the men was familiar. "Kospero!" he whispered.

There was no response. The eyes stared straight ahead.

"Kospero?" he tried again. It was undoubtedly Kospero, or it had been. Then he lost sight of him.

The knowledge was peculiarly frightening. All this time he had thought Kospero was dead, and now he found him turned into a zombie and serving the Wizard of the Black Mountain.

They were taken into a small room and strapped down on tables side by side. The room was lit by a fresh, bright Monjon globe that hung overhead.

The wizard began in a cheerful-sounding mood. "So, you escaped me temporarily, but you didn't get far enough, it seems."

Evander felt as limp as that rabbit, hanging from the hunter's belt.

"Now, as I recall, I was on the point of blasting you to nothingness when you both disappeared, along with the magic carpet. It was not the effect of my spell. That was a ragnarok spell; you should have glowed with a golden light for a short period before you were completely consumed. No, the blasted Thymnal interfered, it was obvious. Your sudden disappearance left us with many questions."

The wizard moved slowly and with a grimace of pain. It noticed Evander's stare. "Yes, young man, this pain is all because of you. That nasty knife of yours carried a sting. You can be sure I shall linger over your passing from this world."

Evander gritted his teeth. "Do your worst."

"Oh, I shall, I shall. But first, tell me where you disappeared to. Where have you been hiding these past few weeks?"

Neither of them responded.

"Well?" The wizard purred in an evil way.

Evander's mouth was dry.

"Well?" it roared into his face, wafting a smell like that of sour dust.

"We went to a place called Orthond," said Serena.

"How did you go to this place?"

"I don't know; ask the Thymnal."

"Ah, the Thymnal. We'll get back to the Thymnal. First tell me where this place Orthond is."

"I don't know."

"You don't, eh? Or you just won't tell me. Don't want me to find it, eh?"

"Oh no, I'd love you to find Orthond. You'd see what your kind are worth in the world."

"That does not sound like a compliment, my darling. Aren't you forgetting that we are wed?"

"I will never wed you."

"Come now, my dearest, don't make me angry. We were wed fair and square; your father was there, surely you remember?"

"No wedding was conducted, for the ceremony never began."

"Ah, so you wish to stand on formality, do you?"

Serena made no reply.

"Well, my dear, first I will work on your lover. My nemesis, the daring young man who first crossed me in Port Tarquil. Perhaps when you see me flay him alive, you will recall the way to get to Orthond."

Evander found his voice at last. "She's telling the truth. Listen to me, I will tell you what happened; perhaps you will believe it. You are an ancient master of the dark arts. You, more than anyone else alive, might understand what befell us."

The white dough face was still, the eyes fixed on him. "Speak then."

Without hesitation Evander recounted what they had endured since that moment atop the high tower of Monjon. He spoke of ruined Orthond, its cold winds and broken cities. He spoke of the Eleem and their world, and he described what he knew of their enemy, Waakzaam the Great, Dominator of Twelve Worlds.

The wizard listened intently. When Evander had finished, there was a long silence, then a grunt. "So, it has happened as was foretold long, long ago. Zambalestes predicted it. The Red Aeon could not last forever. Waakzaam would escape the clutch of the Sinni. He would eventually seek to destroy them. The game would be lost on this part of the Sphere Board of Destiny."

Evander stared at him with wondering eyes.

"Hah! You two are such small things, but you are deadly. You bring the news of our doom in your innocent mouths. So sweet, so pretty, and so deadly, and you know nothing, almost nothing at all."

Evander found his voice. "So you know this monster called Waakzaam? You know we tell the truth."

The wizard nodded. Evander would have sworn there was a touch of sadness in the wizard's face.

"The world is very old, child. Long before the Red Aeon, other circles of great magic arose and fell. Before the Red was the Cyan, and long, long before that was the Celadon time that some call the Golden Age, when the Great Elves ruled Ryetelth. Some say they rule still, but through hidden ways. Some say that they are the Sinni themselves, somehow transmogrified upon the higher blessed plane of existence."

Evander blinked. The wizard focused and then gave a snort of amused contempt. "But you don't know what I'm talking about. Probably no one alive on this world, but myself, knows these secrets. I shall deal with you later."

The wizard left them. The globe bathed them in warm light. Their bonds were firm, with no likelihood of escape. The zombies stood outside the room anyway.

They were left there for a long time. They did their best to boost each other's morale. It wasn't easy at first. The situation had never seemed quite so dismal, but somehow they found the strength to put it aside and refused to surrender to absolute woe. After all they had been through, it was impossible that they fail now. Gallows humor, without hysteria, came to the surface.

Then the wizard returned. "I have had a wonderful idea. I shall offer my bride her freedom. She shall go back to her father if he will give up the Thymnal."

Serena laughed bitterly. "He will never give up the Thymnal. He cares more for the Thymnal than he does for me."

"The man is thy father, foolish girl! His heart will rend

when I tell him what I will do to you if he does not agree."
The wizard gave her his mad smile again. "And I'll even
throw in your lover as an added inducement, on the one
stipulation that he be thrown to the lions at once."

With this he left them. The Monjon globe continued to
blaze down at them, but they slept nonetheless, for they
were hard worn by all they had endured.

Hours later, Evander awoke. A figure had entered the
room. It hovered about behind his head, out of his line of
vision. It seemed agitated, moving from place to place.
Then it moved around to the other end of the table.
Evander suddenly realized it was Kospero.

"Kospero? Do you recognize me? It's me, Evander."

The blank-eyed figure peered down at him. It was troubled, its forehead wrinkled. "Who are you?" it said at last.

"I am Evander, Danais, your friend, your pupil. We were
aboard the ship, the *Wind Trader,* you remember. We went
ashore at Port Tarquil. I was eager to see the girls who
dance in the taverns there. The wizard afflicted me."

"Danais?" The blank eyes lost their blankness for a
moment.

"We were thrown overboard into the sea. Do you
remember?"

Kospero put his hands to the sides of his head. "I . . ."
he began. Then he gave an inarticulate cry and turned away
and left the room.

"What was that about?" asked Serena.

"It is Kospero, Serena; you remember I told you of good
old Kospero. My friend, my teacher, who was thrown to
the sharks off the Bakan coast."

"But you said he was dead."

"I thought he was, but he's not. He's right there. The
wizard has had him here all this time."

"He's a zombie."

"Yes, but we've stirred his memories, I think."

"Can you get him to free us?"

"I can try."

But to even try required that Kospero come back, which
he did not. Hours slipped by. Eventually, they dozed, even
under the brilliant light of the hot young Monjon lamp.

The door crashed open. Still wearing a black floor-length
cloak, the wizard shuffled in radiating anger. It was plain

that the king had refused to deal. "That pompous little man, he thinks he can defeat my will, my power?"

Something wild and frightening had entered the wizard's eyes. "Bring me the flaying irons!" he shouted over his shoulder.

"Surely, this is beneath you?" said Evander.

The only response was a sickening smile. The zombies rolled in a brazier on a small metal trolley. The flaying knives came in various lengths. The wizard picked one up and began toying with it. "Remove his clothing," he said.

As his shirt was torn away, the wizard gave a gasp of astonishment. "A freak! A marvelous freak of magic! This must have happened when you survived my spell at Port Tarquil. You should have become a hundred toads, which would all have met violent ends by now. Instead, you have grown this wonderful skin. Well, well, well."

The wizard looked down at him with appraising eyes. "Oh, I could get a fortune for you in Ourdh. The curiosities market there is very, um, mature in its tastes."

He suddenly seemed to realize what he was toying with in his hands. "Hah! Won't be needing those for you then. This changes things. Nor will I be giving you up to a bunch of mangy lions. Oh, no. You shall be investigated in the laboratory. I shall keep you in a cage and exhibit you to the curious."

He turned to Serena. "I shall flay her, instead." He flashed a bizarre smile. "And I shall send her pretty skin, intact in one piece, for I am a skilled hand with the flaying irons, to her father."

"No, wait, let me say something," said Evander.

"Ah, it's the 'love' again, is it?" The wizard rubbed his leathery jaw. "Want to sacrifice yourself, is it?"

"No, I have an idea. I think I could get you what you want."

"The Thymnal?"

"Yes."

"How?" The wizard's eyes were alight.

"I know how to sneak into the palace. I could steal it."

"Oh, ho! Do you now? And then what would you do with it?"

"What do you think? I'd bring it back here."

"Ah, and I'm to trust you, am I?"

Evander fell silent for a moment, then glanced toward Serena.

"Of course," murmured Gadjung, "it's all for this 'love' of yours. Or at least that's what you'd have me believe."

Serena was calculating the odds. For herself, she was now certain, there was no hope. The monster would kill her as he had threatened, but for Evander, just possibly there was a chance here. And, she knew, it was important that at least one of them get away and take the warning to the witches in the east. And if she could somehow save Evander's life, then she could face her own death with equanimity.

First, she had to convince the wizard to let him go. She didn't expect Evander to actually steal the Thymnal—Monjon must retain its magical elevation in the world. But he would be set free. She could see that the wizard was seriously considering Evander's brash proposal.

She jumped in. "I know where the key is kept. It's not impossible. It might even be easy; the place isn't guarded that heavily. It's hard to get onto the private floors of the palace, but the Thymnal is kept in a vault in the temple. There is a private accessway from the royal suite. The king always keeps open access to the Thymnal."

The wizard's head snapped around, his eyes boring into her. "Ah, I had suspected something of the kind might exist. Go on."

"The key is in my father's study. It is the head of a decorative brass cat. I can give Evander directions. He has been in the palace before."

"If I let him go, he will try not to come back."

"But you won't let him stay away, will you?"

The wizard smiled. "No, of course not. He'll come back whether he likes it or not, because if he doesn't, I really will flay you, and he is in love with you, Princess. So he has no choice in the matter. I don't even need any magical hold."

"Then you'll let him go?"

"Possibly. I will consider."

Gadjung left them.

The globe burned down on them. Hours went by.

He returned. "Such treachery on your part, Princess Serena. I admit that I am shocked. You abandon your city very easily. I am most fortunate not to have been formally wed to you after all. To think that I deluded myself into imagining that there might grow a fondness, even a love between us. Oh, I am stricken with remorse. Such a cold heart you must have."

Gadjung put a hand to his brow in mockery, then laughed noisomely. "To think that you would betray your city like this. What will they say of you when I tell the world of your perfidy? Serena the traitress, who slew her own people with a word!"

Serena checked her first, hot response, then replied coolly. "I think you will defeat the city in the end, oh mighty one. You are a master of evil; my father cannot match you. Eventually, you will have the Thymnal. So I would bring only a swifter end to our torment. Once you have the Thymnal, you will have no further need to assault us."

"And you hope, you will save your own skin," he said chuckling again, "quite literally."

"Why not? Why die for no purpose?"

Something cruel hardened in those ancient eyes. Gadjung snapped his fingers. Zombies entered and took up Evander and bore him away.

He was strapped to a chair in a small, darkened room. The wizard came to him and used a subtle enchantment and a swinging fob on a chain to put him under hypnotic sleep. Evander's gaze grew dim, and his mouth slackened.

The wizard questioned him intently, but detected no falsehood. The youth was simply trying to save Serena. He would happily die for her.

Finally, he had the zombies take Evander back to the other room while he pondered his decision.

He might lose the boy, a valuable freak and one that he most dearly wished to investigate in the laboratory. Would it be possible to reproduce this effect again? At will? It would be a most amusing effect if one could master it. All that would be lost if the youth simply fled.

But the young man was in love. And love would make men do the strangest things. He would come back, no matter what. And there was a distinct possibility of success in the primary mission. The thought that the Thymnal could be in his hands in the matter of a few hours was enough to bring on euphoria in his ancient, fell heart. After careful consideration he made his decision.

He swept in on them, rousing them from sleep. "I have decided that this is a wager I'm prepared to take. He can't go over to the other side; the king will throw him to the lions. And he knows what will happen to you, with whom he is desperately, moonfacedly in love, if he does not return. So I think I will risk it. He will go. You will give him all the assistance you can. My batrukh will take him."

Chapter Forty-two

He rode the batrukh, sitting on a small saddle set across the creature's neck. He rode, amazed at the act of flying with the world far below. The batrukh's enormous muscles bunched and released behind him, causing him to sway up and down in the saddle. He could actually feel its heat.

He had no need to guide the creature. It knew where to take him. For the return, he had been provided with a silver whistle to summon it when he was ready.

Beneath him the land rushed past, covered in darkness. Distant clusters of lights showed where the river towns of the Skola valley lay. The air rushing past was cool, but to Evander it seemed warm after the chill of Orthond. He tried to use the time well, by going over the information Serena had given him. The brass cat sat on the left side of her father's private desk. To enter that room, one used a key that was hidden in a blue jar on the windowsill outside.

After a while, though, his thoughts strayed. To fly through the night air like this was as magical as anything he had experienced, and yet he was not thrilled by the distant lights. They offered a mirage of safety, but he knew better. There was no safety in his life. He would go back, no matter what. He would do it on the slight chance that the wizard would spare the princess. He would do it even though it meant the rest of his life would be spent in a cage.

Evander tried to fight off the feeling of doom, but it was hard. They had escaped Orthond only to find themselves recaptured by Gadjung. The Gods must have laid a curse upon him. Perhaps it would have been better if he'd just stayed in Sedimo and fought the usurpers. He would have lost and they would have killed him quickly and quietly. That way he would have had to suffer none of these agonies.

Then Evander roused himself from these defeatist

thoughts. While he was alive and free, there was still hope
left! And if he'd been slain in Sedimo, then he never would
have met Serena of Monjon and thus would never have
known the greatest love of his life.

The batrukh was swift. Within the hour it flew in over
the walls of Monjon and made a landing on the top of a
domed mausoleum in the cemetery of notables, just outside
the palace.

Evander scrambled off and slid down the copper tiles of
the mausoleum. When he reached the edge, he swung from
the gutter to a railing and then to the ground.

The batrukh's enormous wings cracked over his head as
it hurled itself back into the air, and he threw himself flat.
The wind ripped up a storm of dust and leaves for a few
wing beats, and then it was gone. Evander got to his feet
and looked around for the landmarks Serena had shown
him the first day they met.

The batrukh's passage had been observed, of course, and
men with lamps were already approaching the outer edge
of the cemetery. Voices echoed from the windows of the
palace above the trees.

He spotted the looming mass of Ludiz the Great's tomb
and turned left, toward the palace wall. The soldiers were
calling down from the battlements. The lights were closer.
He ran to the small mausoleum of the Goose of Gold. On
the south wall he found the brass plaque and touched the
four stars in the corners. Then he reached up to the brass
bas relief of the Goose of Gold and touched the right foot.

Something in the wall clicked. With a creak and a groan,
part of the lower wall slid aside. He pressed himself into
darkness, treading carefully down the steps he felt below.
Suddenly, the stone slid back, and he was plunged into total
darkness. He pulled out the small Monjon globe given him
by the wizard to light his way.

Now he made swift progress. Once again he passed the
curving walls, and the dank areas where water covered the
floor of the tunnel. After his experience with tunnels in
Orthond, this seemed like a childish scramble, and he soon
reached the Pit of Donzago beneath the great vaulted ceiling. A ceremony was in progress. Into the great pit, priests
were throwing flowers, which fluttered for a moment and
then vanished into the darkness. A choir sang of the mo-

mentary nature of life and how swiftly it would run its course.

Evander sidled past unnoticed. He hurried on through the semi-public parts of the labyrinth and passed one set of guards, who took no notice of him either.

He reached the lower dial, where seven tunnels met at the bottom of the labyrinth. He took the second tunnel to the left and soon reached the chimney stair. He met no one and climbed as quickly as desperately sore limbs would allow.

At last he reached the sixth floor and the panel that opened into an alcove inside the royal apartments.

Now he went on the balls of his feet, ears alert for the slightest sound. The apartments were well lit, but quiet at this time of night. The king and queen would be asleep.

Serena thought there might be a guard on the corridor leading to her father's study. Her father disliked having guards inside the royal apartment at all, but had to allow one to calm the fears of his advisers.

On the other hand, since it was late at night, the guard might be stationed inside the front door of the royal apartment, where there was a comfortable chair beside the old Storch-made grandfather clock.

Evander passed a painting of Donzago the Great and went on down a red-carpeted passage, past tall wooden doors with immense silver doorknobs and then to a junction. There was no guard. To the left was a green-carpeted corridor, to the right a polished wood floor running past more doors to a window. A blue vase stood on the windowsill. He reached inside the vase and felt around for a moment before he found the key.

Agrant was a forgetful person, who would have preferred not to have to lock his study door at all. Serena knew her father all too well.

The key turned easily in the lock, and he was inside. Evander exulted for a moment. He had scarcely dared to believe he could get this far. He closed the door silently and recalled that the Goose of Gold had done this trip many times, going to and from her lovers, so it was not impossible.

He used his little Monjon lamp to examine the room. Walled with books on two sides, with a large window that overlooked the gardens, it was sumptuously furnished. An

immense globe of Ryetelth sat in one corner, turned so that
the northeastern coast of Eigo was most prominent. Above
the fireplace was a pair of crossed swords and a shield
bearing the royal arms of Monjon. A table was covered in
scrolls and papers, and a large desk littered with more papers, crystal paperweights, sealing wax, and quill pens.

In a moment of panic he failed to see the brass cat. It
wasn't on the desk. He hastily darted around the room until
he found the cat holding down some papers on a small
side table.

It was a moment's work to unscrew the head. He had
the key! The secret passage to the chamber of the Thymnal
was entered through a hatch hidden inside the large brick
fireplace that dominated the far end of the room. He was
en route to the fireplace when he heard footsteps outside
the door.

He sprang into the fireplace and flattened himself against
the back. The door opened, and the king strode in, muttering to himself in Monjonese. He closed the door and
without a glance in the direction of the fireplace went to
the desk, sat down behind it, and began to search through
the loose scrolls and papers upon it. The king did not keep
a tidy desk, and there was a fair amount of litter.

The king rummaged for a while, and then his hand
chanced on the brass cat. He noticed the absence of the
head and stood up with a cry of distress.

Evander slipped out of concealment and darted forward.
The king looked wildly through the papers, and then on
the floor behind the desk. When he looked up next, it was
to find Evander standing over him, armed with one of the
crossed swords from the fireplace. It was blunt, but still
sharp enough to be driven through someone.

"You?" whispered the king, who had gone white. "But
how? You are dead. I saw you vanish into thin air with my
own eyes."

"We didn't die, Your Majesty."

Agrant touched Evander's knee, then shrank back with
a groan. After a moment he looked up again. "Then what
happened? Where is my daughter?"

"It's a long story, but let it suffice to say that we were
catapulted to another world. There we discovered the grav-
est threat to our own world that could be imagined. We
bear a warning that must be taken to the Emperor of the

Rose. He alone on our world has the authority to combat this threat."

As he listened, Agrant's fear dissolved and was replaced by rage. "What nonsense is this? Who are you, anyway? Where is my daughter? How in hell's name have you managed this deviltry?"

Evander put the sword up to the king's throat. "Be calm, Your Majesty. Listen carefully. I don't have time to make a full explanation. Serena will die a horrible death at the hands of the wizard unless I bring him the Thymnal." Evander looked around for something to bind the king with and noticed the heavy silk cords that held back the curtains. "Lie down on the floor and don't move, or I'll be forced to kill you, do you understand?"

Agrant's eyes blazed, but when Evander pressed the sword harder yet against the royal throat, he knelt and than lay prone.

It was the work of a few minutes, and then Evander had bound the king hand and foot and gagged him with strips cut from the royal nightrobe. As he worked, he tried to explain some of what had happened to them.

Agrant's eyes now bore a look of pitiful frustration, rage, anguish, and something akin to despair. Evander finished with him and then searched out the doorway hidden in the side of the fireplace and pressed it open. He stepped through into another secret passage, this one known only to members of the royal family. He moved cautiously down a winding stair and then along a whitewashed passageway lit dimly by an aged Monjon lamp now shining in the red range.

A door at the end opened out onto a little gallery above the vault of the blessed Thymnal. A narrow stair spiraled down to the floor.

He approached the vault. The door was of heavy, polished steel, the lock massive, but he pressed the brass cat's head into the keyhole and turned, and with a smooth sliding of tumblers it opened.

The Thymnal lay in a casket, inside a steel case the size of a coffin set up in the center of the chamber. There was a circular row of seats for those fortunate individuals who were to bathe in the light of the Thymnal. At other times the case was lowered into the water tank at the far end to begin the process of manufacturing Monjon globes.

The chamber was deserted. The guards were outside the main door.

Evander moved quickly to the case. He looked in and saw the golden casket of the blessed Thymnal reposing inside, sitting on a scarlet cushion. There was no doubting the power of the Thymnal. It was a palpable thing here, this close. Evander felt a wave of warmth go over him, coupled with sudden exotic sweet scents, and then a feeling of calm beneficence spread through him.

The golden casket was the size of a man's head and had handles on either end. It looked heavy. Evander reached down and lifted it out. It was heavy, as if it were truly made of gold and filled with golden coin. He hefted it up to his chest and returned to the stair.

It was heavy, indeed, and by the time he'd reached the king's study again, his arms were aching. Nonetheless, he had a lot farther to go.

He returned through the fireplace hatch. The king was still lying there on the floor, though he'd managed to wriggle halfway to the door. At the sight of Evander carrying the golden casket, the king's eyes bulged with horror.

Evander was moved to pity, even to the king who had planned to feed him to the lions—and would still do so instantly if given the chance—and he tried to explain. "I have to take the Thymnal; it's the only way to save Serena."

Agrant's eyes threatened to explode.

"Look, the wizard would have won anyway. I'm saving you from a long drawn-out agony."

The purpling face suggested that His Majesty was going to expire any moment from apoplexy. Evander backed away.

He rested for a moment, then gathered himself and opened the door into the royal apartments. A quick look showed that the coast was clear. He lifted the casket again and moved down the corridors. Soon he was back on the red carpet.

There was a bad moment just before he reached the secret panel once more. A door opened somewhere ahead of him, and someone sleepily called out a name. Another door opened at once. Two voices spoke, and then the doors closed again.

Evander stood there sweating a moment and then tiptoed

past those doors and down to the secret panel. Once inside the secret part of the palace, he retraced his steps until he came to the great hall of the pit.

It was a quiet time at the side of the pit. The ceremonies were finished, and only a couple of acolytes were left, praying in the pews at the far end. Some guards were dozing at their posts just outside the main doors.

Having scouted the space, Evander decided there was nothing to be done but to step boldly across the floor to the passage that led to the upper choristry, and from which there was a secret way to the outside world. By moving boldly, one would seem quite normal and above suspicion. With a little luck no one would spot the heavy little casket.

He set off and struggled to walk upright, without lurching under the weight of the gold. The acolytes were deep in prayers, their heads bowed so they might never see him. At this distance they might not notice the casket, even if they did look up.

Shoulders burning and arms trembling at the end, he made it across the floor and started up the choristry steps. Climbing steps brought out a new set of aches and pains in his worn-out legs. He stumbled on the third step and to his horror, dropped the casket.

It clanged down the steps like a bell, nicking his ankle as it went and leaving him grimacing in pain and hopping on one foot, before it crashed to the floor.

The acolytes looked up. Worse, the doors opened a moment later, and the guards stuck their heads inside.

A question was shouted in Monjonese.

Panic. He started down the steps. The guards were bellowing at him, and the acolytes were on their feet.

Now the guards had entered the chamber, calling for their fellows. The sound of heavy-footed men running echoed in nearby halls. Evander felt his heart sink. The acolytes were coming. One of them started screaming at him. The news was out. The Thymnal had been stolen.

Evander found himself on the gallery above the pit. Guards were approaching. The acolytes were even closer. He could never escape them with the heavy Thymnal, and without it his life was worth nothing and so was Serena's.

A voice seemed to whisper in his ear. "Jump."

He looked over into the pit.

Why not jump? It would be a better end than going to

the lions. He stepped closer. The casket seemed to weigh
more than ever. It was dragging him toward the pit.

"Jump, you'll not die."

It was now or never. The acolytes were just a few steps
away. He lurched and was over the edge and falling, the
Thymnal tumbling ahead of him, directly into the pit.

Chapter Forty-three

He was falling into forever, or so it seemed. Time slowed as he fell through an absolute nothingness toward more of the same. He couldn't look back, but he was certain he would see nothing there either. He was aware of just himself and the casket, floating through emptiness.

Fortunately, there was none of the freezing and drying from his crossing from Orthond to Ryetelth. The sensory impressions were minimal; he felt neither cold nor heat.

The fear of falling was fading as seconds crawled by. He began to wonder if this was death. If so, it was remarkably painless. The only thing that was certain was that he did retain a sensation of forward motion.

And then with extraordinary suddenness, the nothingness seemed to implode away in all directions, and he was standing on a flat expanse of silver—a silver plane that stretched away for miles in all directions. The golden casket lay on its side ten feet away. Beyond ran the shimmering silver landscape. Humped out of it here and there were cubes of various sizes, from small rocks to small hills.

He looked up into a pink sky and observed flat, pinwheeling polygons made of the same silver material, arranged in a vast daisy chain that was itself slowly spinning. The polygons were other silver planes, like the one he stood on. The scale of it all crashed home as he admired these great pieces of geometry, all in slow grandiose motion about some invisible center of gravity.

Heaven?

Had he died? If this was heaven, he had a feeling he was going to be disappointed. If it was hell, then it might prove preferable to more popular notions of the fiery afterlife. Either way, it seemed unlike the popular conceptions of either place in the hereafter.

He noticed a small book lying facedown and open just a

few feet away. A human skeleton lay close by. The shock of this sight was amplified almost immediately, for he noticed that there were more bones nearby and more skeletons, quite a few of them. They were the remains, he surmised, of those who had thrown themselves into the Pit of Donzago over the centuries.

Clearly, this wasn't heaven.

He took a deep breath. He was warm, and light suffused the land, but no visible source for any of it, no sun in the sky, no clouds, just the ring of silvery mirrors.

He picked up the book. It was bound in heavy black leather. The pages were soft, as if they were actually living things, and the text written on them changed constantly, black amoebae squirming across the pages. He closed the book hurriedly. The wriggling black marks made him dizzy.

He noticed drifts of withered brown threads scattered just past the golden casket. They crunched underfoot as he moved across to examine the Thymnal's chest. The threads were dead flowers. A further scattering of human skeletons could be seen dappling the silver-plate background.

He shook his head, stepped over to the chest, and set it upright. It was unmarked from the fall. As his eyes rested on it, a small voice spoke within his head. It wasn't so much a small voice as a muffled voice, he realized after a moment and he strained to hear it.

After his experience with the Neild and the ancient mage, Shadreiht, Evander was becoming more sensitive to psychic communication. This voice was different from the ones he'd felt before; it had a different tone, exuberantly cheerful.

He examined the lid and tried the lock and discovered that it had broken at some point, perhaps when it pitched to the floor of the pit chamber. He lifted the lid, and a golden light burst forth, and he felt his skin warm beneath it. The radiance of the Thymnal was falling on his toadlike skin at last!

Evander laughed. He roared. Had he paid enough to satisfy the thirst of the Thymnal?

The glow faded, seemed to dim, and then a small orb, glowing softly between gold and brass, rose out of the casket and into the air and spun slowly in place.

The voice in his head suddenly became much louder. "At last, at last, at last, oh thanks be to the Gods at last!"

Evander stared, openmouthed.

"And you!" continued the voice. "You are the one I must thank for freeing me from eons of torment. The boredom I have endured these past two hundred years you cannot imagine."

Evander shook himself. Though why should he find this surprising, after all that had happened to him since he'd first stepped ashore on the Bakan coast? "I, . . ." he began, and then words failed him.

"You are the Prince Danais Evander of Sedimo Kassim. Yes, I know. I have read your thoughts since you first seized my portable prison. I am Donzago the Great."

Evander gasped. "You are Donzago?"

"You see that book lying by the skeleton?"

Evander nodded.

"That was the book of spells I used, which included the one for ascendance into the Higher Realms. That is where such wonders as Thymnals can be found."

The little globe of gold spun slowly.

"Are these the higher planes?" asked Evander.

"Yes." The globe seemed to consider for a moment. "I, impious fool that I was, wished to enter the Higher Realms of the Sphereboard of Being. I tried that damned spell for ascendance and was transported here. The rulers of this realm were displeased and cursed me with the burden of the Thymnal."

"What happened? I know a little about being cursed."

"I was given the Thymnal, the orb that you are now looking at. I was sent back to Monjon. With the Thymnal I had tremendous beneficent power. I could heal the sick. I could make the lamps that are the basis for the city's great wealth. You have seen the power of the Thymnal."

"Oh, great Donzago, I have felt the power of the Thymnal!"

"Intoxicated with new power, I intended to rule forever. I would have been the greatest king the world has ever seen. And then I discovered the awful truth. My body was feeding the Thymnal, and in a few hours I was consumed. I grew weak. My vision blurred, and my senses were stripped away one by one. My mind died in my body, but continued in the Thymnal. In effect, I became the Thymnal."

Evander nodded, groping at the implications of this.

"The high ones had punished me, you see. I would have to serve as the Thymnal, giving good energies to the people for as long as the Thymnal remained on Ryetelth. I could not move. I could not control my own fate.

"The only way out was for someone to throw the Thymnal into the pit that was created when I first broke in on the blessed realm. So I was trapped there in Monjon, when all I wanted was to come here and join the High Ones in the Blessed Realm."

Evander wondered what was so blessed about this realm of silver planes in silent motion. What were all these cubes, and were they actually moving, very slowly? Creeping about on the silver plane? It was hard to say, but now he noticed that there were many small cones, and these were definitely moving.

From the look of the bones scattered about here, this wasn't a place where people could survive.

"So, I am free at last, and I am in your debt, young man. And so I must help you. You cannot stay here. The energies of the Blessed Realm are too strong for the human form. You will weaken and die within a few hours if you linger. Fortunately, I can send you back. That will also close the pit that I opened up with my ill-considered spell long ago."

"You were the Thymnal, and that means there is no Thymnal in Monjon anymore?"

"That is correct. Monjon will be descending to the ground once again. I was imprisoned there a very long time, so it will take as much as an hour, I think, but the city will fall, and the lights will dim. The era of the magical city of Monjon is over."

"Will the rulers of this realm make a Thymnal out of me?"

"No. You are innocent of any lust for the beatitude of the Higher Realm. You will be unmarked."

Suddenly gripped by a thought, Evander put a hand to his chest. The warty skin was still there. He sensed a difference, but he wasn't sure what it was. New hope burst into life in his heart. "If you don't mind," he said, "I will take this spell book."

"Be careful, dabble not in sorcery beyond your strength."

"I understand."

"Now prepare yourself. Take a good deep breath."

Evander slipped the spell book inside his shirt.

The next moment he felt himself lifted, spun about, and propelled back through the membrane of the pit of Donzago. Again he hung in empty darkness for a long moment of suspense. And finally he was ejected onto a hard surface, the floor of the former pit of Donzago. It had magically transformed itself into a black slab of adamant.

Hoarse voices roared in astonishment. Wails of lamentation came from dozens of throats. A great throng of priests and acolytes were gathered around the former pit, but they were blind. The closure of the pit had involved a tremendous flash of light. Evander was the only person in the chamber who could see.

No one noticed him slip into the choristry a moment later. He was through the secret door in a few more moments and into the adit of the Goose of Gold.

A few minutes later, Evander stood in the shadow of the tomb of the Goose. It was raining. There was panic abroad in the streets; he could hear a continuous dull roaring sound of human voices. It seemed to come from all directions.

He took stock of the situation. He had the silver whistle to call the batrukh, but he didn't have the Thymnal. Worse than that, the Thymnal didn't exist anymore.

Evander knew that the wizard would not be pleased. The wizard had no real use for Serena. Gadjung was thousands of years old and had no more sex drive than a peanut. Everything he'd done was to gain control of the Thymnal.

Evander would return. While there was life, there was hope, and he could not abandon Serena to die there alone. But first he would take care of another matter.

Chapter Forty-four

Evander made his way through crazy streets to the outer ward, where the marketplace was strewn with wreckage from a fallen house. A mass of people was trying to get out of the main gate, and they were backed up into the lower part of the market. A jam of wagons was blocking most of the road.

He slipped behind the Wheatsheaf Tavern into the narrow, cobbled alley between two high brick walls. He hunted up and down until he found the place where they'd fallen after leaving Orthond.

He vaguely recalled the heap of rubbish along one wall and shallow mudpools down the center. A doorway into the Wheatsheaf's courtyard broke up one wall. The narrow door into poor old Feerd and Unta's house was broken open. He put his head in and called, but found no response. They had already fled. He prayed they were not harmed.

Outside, he hunted through the rubbish piles, poking with a stick. There was soiled straw, vegetable peelings, broken crockery, a stoved in barrel or two, and a heap of rotten wood.

At last he saw what he was looking for. At the bottom of a heap of garbage a muddy corner of a rug was poking out. The Nob Hat's men had completely missed the rug, probably because it fell into a pool of muddy water and was hard to see in the dark.

He pulled it free. The rug was soaked and muddy and stank horribly.

Evander grinned, knowing how much Konithomimo hated being unclean.

"I can almost hear you complaining," he whispered. "Console yourself with the thought that at least I came back for you. I'm going to try and get you to the Ugoli."

Konithomimo had assured them that he could hear

human speech, so he felt no qualms about addressing the mud-stained, bedraggled little rug.

He rolled it up and toted it under his arm, pushing back up Avenue Fagesta through the crowds until he came to the inn. Inside was more of the same chaos that afflicted the streets. Every guest was trying to leave at the same time.

Merchants got out of the way of the muddy rug to let him by, and he climbed the stairs to Yumi and Elsu's room. They were gone.

He returned to the street and made his way to the house of Ornizolest. He rang the big street bell. After a wait of several seconds the door creaked open.

"Evander? Is that you?" said a familiar voice.

"Yumi! Yes, it's me, and I've got the carpet here. I'm afraid it's going to need a hell of a cleaning."

"Evander!"

The door opened wider, and he was embraced by Yumi and Elsu, and all the other Ugoli folk. The house was full of them. At times of national disaster, the Ugoli found it was wisest to group together in the homes of their wealthy folk. This gave them sufficient numbers to deter attacks by looters.

Ornizolest insisted he come in and stand before the fire, while dry clothes were sent for. Food and drink was on its way before he sat down.

The rug was unrolled. It was a stinking mess, but it was intact. Evander tried to explain what had happened.

Of course everyone in Monjon already knew what had happened. The Thymnal had reacted against the wizard's magic and caused the annihilation of the Princess Serena and an impious interloper and escaped prisoner. There had been a red flash and a blast that rocked the city. The princess was gone, no one knew where.

The king had taken to his bed, overwhelmed by sorrow. The wizard had been driven forth from the city and told to do his worst, for Agrant would never give up the Thymnal.

The Wizard of the Black Mountain put out a huge reward for any information concerning the missing princess or the interloper.

And now the word had leaked out that the Thymnal had been stolen and cast into the Pit of Donzago. All the lamps in Monjon had flared brightly for a moment and then begun to dim. At the same time the city started to fall out of the air, lowering slowly toward the ground.

That had started a raging panic. First the wretches under the city had fled in a convulsive chaos. Dozens had been trampled to death. Meanwhile, in the city proper, buildings were tumbling, walls cracking, the folk milling in the streets.

Evander heard the Ugoli out and then told them what had happened to him and Serena. Their eyes went wide as he described Orthond and its strange, ruined civilization. They stared at the rug as he told them of Konithomimo. They stared at him anew as he made his plea for a finite term of imprisonment for Konithomimo.

He told them what he had learned about the Thymnal and tried to describe the higher planes of being. The Ugoli were stunned to silence.

Then, when he told them of his fate, and that of Serena, they wept in the open, unself-conscious way of the Ugoli folk. They saw that he was doomed.

Yumi said as much.

Evander would not agree, however. He had one card left to play. They listened in wonder as he told them that he was going to summon the batrukh and return to the Black Mountain.

The Ugoli tried to dissuade him. It would be certain death. Everyone knew that the wizard had wanted only one thing, and that was the Thymnal. If Evander went back, he would never escape again. He would become a caged freak, to be exhibited. The princess would die one way or another. And now the Thymnal was gone, there would be nothing to protect Monjon. The wizard would probably come and take control of the city himself. The Ugoli were already close to their own departure. It was time to leave the city of lights. Perhaps the Bakan coast was completely ruined now. The Ugoli would go back across the Merassa to Molutna Ganga. In that huge city they were always welcome.

Evander promised them that he would see them again, someday, somewhere. His Neild-made clothing was brought back. It had been partially washed, dried with hot irons, and thoroughly brushed. The Ugoli commented on its extraordinarily fine workmanship. Evander laughed and told them it had been made by "good Neild." Then with warm embraces, a few stifled tears, and even a final pat for Koni-thomimo, he made his farewells and left.

The rain had stopped, but the streets were still filled with hurrying people, carts, donkeys, and horses. The jam at the gate had broken up though, and traffic was rolling. Evander walked through the crowds to the cemetery and made his way to the domed mausoleum. Climbing up on top of the mausoleum was painful on bruised knees and sore muscles.

There was also a strange feeling in his chest and shoulders—somewhere between a burn and an itch, vaguely pleasurable almost, suffusing his skin. The rays of the blessed Thymnal had fallen on him. Something was happening. Maybe the tide was really turning in his favor at last.

He pulled out the whistle and blew for the batrukh. It made no sound audible to human hearing, but a few moments later the batrukh descended with enormous wing beats that almost blew him off the dome and took up its perch on the heavy brass orb at the top. Quickly, he scrambled up the furred muscles onto the saddle and patted his front to make sure that Donzago's strange little book was still there.

The batrukh hurled itself from the ground, and he clung on tightly as the falling city of lights was left behind.

Chapter Forty-five

Once more he stood before the wizard in his hall on the Black Mountain. He did not know if Serena lived, though he thought she did. Evander had one hope left, and he knew he must play for it with all the skill he could muster.

To the insistent question, he could only spread empty hands. He did not have the Thymnal.

The wizard raged at him. Evander begged for the chance to explain. "I have something that will interest you even more," he pleaded. Eventually, Gadjung calmed enough to listen.

Evander recounted the events of his mission in Monjon. He showed the brass cat's head and explained how it opened the vault of the Thymnal. He described his subsequent flight with the heavy little casket and the disaster that befell him in the chamber of the pit.

"You fell into the pit?"

"Yes."

The wizard's face betrayed astonishment. "What happened? How is it that you are standing here? Where is my Thymnal?"

Evander described the blessed realm with its silver planes floating about each other in a pink sky, but as he confessed, the experience had been overwhelming and he scarcely knew what any of it meant. The one incontrovertible fact was that the Thymnal had been freed.

The wizard's face showed stony rage.

Hurriedly, Evander explained that the Thymnal had taken pity on him and shown him the spell book of Donzago. Evander produced the heavy little book from within his shirt. Gadjung's eyebrows rose almost to the top of his withered skull.

"What is that?"

"The book."

"Give it to me." The wizard almost tore it out of his hands.

"Oh, my!" Gadjung exclaimed. Evander could feel a sea change in the air. The wizard was pleased.

The gimlet eyes pierced him once more. "So, you brought something out of this ruin."

"The Thymnal said Donzago used a spell in that book called ascendance to the Higher Realms. It was there that he obtained the Thymnal."

The wizard stared into his eyes. "I see some shadow of dissembling, but I see that in this at least you speak the truth. You're lying about something, of that I'm sure. I suspect that you tried to steal my Thymnal, and that caused your bungling! You dropped it! You fool! I ought to grill you slowly over hot coals to extract the truth, but your precious skin will save you, for now."

He fingered the book greedily and cut short the interrogation.

Evander was taken away and placed in a small cell, and there shackled to the wall.

With lust in his eyes the wizard hurried to his library. The book was a bizarre artifact. From the age of the Golden Elves themselves, he guessed. The characters used were in a version of their tongue, Intharion. To read them required great strength of mind. He took down the dictionary and began to translate the texts.

In the cell time passed. Evander prayed that Serena still lived and was unharmed. He dozed intermittently and grew very thirsty. He called out for water, but nothing happened for a long time. Then, suddenly, the door opened and a jar of water and a piece of rock-hard bread were thrust in. He drank and ate and slept.

He was awakened next by a strange sensation. An odd ecstasy was in the air; he felt alternating bouts of fright and excitement. The hair on his neck rose up, and he began to sweat profusely, though it was far from warm. Evander's hope soared. The wizard was making great magic! It could mean only one thing; Gadjung had taken the bait and was forging the spell that Donzago had used to break through to the Higher Realms.

Soon afterward the door opened. The zombie of Kospero looked in.

"Kospero, it's me, Danais."

Kospero stared at him and absently chewed his lip. "I bring water, Prince."

"Kospero, you do remember me!"

"I ..." The face went suddenly slack. The zombie set down the water and closed the door.

"Kospero!"

But Evander's cries were in vain. Kospero was gone.

The next time the door opened, it was another of the zombies.

Evander ate the hard bread and prayed to the Gods. He slept, woke, slept again.

The door opened, and two zombies released him from the shackles and hurried him down the passage and up the stairs to the hall of the wizard.

Gadjung was in a triumphant mood. A purple orb spun quietly in the air above his right shoulder. His very own Thymnal, freshly created by the lords of the higher plane.

"Ah, my curious freak, my pretty one," he said at the sight of Evander. "It is time to deal with you and your lover."

"The princess—is she all right?"

"Of course, what do you take me for? A monster?" The wizard cackled happily for a long moment. Evander saw pure evil glaring from those eyes.

"You have a Thymnal now."

"I do. Isn't it wonderful? It gives my magic such strength. I have never felt so wonderful, so powerful. Watch!"

The wizard extended both hands, concentrated, and spoke a set of harsh syllables. The air seemed to grow tense. His ears tickled. Then Evander felt himself lifted off the ground by an invisible force. All the hair on his body stood out on end. He rose five feet, hovered a moment, and was then tossed down. He landed and went to all fours.

"Yes," snapped the wizard. "Crouch there, you dog! You dared to try and get in my way! You almost killed me with that knife!"

Serena was brought in by the zombies.

Evander opened his mouth to welcome her, but his tongue clove to the roof of his mouth and no words came. Serena was also in the wizard's grip. Her eyes were downcast, her face contorted as if she was fighting to free herself and scream defiance.

Zombies pulled Evander to his feet.

The wizard gestured, and zombies roughly ripped off Evander's beautiful Neild-made shirt. In the process one of them gouged his chest and tore away a six-inch strip of the toad skin.

The wizard gave a grunt and stepped down from his dais. "What has happened to my lovely freak?" he said, while stroking the strange, mottled gray skin.

Where the skin had been ripped up, there was now fresh, normal skin, pale pink and wholesome.

"What is this?" The wizard dug his fingers into the thickest, wartiest section and tugged. A piece as big as his hand came away with a soft ripping sound.

It wasn't painful in the least. Evander's heart was soaring. The wizard's magic had been overcome by the rays of the blessed Thymnal of Donzago. The toad skin hung in long tatters from his chest.

The wizard snarled to himself and then squinted at Evander. "You realize you are now completely worthless to me. I have no reason to deny myself the pleasure of killing you." The wizard lifted a hand and snapped his fingers.

"Wait. Didn't I help you get your own Thymnal?"

The wizard laughed humorlessly. "Do you think there is anything you could do that would make up for stabbing me? I lost my ability to change shape. I lost half my strength. You almost crippled me. You think I would deny myself adequate revenge?"

Gadjung had Serena brought to his side. He put his arm around her and fondled her.

Evander wanted to kill him.

Gadjung noted the hate in his eyes and smirked. "My bride-to-be will watch your demise, and then I shall take her to the nuptial chamber. So much for your great love!"

Serena's face was contorted as the wizard strove to control her with his magic and keep her from crying out.

Zombies rolled in a glass tank six feet high and long and three feet wide. Behind came a stepladder. Evander was lifted and placed inside the tank. The glass was thick and beyond his power to break.

A black lacquered box was opened. A zombie lifted out a small struggling creature, then dropped it into the glass tank.

It was a strangely distorted rat, a rat with saber-tooth canines and the build of a miniature lion. It sprang at Evander, who could hardly turn around in the glass tank. It sprang past him, and he felt it sink its fangs into his shoulder.

With a grunt at the pain, he slapped at it, but too late. It was already running across his back and biting him as it went. With oaths and sharp cries he spun around and slapped at the horrible little thing. It was quick and its bite agonizing. Blood ran down his arm.

It evaded his foot and sprang between his legs. In passing it bit him on the thigh. He spun around and leaped after it, but missed and felt it bounce into his back, bite him, and bounce away as he rolled over and tried to grab it.

Once he almost caught it around the body, but somehow it wriggled free long enough to bite his hand and was away again, scampering down the length of the tank while the wizard cackled happily from his throne.

Evander was bleeding from a dozen places now, and the inside of the tank was getting smeared and slippery. He lost his footing on the next pass, and the little monster tried to get at his throat when he fell on his back.

This proved to be its undoing. He caught its tail under his fingers with a lucky slap and then punched it flat against the glass.

A little unsteadily he got to his feet.

"Ah, hah!" chortled the wizard. "Good sport, eh?"

"Let Serena go. You've got no reason to harm her."

"Impertinence! In a few moments we'll see how you do against ten of the little beasts. I wager they'll strip you to the bones in no time."

Evander swallowed heavily. Ten?

The wizard pulled Serena to the glass. "Of course, if you say the word, I'll exchange her for you. Think about it; you can stay in there and be eaten alive, or you can stand out here and watch her being eaten alive. What will it be?"

"Rot in hell."

"Ah, the frankness of youth. Such nobility. Bring in my pets!"

Two zombies entered, carrying a large lacquered box on a tray. They approached the tank. Dully, Evander noticed that one of them was Kospero.

They stood beside the tank and raised the box over their

heads. Evander heard the shrill sounds of the excited super rats. He prepared to die fighting.

Kospero locked eyes with him.

"Kospero!" he shouted.

The eyes blinked. The forehead creased. Something changed. "My prince," said Kospero in a strangled voice.

Kospero kicked the other zombie in the legs, causing him to release his end of the box, then dropped his own. The box splintered on the floor, outside the glass tank.

With shrill squeals of joy the tiny horrors were released. In moments the zombies, Serena, and the wizard were jumping and slapping in place while fierce cries of pain echoed in the chamber. They ran, dodging and colliding with one another. A zombie knocked the wizard off his feet at one point, and he was bitten badly on the head. Then the doors slammed. From the far side came the sounds of vigorous blows as one or two overeager rats were hunted down and dealt with.

Inside the hall the rest ran in circles around the glass tank. They could not scale the walls, nor jump that high. Their squeals sent chills down Evander's spine.

The door burst open again, and the wizard strode in. The rats sprang toward him, but he conjured with both hands and roared a syllable of power. The ferocious hearts that beat inside the terrible rats were stopped. They keeled over where they stood.

The zombies and Serena followed the wizard, stepping gingerly through the door. Gadjung had blood dripping down his face from a slash on the forehead. He raised a fist and bellowed two words of command.

Kospero gasped and sank to his knees, his hands at his throat. His eyes rolled up into his head. He pitched forward onto his face and lay still.

Evander pounded on the glass.

The wizard flashed him a look of hatred. The other fist came up, and Evander was pulled to the floor, slowly choking to death on his own tongue.

Serena, too, was hauled down. They were going to die together.

Evander tried to meet her eyes. He had gambled, and it seemed he had lost. He had hoped that Gadjung's new Thymnal would have consumed him in time. He wanted her to know that he had tried, and that he still loved her, more than anything else, even life itself.

And then the wizard gave an odd cry.

Evander looked up. The grip on him was weakening. With an explosive gasp he expelled his tongue from the back of his throat and sucked in a breath of air. The red haze retreated from his vision.

The wizard was staggering, hands waving in the air.

"No!" he cried. "No, not me!"

The ancient sorcerer felt a fast-creeping death overcoming his body. So intent on his petty vengeance had he been that he had never noticed the fatal draining of his life force by the Thymnal that glowed balefully above his shoulder.

Gadjung choked, staggered, and raised his hands to the Thymnal. "Can't be," he said.

Evander watched through the glass as the wizard fell to his knees. His flesh was hardening, his skin turning to ash and flaking away. The eyes were gone, the teeth exposed, and then what remained of the skeleton fell to the floor and shortly evaporated into thin air. All that was left were thin lines of gray dust.

The wizard Gadjung, survivor of the Old Red Aeon, had passed on, his life force now compressed within the purple Thymnal that was left hovering a few feet from the floor.

The other zombies awoke from the spell that had gripped them for so long. Some broke into tears of joy. Others stared around themselves, completely witless. A few bellowed in emotional rage.

Serena staggered up and collapsed against the glass. Evander let out a wild whoop. He jumped up, caught hold of the top of the tank, and hauled himself up and over, ignoring the pain, and swept Serena into his arms.

Chapter Forty-six

Evander and Serena were quite giddy until they noticed the body of poor Kospero. Evander shook off the euphoria and fatigue. He pointed to the hovering, purple Thymnal of Gadjung.

"Kospero! Let us expose him to the Thymnal. Perhaps we can save him."

Together they manhandled Kospero's body across to the dais, where they laid it out beneath the Thymnal. Evander stood up and gingerly took hold of the Thymnal.

It felt warm and massive to the touch and moved with only the slightest pressure. He brought it down and pushed it against Kospero's head and then against his chest.

For a long moment nothing happened, and Evander was about to conclude, sadly, that his friend was beyond the healing powers of the magic Thymnal.

A moment later, Kospero's body jerked. His mouth opened, and he expelled fluid and air, his eyes open. He lay there sucking in deep breaths.

Evander let out a whoop.

"Where?" Kospero said weakly.

"Kospero, 'tis you. You live again."

"I live, my prince. I live."

They made their way slowly out onto a high battlement of the wizard's fortress atop the mountain. Beneath them was the land of the Bakan coast. Inland in the distance lay Frungia and the Skola valley. In the other direction was the distant sea.

Evander pointed to the sea.

"We must go to the eastern empire. We must warn them."

Serena pulled away the last strip of the horrible wizard skin. "You are whole once more, free of this dreadful curse."

"Thanks to the blessed Thymnal for that."

Kospero turned to him. "My prince, I don't know how I come to be here, or even where this is. I remember a ship, the *Wind Trader* I think she's called. We were beating up the coast to Port Tarquil. Then my memory fades, and everything is vague. I saw you, but as if in a dream. I could not speak. It is as if I have been asleep for a long time."

"You have been in thrall to the Wizard of the Black Mountain. He struck at us first in Port Tarquil. I was accursed with a hideous skin. The crew of the *Wind Trader* threw us overboard. The wizard's creature captured you. I was found by some wonderful Ugoli people who took me to the city of Monjon."

Seeing Kospero's stunned incomprehension, Evander clapped him on the shoulder. "A long story, my friend, and I will happily tell you all that I know in good time."

"My prince, I feel as if some great victory has been won here. What has happened?"

"You are correct; we have won a victory. And I have won the fairest bride in all the world."

Serena laughed, her heart soaring with unanticipated release from the dire fate she had expected until so recently.

Evander pulled her to him with a laugh and kissed her cheek.

"Look," she said, wonderingly. "Your wounds are healing."

It was true; the bites had stopped bleeding. Even his poor battered knees were improving fast.

"The new Thymnal is very strong. It reflects the power in its maker."

Serena looked down sadly at the mention of the Thymnal. "You said that the Thymnal is gone from Monjon. The city has fallen."

"The lights have dimmed."

"I am so sorry for my people; they will suffer now as they have not suffered in many years."

Evander shook his head. "Fear not, my love, for we shall take them the new Thymnal to replace the old."

Her eyes leapt. "You would do that? Even after all my father tried to do to you?"

Evander nodded. "I think the Thymnal will be safe in Monjon, and we will make sure that it is used to do good.

The tyranny of the priests must end, and access to the rays of the blessed Thymnal must be opened to the masses."

"Oh, yes, that would be wonderful. We shall insist on it. If they want the Thymnal, they shall have to reform."

"Good, then we're agreed. The new Thymnal will return Monjon to its place of glory, but the priests will no longer control it as they used to. We will go to the eastern lands and seek out the witches of Cunfshon and bring them our warning."

Serena felt her heart would burst from pure joy. "We have kept the Thymnal and lost a most evil wizard. Let this be a good sign for the world."

An exciting preview of
*The Dragon at the
End of the Worlds,*
coming from Roc in early 1997.

In this next grand adventure
of battledragon Bazil and his
dragonboy Relkin, the two find
themselves separated from
the fighting 109th unit. . . .

Bazil and Relkin stumbled on through the jungle, steering south and east as much as possible. This was the seventh day since they had beached on the forest strand and headed into the jungle in search of food. At first Relkin had been sure they were somewhere on the eastern shore of the inland sea. The strange forest was the same as that which they had traversed during the epic march of the Legions from Og Bogon to the shores of the inland sea. Relkin had thought they should be able to catch some of the more unwieldy animals they had seen during that voyage down the great river.

On both scores he had been wrong. What animals they had seen had invariably slipped away from them. They showed an amazing ability to shift large bodies at great speed through these forests of conifers and cycads. They were also much quieter than one would have expected and were able to fade away into impenetrable thickets with scarcely a sound. As a result Relkin and Bazil had hardly eaten a thing.

During that hungry week, Relkin had come to realize that instead of being on the eastern shore of the ocean, they were in fact on its southern margin. Seven days of heading in an easterly direction had brought them that morning down to an inlet laid out north to south. Down the inlet lay the ocean. Clearly they were moving eastward along an east–west shore. Which, of course, also meant that they were a very long way from the rest of the Argonathi army. They were truly alone and would have to rely on themselves on the long journey ahead. It was even possible, as Relkin was reluctantly coming to accept, that they might never rejoin the army, not until they got all the way back to Bogon on the east coast. One thing he had refused to even consider was that they might never make it back at all. All in all, it was a dire situation, and both of them had been working hard to keep the other's spirits up.

They entered a marshy area. On a mudbank Relkin surprised a scarlet amphibious beast the size of a cat. His sword pinned it before it could reach the water. In a few moments, it was gutted and cleaned and broken into pieces, while Relkin looked around for firewood. There was something wrong though, a strange smell that made the hair on his neck stand up.

The dragon looked askance at the chopped-up, red-skinned creature.

"I don't think this is a good idea," he said carefully, knowing full well how hungry Relkin was, but distrusting that awful smell.

Relkin cut off some hunks and threw them into a nearby pond where some small fish were circling. The fish attacked the chunks briefly. Two or three were almost instantly stricken with paralysis and floated to the surface, bellies up.

With a sigh of frustration, Relkin told his stomach to forget it. He wiped his sword carefully in the sand and washed his hands very thoroughly before they went on.

The mires thinned out and they moved through tropical heathland, with a thin forest cover of dwarf pines. The going became considerably easier and they moved along at a steady pace, eyes peeled for some sign of prey. Ahead were white limestone cliffs.

Relkin heard it first.

"Uh oh," he groaned.

On a breeze from the south came a distant medley of wailing cries.

"Those things again," grumbled the dragon. "They are too common in these parts."

Hurriedly, they moved due east, trying to put a lot of space between themselves and the source of the noise. They had seen a pack of the creatures that made those cries and had faced their ilk on the ramparts of the Legion camp. They had no desire whatsoever to come to grips with a horde of yellow-skinned killers, each with deadly sickle claws on its hind feet that they used to disembowel prey.

The two pushed on, working eastward along a ridge

of drier ground, where the forest cover stayed thin and it was relatively easy to make good time. The wailing cries died away for a while, and they were starting to think they'd left them behind when they were renewed. This time they were nearby. Bazil and Relkin were being tracked. They increased their speed, and now came to an area cut up by the karst canyons of a limestone landscape. Ledges and pinnacles were abundant.

The wailing cries were directly behind them now. Cursing, the two shuffled along, pushing tired bodies into a redoubled effort. A fault had thrust limestone up in a sharp cliff that barred their way. There was no time to waste here, the yellow-skinned killers would be on them very shortly.

Relkin found cause for hope though. A crack in the cliff face offered a chimney they could ascend, legs on one wall, shoulders on the other. Bazil had learned to climb this way when he was a sprat back in Blue Stone county, although it had been a long time since he had tried it.

They climbed. For Bazil it was an exhausting ordeal, and his energy reserves were already getting low. Still the chimney was almost ideal for this purpose—being big enough for a wyvern dragon to wedge his feet on one wall and his shoulders on the other.

Relkin was too small to get the benefit of the chimney effect, but he was able to scale the wall anyway. He too felt the weakness that came from lack of food and found himself drained by the time he hauled himself out on top of the cliff.

The pack of sickle-claw killers had emerged from the forest and formed a stolid, goggle-eyed audience down below them. They made no sound, except an occasional keening cry of disappointment.

Relkin looked down at the stiff-legged pack. He counted more than ten of them, waiting patiently, with their long arms drooping to the ground, their tails held out straight behind them and their big eyes fixed intently on himself and the dragon. Slowly Bazil inched his way up to the top of the chimney. He was sobbing for breath with each heave up the rock. At last he got a shoulder over the top. The maneuver at the end was the worst

SuperLotto PLUS

PLAY MAKE ME A MILLIONAIRE
SCRATCHERS NOW!
QUICK PICK

						MEGA
A	01	02	20	33	39	10
B	06	07	19	25	38	07
C	09	22	28	36	42	02

SAT FEB28 09

013610 $3.00
R0683418   459-037101839-083335

Millions Jackpot paid in 26 annual payments or players may choose the cash value payment in one lump sum. Call 1-800-LOTTERY for more information. Play Responsibly. Must be 18 or older to play. Problem Gambling Help Line 1-800-GAMBLER   ©2008 California Lottery

Care for Tickets:

Do not deface	Do not iron	Avoid heat	Keep dry

REV:01/08

005137600

CM NAME_____
(Print one name only)   Date of Birth

ADDRESS (print)_____

_____

PHONE (_____)_____
          AREA CODE

SIGNATURE_____

Winning tickets must be claimed within 180 days after the draw in which the prize was won. There may be different claiming periods for replays, entries, coupons, and promotions. Check your ticket selections for accuracy. Ticket cancellation rules apply. You must present this ticket as proof of your selections to claim a prize. Determination of winners is subject to the rules and regulations of the California Lottery. You must be 18 years or older to play. Super Lotto Plus and Mega Millions Jackpot paid in 26 annual payments or players may choose the cash value payment in one lump sum. Call 1-800-LOTTERY for more information. Play Responsibly. Must be 18 or older to play. Problem Gambling Help Line 1-800-GAMBLER   ©2008 California Lottery for him, since he was already drained of strength and this required the maximum effort from his upper body.

Bazil took a deep breath, twisted and let his feet leave the opposite wall. His arms and shoulders took the entire strain for a moment, while his claws gouged out dust from the rock face beneath him, and then he managed to boost one leg up and get a talon grip on the edge. For a moment he teetered there and might have fallen back, but for a final convulsive heave, plus Relkin's frantic hauling on his joboquin that brought him over the edge and left him panting flat out on the upper surface.

The mob of killers below were still staring up at Relkin with solemn eyes. He was tempted to find some rocks to heave at them.

Bazil got back to his feet with a groan or two.

"Time we was moving on," whispered Relkin.

Carefully, the boy and the dragon inched backward from the cliff until well out of sight from below. Then they rose to their feet and retreated across the plateau to the far side. The limestone region formed a scarp with the steep side facing east. They came to the top of this steep slope and found the country spread out below them. Dimly, far off to their left, Relkin glimpsed an expanse of blue that he knew at once was the Inland Sea. Directly ahead lay a river plain, with the river's serpentine coils spread across it.

His fears were confirmed then. They were way to the south of the legions and essentially on their own.

"What now?" said Bazil, whose own grasp of geographic details was considerably vaguer than Relkin's.

"Got to get down this slope, get across the river and continue east. Somewhere over there we ought to find the big river we took through the mountains. Maybe we can hook up with the Legions. Find where we left the rafts."

"Not going to be so easy to raft up the river as it was to float down."

"I know. But it'll still be easier than walking the whole way."

The dragon fell silent, struck by the hard, obvious truth of this statement.

"Come on, let's take this carefully. Don't want a fall," said Relkin.

"By the fiery breath," grumbled the leatherback, but he fell in behind Relkin as they started down.

Cautiously, they descended the steep slope, scrambling down through thickets and dense patches of vines. By late afternoon, they were far down the slope, deep in a murky forest fed by springs rising at the bottom. At one spring they paused to take a drink. Behind the spring Relkin discovered a cave that went back into the hill a considerable distance. The air coming up from the cave was cool. Relkin detected nothing more than the smell of cool, moist stone. Bazil noted the presence of some bats in a sidecave, but nothing else. They huddled there for a moment, to get their breaths back and plot their next move.

"I think we should stay here, sleep, and move on in the morning."

"You not as hungry as this dragon."

"I'm not so sure about that, but the river's too far for us to reach before dark. I bet there'll be a lot of mosquitoes down there. You know what the witches said about mosquitoes and the plague."

Bazil remembered the plague too well. He shuddered.

"We stay here tonight," he said.

They cut down some boughs and made nests for themselves just inside the entrance. Relkin went off to scout for small game.

He passed down by the spring, which had formed a wide circular pool at the base of a cliff of white limestone. Palms grew around it in a grove that trailed off into the deeper woods where the conifers grew thick.

He wended his way down this path of palm trees seeking something small that he could hit with one of the half dozen smooth stones he'd picked up earlier. There were lizards, but they were high in the trees, and wary. At the sight of him, they flitted upward. He groaned and shifted weary limbs on down the path. They really had to find something to eat or he was going to get too weak to carry on. Relkin could have wept for his lovely little Cunfshon bow. Those fat lizards would have fed him well and given the dragon a little something to stave off the worst pangs of hunger. With the bow, they would have been easy targets.

Suddenly he heard a triumphant shriek behind his

back. Three of the pack carnivores stepped out of concealment. Another shriek came from ahead and there were the rest of them. He was trapped between them.

Relkin never hesitated. He hurled a stone at the nearest and scored a good hit, high on the forehead. The creature hissed and shook. Relkin was gone, running for his life beyond the palms through a mass of young fir trees no taller than Relkin himself. He was able to force his way through and stay ahead of the ululating pack, but they were right on his heels.

The trees grew larger. He ran bent over low and managed to get along beneath their lowest branches. The predators were not as agile here. They did not use their forelimbs effectively to grasp and raise the lowest branches. They bulled through with their heads and they were inevitably slowed. Relkin sensed after a while that he was gaining.

Then the firs ended and he burst out into a wide clearing. Tall trees lined the eastern side, the scarp cliff was visible on the other. He doubled for the cliff. There were scattered palms and a few pine trees as he approached the farther side. Behind him he heard the first shrieks as the pursuit emerged from the firs. They had him in their sight. Now it was simply a footrace and Relkin was sure he would lose that. He'd seen these creatures run and they were better than any human athlete in the world. . . .